DATE DUE

9-27-00

FALL

OF A

COSMONAUT

FALL

OF A

COSMONAUT

STUART M. KAMINSKY

THE MYSTERIOUS PRESS

Published by Warner Books

A Time Warner Company

Mysterious Press books are published by Warner Books, Inc.,
1271 Avenue of the Americas, New York, NY 10020.

Visit our Web site at www.twbookmark.com

A Time Warner Company

The Mysterious Press name and logo are registered trademarks of Warner Books, Inc.

Printed in the United States of America

First Printing: September 2000

10 9 8 7 6 5 4 3 2 1

Library of Congress Cataloging-in-Publication Data
Kaminsky, Stuart M.
    Fall of a cosmonaut / by Stuart M. Kaminsky.
        p.   cm.
    ISBN 0-89296-668-8
    1. Rostnikov, Porfiry Petrovich (Fictitious character)—Fiction. 2. Police—Russia
(Federation)—Moscow—Fiction. 3. Moscow (Russia)—Fiction. 4. Astronauts—Fiction. I.
Title.

PS3561.A43 F336 2000
813'.54—dc21   00-038030

To Elliott Gould, fan and friend,
from a fan and friend.

I, son of Ether, will take you to orbs that lie beyond the stars, and you will be queen of the universe, my bride. And from above you will look back without regret, without concern at the earth which, you will then know, has no real happiness and no lasting beauty.

—Mikhail Lermontov, *The Demon*

The stars, as if knowing that no one was looking at them, began to act in the dark sky; now trembling, they were busy whispering with pleasure and mysteriously to one another.

—Leo Tolstoy, *War and Peace*

Prologue

★ ★ ★ ★ ★ ★ ★ ★ ★ ★ ★ ★

The *Mir* space station was launched in February of 1986. It followed the Russian space program's seven smaller manned space stations, beginning with *Salyut I*, launched in 1971, which orbited the earth for six months.

Mir, which means "peace," is forty-three feet long and fourteen feet wide. It has ninety-eight foot-long energy-generating solar panels. *Mir* can accommodate six cosmonauts for short stays and three for longer periods. Fifteen months is considered the maximum time for a cosmonaut to remain in space.

Mir has six docking ports, and when most or all are in use the attached units make *Mir* look like a metallic dragonfly being attacked by space parasites.

Mir has four areas—a docking compartment, living quarters, a work area, and a propulsion chamber. The docking compartment houses television equipment, the electrical-power supply system, and five of the six ports.

In the living space are two small sleeping cabins and a common area with dining facilities and exercise equipment, plus a toilet, sink, and a water-recycling system.

The work compartment contains the main navigational, communications, and power-control systems. Attached to the sides of this compartment are two solar panels that provide *Mir's* electricity.

Space suits are needed only in the propulsion compartment, which is not pressurized. This compartment has rocket motors, a fuel supply, a heating system, and the sixth docking port, used only for unpiloted refueling missions. Outside this compartment are the antennae for all communication with the earth.

In the docked modules are an observatory with x-ray and gamma-ray telescopes. Another module, with an air-lock system, is used for repairs outside the station. A third module is used for scientific equipment and as a docking port for heavy spacecraft. Two more modules with various functions complete *Mir*.

Mir is a marvel of technology, the pride of Russian science, and for the last five years of its existence it has been rapidly decaying and experiencing a series of disasters—some small, some large, and at least one that began as . . .

Tsimion Vladovka sat before the console in front of the axial docking port, wondering if dreams were different in outer space. He pressed the buttons on the panel in front of him and watched the lists and numbers scroll by, certain that if something was wrong the automatic part of his mind would notice and nudge him into action and out of the memory of his dream.

Tsimion had been on the *Mir* space station for eight months. Early in his stay he had decided that there were three things about the journey around the earth to nowhere that he did not like.

First, he did not like the loud squawk of the alarm that woke the cosmonauts each morning and blared when there was a problem or potential problem. At first he had slept just below the level of consciousness, strapped in to keep from floating about the cabin, slept without dreams, dreading that blare. Now he had learned to anticipate it, check his watch, unstrap himself, and float past whoever might be sleeping just below him. Long before the others awoke, Tsimion was drifting weightlessly about the communal cabin, eating alone at the work and dining table. At forty-two, he was the oldest of the three cosmonauts on board the space station. If he took after his father, whom he already resembled, he would soon be white haired. At first, Tsimion had routinely shaved carefully, finding even the smallest hair on his throat, cheekbones, and beneath his ears. His beard was dark and grew quickly. Lately, he had begun to shave just enough so that there would be no questions from ground control about his appearance. There was a slightly Asian look about his face, a look of eastern Russia and the farming village in which he was born, that weightlessness somehow accented. His family went back at least a thousand years in that village not far from St. Petersburg, inbreeding with other potato-farming families till everyone in the town looked as if he or she had been cloned from the same original, with more than a touch of the Mongols who had long ago raided and raped their way through the plains.

When he brushed his teeth, Tsimion had to remind himself to keep his mouth closed tightly so that the toothpaste would not drift about the cabin. Even with frequent warnings and reminders it was inevitable that food particles would get away. It was routine for the cosmonauts to gather in stray floating bits as they came upon them and dispose of them in safe boxes. Washing was not so bad, but it had its own problems. Globules of water clung to the skin and had to be coaxed with a sponge to do their job. Capturing a fleeing globule of water in a plastic bag was a daily game.

"You sound tired, Vladovka," Mikhail Stoltz had said once, his voice deep with years of smoking Turkish cigarettes. "*Kahk dyehlah,* 'how are you?' "

"*Pryeekrahsnay,* 'fine,' " Tsimion had answered.

Tsimion had wondered at first why Stoltz, who was head of security at the Star City cosmonaut training center twenty miles outside of Moscow, had recently begun communicating with *Mir.* There was no point in asking and it wasn't Tsimion's concern. If there were a security problem on the space station, Tsimion was reasonably certain which of the other cosmonauts might be involved.

"I have been working on the fungus experiments," Tsimion had said. "I lost track of time."

"That is what your watch is for," Stoltz had said with a laugh, a laugh patently false and carrying a hint of warning.

Their brief daily conversations, both men knew, were monitored by countries around the world, but they were most concerned with convincing the Americans that these communications were light and confident. There were breaks in radio contact with space control in Karolyov and Star City resulting from *Mir* being on the opposite side of the earth from Russia. In fact, acceptable radio contact lasted only minutes a day. Though he did nothing different from his normal routine during these breaks of contact, Tsimion looked forward to them precisely because they isolated him and the others from all earthly control.

The second thing that Tsimion disliked about his mission was his company. It was natural, he knew, that in such confines people would begin to get on each other's nerves. They had all been taught that, all been trained in techniques of dealing with each other. Tsimion had spent much of his free time in the *Spektr* module, sending long e-mails to his wife at the Star City cosmonaut training center. He knew the correspondence was being monitored and analyzed by psychologists and military officers, and so he kept his innermost thoughts to himself. For much of his time, Tsimion had taken to keeping a journal and recording his dreams. The journal was a neat, thick, blank-paged book with a hard cover. He had, when he first began keeping it, asked the others aboard *Mir* about their dreams. Early on they had cooperated. The most cooperative had been the American, Tufts. Tufts's Russian was grammatically correct but heavily accented. Tsimion's English was no better. The two had become friends and had once been chastised by Vladimir Kinotskin for playing catch in the communal room with a ball of rolled aluminum foil that floated wildly across the small area.

"You could break something," Kinotskin had said, suggesting but not exerting his command as senior officer, though he was more than a decade younger than Tsimion.

Tsimion was a botanist with no great ambition. Space was not the final frontier but an escape from his routine and badly paid future of agricultural research in Siberia. He had volunteered for the training, threw himself into it, and succeeded in qualifying.

"Everything is already broken," Tsimion had said.

"Nevertheless . . ." Kinotskin had said, and the game had stopped. Kinotskin was muscular, blond, and humorless, with a doctorate in aeronautical engineering from Moscow State University. He was ambitious, handsome, unmarried, and slated to be a spokesman for the Russian space program when he returned to earth, his uniform covered in medals, his teeth covered in caps of artificial whiteness, and the small mole just below his left eye neatly and surgically removed without leaving a scar.

The American was gone now, taken back to earth by an American space shuttle at 17,500 miles an hour, replaced by another Russian, Rodya Baklunov, who had joined the crew carrying specimens of fat white worms in carefully sealed canisters. In addition to his other chores Baklunov, a small, powerfully built, and nearly bald man, spent most of his time with his worms. He did not share the nature of his experiments with Kinotskin or Tsimion, who now sometimes dreamt of those worms. In his dreams, the worms, hundreds of them, had escaped and were floating around the cabin. Baklunov was floating after them and with gloved hands slowly recapturing the worms and placing them back in a canister from which they immediately escaped.

"Don't touch them," Baklunov said in the dream. "Just a touch will make your skin burn and peel off in seconds, leaving a bloody screaming Vladovka begging to be shot because when the bleeding stopped, Tsimion Vladovka would turn into a giant, bloated white worm."

In fact, in the dream, one fat white worm squiggled through the air and clung to the exposed hand of Tufts, the American, who immediately began to peel to near screaming death. And then Tsimion saw that three more worms were heading toward him. Beyond these worms, Baklunov was still patiently, calmly plucking worms from the air and putting them in the canister from which they would immediately escape. This was always the point at which Tsimion awoke.

Tsimion had recorded that dream and the variations in his journal. He wondered if when he returned to earth the dream would continue to come. He felt sure it would.

The third thing, and most important, that he disliked about *Mir* and that caused him to think, "if I get to earth," was the gradual disintegration of the space station. Systems were dying and had to be jury-rigged and frequently repaired. The inside of the spacecraft, so clean in photographs and diagrams shown to the world, was beginning to look like the messy workshop of a weekend tinkerer. Cables with fraying wires were wound with tape, panels once lit were permanently dark, and small metal boxes on the floor were tied in to perform tasks that should have been part of the internal system of the station. Solar panels shut off without reason. One of two oxygen generators in the *Kvant I* module seldom worked. The backup generator frequently failed. Their backup was an emergency cylinder that could be started to create a chemical reaction which produced oxygen. Tsimion was not at all sure the emergency cylinder would work. The last backup was individual oxygen packs with a supply of a few hours, supposedly enough time for the three cosmonauts to make it through the docking passage and into the *Soyuz* capsule, which could detach and return them to earth.

But there had been problems in the past, even a fire before Tsimion's time on *Mir*, and it had become clear that even following emergency procedures there would not be enough time for all the cosmonauts to get to the *Soyuz* and detach while a major breakdown was underway. Even if they could detach, an explosion destroying *Mir*, which might happen in seconds, could overtake and destroy the *Soyuz* before it could distance itself from the station.

Ground control knew and Tsimion and the other cosmonauts knew that they were sitting inside a space bomb continuing to circle the earth, performing meaningless experiments simply to demonstrate to the world that the only space station, the first real space station, in orbit was Russian.

There had been a time when Russian children wanted to be cosmonauts, treated when they returned from space missions with the welcome of heroes. Parents gave their children the names of cosmonauts. Russia was overcrowded with Yuris named in honor of the iconic Yuri Gagarin, who was overwhelmed by his being a national treasure for simply sitting in a sphere he didn't control and circling the earth a few times.

Now Russians did not even know the names of the cosmonauts who orbited the earth. Children wanted to be economists, bankers. They wanted to earn degrees in business. Engineering schools and research institutes, like the one Tsimion had attended, were closing down. Science and space were of little interest. The young were looking to the earth and their bank accounts, not to the skies.

And so, Tsimion spent each day in nearly resigned anticipation of that squawking alarm that would tell them yet another system had failed, another crisis was about to begin.

Tsimion Vladovka did not blame the solar-winged tomb in which they sped. *Mir* had been launched more than a decade ago. It was not intended for existence beyond a decade. It had done its job. It was tired.

Mir reminded Tsimion of the little horse in Raskolnikov's dream in *Crime and Punishment*. It was Raskolnikov's dream that had haunted him for more than two decades and was responsible for Tsimion starting his dream journal, which, he rationalized, might be of scientific interest back on earth.

In Raskolnikov's dream, he is once again a small boy in the village where he was born. He is with his father. A big man comes out of a tavern and climbs into a cart. The cart is to be drawn not by the large horse with thick legs who normally pulls it, but by a small horse. The man takes the reins and invites people to join him on a ride.

"Come," the man shouts drunkenly. "Climb aboard."

People come laughing and climb onto the cart, crowding together.

The small boy tells his father that the horse cannot pull all those people. The father tells the boy that there is nothing they can do.

The big man yanks the reins and orders the small horse to pull. The horse tries valiantly, stumbles, breathes cold air. The big man whips the horse and then climbs down to beat him. The boy breaks away from his father and runs to help the fallen horse, who is now being clubbed and whipped. The big man turns to the boy, saying, "This is my horse. I'll kill him if I wish." The horse dies and as he dies the boy kisses his mouth.

Tsimion thought of *Mir* as that small horse and himself as the young Raskolnikov. The difference was that the man who owned *Mir* was faceless and on the ground, and Tsimion Vladovka did not dare protest as he rode the horse through starry blackness and red-white sunlight high about the clouds of earth.

It was a gamble. All others had gone. They had managed to leave the dying horse before its last breath.

"It is safe," spokesmen at ground control had announced. "Our problems have been small and we have planned for their correction and executed all needed repairs. No one has been seriously injured or died on *Mir*."

There is always the possibility of a first time. In the history of chance, there was always an inevitable first time that altered the odds forever.

Mir had floated for well over eleven years at three hundred and ninety kilometers above the earth, had circled that earth close to seventy thousand times.

Tsimion had recently developed a fourth concern. Baklunov had begun to talk to himself and he had developed a dreamlike gaze and a knowing smile. When spoken to he answered, but he seldom looked at Tsimion or Kinotskin when they talked to him. The little man performed his duties, kept himself immaculately clean and well shaven, ate with the others, and seemed to Tsimion to be going slowly mad, a condition with which Tsimion could sympathize. Though Baklunov had been on the space station working in his own module for only a month, Tsimion thought the stay was long enough. He had tried to convince Kinotskin, whose responsibility it would be to make the recommendation that Baklunov return to earth, but Kinotskin had his own future on earth to consider. To request the early return of one of the men under his command would be an admission of failure, an admission that would cost the Russian government a massive amount of money to remove the worm man.

"He is all right," Kinotskin had told Tsimion only two days earlier as the two went over routine data and monitored the telescope telemetry.

"He is going mad," said Tsimion.

"Ridiculous. He is eccentric. Biologists are often eccentric."

Tsimion had wondered what extensive experience Kinotskin had with biologists that led him to this conclusion, but it was not an issue to be debated. Tsimion had long come to the conclusion that, though Kinotskin could easily beat him at chess, the poster boy with the blond hair and small mole was not particularly bright and possessed no imagination. He claimed, for example, that he never dreamt. Tsimion was inclined to believe him. The only subject outside of his work that Kinotskin entered into with any zeal was women. Vladimir Kinotskin never tired of talking about the women he had been with and the women he would be with when he returned to earth and toured the world.

"American women, perhaps the wives of diplomats, African women. You know, the women of Somalia are among the most beautiful on earth. And Mexican women, I have seen them with large breasts and lips that . . ."

Kinotskin had been at a loss for words. He had the soul of a satyr without the wit or words of a poet. His talk of women bored Tsimion, who was forced to endure it.

Five more weeks, Tsimion thought. Five weeks and I will be leaving. I can make it for five weeks. I have many dreams to record and to dream. I have my experiments.

The alarm went off, squawking, bleating. It was about time for the others to wake up, but there was something wrong. It was five minutes too early. Another system breakdown? Would they have to endure that maddening sound for hours till they could dismantle it?

Kinotskin shot through the opening to the command module.

Tsimion watched him bump into the side of the small tunnel, grab the bar next to the seat beside Tsimion, and say, "It's . . . he . . ."

"*Shto*, 'what?' "

" 'Come,' *typeeyehr*, now."

It was the first direct order Kinotskin had issued to him.

Tsimion Vladovka had visions of worms floating through the passage into the module. He glanced. There were no worms. Not yet.

They were just coming into radio contact with the earth. Quickly the white-faced Kinotskin told him what had happened. The younger man spoke quickly, efficiently. It took less than fifteen seconds. There was nothing more to say to each other. They knew what must be done. Kinotskin began to transmit.

There was no television contact. Ground control had ended

almost all such transmissions since problems had begun more than a year earlier. Voice contact was not perfect.

"Ground," said Mikhail Stoltz, his voice weary.

"We have a *Syehm*, a 'Seven,' " Kinotskin said calmly.

There was a silent pause on the earth before Stoltz came back, now alert.

"Prognosis?" he asked.

Kinotskin saw his future disappearing, but he managed to pull himself together and speak. "Unable to give one at this time," he said. "We must go now. We will return with a report as soon as possible."

Possibly never, thought Tsimion, who said quickly, "Ground, please tell my wife I love her."

"Come," said Kinotskin, tugging at Tsimion's white T-shirt.

"And," Tsimion added, reaching to turn off the ground contact, "if we go to *Vossyeam*, 'Eight,' please inform Porfiry Petrovich Rostnikov."

Chapter One

★ ★ ★ ★ ★ ★ ★ ★ ★ ★ ★ ★

One Year and Five Days Later

Porfiry Petrovich Rostnikov, chief inspector in the Office of Special Investigation, had not witnessed such a sight in his more than half century of life.

He had been heading across Petrovka Street after getting off the bus. The central police headquarters, two ten-story, L-shaped buildings surrounding a landscaped garden protected by a black metal fence, was no more than fifty steps in front of him.

It had been raining lightly when he kissed his wife, Sarah, and left his apartment on Krasikov Street. The rain had grown worse, out-of-season rain blamed by the television weather people on something called *El Niño* or *La Niña*.

When he got off the bus, it was coming down heavily and he could hear the crack of thunder. To his right he saw a bolt of lightning and the crackle of its electricity. It was at times like this that he missed his left leg. He had learned to talk to the leg, which had been shattered by a German tank when he was a boy soldier in Rostov. He found it difficult to talk to the leg-shaped mechanism of plastic and metal; it had resisted all conversation for the year or more that it had become a reluctant part of the burly man known to the various branches of the police, Mafias, and petty criminals as "the Washtub."

The bus had pulled away down the street. Rostnikov looked

after it. The bus swayed dangerously though it was moving slowly. The wind suddenly went mad. People scattered. No one screamed. The two uniformed officers at the Petrovka station gate backed into the relative safety of their small bulletproof guard box.

Porfiry Petrovich swayed and ordered his leg to stand firm, knowing that it would not listen, had no mind. It was efficient but poor company. He was about to fall. The wind pulled open his coat and tugged at the buttons of his shirt. Rostnikov avoided a car that pulled past him and stopped in the middle of the street. The Washtub managed to make it over the curb to a small tree whose bare branches chattered as he clung to the trunk.

In the kennels of Petrovka, the German shepherds howled.

It was then that the bench, iron and wood, came flying down the street, touching down on top of a stopped car, creating a streak and scratch of sparks before continuing away about six or seven feet off the ground. The bench paused, twisted, rose as if deciding what to do, and then darted with the wind and rain down the street and into the drenched darkness. Now Rostnikov could hear the sound of windows breaking in Petrovka head-quarters.

It reminded him of something in a book he had read. No, it had been Chekov's notes on Siberia, the description of something like this, only in Chekov's tale it had been snowing.

Rostnikov clung and watched, waiting for more wonders. Across the street, well behind the bus and not far off, a slightly larger tree than the one to which he clung cracked low on the trunk and slowly toppled, brushing the sidewalk with a dying sigh.

And then it was over.

The rain continued but it was only a drizzle now, though the street was puddled and rivulets cascaded down the gutters. There was no wind, just a breeze. The sound of thunder was distant now and there were no more crackles of lightning. The entire marvel had taken less than a minute.

Rostnikov examined himself, touched his body to be sure he

had not been stabbed by some stray flying screw or broken twig, and continued his walk to Petrovka headquarters. The guards nodded him in as they emerged cautiously from their shelter.

He was not the first to arrive on the fourth floor, which housed his office, that of the director of the Office of Special Investigation, and the cubicles of the investigators who worked under the direction of Porfiry Petrovich Rostnikov, who, in turn, reported to the director. The cubicles of the investigators were behind a door directly across the hall from Chief Inspector Rostnikov's. It was only seven in the morning. The sun was barely out, but the light was on in the investigators' office.

Rostnikov knew who was behind the closed door. He went to his own office, closed the door, and began to remove his soaking clothes and put on his spare suit, which was in his very small closet. He hung his damp clothing neatly on hangers and then brushed back his hair with his hands. His hair, like his father's before him, was bushy. There was more than a bit of gray in it now, but Sarah, his wife, said it made him look distinguished, even stately. To keep him looking respectable, Sarah checked his shirt, suit, and tie each morning. There wasn't much of a selection, but with three suits, a dozen ties, and a reasonable selection of shirts and two pair of shoes, one black, one tan, she could certainly keep him respectable.

He moved to the window of his office and looked out. There was a scattering of tree branches in the street, and some of the shrubbery and flowers in the courtyard of Petrovka had been broken, plucked, and tossed about by the storm. Now the heat would come back. The mad rain would drop the temperature for a few minutes, and then the summer heat, worse than any Rostnikov could remember, would be back.

Air conditioning in Petrovka, driven by the city's gas system, if working, made the offices too cold, just as they were too hot in the winter. Stepping into the heat of the outdoors from the chill of the protected building was a blow for which one had to prepare.

His window was not broken but he could see that several across the courtyard had imploded. Behind one of the broken windows on the third floor a heavyset woman in a dark dress looked at the jagged broken glass and then across at Rostnikov, who nodded his head in sympathy. The woman turned away.

Rostnikov's office was wired by the director, Igor Yaklovev, "the Yak." Rostnikov knew his conversations were recorded and listened to, and the director knew that Rostnikov knew. The offices across the hall were similarly wired and every inspector knew it. Everyone pretended that their conversations could not be overheard. Everyone knew that if they wanted privacy they had to leave the building. The director did not really expect to learn anything from his hidden microphones, but he wanted the devices to remind those who worked for him that he was in charge. The only one who was upset by these hidden microphones was Pankov, the director's secretary, a sweating dwarf of a man who had lived in near panic since learning of the wiring, long after the discovery had been made by the entire investigative staff.

Rostnikov was suddenly hungry.

His phone was ringing.

He picked it up and said, "Chief Inspector Rostnikov."

"Are you all right, Porfiry Petrovich?" his wife said.

"I am fine," he said. "The storm hit where you are?"

"I think it hit everywhere in Moscow. The television said that part of the roof of the Bolshoi was torn off and that people ran in fright as the pieces of roof chased them into the square."

"Was anyone hurt?"

"I think so. The television said so."

"You are well? The girls are well?"

The girls of whom Rostnikov spoke were twelve-year-old Laura and her eight-year-old sister, Nina, who lived with the Rostnikovs in their one-bedroom apartment along with the girls' grandmother,

Galina Panishkoya. They had no place else to live yet. Galina had recently been released from prison. She had shot a man in a state-owned grocery. It had been an accident. The man had been arrogant. Galina had been desperate for food for her grandchildren. Rostnikov had arrested her. Rostnikov and his wife had taken in the girls. Rostnikov had gotten Galina out of jail and had gotten her a job in the bakery on the Arbat owned by Lydia Tkach. And so the Rostnikovs found themselves with a new family. Porfiry Petrovich didn't mind. Sarah welcomed them and their company.

"Yes, the girls are fine. Galina took them to school."

"Then maybe the mystery we call God and cannot understand has chosen to keep us alive another day. I saw a bench fly down the street."

"A bench? What is happening to the world, Porfiry Petrovich?"

"It went mad long ago, Saravinita. Most of the world refused to acknowledge it, but you and I have not been given the luxury of blindness."

"Take care of yourself today, Porfiry Petrovich. It is a dark day."

"I will try to be home at a reasonable time," he said. "You take care too."

He hung up, removed his artificial left leg, placed it on his desk, and in English softly sang, "Looks like we're in for storm in the weather. Don't go out tonight. There's a bad moon in your eyes."

Rostnikov knew he didn't have the words quite right, but the melody was close and the meaning clear.

The phone rang again and Rostnikov picked it up.

"The director would like to see you in his office in fifteen minutes," said Pankov. Rostnikov had long ago decided that Pankov was the only human he had ever met who could sweat over the telephone.

"Please tell Director Yaklovev that I will be there in precisely fifteen minutes."

"I will tell him, Chief Inspector. Would you like coffee when you come?"

"I would," said Rostnikov.

"A cup will be waiting," said Pankov, hanging up.

Pankov was definitely the dog who did the bidding of the director. He had hidden in the shadow of the previous director, the preening but surprisingly cunning Colonel Snitkonoy, who had gone on to the position of chief of security at the Hermitage in St. Petersburg and been promoted to general. The current director was a bit more difficult than had been Snitkonoy, who'd been known as "the Gray Wolfhound." While the Wolfhound had been tall, stately, almost always uniformed, the picture of a historic officer, Igor Yaklovev was of normal height, lean, given to dark suits and conservative ties. He spoke softly and kept his brown hair cut short and his bushy eyebrows untrimmed. The Yak, who had been a KGB officer, was ambitious and didn't bother to hide it. He was not above manipulating his office or the law, not for wealth but for the promise of power. The Yak had made an unwritten agreement with Rostnikov. Porfiry Petrovich would be in charge of all investigations turned over to the office. In turn, the Yak would decide how to handle the results of all investigations. Rostnikov would have a free hand and the complete support of the director in carrying out his investigations. In turn, Rostnikov would not question his superior's use of information gathered.

There was room for negotiation with the Yak but not a great deal of room. Rostnikov and his team had been responsible for notable successes even before the fall of the Soviet Union. Each additional success made the Yak look better. He did not long for the prestige and public circle of the Hermitage. He sought the quiet power of Moscow. Though it was no longer fashionable or politically correct to put paintings or photos of Lenin on the wall, the Yak kept a clear mental picture of the fallen leader in his mind as a model and inspiration. Were it acceptable, he would have grown a small beard.

Rostnikov put his artificial limb back on after sliding up his trousers and being careful not to snag the cloth on the prosthesis. He stood, hesitated, and then with a sigh of resignation reached into the pocket of his drying jacket and took out a plastic Ziploc bag containing two sandwiches of Spam, wilted lettuce, and butter. Sara had sliced the sandwiches neatly in half. Rostnikov stood eating one of the sandwiches, knowing he would be hungry again in a few hours. The morning was just beginning but it already seemed long. He vowed to wait as long as he could before he ate the other half of his lunch.

Across the hall in his cubicle Emil Karpo sat alone, neatly writing a report and preparing for the day. Karpo, tall, gaunt, and ghostly, known to those around him and those who kept their distance from him as "the Vampire" or "the Tatar," had been given an assignment by the chief inspector that he would have preferred to avoid. Karpo had simply nodded and taken the report. The case was murder, the victim a research psychologist at the Moscow Center for the Study of Technical Parapsychology, which, Karpo knew, was doing classified work for the government.

Akardy Zelach, "the Slouch," had been assigned to work with him. That was acceptable. Zelach was not bright, a fact of which Zelach was well aware and which he accepted. He took orders well, was loyal, and never complained. He was large, though of average strength. Karpo, who was taller but much thinner, was far stronger, but Zelach was not afraid of trouble, though he had almost lost his life several years ago aiding a fellow investigator.

Karpo had been a loyal Communist. Even now he refused to acknowledge that there was anything wrong with the philosophy. It was the weakness of humans that had brought an ideal to ruin.

It had not been the lure of capitalism but the drive for power that had begun even before Stalin. Humans were, Karpo had decided when he was quite young, ultimately animals. A reasonable utopian ideal like Communism was probably beyond the conception of animals, even those wearing clothes.

Karpo had become a policeman to protect Communism and the state from the eroding effects of crime. Then, for several years he remained a policeman because it was what he knew how to do and he could lose himself in the work. Recently, he had come to a new commitment to his work. A woman, her name was Mathilde Verson, had been killed in the crossfire of a battle between two Mafias. She had been the meaning for his existence. Now his crusade was to rid the city of Moscow of as many as possible of the worst of the two-legged monsters who prowled the dark streets.

But psychics? Had Porfiry Petrovich given the assignment to him as some kind of joke? Rostnikov was not above such a joke. Emil Karpo was surely the wrong man to deal with people who believed in and studied such things. The world was tangible. Nature had its laws, even if we did not understand them. So-called psychic phenomena were strands of false hope that something existed beyond the natural world. Yes, some things called psychic phenomena were certainly explainable if the research and experiments were possible to demonstrate that they were natural and not supernatural. The problem might be that research did not exist to prove the natural where the unnatural seemed to be taking place. It mattered little to Emil Karpo. It was sufficiently challenging to accept the terrible reality of the tangible world in which he existed.

Rostnikov entered the room. Karpo did not have to look up. It was too early for anyone else, and the sound of the limping leg on the wooden floor was unmistakable.

The chief inspector entered the cubicle and stood before Karpo's desk. Karpo put the top back on his pen, closed his notebook, and looked up. He was dressed as always completely in black: shoes, socks, trousers, and jacket over a pullover shirt.

"Are you aware that we had a storm, Emil?"

"I am aware, Chief Inspector."

"Windows broke, trees fell, a bench flew down the street and into the darkness."

Karpo nodded. "It seemed unduly loud."

"Thunder and lightning. At this magnitude in the middle of the usually calm summer. Nothing like this has happened before. Perhaps at the parapsychology center you will witness things that haven't happened before?"

"I do not expect that to occur," said Karpo.

"I know. Do you like Spam?"

"No."

"If you are here when Iosef arrives, please tell him to come to my office and wait for me."

"I will be here till the institute opens at nine."

"Keep smiling, Emil Karpo."

"I do not smile, Chief Inspector."

"I know," said Rostnikov.

"And I know that you know," said Karpo, without humor or emotion.

"We have too many levels to our conversations," said Rostnikov. "Even the most trivial. I believe it is endemic to Russians. It comes from having a history in which survival is often dependent on being cryptic."

"That is possible."

"We will talk later. As always, take care of yourself. Today especially. Omens from the sky."

"I do not believe in omens," said Karpo.

"Which is one reason you have been assigned this investigation," Rostnikov said as he nodded and left the cubicle.

He arrived in the outer office of the director one minute before his scheduled appointment. Pankov stood up and handed him a dark mug of steaming black coffee. Rostnikov took it with thanks. Pankov bit his lower lip, waiting for the chief inspector to taste the brew. Rostnikov did so. It was not foul. It was not good, but it wasn't foul.

"Very satisfying," said Rostnikov.

Pankov smiled, having lived through another of the thousands of ordeals in his daily life.

There was no time to sit and, besides, Rostnikov did not want to go through the trouble of sitting for less than a minute. The maneuvering of his leg was more than the moment of repose was worth, especially when he was holding a mug of hot liquid.

The door to the inner office opened and Pankov rose behind the desk to look at the director, who stood in the doorway.

"Pankov, sit down. Inspector, come in."

Yaklovev left the door open and turned back into his large office. Rostnikov, still carrying his coffee, followed him and closed the door. The Yak sat at the far end of his conference table.

"Sit," said the director.

Rostnikov placed his mug on one of the brown cork circles provided for drinks and eased himself down to one side of the director.

"Do you know a man, a cosmonaut, named Tsimion Vladovka?" asked the director.

Sasha Tkach made a sound, perhaps a groan, probably a reaction to the dinner of oversalted barley-and-beef soup his mother had prepared the night before. He rolled out of bed and tried to see the clock on the bed stand. Normally Maya would have awakened him by now. Instead he had been awakened by the electric crackle of nearby lightning and the sound of rain hitting the windows across the room.

It was late. He would have to hurry, to shave, take a cold shower in the little tile cubbyhole in the bathroom. To accomplish this he would have to get past his mother in the bedroom.

Lydia, in spite of her loud snoring, was a light sleeper. He did not want to wake her. He wanted coffee, though he was sure the acid in it had been giving him stomach pain. Perhaps he would switch to Pepsi-Cola. He had appropriated a large supply from a tourist hotel that wanted no trouble with the police. There were six bottles in the refrigerator and a carton of them next to it.

Tomorrow, he told himself, tomorrow I'll start drinking Pepsi-Cola. Today I need coffee. Who could deny me coffee in a life like mine?

Sasha was thirty-four, an inspector in the Office of Special Investigation. When he had begun as an investigator, he had been in the procurator's office under Porfiry Petrovich Rostnikov, who reported to Procurator Anna Timofeyeva. Looking a decade younger than his years, lean, handsome, with straight blond hair that often hung over his forehead, he had done undercover work, pretending to be a student, a naive computer salesman, a manager of killer dogs, a black marketeer, an innocent file clerk, and many other things, but now . . .

He looked around the living room–dining room–kitchen. It was empty. There was no Maya in the bed. The baby was not in the crib, though the crib was still there, and he knew his four-year-old daughter, Pulcharia, wasn't in the next room. His wife, Maya, had taken the children and gone back to Kiev to live with her brother and his family, indefinitely.

Sasha took a deep breath, heard his mother snoring in the bedroom, folded the bedding and pillows, and closed the bed back into the sofa.

Sometimes, during the past few weeks, he had concluded that it was his own fault. He had staggered, fallen, been with other women, unleashed periods of brooding anger and sullen silence. In short, he had been less than a joy to his family. However, with Rostnikov's help, he had convinced Maya to give him one more chance, twenty-two days. She had reluctantly agreed, partly, he thought, because it had been a strangely specific number to choose.

She had remained the entire time and he had tried, really tried, to change. But change does not come easily. He had loved his children, held his wife in the darkness of night when he came home, avoided other women, and done his best, though his moods had still come. And at the end he had the feeling that it was she who was becoming sullen, that somehow she had taken on his moods of depression as if they had been a disease transmitted from one person to another.

He moved to the small sink in the kitchen area near the window and turned the water on, but not full blast. The pipes were noisy and there was a precise point, which he could never quite judge, when they would begin to rattle and shake. Porfiry Petrovich, who for reasons Sasha did not understand had a great interest in plumbing, had during his last visit to the apartment offered to look into the problem. Sasha had said he would let him know. He cupped cold water in his hands and plunged his face into his palms. He let the water drip onto his extra-large gray Nike T-shirt and he rubbed his eyes. He could see somewhat clearly now.

When Maya had moved out, Lydia, who was retired and supposedly on pension from the Ministry of Information, had insisted on moving in with her only son. At first Sasha had protested, said he would be all right, that he was sure his family would be returning soon. She had insisted and, he admitted, he really did not want to be alone.

There were times, however, in the last weeks when he was sure he had made a mistake. Lydia could barely hear. She had a hearing aid but she either didn't use it or turned it off. Lydia issued commands and criticism. Until Maya had left, Lydia's favorite topic had been Sasha's dangerous work and her insistence that he seek safer employment. She had not given up on that quest, but she now had a list of her son's shortcomings that required addressing.

Lydia had money. She had invested most of her salary for

decades in property. It had all been done quietly and with advice from her superiors, who taught her how to make such purchases and protect them even within the Soviet system. Now, having sold much of that property and placed the money in high-yield foreign investments, Lydia was more than comfortable financially. Her prize investment was a bakery and pastry shop on the Arbat. It had been a state-run bakery, with sad loaves and lines of shuffling people. And then the revolution ended: crime, punishment, money flowed next to poverty even worse than that during the Soviet reign. But those with many new rubles, some with hard foreign currency, and even a few with very little flocked to the bakery on the busy Arbat to buy sweet cakes and brown healthy breads.

When even the new ruble had fallen to near nonexistence, Lydia, whose investments and money were all secure in German banks, had become even richer.

Maya had more than once suggested that Sasha stop being a policeman, manage the bakery, perhaps open a second one, maybe a chain of bakeries in various Russian cities. He would make money. He would have time to be with his wife, his children, his mother.

The idea, when presented to Sasha the first time, had made him seriously consider that suicide would be a better alternative to a career in bakery management, a career in which he would work for his mother.

Sasha liked being a policeman. He liked having new problems almost daily, dealing his way in and out of dangerous situations, meeting challenges, carrying a weapon. Anything else, particularly managing a bakery, would mean a slow death.

Now, with Maya and the children gone, he needed his work more than ever and, surprisingly, in the few weeks since she had been gone, he was sure that he was becoming a better policeman. He got along better with the partner assigned to him for each case. He wrote his reports without complaint and he did not frown or sulk when given a case he normally would not have liked.

But at the same time he missed Maya and the children and lived for the day they would return. He would be a better husband and father as he had become a better policeman. At least he thought he would.

He moved slowly to the bedroom door and opened it, inch by inch, pausing when he heard the slightest creak. When it was open just enough to slide through, he eased in carefully to the snoring of his sleeping mother. By all rights, the nearly deaf woman would not have heard a medium-range missile rip through one wall and out the other. But her son's slightest move would sometimes bring her upright in bed, squinting toward the hint of a sound.

This time he was lucky. He moved with the trumpet of her noise to the tiny bathroom and closed the door before turning on the light. There was just enough room to stand and carefully take off his T-shirt and boxer shorts. And then he turned on the water. With luck, he could shower, shave, shampoo, dress, and be gone before Lydia woke up.

As he shaved in the cool water Sasha became angry, angry with Maya. What had he done? She had given him a deadline. He had done his best. She knew what he was, how he was. He had done much to change, but one doesn't change in days. It takes weeks, months, if it can be done at all.

She has another man, he thought, and not for the first time. This is all a sham, a trick to make me look responsible, guilty while she is with him, probably someone she met at the Council for International Business Advancement, where she had worked. Why had it been so easy for her to be reassigned to Kiev? Was the man someone higher up in the trade center?

Maya was beautiful. Perhaps she had become vulnerable.

Yes, it was her fault. He had done his best. He turned off the water in the shower and, as he dried himself with Maya's favorite towel, changed his mind again and was sure that he was to blame. Fully, certainly. There was no other man. There was no other reason. The fault was his. She had simply endured as much as she could. He longed for Maya, for his children—for Pulcharia to run into his arms and announce that she had a story to read to him.

Sasha wiped the steamy mirror and looked at his face, toothbrush in hand. The face looked tired, the eyes heavy, the hair not as lively as it should be in spite of just having been shampooed. The body looked pale. He could no longer pass for a student. He looked thirty or more. It was not a bad-looking face and body, but it was not the face and body that could convince anyone he was a naive twenty year old. He had been through too much, had seen too much.

He dressed, compensating for his feeling of self-pity by putting on his best suit, the one he had hung on the bathroom door the night before. A reasonably eager smile and good grooming might compensate for the fact that he was going to be late. Sasha and the rest of the inspectors had no given hours unless Rostnikov or the Yak himself told them to be in at a specific time. But Sasha had arranged to meet Elena Timofeyeva at Petrovka at eight o'clock. Elena was always on time. Elena, the only woman in the office, made it her business to be on time and do her job with as much energy or more than any of the men.

Elena was plump, pretty, serious, and smart; smarter, Sasha thought, than Sasha Tkach. He had seniority, but she was two years older than he and more likely to get ahead somewhere in the Ministry of Interior, which oversaw all criminal investigation. At first, when he came to this realization about Elena, he had been sullen and felt sorry for himself. That was no longer the case. He belonged exactly where he was. Promotion meant responsibility and greater vulnerability. He had no passion for power, and the greater salary was not sufficient incentive.

Sasha was dressed, ready. With the money from Maya's salary, which was larger than Sasha's, not coming in, Lydia had found ways to try to buy her son's happiness. She had urged money on him, far too much, to pick up a few things on the way home if he ran into them. She would not ask for the change. She found other ways. At first he had been reluctant to take the money, but he had soon found himself accepting, wondering if he was being lured into an emotional debt to his mother, a debt that he would be unable to escape. However, that easy money did provide compensations.

He would take two sweets from his mother's bakery out of the refrigerator and buy a large coffee from the nearest kiosk today. She was snoring still as he eased out of the bedroom door, deciding not to close it.

Luck was with him as he opened the refrigerator, selected something small and cakelike, covered with chocolate, and a French croissant, dropped them in a brown paper bag, and headed across the room to the front door.

Suddenly the snoring stopped. Sasha could either break for the door and hope she would not hear him leave or move slowly while she got up, hoping to make it out of the room before his mother came through the partially open door.

Neither turned out to be possible.

"Sasha? I hear you. I have to talk to you."

He was doomed.

She sat in her small office, looking at her cooling cup of tea. It was a bleak, white-walled office. That was the way it was supposed to be. It had no windows. That was the way it was supposed to be. The door was closed. That was the way it had to be.

The woman's desk was almost completely clear and the dark wood shone with neatly applied polish and without a bump, mark, or scratch. The only object on the desk was her cup of tea in a simple white porcelain cup. The tea strainer had been removed, the grounds dumped into the wastebasket.

The only outside distraction this early in the morning had been a rattle of windows down the hallway outside of her office. She thought she heard the sound of rain on glass and was sure that there had been lightning and thunder. The weather had never intruded this deeply into the Center for the Study of Technical Parapsychology. She had waited till it passed.

Now she tried to clear her mind as she sat, tried to relax, used her techniques for concentrating on nothing. She hummed the single note she had chosen and paid attention only to it. After seconds or minutes, she didn't know which, she let her eyes fall slowly to the cup. It was nothing. Some object. She continued the hum. A circle of nothingness surrounded her hum, and deep within she let the power unto itself reach out to the cup. Something was happening. She tried not to let thought enter her being. The cup. She gently allowed the power to engulf the cup almost lovingly. She waited, distanced, for the power to move the cup. It would not take much of a move, just a distinct small motion, an indisputable motion.

And then her meditation broke, as she knew it would. Thoughts, fears, reality crept in, and the murder of the day before danced before her. Sergei Bolskanov at the table in his laboratory in his white laboratory coat. He had been listening to a CD, Mozart perhaps? He had turned. There was no look of horror or surprise on his face. There was a look, perhaps, of pleasant surprise. And then the hammer came out and fell hard upon Bolskanov, the claw side digging into his beard just below his lips. Bolskanov tried to rise, ward off the attack, but he was bewildered, dazed. The second blow dug deeply into his forehead. He yelped like a dog and tumbled back. No longer able to protect himself, blood spurting, he ripped off his glasses and flung them into the corner of the room.

The blows continued. Four, five, six, until there was no doubt that the heap of blood and flesh on the floor was no longer alive. The hammer was wiped on the bottom of the dead man's blood-spattered white smock, dropped on the floor, and kicked across the room to rest next to the pair of glasses.

And so, she asked herself, reaching out for the cup of tea, how can one perform an experiment with such thoughts, such memories, such images?

Her hands trembled but only slightly as she lifted the cup and took a sip. Tepid but with its flavor still intact.

The police were coming back. It would be a long day.

Chapter Two

★ ★ ★ ★ ★ ★ ★ ★ ★ ★ ★ ★ ★

"Tsimion Vladovka."

Rostnikov's pad was open before him. His pencil was in his right hand, his alien leg stretched out under the table at a slight angle so it would not touch Yaklovev's foot.

"Tsimion Vladovka," the Yak repeated, leaning over, head cocked at a slight angle, hands folded on the table as he looked at Porfiry Petrovich for a reaction. "Do you know him? Does the name mean anything to you?"

"It is vaguely familiar."

"He was a cosmonaut," said the Yak evenly.

Rostnikov nodded, his eyes on the director, waiting for the point to come as it inevitably must. "There have been many cosmonauts," he said.

"Many," agreed the Yak.

Rostnikov reached for the mug of coffee before him and drank slowly, waiting.

"You remember the *Mir* flight of perhaps a year ago, the one in which the three cosmonauts came down prematurely?"

Rostnikov did not particularly remember.

"There was a problem during that particular flight."

Rostnikov said nothing.

"Yes," the Yak went on. "There were always problems. But this one prompted an early change of crews and the rather unceremonious return to earth of the three cosmonauts on board. Vladovka was one of the cosmonauts. He is missing. National Security has been unable to find him. The Space security force has been unable to find him. Military Intelligence has been unable to find him. We have been given the task of finding him."

Rostnikov nodded, let his eyes take in the thick file that lay behind the protective wall of the director's arms, and then began to draw without thinking of what he might be drawing.

"And? . . ."

"You personally are to find him," said the Yak.

"Question. Why does he have to be found?"

"He has information about our space program which might embarrass us, which should not be allowed to fall into the hands of other nations. He may have been kidnapped. He may have defected. He may have committed suicide somewhere, or he may simply have gone mad and run away."

"And when I find him?"

"If he is alive, you are to inform me of where he is, be sure he remains there, and leave the rest to me, but if you believe he is trying to leave the country, take him into custody and bring him to me. It is better for you, better for me, if you do not ask him about the information he has. And it is essential that if he tries to tell you, you do not allow him to do so. There are secrets it is not safe to keep."

The Yak unclenched his fingers, opened his arms, and slid the folder over to Rostnikov. Rostnikov drew it in past his coffee cup, opened it, and found the photograph of a very serious dark man with the face of a peasant, a face not unlike his own.

"I would like to work with Iosef on this," Rostnikov said, putting down his pencil.

"The choice, as always, is yours, Chief Inspector," said the Yak. "You wish to work with your son. Do so. As I say, the choice is yours. You have any questions?"

"One," said Rostnikov, pocketing his pencil. "Why did you ask me if I knew Tsimion Vladovka rather than if I had heard of him?"

The Yak smiled. It wasn't a very good smile. It was touched with the suggestion of a cunning secret knowledge, to make those who witnessed it slightly uncomfortable.

"In the last transmission before the rescue, Vladovka mentioned your name."

"In what context?" asked Rostnikov, pausing as his hand reached over to close the notebook.

"There was no context. He simply said 'Porfiry Petrovich Rostnikov.' "

"And was he not asked of this when he returned to earth?"

"I do not know. The fact that he mentioned your name is in the file before you. The reason he did so is not in the file you have before you."

"Then I will begin by finding someone to whom I can ask the question," said Rostnikov, rising far less awkwardly than he had when he first acquired his unresponsive leg. "He has a wife, children?"

"Wife died several months ago, cancer. No children. He has a father, brother, somewhere on a farm near St. Petersburg. He hasn't seen them in years."

"Then . . ."

"I have arranged for you to meet with the director of security at Star City. His name is Mikhail Stoltz. He spoke to the cosmonauts when they were brought back to earth."

Rostnikov was up now. The Yak joined him.

"He had friends?"

"Vladovka is known to be a rather solitary man."

"The other two cosmonauts on that flight?"

"One, Rodya Baklunov, died during an experiment on earth. He was a biologist. The other, Vladimir Kinotskin, works at Star City. It's all in the file before you."

"Final question," said Rostnikov, tucking his notebook into his pocket and picking up the mug. "Why has it taken a year before anyone contacted me about this mention of my name in outer space?"

"That," said the Yak, "you will have to ask Stoltz. And remember, do not question Vladovka when you find him. Simply find him and report his whereabouts to me."

"And," Rostnikov added, "I am to see to it that he remains where I locate him, or bring him to you if I believe he will run."

"Precisely."

Rostnikov nodded. The Yak had not said, "if you find him." He had said, "when you find him." This could be a sign of confidence in his chief inspector, but, Rostnikov knew, it also could be a warning. Find him, Porfiry Petrovich. Do not fail.

In the outer office, Rostnikov handed the cup to Pankov.

"You didn't finish."

"I had enough. It more than served its purpose. I thank you, Pankov."

"You are welcome, Comra . . . Inspector Rostnikov."

"It is hard to get rid of old habits, Pankov."

"Very hard," the little man said, sitting back in the chair behind his desk and placing the mug before him.

Rostnikov clasped his hands together and very gently tapped his knuckles against his chin as he looked toward the window, lost in thought.

"Can I help you with anything?" Pankov asked.

"No," said Rostnikov. "I was thinking of flying benches and flying spheres and how thoughts come to us and sometimes make contact with flying mysteries which cannot be explained by our science. Where were you when the sky went berserk, Pankov?"

Not for the first time Pankov wondered if the chief inspector were more than slightly mad, not the everyday madness of almost all Russians but a special puzzling madness.

"You mean the storm? I was here, at my desk."

"You heard? You felt?"

"Yes."

"Were you frightened?"

"No, yes, maybe a little."

Pankov did not like these odd conversations with Rostnikov, but at the same time Rostnikov was the only one who talked to Pankov as if he actually existed, had feelings, ideas.

"Good, sometimes it is good to be a little frightened."

Pankov knew his office was wired by the director. He had learned this accidentally only a few months earlier, but he should have known, should have guessed. Now he was careful and spent much of his time trying to remember if he had said anything disloyal about the director since he had replaced Colonel Snitkonoy. Pankov longed for the old days when he served as loyal lap dog and admirer of the Gray Wolfhound. But they were gone and he had yet to figure out what his role should be with his new superior.

Inside his office, Director Yaklovev was not listening to the conversation between Pankov and Rostnikov. He was taping it but he had no intention of listening to it later. In fact, it had been weeks since he last eavesdropped on his secretary. The conversations he heard yielded nothing of interest. Pankov was nearly a perfect assistant. He did what he was told to do out of fear, and he was loyal to the director for the same reason.

The Yak had come to a conclusion soon after the Soviet Union had collapsed. Some of that conclusion was the result of observing the obvious, and some had come from drawing cautious conclusions about the future.

The obvious part of his conclusion was that there was no Russian governmental, political, or economic system. Communism had gone and been replaced by a loose confederacy of flexible and inflexible powers with Yeltsin as the spokesperson, a spokesperson posing as a strong man, with little or no idea of what he was representing. There was no system. There were no checks and balances. There was a duma that complained about, supported, and waited with fear for the fall of what now served as the government.

To the Americans and the West in general, Yeltsin and his ever-changing cabinet had asserted that Russia was now a capitalist democracy in which the people voted and the government acted on their behalf. Yes, thought the Yak, they voted, but in a system in which they had no idea of what the candidates really believed or what power they actually had. Perhaps there had been no time in history when a nation was run by leaders who had no idea of what the law was or what their own philosophy might be. The new president, Putin, was no better than Yeltsin, only more sober.

Yaklovev was reasonably sure the economy would collapse again, and perhaps again, and the government would fall, each time to be replaced by a leadership that walked the line between limited reforms and capitalism and a tempered socialism that would go by the nostalgic name of Communism, socialism, or something else it really was not.

The Yak was prepared. He had weighed the names of those who were likely to take over not only the next government but the one beyond that, and he had, through his office, systematically continued the agenda he had begun when still with the KGB. He would build a collection of evidence that could be used to obtain the gratitude of any faction or factions that succeeded. It was, perhaps, a unique agenda, one that would take him quite far if he was careful, and he intended to continue to be careful.

Yaklovev was not far from making his next career move. In little more than a year he had compiled documents and tapes that would embarrass some members of the government and the business community to the point where they would be happy to cooperate with him, providing he did not ask too much. The Yak did them all favors. He asked for little or nothing beyond their support, and he did not intend to ask for more than they would be willing to give. He was not after money. He wanted to be deputy minister of the Interior, to stay there and amass more for his files and to move up to the head of the ministry if and when the times were right.

Rostnikov had helped him. Rostnikov could help him even more. With this very case, Rostnikov could provide enough for Yaklovev to consider making that move. If the times were right.

He moved to his desk and thought for an instant of the sketch Rostnikov had made in his pad while they were talking. Yaklovev had caught only a glimpse of it, but the memory was clear.

Rostnikov had drawn a very reasonable likeness of a bird in flight. The bird's right wing was bent at an odd angle, possibly broken, and there was a distinct tear in the bird's eye as he looked downward, toward the earth, possibly for a place to land.

Rostnikov was eccentric. Igor Yaklovev had been told that before he became director. But Rostnikov was good, very good at his job, and those who worked with him were also good and loyal. That loyalty did not, Yaklovev knew, extend to the director, but he had an agreement with Rostnikov. Rostnikov would be given the assignments and have a free hand. When trouble arose, Yaklovev would do his best to protect Rostnikov and his group. He had proven many times that he would do so. Yaklovev knew that he was only as good as his word. Those he dealt with, friends and enemies, knew that if he declared or promised, the Yak would keep that declaration or promise. There were two conditions to his agreement with Rostnikov. First, Yaklovev would receive all the credit for the difficult cases resolved by the Office of Special Investigation. He would also accept all the responsibility for those not resolved. And so it was important that those cases which no one else wanted, those cases which were dumped on his office because they were politically sensitive or unlikely to be resolved, be dealt with successfully. The second condition was that Rostnikov and the other inspectors ask no questions about the disposal of cases. They were to bring in the information, and the director was to decide on its resolution with no questions asked.

So far, it had worked well. Yaklovev was determined that the system continue to work.

When Akardy Zelach slouched in precisely on time, precisely on the hour, Emil Karpo put down his pen, closed his notebook, and walked past him with only the slightest motion of his head to indicate that Zelach should follow.

Zelach had just enough time to place the bag of lunch his mother had prepared on the desk in his small cubicle. The bag was brown paper. The bag was wet. He didn't have time to take off his coat as he hurried to keep up with the man in black with whom he had been teamed.

Zelach was forty-one but looked older. His eyesight had been deteriorating and he had been forced to wear glasses. The glasses were round with thin rims of brown. Unfortunately, they did not make him look any more intelligent. At first he had been reluctant to wear the glasses, afraid Chief Inspector Rostnikov or even the Yak would see his poor eyesight as a reason why he should not be a policeman.

Zelach's mother had gotten him to wear the spectacles by pointing out that if the Office of Special Investigation had a one-legged chief, it would certainly not mind having a nearsighted inspector.

"Where are we going?" asked Zelach as he nearly ran to keep pace with the Vampire.

"Down," said Karpo.

"Down," Zelach repeated as they started down the stairs. "Did you see the rain?"

"I heard the storm," said Karpo.

"They say the roof of the Bolshoi was ripped off, cars were overturned, children picked up and tossed about like . . . tossed about."

"Probably gross exaggeration."

"Probably," said Zelach as they passed the main floor and headed down. He knew where they were going now. Perhaps he should have brought his wet lunch bag. It was not going to be a pleasant morning.

Two flights below ground level, Karpo walked to a steel door and opened it. Zelach reluctantly followed. The room was large and had the smell of the dead. Zelach knew the smell. He had been a policeman for half of his life. But the laboratory of Paulinin was something different. It was low-ceilinged, large, and cluttered with tables and shelves filled with objects and jars. Inside the jars of liquid floated specimens taken from the recently and sometimes long-dead that Paulinin had examined. Knives, saws, lamps, boxes, machine parts, clothing, table legs, and books—hundreds, maybe thousands of books—were piled on the floor. The room was a death trap if fire should break out, and the only way to the rear of the room where Paulinin now stood over a corpse was through this labyrinth of books, shelves, and objects.

Zelach followed Karpo to the rear of the room, the most lighted area of the dark space. Lights shone down on the white corpse.

Paulinin was concentrating on the hole he had opened in the skull of the bearded, slightly overweight corpse on the table before him. Paulinin's hair was, as always, wild and his white coat stained with things that Zelach did not wish to think about.

Paulinin looked up and saw Karpo wending his way toward him. "Emil Karpo," he said with clear pleasure. "And who is . . . ah, Zelach. Coffee?"

"I think not," said Karpo. "Not at the moment. We must get to the center by ten."

"But we are still scheduled for lunch Friday?"

"Yes," said Karpo.

"Zelach, you are lucky to be working with this man," Paulinin said, pointing a scalpel at Zelach but not looking up from the corpse. "Very lucky."

Praise coming from Paulinin was always suspect. It was acknowledged that Paulinin, as good as he might be—and he was very good—was rather mad, and if he did not like you, you were certain to be subjected to undisguised scorn, abuse, or ridicule. Normally, Paulinin reserved his anger for the pathologists "upstairs."

As good as Paulinin was, there were few in either the procurator's office or uniformed police divisions who came to him. They preferred second-rate scientists to one who attacked them about amateur work and befouling crime scenes.

"I have been talking to your friend here," Paulinin said, putting his hand gently on the shoulder of the corpse of Sergei Bolskanov. "He has told me a great deal. The hammer you found was, indeed, the murder weapon. Even one of the idiots called in by the fools upstairs should know that; even Doldinov, the new young one, destined for increasing incompetence and promotion, would know the rest. No, he probably would not."

"What would he not know?" asked Karpo, standing with Zelach across the table on which the corpse lay, eyes open.

"Ah," said Paulinin. "Our killer was not particularly powerful. The blows were not deep. Our killer was angry, in a rage, frantic. The blows were many. Our killer was in a state of panic, searching for the brain. There was probably premeditation, an incompetent premeditation. The hammer is not large. It is not the best weapon for someone planning a murder. And Sergei here almost certainly knew his killer."

"How do you know?" Zelach said before he could stop himself.

Paulinin smiled. He welcomed the question.

"There are no defensive wounds on Sergei's arms. Someone approached him, raised a hammer, probably one hidden behind his back, hit him twice in the face. Baklunov did not raise his arms, made no move to protect himself. After that he was in no condition to protect himself. He was killed by someone he knew, someone he did not expect to attack him. Someone he didn't even turn to more than glance at. Someone he didn't consider a physical threat."

"What else did he tell you?" asked Karpo, standing with his hands clasped before him at waist level.

In the shadows of the bright light pointed downward, Karpo looked particularly ghostly to Zelach.

"A few whispers, a few whispers," Paulinin whispered. "Our Sergei's skull has an old scar beneath the hair, and his brain has a healed lesion where something, probably a tumor, has been removed, perhaps a decade ago or longer. Sergei is suggesting his killer was going after that very spot with the hammer, that very spot. I can't be sure yet, but it appears to be the case."

"Did he tell you why?" asked Karpo.

"Not yet, not yet. But if it is so, and I think it is, our murderer knew Bolskanov well, knew his skull hid a vulnerable secret. Would you like to know what he had for his final meal and approximately when he had it?"

"If you believe it is relevant information," said Karpo.

"Interesting information but probably not relevant. I would tentatively conclude that Sergei was a vegetarian. You might ask some of his colleagues or his family. I am curious. It might or might not mean anything."

"We will ask," said Karpo.

"Well," said Paulinin, looking at the open skull on his table. "In addition to the brain injury, he has had two broken ribs in his life, but they are not recent. I would conjecture that the ribs were broken about the same time he developed the tumor or whatever it was that was surgically removed from his brain. That is about all that is pathologically interesting. His killer left no blood of his or her own at the scene, as far as I can tell at this point. The hammer, however, is a bit more interesting. The murderer wiped the handle on Sergei's laboratory coat. How do I know? Because there is a smudge of blood from the handle at the bottom of the coat where there is no splattering of blood from Sergei's wounds. The killer either flung the hammer, holding on to the bloody head of the hammer to which clung bits of brain, into the corner, protecting it from prints with the coat, which would be very awkward and make it difficult to throw that far, or the killer let it fall to the floor. Most people would choose not to do that. In addition, the head of the hammer did not appear to have been handled. Skull and brain fragments, not to mention blood drops, seem reasonably intact."

"Then what?" asked Zelach.

"The murderer," said Paulinin, standing short but erect in the pose of a lecturer, "simply dropped the hammer and kicked it into the corner. A very close examination of the floor yielded very small scratches from the hammer as it slid along, leaving tiny fragments of brain, blood, and bone too far from the body to have been there as a result of the attack. So what do we learn from this?"

Zelach had no idea.

"The murderer may have stepped on these traces of blood, brain, and bone," said Karpo. "The solution to your murder lies in a pair of *tufli*, 'shoes.' "

"You are nearly perfect, Emil Karpo, very nearly perfect," said Paulinin with delight. "Only Porfiry Petrovich himself approaches you. Our killer certainly washed or got rid of clothing, but being Russian and seeing no significant trace of anything on his shoe, he would, at most, merely have wiped it as a precaution. Maybe not even that. I prefer it if he did wipe it. The game is only good if there is a challenge."

"As always, Paulinin, you have been *vyeelyeekahlyehpnah*, 'magnificent,' " said Karpo.

"Only from you would I find such praise meaningful," said Paulinin, looking at Zelach, who nodded, praying that they could now get out of this dungeon. "One more observation. Our friend here was slovenly, probably very slovenly. His fingernails are uneven, bitten. There are signs of old dirt under those fingernails. The trousers he was wearing were badly in need of cleaning. His socks had holes and there was a significant hole in one pocket. In the other he had accumulated four pens, three paper clips, some keys on a ring, coins, and lint. I would guess that his home and work space are a mess."

Zelach avoided looking around the cluttered room. The word *mess* would be inadequate to describe what he knew and didn't know was around him.

"Lunch Friday," said Karpo.

"And a game of chess?"

"Certainly, a game of chess."

"We are talking about the life of Tolstoy. We are talking about an announced major screening at the Cannes Film Festival, at festivals all over the world. We are talking about an international cast and the brightest, most creative young Russian film director. We are talking about Cinema Russia Production Company, my life."

The man making this small speech was pacing back and forth, smoking, looking at Elena Timofeyeva and Sasha Tkach, who were seated on wooden chairs facing him.

The room was clean but smelled of smoke, stale smoke. There was a conference table, one end of which was covered with scripts, mail, and papers with an overfull ashtray nearby. The end of the table where this clutter resided served as the desk of the man who was pacing and rambling.

His name was Yuri Kriskov. Sometimes he used the *v*. Other times he ended his name with the older *ff* and became Kriskoff. It all depended on his audience. Everything depended on his audience.

Yuri Kriskov was reasonably well known. He was not quite famous. He was a movie producer. His job, at which he had been mildly successful before the fall of the Soviet Union, was now busy and lucrative. Yuri had once been a businessman with connections in the government, some of which he still retained. He was fifty-two years old, of average height and weight, with a full head of dark hair which he carefully touched up each morning to keep the gray away. Yuri had two children by his current wife, Vera, his third, who had starred in his first film, *Strange Snow*. Yuri also had a young mistress. The mistress was primarily for show. Yuri had almost no sex drive, a fact about which his wives had frequently complained. Yuri's passion was reserved for movies.

"Where was I?" he asked, looking at Elena.

"The Cannes Film Festival," she said.

"Yes, the Cannes Film Festival."

"May we summarize what you have told us so far?" Elena asked.

"If you wish," Yuri said, sitting at his end of the table and searching for another cigarette.

Sasha looked at his watch. They had been in this room for almost an hour and he knew that Elena would and could summarize the whole situation in a few minutes.

"You were called at home at approximately three in the morning. A man said that he had the negative of your Tolstoy film and he wanted two million American dollars for it or he would destroy the negative and kill you. You told him he was crazy and hung up. He called again and told you to go check, that he would call you back in two days. That means tomorrow?"

"I think so. I think it must. He didn't call this morning," said Yuri, searching for the package of cigarettes now lost somewhere under the papers on the table. "He wants the money tomorrow."

"You got dressed," Elena continued, "called your editor, came to your office, where your editor met you to tell you that the negative was indeed missing, that the cabinet in which it was being kept had been broken into. You then made a call and discovered that the backup negative . . ."

"Of inferior quality because it is a copy," Yuri said impatiently.

"Of inferior quality," Elena continued, "was also missing. The film cost approximately thirty-six million American dollars to make, that's a million dollars more than *The Barber of Siberia*, making your film about the life of Tolstoy the most expensive movie ever made in Russia and . . ."

"But that's not the point," Yuri said, standing and pointing his cigarette at the two detectives. "It took us two years to make that movie. The world expects it, awaits it. Our film industry is trying to earn worldwide respect. If we don't have the film, and quickly, our country, our government, *I* will be humiliated, ridiculed, laughed at. Our government doesn't want this. I don't want this and our backers do not want it."

"Your backers?" said Sasha.

Yuri sat again.

"They are not important in this discussion other than the fact that they want the movie finished and shown. They want awards. I don't think they would simply be satisfied to get their money back."

"You can go to them for the two million," Sasha said. "If you have to give it to the thief, we can track him or them down and get the money back."

"Hah," said Yuri. "And hah again. I could pay these criminals and they could destroy my negatives and murder me."

"Why?" asked Elena. "What could they gain?"

"They could do it out of spite," Yuri said slowly, as if explaining the situation to a backward child. "They could do it for fun. They could do it to destroy me. There are people on the streets of Moscow who would kill you if they asked you for a match and you didn't have one."

"Your backers are Mafia," Sasha said.

"I did not say that," Yuri said, backing off. "I said nothing like that, implied nothing like that. If you choose to draw such a conclusion, I cannot stop you, but think, if my backers were Mafia, I could not go to them for money to pay a . . . a . . . a negative-kidnapper. Even if they gave me the money, even if I got the negative back, they might suspect that I was doing this just to get two million dollars. They might simply think I was incompetent. They might do anything. You never know what such people will do. No, no, I cannot go to my backers for money."

"The government might . . ." Sasha tried.

"No," said Yuri, pacing again. "I called people this morning, early, before you came. The government cannot be a part of this, will not. The embarrassment—no, it is clear. The government has enough problems. It will not get involved in a possible cultural disaster. I am alone."

He ran his right hand through his hair as he paced in anguish.

"When do they want the money?" asked Elena.

"Tomorrow. I told you. They want the money tomorrow or they will destroy the negatives and kill me, or so they say. They will call tomorrow in the morning, early, at home, and tell me what to do."

"How are you to deliver it?" asked Sasha.

"Cash, American dollars, nothing less than hundred-dollar bills and nothing more than thousand-dollar bills. They said they will meet with me alone and will give me phone directions about where to bring the money. I'm to have it ready at my home and be prepared to move quickly. They warned me that they would know if there was anything traceable on the bills, any markings or any dyes in the bag, they would come back and kill me and my family."

"Unfortunately, you will be unable to go to this meeting," said Sasha.

"Of course I can't. I don't have the money."

"You will tell them you have the money but you can't go," said Sasha. "You have a bad heart. You had a sudden attack today, angina because of all this. You will send your nephew in your place."

"You will send your niece," Elena said.

"Nephew would be more convincing," said Sasha.

"Do I get a vote?" asked Yuri.

"No," said Sasha.

The two detectives were looking at each other now and not at the confused producer.

"We will discuss it and tell you in a few hours," said Elena. "If the thieves call before the morning, tell them you are getting the money together. Say nothing about your bad heart, tell them you'll be home and waiting for their call. We will be with you. They said they will call early. We'll be at your home at five in the morning. If the phone rings before we arrive, don't answer it."

"But . . ."

"Don't answer it," Sasha said.

"All right," said Yuri, going back to his space at the end of the table. "This is a great movie, a truly great movie. They've stolen the life of Tolstoy. Could anything be worse for a Russian to do? What has happened to national pride?"

"We will get your negative back," said Elena, rising.

"We'll get it back," echoed Sasha, rising.

"Here," said Yuri, pushing some papers across his desk and picking something up. He moved to the seated detectives and handed two yellow cardboard rectangles to Sasha. "Tickets for tonight. The Khudozhestvenny Theater. I don't know what the movie is."

"Thank you," said Sasha, pocketing the tickets.

"And now," Elena said. "We would like a list of everyone who had access to the negative and we would like to meet them."

"Then," said Yuri with alarm, "they'll know I've brought in the police."

"We are not the police," said Sasha. "We are potential investors in your next film. We represent a French production company. Gaumont. No, Canal Plus."

"I don't know," said Yuri, lighting a new cigarette, his hands shaking.

"Fortunately," said Elena, "we do."

"The list is long," said Yuri. "Editors, assistant editors, me, cleaning ladies. The list is long. And who knows who these people might let in? We keep the negatives locked in a cabinet in a temperature-controlled room, but we don't do anything particular to keep people out except for the sign on the door that says Keep Out."

"Humor us," said Sasha. "Make the list. Take us on a tour."

"A tour and a list," Yuri said, shaking his head. "A list and a tour. Yesterday I was happy, ecstatic. Today I am despondent. Tomorrow I may well be dead."

And with that they left. Yuri Kriskov or Kriskoff led the two detectives out of the room, walking in front of them, smoking nervously, and pondering his fate.

Valery Grachev pondered his next move. He did not look up at the fat, bald old man across the table who sat with his arms folded, no expression, his large lower lip pouting out. Was it a trap? The path was too open. His opponent too clever. No, he would not move his queen to check the old man's king. He would wait. Valery moved his queen's knight's pawn two spaces forward.

The Central Chess Club was crowded. It usually was. This was the home of Russian chess champions. The photos of those champions lined the gray walls, lit by chandeliers hanging from the center of the room. Though there were many people, there was almost total silence, with the exception of someone moving a chair to rise or sit, or the occasional cough, throat clearing, or sneeze.

The fat man wore an incongruous red blazer. It looked new. He was probably uncomfortable but he didn't show it. Two gangly boys with strangely colored hair played at the table next to that of Valery and the fat man. Both boys wore T-shirts. On the shirt of the boy next to Valery was the word *Guts* in English and the colorful picture of a full-lipped mouth open wide and a massive tongue protruding from it. The boy's hair was red and green. His opponent's T-shirt bore the words *Bad Ass* and depicted a woman leaning over to reveal her naked rear end. This boy's hair was orange with white streaks. He also had a tattoo on his left biceps. It was the picture of a woman winking.

Valery had played against the boy with the tattoo several times in Timiryazevsky Park. They were even in games.

On the other side of Valery and the fat man, two women, intense, dark, maybe in their forties, wearing dreary dresses and short hair, were glaring at each other, only a few pieces remaining on their board.

Gary Kasparov, the world champion, had played here. Vladimir Kramnik, the second-ranked player in the world, played here.

The old man still had not moved. Valery should have insisted on a clock, but, if he had, the old man would probably not have accepted his challenge and Valery would be standing and watching others play. The old man was good, probably better than Valery, but the old man could make mistakes. He had already done so trading pawns at mid-board.

Valery was twenty-four. He was five-feet four-inches tall, had the build and face of a bulldog, and a passion for chess which led to the nickname he bore proudly—*Kon*, "the Knight." He lived in a small apartment with his uncle, who sold used goods from a cart in a small open-air market in the rubble of a fallen building on Yauzsky Street. Valery's salary was more than his uncle earned, and so Valery contributed a bit and had a place to live and no privacy. Soon Valery would have more than enough money to move out.

Valery was playing two games at the same time, one with the fat man, the other with Yuri Kriskov. He was not certain that he would beat the fat man, but Kriskov was a fool, a clever fool but a fool nonetheless.

The game had begun. The bulky rolls of negative were well hidden along with the gun, which he fully intended to use if Kriskov did not pay. Tomorrow he would call, make the next move. He had already anticipated that Kriskov would turn to the police, that a simple exchange would not be possible. He would change the direction of the game, make moves Kriskov could not follow. Check was close by and checkmate not far behind. Valery had an advantage his opponent did not anticipate, an advantage that would make the next move and even the entire defensive game of Yuri Kriskov known to him.

The fat man grunted. His left hand hovered over the board for an instant and then he moved his king's knight over the pawn to the left.

Valery didn't hesitate. Before the fat man's hand was back across the chest of his red blazer, Valery moved his queen's bishop across the board to a square at the left side of the board.

The fat man had made exactly the move Valery had hoped for. The game would not be quick, but the advantage definitely belonged to Valery Grachev.

Chapter Three

★ ★ ★ ★ ★ ★ ★ ★ ★ ★ ★ ★

Mikhail Stoltz was a very big, bulky man with close-cropped white hair, a bit younger than Rostnikov. He wore a blue tailored suit, a light blue button-down shirt, and a red-and-blue diagonally striped tie. His black patent-leather shoes were well polished. Stoltz, Porfiry Petrovich, and Iosef were seated on a bench in Pushkin Square outside of the McDonald's. The meeting place was Stoltz's idea. The rain had long stopped and the park looked as if the storm had not touched it.

Stoltz smoked a cigarette and looked at the father-and-son detectives.

"You recognize me?" Stoltz said.

"Three years ago. The Sokolniki Recreation Park," said Rostnikov. "Senior weight-lifting competition."

Stoltz nodded, looked at his cigarette, and said, "You easily won the bench press, but, as I recall, you couldn't compete in some of the other events because of . . ."

Stoltz looked down at Rostnikov's legs. The day was warm and humid. Rostnikov was sweating under his lightest suit. He would prefer to be in the air-conditioned noise of McDonald's, eating a Big Mac.

"My leg is gone," said Rostnikov. "It is in a large bottle two floors below ground-level in Petrovka. We have an eccentric technician who collects such trophies."

"Paulinin," said Stoltz.

"Paulinin," Rostnikov confirmed.

"His eccentricity and skill are known to many of us," said Stoltz. "Your leg?"

"It has been replaced by a leg of metal and plastic," said Rostnikov. "Perhaps I can persuade it to cooperate so that I can compete in other events this year. As I recall, you won both the dead lift and the clean and jerk."

Stoltz nodded.

Iosef tried to keep his mind on this foreplay, but his thoughts were of Elena Timofeyeva. She had agreed to marry him. He was sure she did not think it a particularly good idea, at least not a good idea for either of their careers. The Office of Special Investigation would have three Rostnikovs. That might be one too many for Yaklovev, who, Iosef knew, was not particularly fond of him.

Iosef was a bit taller and certainly leaner than his father. His father's hair was dark. Iosef's was light. His father had the face of hundreds, no, thousands of Russians one sees on the street. Iosef had the look of Scandinavia. His looks were certainly the gift of his mother.

". . . why he would disappear," Stoltz was saying when Iosef managed to rejoin the conversation.

A man in a ragged coat far too warm for the weather staggered to the bench and paused, hands in his pockets. The man was bearded. His hair was a bush of dirty darkness and his eyes were red with alcohol.

Stoltz paused and looked up at the man. "What?"

"This is my bench," the ragged man said. "I need to sleep."

"You need to go away," said Stoltz with irritation. "These men are the police."

"Then," said the man, "they should take responsibility for vacating this bench. This bench is mine. Ask anyone. This bench is mine by virtue of the law of primogeniture."

"Do you know what that means?" asked Rostnikov, looking up.

"Of course," the ragged man said, swaying. "Property of the father goes to the firstborn male. This bench belonged to my father. Many was the time when my mother sent me here to drag him home, if you call the hallway we lived in home."

"We're touched by your troubles," said Stoltz, rising to face him. "Now go away and come back in an hour."

The ragged man swayed, but he did not move.

"You have a name?" asked Rostnikov.

"Everyone has a name," the ragged man said, hands still in his pockets, eyes meeting those of Stoltz, who could have lifted the filthy creature above his head and thrown him for a new park record.

"And yours is? . . ."

"Dovnikovich, Andrei Ivanov Dovnikovich. I used to be a teacher of Russian to people who spoke only Spanish. I had Cubans, Mexicans. I made a living. Now the Cubans don't come anymore and the Mexicans are learning English."

"Would you be willing to tell your obviously interesting story to my son here over a cheeseburger?"

"I have my pride," said the ragged man. "Does he want to hear my tale?"

"I can think of nothing I would prefer," said Iosef, standing and looking at his father with a sigh.

"Two cheeseburgers, fries, and a Coca-Cola. No, a milkshake, strawberry," said the ragged man, finally moving his eyes from those of Stoltz to those of Rostnikov, who was the only one still seated.

"That sounds reasonable," said Rostnikov. "Iosef, break bread with Andrei Ivanov Dovnikovich and hear his story. Then later you can tell it to me. I'm sorry we cannot join you, but with your permission we would like to conclude some business on your bench."

"You have my permission," said the ragged man, closing his eyes and bringing his head down with a bow.

Iosef and the man moved away, across the grass, toward the short line waiting to get into the McDonald's.

Stoltz looked down. "His life story," he said, shaking his head.

"I look forward to hearing it," said Rostnikov, turning his head to watch his son and the ragged man move toward the line. "My son will tell it well. Iosef used to be a playwright."

"And now he is a policeman," said Stoltz.

"He was not a good playwright," said Rostnikov. "He may become a good policeman. Vladovka."

"Vladovka, Tsimion Vladovka," Stoltz repeated, sitting again on the Dovnikovich bench. "You have the information you need in the file we gave to Director Yaklovev, but I understand you have questions . . ."

"Many. Where can I find the other cosmonaut? Kinotskin? His location is not indicated in the file."

"Why talk to him?" asked Stoltz, throwing his cigarette stub in the general direction of a metal trash basket.

"I want to know what he knows about Vladovka, the last flight, perhaps why he mentioned my name. Do you know why he mentioned my name? Did he ever tell you when he was back on earth?"

"No," said Stoltz. "Perhaps you can ask him if you find him."

"When I find him," Rostnikov corrected, shifting uncomfortably on the bench. "Director Yaklovev has given me no option."

Rostnikov could not imagine the ragged man sleeping here. It would take a decidedly unhealthy intake of vodka.

"I suppose I can give you Kinotskin's address," said Stoltz. "He would be easy to find in any case. He works for the space program, for me, in fact, in security at Star City. I'll set up a meeting, but I warn you, there is nothing he can tell you that will lead you to Vladovka."

"Perhaps not, but . . ."

"You have information on Vladovka's entire life," said Stoltz, a bit impatiently. "We sent your office a copy of our file. Where he is from, who his friends and relatives are, and what he looks like. Why not start with his family?"

"I think, perhaps, our office has the case because others, State Security, have talked to them and come away with nothing. I will talk to his family, but first another direction."

"The other cosmonauts," said Stoltz.

"Yes."

"Well, it will be but one meeting. Baklunov is dead. Cancer of the liver. He went quickly."

"On the flight, he was . . ."

". . . conducting experiments. He was a biologist. Very promising. His death was a tragedy for the program, for Russia," said Stoltz. "Other questions?"

"What happened on that last flight that required an emergency rescue of Tsimion Vladovka and the others?"

"Test results came in," said Stoltz. "Results of tests taken routinely on all cosmonauts. Sometimes the results take a long time to get to us. We learned of Baklunov's cancer and were told that he had to come back for treatment."

"Why did the others not stay in space?"

"Vladovka and Kinotskin had been on the mission for many months. A new team was ready. Since we were nearing the end of the *Mir* program and the expense of sending a shuttle to the station was so great, we would simply make the replacement planned for two months later and save the expense of another shuttle flight. Kinotskin will verify and give you details if you like."

"And the cosmonauts who replaced them," said Rostnikov. "I would like to talk to them."

"I'll see what I can arrange, but it may well take a while."

"May I ask why?"

"Oh, two are out of the country, an extended stay in the United States to consult on their proposed manned space efforts. An attempt to continue to build relations with the Americans. Actually, I do not trust the Americans, but I do not make policy."

"And the other cosmonaut who took over the mission?"

"Bobchek is in China now," said Stoltz, looking across the square at two old men engaged in a bitter argument. "Went with our blessing, reluctant blessing, but a blessing nonetheless. He is a consultant to a computer-chip development company. Eventually they will discover, if they have not already, that Bobchek was the least bright of all the cosmonauts in the last forty years. His conciliative powers are negative. We could not plant a more effective agent with the Chinese to impede their electronic research if we planned for a decade. There are no plans for his return."

Rostnikov nodded and began the awkward process of getting up. "You have no idea of why Vladovka would run, hide?" he asked. "No theory of your own?"

Stoltz shrugged. "Who knows? A woman perhaps. An offer from a foreign government, possibly the French, possibly the English. Vladovka knows a great deal about our space program."

"A great deal that we have not shared with other countries and that they do not already know?"

"Who knows what other countries will pay for? The space race is on again. We are behind on launching a new station with the Americans. Vladovka could possibly embarrass us with what he knows of our problems. We would certainly survive such embarrassment but . . . You know. You have superiors. I have people to whom I must report. Those in charge, as you well know, have but a tenuous grasp on their power. Embarrassments can be used to destroy people."

Rostnikov, now standing, nodded. He believed very little that

Stoltz had told him. The man was too cooperative, too ready with answers. More was going on than Rostnikov was being told, or was likely to be told by Kinotskin, the one cosmonaut other than Vladovka who knew about the flight, but still . . .

The two men shook hands.

"I'll call your office with a time and place to meet Kinotskin."

"Soon," said Rostnikov. "Preferably today."

"We all want Vladovka found soon," said Stoltz.

"Do you like Vladovka?" Rostnikov asked, his hand still in that of Stoltz. The hand he shook remained firm and strong, but Porfiry Petrovich felt something, the hint of a small, deep tremor perhaps.

"Does that make a difference?" Stoltz said, removing his hand.

"Who knows? The question came to me. I asked it. I'm curious. It is my job to be curious."

"No, I do not like Vladovka," said Stoltz, now meeting Rostnikov's eyes. "He is too much of a dreamer, too difficult to gauge. A botanist. He prefers the company of plants to that of people. I had the feeling he was elsewhere during many of our conversations, and he said odd things that he could or would not explain."

"Like my name?"

"Yes, precisely, like your name. Where he got it or why he mentioned it in space to me, I do not know; he never said when he returned to earth, but I think it ironic."

"How so?" asked Rostnikov.

"He chose the man who would track him down," said Stoltz.

Rostnikov nodded and looked around the small park. Not far from here was an old Russian Orthodox church that had been sold to Jews who had, as inconspicuously as possible, converted it to a synagogue. The rabbi, a young Israelite named Avrum Belinsky, was a friend of Rostnikov's through tragedy. Several young Jews had been murdered in what had appeared to be an anti-Semitic act of terror. Rostnikov had found the murderers with

Belinsky's help. The crime had been one of greed and not of
hate. Rostnikov and the young rabbi shared some secrets about
the case. Perhaps Rostnikov and Iosef would walk over to see the
rabbi after lunch.

"I'm going to join Iosef and Dovnikovich for lunch. Would
you like to come, talk about weights and competition?"

"No, thank you," said Stoltz. "I have to get back to our Moscow
office. Every day is problems."

Rostnikov nodded and said, "Then I look forward to your call
and to seeing you again. I am sure I will see you again."

It was Stoltz's chance to nod before he turned and walked
quickly away.

The Center for the Study of Technical Parapsychology was
within easy walking distance of the Kremlin. There was no sign
outside the gray-stone building indicating its purpose. Wedged in
between an eight-story red-brick office building and an Atmo-
spheric Research Center of hard concrete and proud sign, the
Center for Technical Parapsychology remained relatively anony-
mous. It had once housed the offices of the International Institute of Communist Parties and Development. Since then it had
gone through a massive renovation. The rooms they were shown
were all on one floor, the second floor. The first floor was reserved for offices, meeting rooms, a library, and a business-and-
records office.

Nothing in the brief explanation they had been given made
much sense to Zelach, who simply adjusted his glasses and followed Karpo and the woman in the gray suit who wore glasses
far more stylish than his. She was about forty, a bit on the thin
side, and plain of appearance with short dark hair. She wore a
white laboratory coat. She used no makeup and walked with her
hands folded across her small breasts. Her one attractive feature,
as far as Zelach was concerned, though he would not admit it

to himself, was her ample mouth. She spoke slowly, deliberately, but it made no difference in Akardy Zelach's comprehension.

"We, I mean the Soviet Union, were the first to officially sanction the study of psi phenomena," Nadia Spectorski said as she had opened the door of the first room, which contained a wall of steel-colored machines, some with metal arms jutting out. "Do you know the term *psi?*"

"Psi," said Karpo, examining the room, "is the twenty-third letter of the Greek alphabet. It is a general term for the entire spectrum of paranormal phenomena."

"Ah," she had said. "Then you have followed our findings and publications."

"No," said Karpo, "but I am aware of the field of study."

"And you are skeptical?" she asked.

"I am skeptical about all things," Karpo said.

"Well, perhaps you should see some of the films of our experiments," she said, arms still folded.

"Perhaps," Karpo said.

"We are scientists, Inspector, not mystics. We objectively examine telepathy, prophecy, and above all dreams and psychokinesis, the ability to move objects with the mind alone."

"I am aware of your studies," Karpo said. "This room?"

"Measures electrical and magnetic changes in subjects engaged in experiments," she said. "We are not the largest center in Russia for the study of psi phenomena. That is in St. Petersburg at the university, but our work is critical and quite different. And, I might add, underfunded. We used to receive our primary budget from the government, but now we have been forced to seek outside support through our Psychic Research Foundation. We even get money from Americans and the Japanese."

"The room where the murder took place," said Karpo.

Nadia Spectorski nodded and moved down the hall, now passing numbered white doors, and stopped in front of room 27.

"Here," she said.

"The dead man, Sergei Bolskanov, what was his area of specialization?"

"Telekinesis, dream states, several things," she said, opening the door and reaching in to turn on the fluorescent lights, which tinkled to life. The room was clean and relatively empty. A table sat in the middle of the room, a small table with a white top. There were chairs facing each other across the table and, in the wall to the right, a large mirror.

"Sergei Bolskanov was a brilliant physiologist," she said. "His experiments, more than twenty years of them with every kind of person, children, politburo members, catatonics, self-proclaimed psychics, cosmonauts, were conducted in this room, filmed through that one-way mirror. They were simple experiments but controlled. The floor, for example, was specially installed and insulated. It floats on designed material so that there are no external vibrations. Objects would be placed on the table. Sometimes Bolskanov would be in the room. Sometimes he would not. Various small objects of widely different material would be placed on the table. The subject would be connected to nonintrusive wires to monitor his or her breathing and physiological responses."

"Objects," said Karpo.

"Oh," said Nadia, pursing her lips, "blocks of wood, glasses of water, toys, books, individual sheets of paper, batteries, the list was long. The results impressive."

"Tools? A hammer perhaps?"

"The one that was used to kill him? Perhaps. He experimented with hundreds of objects."

"Could the camera have been running when Sergei Bolskanov was murdered?" asked Karpo.

"I checked. The director of the center, Andrei Vanga, checked. It was not."

"I would like a list of everyone who was here when Bolskanov was murdered," said Karpo.

"That should be no problem," she said. "I'll show you the

sign-in book, which includes the time people checked in and the time they checked out. I have already examined it. There were only five of us, including Sergei. It was late at night."

"You were here," said Karpo.

"I was."

"And?"

"I was in my office downstairs. It is down the corridor away from the entrance. I saw and heard nothing. Even if I were standing directly outside this room, I would have heard and seen nothing. No sound escapes. That is true of all the laboratories."

Karpo looked around the room slowly and at the mirror. Zelach did the same but saw nothing of interest, and though he did not speak, he felt uneasy in the room. Normally he felt nothing particular, even when he was at a bloody crime scene in which more than one mutilated body was still lying. But this room made him decidedly uncomfortable.

"And your work?" asked Karpo, walking out of the room.

"Psychic probability and telepathy," she said. "I studied in England. My degree is from Moscow State University in psychological studies and anatomy."

"And you are not married?" Karpo said.

Nadia Spectorski took off her glasses and cocked her head to one side to examine the gaunt creature in black.

"I am not examining the possibility of a relationship," Karpo explained. "I am trying to obtain information."

"So that you can construct a series of possible scenarios, imagine the murder?" she asked.

"I have no imagination," Karpo said flatly. "I collect and analyze information. If the situation requires what you call imagination, I consult with my superior, Chief Inspector Rostnikov, who has a large imagination. Now, I would like to see the sign-in book and interview everyone who was here at the time of the murder. My colleague will then interview everyone in the employ of this facility who was not present."

"Certainly," she said. "Are we finished in here?"

"Yes," said Karpo. "The room next to this one, the one in which we can look through that mirror into this one."

Nadia Spectorski nodded, opened the door, and led them to the adjacent room.

"Why were you chosen to take us on this tour?" Karpo said. "You are not the director or even the assistant director."

"I volunteered," she said. "Sergei was not a well-liked man. To call him gruff, unpleasant, and secretive would be to minimize the extent of his clear and open dislike of the human race. I was probably the only one who had anything like a relationship with him, and that was simply cordial. Even Sergei needed someone with whom to discuss his ideas."

"He was not married," Karpo said.

"He was not."

Nadia Spectorski entered the second room but did not turn on the light. Through the mirrored window, they could see the scene of the murder. Nadia had intentionally left the light on. To one side of the mirror, on a tripod, stood a video camera.

"I should like to see the last tapes he made," Karpo said.

"That is no problem," she said. "However, the timing mechanism indicates that nothing has been recorded for several days."

"Still, I wish to see it."

"Easy enough," she said, opening the camera with a push of a button. "Here."

She handed the tape to Karpo, who placed it in his pocket. "And now I should like to talk to the others," he said.

"Before we do that," she said, leading the way back into the corridor and closing the door, "would you indulge me in a quick and simple experiment? It will take only a few minutes of your time. I have never worked with policemen before."

"Experiment?" asked Karpo.

"A deck of cards. It is something I do. Right down the corridor. I am being cooperative and will continue to be so. I could make your investigation difficult, though I have no reason to do so. Indulge me. It is something I do with all visitors."

Zelach shifted uneasily and considered speaking but decided against it.

"Ten minutes," said Karpo.

"And since I am obviously a suspect because I was here, you can also observe how I work and see if it yields anything about me you might be able to use."

Two minutes later they were in a room not much different from the laboratory of Sergei Bolskanov. This room was smaller, with no mirror. It was completely empty except for the table with four chairs. Nadia Spectorski sat on one side, the detectives on the other, facing her. She held something small in her lap and with her free hand passed a deck of cards to Emil Karpo. As they proceeded, she took notes on a lined pad on the table to her right.

There were three experiments with each man, each time with a fresh deck, six decks all moved to the side after each experiment. First they were asked to concentrate on the deck before them and tell what the top card would be. They were then to turn over the card. When that experiment was finished with each man, Nadia repeated it, only she turned over the cards. Finally, with yet another deck, she picked up each card, looked at it, and asked each man what card she was looking at.

"Are we now finished?" asked Karpo.

"We are," she said, standing.

"And?"

"You were well within the law of averages," she said, looking at her notes. "No significant sign of telepathy or projection. You," she added, looking at Zelach, who blinked nervously behind his glasses. "You got nothing right. You are phenomenally below the law of averages. It is extremely rare for someone to get not a single correct card in all three experiments. I'll have to recheck the data."

"I'm sorry," said Zelach.

"No," she said. "It is interesting."

"You do not seem to be particularly disturbed by the murder of your colleague," said Karpo suddenly.

"We each carry our grief in our own way, Inspector," she said. "As you well know, as you have done."

There were few times in his life when Karpo was unprepared for an eventuality. This was one of those times. Karpo's loss had been enormous. The only woman who had gotten through to him emotionally—no, the only *person* who had gotten through to him—had been Mathilde Verson, the redheaded part-time prostitute who had been full of life, and who had seen something in the pale specter that challenged her. Mathilde had been killed in the crossfire of two Mafias while she drank coffee in a bar on a bright summer day.

"What do you know of me?" he asked.

"Little," she said with a shrug. "But what you should know of me and would probably learn from the director is that I entered this line of research because I have psychic insights. I have, as they said in past centuries, visions. I cannot control them. I usually don't know what they mean or what I am even seeing, but they are there. I am, in fact, in addition to my own research, a primary research source for Boris Adamovskovich. Who was also here during the murder."

Zelach was looking from Karpo to Nadia Spectorski. He felt a tension but wasn't at all sure what it was all about.

"It was an intuitive observation," Karpo said.

"She had red hair," responded Nadia Spectorski.

"You have done research on me in the last day," Karpo said.

"No," she answered. "I have not, but my job is not to convince you of anything. I have encountered hundreds of nonbelievers in psi phenomena. I have learned not to argue with them. Let's go see the director now. I know he is expecting you."

"Psychic knowledge?" asked Karpo as they all rose.

"No, you are scheduled."

"Shall we argue now?" asked Elena.

They were seated at one of the hundreds of new outdoor cafés and coffee shops that had sprung up in the new Moscow. This one was on Gorky Street. The coffee was exceptional and the owner never charged the police, which was good for Elena and Sasha because they could not have otherwise afforded the two cups and the pastry they had been served. Elena had pushed the sweet *ahlahd'yee s yahblahkalmee*, "apple puff," across the table to Sasha. Elena was watching her weight. She was about to be married, maybe, and she did not want to go the way of her mother and her Aunt Anna, who were decidedly overweight. Elena, as men had told her, was well toned and amply plump.

"No argument," said Sasha, picking up the sweet and taking a bite. He looked at the people at the other tables and smiled.

"I will go to the exchange. I will pose as Yuri's niece."

"As you wish," said Sasha. "You are sure you don't want a small piece of this?"

"A small piece," she said with a sigh as he pushed it back toward her. "You've changed, Sasha Tkach. Your wife takes your children and leaves you. Your mother who drives you mad moves in with you. And instead of being miserable, you've grown more cooperative. If one did not know, one might say you are content."

"And this bothers you?" he asked.

"No, but it puzzles me. Are you happy that Maya left?"

"No. I want her back. I call her, write to her. I miss both of my children, perhaps Pulcharia most of all. It is almost her fourth birthday. I tell Maya I am changing. She doesn't believe me. And, yes, even a day with my mother would have been enough to drive Lenin mad. I cannot explain my mood."

"Nor can I," she said, eating the rest of the apple puff. "But I will cease questioning it."

"Proof," he said, reaching into his pocket. "Here are the tickets for the movie Yuri handed me. Take them. Go with Iosef."

"Can't," she said. "We have other plans. Perhaps the new Sasha Tkach would like to take his mother."

"It would be a true test," he said, rubbing his chin. "I have taken my mother to movies in the past. It would be a true test. This morning, before I could escape, she followed me around, screaming that I should go to Kiev, beg Maya to come back. She said she would give me the money, that she would talk to Porfiry Petrovich. She misses her grandchildren. You know the Protopopovs, downstairs from us?"

"No."

"It was so early and Lydia was so loud that they banged on the wall," Sasha said. "I'm a policeman. They know it. Policemen don't have their walls banged on. Even if you hear shots you don't bang on a policeman's wall. They banged."

"What did you do?" Elena asked.

"After I escaped from my mother I knocked on their door and apologized," he said. "Before Maya and the children left I would have pounded back and told the Protopopovs to be quiet. You see before you a very changed Sasha Tkach. Taking my mother to a movie will be the true test."

There was a pause while Elena finished her coffee and Sasha gently drummed on the table with the fingers of his left hand and hummed tunelessly.

"Then I'm the niece?"

"Yes," he said. "If you wish. And I will be a visiting producer from France. Would you like to hear my French accent?"

"I have heard it. It is fine. I will be the one making the exchange?"

"Yes," said Sasha.

"I know what the movie is," Elena said. "It's English. Something called *The Full Monty*, a *kahmyehdyeeyoo*, 'a comedy.'"

"What is a monty?" Sasha asked.

"I don't know. Some kind of container, I think."

"You know if it has subtitles?" Sasha asked hopefully, mindful of the dangers of his mother's poor hearing, which, coupled with her willfulness and determination, could easily bring an entire audience to its knees or send it in flight from the theater.

"I think it is dubbed," she said.

"A true test," he repeated.

Porfiry Petrovich had gone to see Avrum Belinsky alone. Iosef had no interest in joining him. Iosef's interests lay elsewhere. Besides, Rostnikov had a reason for seeing the rabbi alone.

The walk from Pushkin Square was short so his leg did not protest as he moved. Rostnikov entered the small synagogue that had gone through several incarnations, from church, to government office where work permits were issued, to a minor tourist attraction with minimal restoration so that it resembled a church, and then to a synagogue.

Belinsky was by himself, not in his tiny office just to the left of the entrance, but at the rostrum on the small platform which Rostnikov knew was called a bema. Belinsky seemed to be lost in thought, a pen in hand, looking down at some papers.

Belinsky had been in Moscow only a few years. He had started a congregation and almost immediately had found the young men in his small congregation being murdered. Belinsky himself had almost been killed by the murderers, who had acted not out of a commitment to anti-Semitism but to drive the congregation out of existence and out of the synagogue where they knew a valuable bejeweled artifact was hidden. With Belinsky's help, Rostnikov had caught the murderers. Now, the policeman and the rabbi were close to being friends.

Belinsky was a powerfully built man of average height. He had been a soldier, an extremely well trained Israeli soldier who was familiar with confrontation, sacrifice, and death. He had been chosen to go to Moscow precisely because he was determined and capable of taking care of himself and his congregation.

"Porfiry Petrovich," Belinsky said, looking up with a smile and touching his short black beard.

"Avrum," Rostnikov answered, deciding not to sit in one of the several dozen folding chairs that faced the platform on which the young rabbi stood.

"I was working on a sermon," Belinsky said, moving away from the bema and approaching Rostnikov with his hand out.

The two men shook hands and Belinsky motioned for Rostnikov to take a seat. He could not refuse. Rostnikov did not trust wooden folding chairs. They had disappointed him in the past. He sat carefully and the rabbi turned one of the chairs around to face him.

"I was in Pushkin Square," Rostnikov said.

"And you decided to pay me a visit," said Belinsky.

Rostnikov nodded. "But that is not all," he said.

"Sarah," said the rabbi.

"She goes out every Friday night," said Rostnikov. "She says she is going to see her cousin or friends. But she is coming here to attend services."

"Yes, she is Jewish."

"She has been through a great deal," said Rostnikov. "Surgery. I almost lost her."

"I know."

"It does not surprise me that she would turn to the religion of her grandfather," said Rostnikov. "And it is reasonable that she would come here, to you."

"But?"

"I do not understand why she has not told me. Are you under some rule, like a Catholic priest or something, that prevents you from telling me?"

"No, but I think you should ask her. Would you like a drink? Water? I even have some wine and Pepsi-Cola in my office."

"No, thank you. I plan to ask her, but I have learned that it is a good idea if at all possible to be prepared for what might turn out to be a difficult situation."

It was Belinsky's turn to nod. "She is concerned."

"Afraid," said Rostnikov.

"Yes. She is seeking some deeper meaning in life and has turned to a reasonable place for that meaning."

"And has she found it?" asked Rostnikov.

"I don't think so. Not yet. Maybe never. Let me tell you a secret, Porfiry Petrovich. There is no meaning we can find. Our God does not give us simple answers. His only answer is in the enigma of the Bible, of our Torah. I have come to the conclusion that if we seek openly we come to realize that the Bible is telling us to accept what is—the good, the evil. God makes no sense we can understand, just as the world makes no sense we can understand. We can only accept what is and we can find solace in that acceptance. Accept life. Do not ask God for justice, mercy, goodness. God is, like man, a mystery. He can act in ways that make no sense to us. He can change his mind. He can destroy us or grant us mercy, and there is no fathoming why he does any of this."

"That is the sermon you are working on?"

"Yes," said the rabbi, touching his dark beard and smiling.

"You do not wish to answer my question," said Rostnikov.

"In a way, I have. Ask Sarah."

Rostnikov rose.

"The heating system working well?"

"Yes, you did a good job. This winter will be the real test."

"The toilet?"

"A work of art. Thank you."

"Then," said Rostnikov, "there is no more to say."

"Not now," said Belinsky.

They shook hands again and Rostnikov made his way out onto the street. He was lost in thought, half a block away, when he remembered that he had meant to ask Avrum Belinsky where he had been during the morning storm.

Chapter Four

★ ★ ★ ★ ★ ★ ★ ★ ★ ★ ★ ★ ★

The director of the Center for the Study of Technical Parapsychology, Andrei Vanga, was clean shaven, white haired, and wearing a rather rumpled brown suit and a tie that was no match for it. He was a slight, nervous man who habitually played with the gold band on the small finger of his left hand. His office was large. The furniture was well-polished wood with comfortable chairs and even a small brown leather couch. The paintings on the wall were originals, though a close examination would reveal that the artists were not particularly well known.

Nadia Spectorski had left them to return to her work. Zelach and Karpo had been guided to the sofa by the director, who took Zelach's arm.

"We would prefer the chairs," Karpo said.

"As you wish," said Vanga, backing off and moving three of the four chairs in the room into a mini circle so they could face each other.

Vanga's face was pink and solemn. He leaned forward attentively, playing with his gold band, ready to help.

"Do you have any ideas about why someone might kill Sergei Bolskanov?"

"None," said the director.

"No enemies?" asked Karpo.

"None," said the director sadly.

"Everyone liked him?"

"Everyone," said the director. "He was a quiet, pleasant, hard-working scientist. We all admired him."

"We have heard otherwise," said Karpo.

"Well," said the director with a knowing smile. "He could be a bit . . . how shall I say? A bit gruff, but just a bit."

"Someone hit him repeatedly with a hammer," said Karpo.

"I know," said the director.

"It is possible that it was done by someone who did not like him."

"Of course," the director said with a shrug.

Zelach was paying close attention and had concluded that they were going to get little from Vanga, but Karpo persisted.

"Could someone profit from stealing the results of Bolskanov's work?"

"Profit? Make money?"

"Make money, win acclaim, respect."

"I don't know. Maybe. We don't think like that. We're afraid to. Someone around here might read our minds," said the director with a smile.

Neither of the detectives returned the smile.

"It was just a joke," said the director earnestly, "an attempt to lighten . . . I spend much of my time raising money. I sometimes use that . . ."

"And your research?" asked Karpo.

"Psychic phenomena during dream states," he said. "I have written forty papers presented at conferences all over the world. I've written two books. I'd give you both copies but they are a bit old and I have only a few left. But I'm working on a new article which I believe will be modestly important in the field. I . . ."

"Bolskanov also did dream research," said Karpo.

"Correct," said Vanga. "I brought him into the center. We

worked together on many projects. He often came to me for advice, to review his findings, to . . ."

"We would like your shoes," said Karpo.

"My . . . I beg your pardon."

"Your shoes," Karpo repeated.

"Now, these?"

"Yes."

"Why?"

"You will get them back before the end of the day," said Karpo. "Please take them off and give them to Inspector Zelach."

A bewildered director began removing his well-polished brown patent-leather shoes.

"I'll have to wear my spare pair," he said. "They are black and . . ."

"We will take those also," said Karpo.

"I'll have to walk around all day in my stockinged feet."

"You will not be alone," said Karpo.

Vladimir Kinotskin had been warned that policemen were coming to talk to him. He had been told that it could not be avoided. He had been informed that it was about Tsimion Vladovka, who was, as he well knew, missing.

Vladimir had changed greatly since he had returned to earth. He had lost weight and his once-blond hair was almost completely white. His youthful handsome face had darkened too and taken on several rigid lines. He did not smile. His ambition had, for good reason, deserted him. He had no goal beyond continuing his routine work and keeping to himself. He had given up all hope of marriage and family. He could not imagine subjecting a woman to his moodiness, and he knew he could not pretend to be happy or even content. All he hoped for was an eventual truce with his memories, a fragile peace of mind with which he could live, but he doubted he would achieve it.

Perhaps he should have run like Vladovka, if that is what

Vladovka had done. They had seen each other infrequently since the moment the shuttle had landed. They never spoke when they passed.

Vladimir had two hours before the police arrived. He had decided to walk, to walk aimlessly, to think about how he would answer the questions Mikhail Stoltz had posed to him.

"Just tell the truth," Stoltz had said.

"You want me to tell the truth?"

"Yes."

"But . . ."

"The truth," Stoltz had repeated.

The boyish exuberance that might once have been enough to protect Vladimir was gone. The confrontation would be difficult. Stoltz had put a hand on his shoulder and told him he would be just fine. Then Stoltz had him driven from Star City to the Moscow office of the space program.

Vladimir Kinotskin was not sure he would be fine, but he thought he could be good enough.

It was growing humid and hot after the morning rain, and Vladimir had left his jacket on the back of a chair in the office that had temporarily been assigned to him. He had sweated through the white shirt he was wearing. He had loosened his tie and he had gone out to walk and try not to think.

Now he found himself before the Church of Simeon Stylites. He remembered something, something Vladovka had mentioned during the long flight. Vladovka had read some poems to him, poems by Mikhail Lermontov, who had lived more than a century ago. Lermontov, whom Kinotskin had read but not remembered, was also an artist. Vladovka had read but Vladimir had not really listened. Now he remembered.

He went around the church down to Vorovskogo Street and into the small alley which is Malaya Molchanovka Street. The house was there. Now a museum, the house where Lermontov lived with his grandmother stood, restored, modest. Nine windows downstairs, three up, a small gable. Perhaps Vladimir was paying homage. He wasn't sure to what he was paying homage, but it felt right, the proper preparation for the interrogation he would soon undergo.

There was no one in front of the wooden house. After all, one had to know it was there and wend one's way back to it to find the unassuming structure.

As he moved along the white fence toward the entrance, he sensed a movement behind him. He started to turn. He felt no more than the sting of a bee, the prick of a pin. It was in his lower back, somewhere near his liver. An irritation. He finished turning and found himself looking at a bare-headed man with curly black hair. The man was walking away from him. The man was carrying an umbrella.

Vladimir turned back toward the house and wondered why the man had come up behind him and then turned away when Vladimir turned. The sting. No, he told himself. It couldn't be. But he knew that it could. He felt fine, but that meant nothing. It wouldn't end like this. They wouldn't . . . but he knew they could.

He made it as far as the front door and then he fell to his knees. No one was around. It would, he knew, make no difference. It was too late. The ground was moist from the morning rain. He didn't want to die here.

The door of the house opened and an old woman stepped out, covered her mouth with her hand, and leaned over to him. She had a look of horror in her eyes. Vladimir did not know that his eyes and mouth were streaming blood. He felt nothing but weakness. He was suddenly very sleepy.

Maybe he should try to say something to the woman, write something in the dirt, but he couldn't think what he might write or say. He fell forward on his face before the woman, who screamed and ran back into Lermontov's house.

When an ambulance arrived fifteen minutes later they found

the body of the young man, whose head was encircled by a large pool of deep-red blood. The two men who had come out of the ambulance had seen sights like this before. They could take the vision. What they couldn't grow accustomed to was the stench of the dead man, who had befouled himself in a last spasm of indignity.

Since Elena was to play the niece, she could not return for the tour of Yuri Kriskov's editing facility. The chances were more than good that the negative-napper worked for Kriskov. The trip from the office to the production center just outside the outer ring on Durova Prospekt, not far from Mira Prospekt, was taken with Yuri Kriskov, who drove, explaining the list he had prepared of employees who had access to the negative.

Though Kriskov maintained an office in the heart of the city, the production facility, including a small studio, was a long, traffic-jammed ride away. On the way Kriskov said, "Normally I go to the production building from home. I live not far away, but sometimes . . ."

"Stop," shouted Sasha.

Kriskov hit the brake and Sasha lurched forward, hands against the dashboard. Kriskov had come very close to ramming into the rear of a very large, rusting blue truck.

"I am more than a bit upset," Kriskov explained.

You are more than a bad driver, Sasha thought.

Traffic was slow. It usually was, but Yuri Kriskov wove his blue Volga with tinted windows through the narrow, momentary spaces between buses, trucks, and cars.

The list Kriskov had prepared was long and, Sasha decided, probably useless at this stage. Besides, he couldn't concentrate on it with Kriskov, who chain-smoked and challenged sanity as he sped past cars, trucks, buses, and an occasional bicycle. There wasn't enough time to check out each name. Yuri had done his work. There were forty-two names on the list and it was possible none of them was the right one. If the thief was not trapped tomorrow, Sasha and Elena would go to Porfiry Petrovich and ask for additional help in checking the people on the list.

The car was thick with smoke. Yuri made no effort to apologize or open a window more than a crack. The car was specially equipped with air conditioning, but it did little and was noisy.

Sasha had the list in his lap.

"I trust everyone on that list," said Kriskov between nervous puffs. "And, at the same time, I don't trust anyone on the list. This is maddening. How can I look at them. Kolya I have known since we were children in Rostov. And his sons I have known since they were babies. Forfonov, Blesskovich, Valentina Spopchek nursed me through the flu, and . . . I may reach out and strangle one of them if they show the slightest hint of deception."

"You won't," said Sasha, opening his window as they nearly missed a rickety little yellow Yugo whose driver cursed and managed to get out of the way, almost hitting a pickup truck in the next lane.

Yuri paid no attention. "We are almost there," he said.

A few minutes later Yuri turned off the highway, sped down Mira Prospekt, made a sharp left onto Durova Prospekt, and drove until they came to a newly paved narrow road. At the end of the road stood a five-story building, white with a dome that looked as if it had been designed for a science-fiction movie. The structure stood alone in an open field of tall weeds. Yuri drove to the building and parked in a space marked by a black-on-white sign nailed to the concrete wall, stating that this was the space of "Y. Kriskoff."

Kriskov threw away what remained of his latest cigarette and got out of the car. Sasha followed him to the large gold-painted double doors.

"My name," Sasha reminded him, "is Sasha Honoré-Baptiste, from Gaumont."

"I remember. I remember," said Yuri impatiently. "I know my lines. I started as an actor. What if someone says something to you in French?"

"My French is fine."

They were passing the empty reception desk in the tiled lobby and heading for a door with a red light over it. The light was on.

"You speak it like a native?"

"I have been told. Relax, Yuri Kriskov," said Sasha. "I know what I am doing."

"Of course," said Kriskov, looking at the young man at his side, decidedly unconvinced at this point in his life of the wisdom of this or any enterprise.

They paused at the door and the light went off. The producer opened the door.

"This is a re-recording studio," said Yuri. "The director works with the actors and sound people to go over lines, repeat, change, make them clearer, or just put them in. In this case they appear to be working on a film that may not exist."

Three people were in the small, tile-walled room. A bearded man, in jeans and a gray T-shirt that displayed a picture of Michael Jordan smiling, was introduced as Peotor Levich, "the famous director." Sasha had never heard of the famous director but he shook his hand warmly and said, "I very much admire your work." Sasha did his best to speak with a French accent.

Levich was big-shouldered and going to fat. He was perhaps forty at most. "Sasha Honoré-Baptiste," he said and they shook hands. "I know you."

"Impossible," said Yuri Kriskov quickly. "Monsieur Honoré-Baptiste has been in Moscow for only a few days and . . ."

"From the movies," said Levich, examining Sasha with a knowing grin. "Policeman. Policeman. Ah, you are an actor. I remember you played a policeman in those two movies with the actor. What is his name? What is his name? Sad face he has. But his name . . ."

"I'm an investor now," said Sasha. "The hours are shorter but it pays better."

"Where did you learn Russian?" asked Levich.

"My mother is Russian. She taught me. My father is a jeweler. He has traveled to Russia many times."

"I saw you in those movies," Levich said. "I greatly admire French movies. What was it? Something about some stolen drugs. You played Belmondo's son and there was that actor."

He looked at Sasha for an answer and then supplied his own.

"Philippe Noiret. I would have loved him for Tolstoy. I would have traded my arm. Both arms."

Sasha smiled and shrugged, unable to deny the man's fantasy.

Levich stepped back, examined Sasha, and said, "Yuri, he is our Montov when we do *Beyond the Steppes*. We change the character's name to Montaigne. He speaks with that accent. The women will love him. Handsome, a touch of fading boyishness, and a look of having been through more than we will ever know."

"He is not an actor any longer," said Yuri, showing his impatience. "He has told you."

"You would play opposite Leonora Vukolonya," Levich went on. "It's not a huge role. You could do it in a week. You would make love to Leonora Vukolonya. Do you know how many men would cut off their right testicle to make love to Leonora Vukolonya?"

"Six," said Sasha to the director, who seemed to have a penchant for cutting off appendages. "And they would all be lunatics."

Levich laughed. "A sense of humor. Think about it."

Yuri introduced Sasha to the other people in the small room, an older man and woman who stood before a dark machine. Behind them was a movie screen. Before them was a glass panel with a projector behind it.

Yuri introduced them and then moved out of the room with Sasha in tow.

"Think about it, Honoré," said Levich as they left.

"Levich is a Jew," said Yuri. "Very talented. Would he be talking about making another movie if he were about to destroy the entire company? He is not that good of an actor . . . we can't smoke in here. Too many things here, film, burn too easily. Too volatile."

Sasha had no intention of smoking then, there, or anywhere.

The tour moved quickly. The editor, who sat working in a narrow room with a wall-to-wall table filled with machines, looked up when they entered. She was a bit dumpy, with dirty-blond hair a bit unkempt, probably nearing fifty. Two young men were in the room with her. All three were hovered over machines with cranks on which reels of film hung. Strips of film hung from clips all over the room, like black decorations to fit the clearly somber mood.

"We can't work, Yuri," the woman said. "We can't pretend. We have nothing to work with here. Bits, pieces. I hold you responsible."

Yuri put a finger to his lips behind Sasha's back and said, "This is Sasha Honoré-Baptiste from Gaumont in France. They are thinking of investing in us. Monsieur Honoré-Baptiste, this is Svetlana Gorchinova, the deservedly honored editor, the greatest editor in all of Russia."

Yuri beamed. Svetlana did not.

"We are busy," she said after shaking Sasha's hand with a quick jerk. "We are busily engaged in the task of putting together enough pieces of film to make a trailer for a movie that doesn't exist."

"Perhaps you could just introduce Monsieur Honoré-Baptiste to your assistants and we can leave you."

She turned in her high swivel chair and looked at the two young men behind her. The taller and younger of the two had long hair, a large nose, and very crooked teeth.

"Nikita Kolodny," she said.

The young man tried to grin but the mood of the room was too funereal.

"And this," she said, pointing to the very short, stocky young man in the back of the room, "is Valery Grachev."

Grachev nodded.

"Any news?" Svetlana Gorchinova said.

"I think we should not talk business before our guest," said Yuri.

The woman shrugged. She made no effort to hide her depression. "No news," she said.

"We must go now," Yuri said, touching Sasha's arm.

"It is a pleasure to meet you," Sasha said.

The two young men nodded. Svetlana turned back to whatever she was editing or pretending to edit and said and did nothing to acknowledge the departure of a possible investor.

Back in the hall with the door closed, Yuri whispered, "She did it. I can tell. You could see. She is not just eccentric. Everyone says she is eccentric because she is a great editor. But she is really just a crazy woman. Crazy women do anything. Believe me. I have known women as crazy as that one. She will do anything."

"She plans to destroy her own work?" asked Sasha.

"For two million dollars," Yuri said, fishing out his cigarettes and lighting one in spite of his earlier warning about not smoking in the building.

"She is well paid? She is in demand?"

"Very much so."

"Then why? . . ."

"She hates me. Can't you see? She hates me. And two million American dollars. Maybe she'll just pretend to destroy the film and then she'll keep it to herself, treasure it like those Japanese who buy Renoir originals and then hide them in vaults."

"Where do we go next?" asked Sasha.

"Deeper into the hell over which I have lost all control," said Yuri Kriskov.

*   *   *

Rostnikov stood, hands behind his back, feet apart, twenty feet away from Paulinin, who leaned over the body of Vladimir Kinotskin, which still lay in front of Lermontov's home. Uniformed guards were at work keeping the inevitable crowd away. It wasn't a large crowd but it was large enough to require half-a-dozen officers. Iosef directed the crowd control while Paulinin, his fishing-tackle box open, his hair wild, looked at the body, ignored the stench, and grumbled.

Paulinin took the dead man's temperature, touched his ankles, took samples of blood and liquid feces, and examined the body as best he could. Finally, he closed the tackle box, picked it up, and moved toward Rostnikov.

"You know what Kaminskov or Pashinski or one of the other dolts who call themselves pathologists would say?"

"No."

"They would say your young man had a stroke and a seizure," said Paulinin. "It would all be over. They wouldn't have looked for the small puncture in his lower back, even though the hole, grant you it is very small, went right through his shirt. All the symptoms of a massive stroke and seizure, and in one sense they would be right, but the cause of the stroke and seizure they would miss. I will need to talk to the young man in my laboratory."

"Murdered," said Rostnikov, who had fully expected this finding.

"Just as clearly as the other one I looked at this morning with his head crushed by a hammer," said Paulinin. "And I could tell you more, much more about the killer, if the ground were not so trampled by the usual idiots. The ground is perfect, perfect for prints, but . . . look at it. It looks as if a World Cup game has been played here."

"Thank you for coming, Paulinin," said Rostnikov.

"Uhh," said Paulinin, looking back at the body. "You can bring him to Petrovka now, down to my laboratory. Don't let the idiots clean him. I don't care how he smells. He comes as he is. I will clean him when it is right. I will apologize to him for the indignities he is suffering and will have to suffer further. I have, as you know, learned to talk gently to the dead."

"I have observed," said Rostnikov. "I'll have you driven back to Petrovka."

"Good. My lunch is waiting."

When Paulinin was gone, Rostnikov waved to his son and Iosef walked over to him.

"What do we conclude from this?" asked Porfiry Petrovich.

"That three cosmonauts were on that mission," said Iosef. "Two are dead and one is missing."

"And?"

"Three cosmonauts relieved them," said Iosef. "Perhaps we should talk to them about what they saw and heard, since Mikhail Stoltz appears unwilling or unable to provide answers."

"So you are convinced that Tsimion Vladovka's disappearance and the murder of Vladimir Kinotskin are connected to the *Mir* flight," said Rostnikov.

"Yes."

"I am inclined to agree. Then perhaps we should move quickly before someone tells us that this murder belongs to MVD and not to our office."

"Or before the Yak tells us to mind our business."

Rostnikov touched his son's arm and nodded his head. "Come, let us break the bad news to Stoltz, though I feel it will not come as a great surprise. Are you hungry?"

Iosef looked at the body. "No. We had cheeseburgers only an hour or so ago, remember?"

"Then later, perhaps. Your mother made me sandwiches. I wonder what it must be like to be weightless in a metal sphere circling in silence," said Rostnikov, looking at the body and then at the sky as they walked away from the scene. "It must be difficult to remind oneself that one is not dreaming, floating, awake but asleep."

" 'A giant will come in the darkness under a cloud,' " said Iosef as they reached the street and stamped their feet to remove some of the mud.

"Lermontov?" asked Rostnikov, looking back at the scene of death behind them and at the gawking, silent little crowd.

Iosef nodded. "More or less."

"Go on," said Rostnikov.

" 'You will know him and the sword he carries,' " Iosef continued. " 'Your doom has come. You beg and weep. He laughs. And then he will stop laughing and will be a sight of horror, a sight as black as his cloak and eyes.' Shall I go on?"

"No," said Porfiry Petrovich. "That is enough."

"The curse of having been in the theater," said Iosef. "One thinks of lines, passages, monologues, the poetry of Lermontov usually distorted by one's needs and memory. Lermontov was only twenty-seven when he died in a duel. Did you know that?"

"Yes," said Rostnikov.

"According to the papers in his wallet, Vladimir Kinotskin was twenty-seven when he died today," said Iosef.

"Perhaps he was making a pilgrimage."

"Perhaps," said Rostnikov, glancing over his shoulder at the crowd behind them.

A man in the crowd, one of several carrying umbrellas, watched not the dead man and those now moving the corpse into a black plastic bag but the two detectives who talked on the street. The man was lean, well dressed, and looked foreign, perhaps English or Dutch. His eyes were quite blue. That morning he had nicked himself shaving. His hand went up to the healing wound, and as the detectives walked away, the man with the umbrella moved through the small crowd to follow them at a very safe and professional distance.

*   *   *

Karpo had been unable to find Rostnikov, who was, at the moment he called, out watching Paulinin examining the body of the dead cosmonaut. And so Emil Karpo took it upon himself to make the decision. Not only did he take the shoes of all those who had signed in to work when Sergei Bolskanov had, but those of all the people in the building. Everyone in the building except the police were walking around in stockinged feet.

"Dignity is lost but comfort may offer compensation," said Karpo.

Zelach nodded and blinked. He had not only rounded up all the shoes, which were contained in three cardboard boxes at the front door of the center, but he had obtained the addresses of everyone and, starting with the sign-ins, was about to go to each house and collect every pair of shoes he could find.

"Emil Karpo," he said, standing in the doorway, looking down at the boxes, "what if the murderer has thrown the shoes away?"

"Unlikely but possible. It makes no difference."

"It will take days," said Zelach.

"I have ordered a car and driver with the approval of Director Yaklovev, to whom I have just spoken. The driver will help you. If you move quickly you can get to all thirty-seven locations before six."

"They will have to go home barefoot in any case," said Zelach.

"I will send an officer out to buy thirty-seven pairs of very cheap sandals," said Karpo. "Now, I think you should begin your collection."

Zelach adjusted his glasses. They had begun to hurt just behind the right ear but he was afraid to fool with the thin wire. There was no chance now that he would get to the lunch on his desk in the damp brown bag.

When Zelach had left, Karpo motioned to one of the two uniformed men. "No one comes in. No one goes out."

The officer, who was twenty-three, very large and undertrained, knew the Vampire by reputation. He said nothing as he stood before the door. Even if Putin himself or the mayor of Moscow would appear, the officer, whose name was Dimitri, would not let him pass. He had no intention of using the Kalishnikov rifle in his hands on anyone of real importance and he was confident that he could handle most who tried to pass him, but he decided instantly that faced with the possibility of failure he would either have to shoot himself or the person who was giving him trouble. He could not imagine telling Inspector Karpo that he had failed.

Nadia Spectorski caught up with Karpo in the hall. She was clearly excited, breathing quickly.

"Where is the other officer?"

"Akardy Zelach?"

"Yes, I must speak to him," she said.

"Whatever you might wish to tell him, you can tell me. I am the senior officer."

"This is not about Sergei's murder," she said. "It is far more important."

"More important?" asked Karpo, wondering if the barefoot woman before him had gone mad.

"Follow me," she said. "Come."

He followed her as she hurried down the corridor to her small office. The offices had windows. None of the rooms upstairs had windows, though there were windows at the ends of the corridor. The view from this window was of a small concrete square with bolted-down wooden fences facing each other.

She went behind her desk, where Karpo saw six decks of cards, a pad of paper with many notes, and a small electronic instrument.

"You remember when I said that the other officer had no guesses that were correct? And I said that was very odd?"

"Yes," said Karpo.

"Do you have an open mind?" she said, looking up.

"Yes."

"Good. I was wrong about your friend."

"Colleague."

"Colleague then, fellow officer, what does it matter? He guessed forty-eight out of fifty-two cards correctly when I looked at each card, but all forty-eight were exactly two cards *after* the card I looked at. He had no connections when I did not look at the cards."

"You said . . ."

"Yes, yes, yes, but I remembered the farmer in England," she said.

Karpo refused to be confused, and he refused to sit. He was not here to talk about cards. He was here to find a murderer.

"A farmer in England. Koestler wrote of him in his book *The Roots of Coincidence*. The farmer appeared to guess none of the cards, but a researcher went back and checked the deck. He was curious. The farmer had guessed not the card the researcher was looking at but two cards later. No, he had not guessed. The farmer knew. Do you know what that means? We are not even dealing with telepathy here. We are dealing with . . . I'm not sure. He must come back for more tests."

Karpo's expression, as always, remained the same. "If he so chooses," he said.

"He will choose," she said. "He will be afraid. He will talk to his mother and she'll tell him to cooperate."

"What do you know of Akardy Zelach's mother?"

Nadia looked up.

"I've seen her in her room," she said. "I know what she believes. Remember, I'm a subject here too. Is your mind still open to what you do not understand?"

Karpo did not answer for a long time, and the excitement in Nadia faded at the sight of the ghostly figure looking down at her, deep in thought.

"You claim you can see Akardy's mother. You claimed you saw Mathilde Verson. Did you see the murder of Sergei Bolskanov?"

Nadia met his eyes and started to say no, but she could not. Instead she shook her head.

"Would you like something to eat or drink?" he said. "I can accompany you someplace nearby where we can talk, outside these walls."

"I have no shoes," she said. "And I want to work on this data, this amazing data which . . ."

"I will find you shoes," he said.

Defeated, she nodded.

It would take much more to convince Emil Karpo that people could move objects with their minds, see through cards, or talk to the dead, but it took no more at the moment to convince him that the woman before him might well be mad and might well be capable, in a state of excitement, of a raging murder.

Chapter Five

★ ★ ★ ★ ★ ★ ★ ★ ★ ★ ★ ★ ★

The good-looking young man with Yuri Kriskov had been a policeman, not a French investor. Valery Grachev was certain of that. He had expected no less. What pleased him, however, was that an attempt was being made to hide the fact that the police were involved.

Valery had been dismissed soon after Kriskov and the policeman left. There really wasn't much to do and so Svetlana had sent him into the city to pick up a package, a simple hand splicer to replace one that had lost its sharpness and was out of alignment. He had taken his scooter with the usual promise of reimbursement for gasoline, a promise that had led him to keep a small notebook of how much the company owed him.

He drove carefully toward the heart of the city inside the Inner Ring and planned two moves ahead. It would be what seemed like a bold gambit but would turn his opponent—no longer Yuri but the policeman who used the name Sasha—looking in the wrong direction. Already Valery had set the offense moving, very carefully.

He had kept his eyes open, planning for this day as he would for a tournament. It was never his intention to simply take the negatives, make the demand, collect the money, and walk away.

That was what he wanted them to think, that it was simple, direct.

Valery had gone through the garbage for weeks, listened to phone calls, watched and mapped the house and neighborhood of Yuri Kriskov.

There was almost no chance that Kriskov could raise the two million American dollars in two days.

Valery parked, locked his scooter, and headed for the film-equipment warehouse near the Moscow Film School.

The police would begin checking the background of everyone in the company. He would not escape the scrutiny, but their search would yield nothing about him that would rouse suspicion. He had never committed a crime, never been arrested.

But they would find much to be suspicious of in Svetlana's history. Mental illness, a massive breakdown two years earlier. A major confrontation with the producer of the last movie on which she worked. Wild shouting matches on two occasions with Yuri Kriskov. Complaints about being underpaid and even outbursts in front of Valery and others about not caring if the damn negative burned if she did not get what she deserved. Many years earlier, Valery had discovered, Svetlana had been arrested for firing a pistol in a department store. Were she not the famous editor, she would probably have been filled with drugs and sent into the streets to wander like the zombies in *Dawn of the Dead*.

And now the police would be watching her, certain that she had the negatives, waiting for her to make a mistake and lead them to the stolen reels. They would know from the voice of the man that Yuri had reported that she had an accomplice, but that was easy. They would deduce that the man was Svetlana's common-law husband, a former screenwriter who had not worked in almost a decade. Even when he had worked, it had been in the days of the Soviet Union and he had made less than an old street-sweeper.

Valery picked up the new splicer, signed for it, put it in his backpack, and went back to his scooter.

He wondered if they had found the note yet. They probably had. If not, they soon would.

He wondered if the policeman would go running after Svetlana. He surely would.

The plan was nearly perfect, but the danger in a good game was overconfidence. Like the fat old man, Yuri had almost made the mistake of luring his opponent into early vulnerability by a seemingly innocuous one-space move of his bishop's pawn. He had underestimated the fat man, though Valery had eventually won the game, but it was a lesson to be learned.

Perhaps he should not have left the note. It was a bold touch. He had twice crumpled it up and thrown it in a wastebasket. And twice he had retrieved it. It was dangerous to sneak into Kriskov's office, but he had been unable to resist, to lure the police farther away from the truth. He had not been caught in the office or seen outside of it. He was not sure how good the police really were at tracing a note like this to a particular typewriter. He hoped they were very good. He had used the one in Svetlana's little office.

Box under his arm, Valery moved to the nearby phone and made a call. When the phone on the other end was picked up and he recognized the voice, he gave the code, "Amlady?"

"No," came the answer. "You have the wrong number."

"I'm sorry," he said and hung up.

Perfect, he thought. By this time tomorrow Yuri Kriskov would be quite dead, and Valery would be on the verge of being a very wealthy young man.

"I'm certain," Kriskov had said, handing the sheet of notepaper to Sasha.

It had been in the middle of the conference table. No envelope. Thumbtacked and sure to leave a small scar in the polished wood.

Yuri had smoked and paced. Sasha had wanted to tell him to sit down.

The note was simple:

> You have told too many people about this. This is between you and me. It must be settled tomorrow or I will do as I have told you I would. I know you have the money. Let us keep this between ourselves. I . . .

Sasha and Elena sat in the office of Porfiry Petrovich, who looked at the sheet of paper and ate a radish-and-tomato sandwich with butter on thick, dark bread from the bakery of Sasha's mother. He had offered to cut the second sandwich in half and share it with them. Sasha had accepted. Elena had politely declined. There would have been a third sandwich, but Rostnikov had eaten it hours earlier.

Rostnikov had excused himself for eating while they talked and was sharing his bag of overly salty potato chips with the two detectives. Rostnikov looked at his watch, a birthday gift from his wife. The face of the watch was large and simple.

"And Kriskov is certain that the note was written by his editor, Svetlana . . ."

"Gorchinova," said Elena.

Rostnikov took another bite and continued to look at the note. "Why," he asked, "does the note appear to have been crumpled up? Is this the way you found it, open?"

"Open and flat," said Sasha. "A thumbtack through it. Perhaps the thief had it crumpled in his pocket and flattened it when he came in."

Rostnikov took a large satisfying bite. Elena did her best not to reach for the open bag of chips. She didn't even like chips, but the tempting fat called out to her.

"No," Rostnikov said, reaching down to scratch his itching artificial leg. "It is a small note. It could simply have been folded once and put in a pocket. And why does the note stop with the word *I*?"

"I do not know," said Sasha. "Kriskov says that Svetlana Gorchinova has a history of mental illness."

"Apparently an attribute that does not interfere with her ability to edit films," said Rostnikov, eyes on the note, chewing.

"Perhaps it contributes to her creativity," said Elena. "Freud believed that the most creative people were neurotic or even borderline psychotic."

Rostnikov thought of the house of Lermontov and wondered if the great poet had been neurotic. He would have to get a biography.

"Was Lermontov neurotic?" he asked.

"Lermontov?" asked Elena.

She did not fully understand this washtub of a man who was going to be her father-in-law in the not-distant future. She respected him, admired him, but found it difficult to follow his leaps and musings.

"Lermontov," he repeated. "Have you ever visited his boyhood home?"

"No," said Elena, puzzled but trying not to show it.

"I have," said Sasha. "Maya wanted to see it. It is bleak."

"This is an old note, probably crumpled and thrown into a wastebasket," said Rostnikov. "It is unfinished. The *I* is the beginning of another thought."

"So," said Elena, "she kept the note, brooded, and decided to send her message to Kriskov after she took the negative. If Kriskov and Freud are right, she may be a bit mad."

"She would write a new note, I think," said Rostnikov. "But who knows? Madness has its own reasons. Did anyone see someone enter the room where the note was found?"

"No," said Sasha. "But I really couldn't make inquiries. I'm a

French film executive from Gaumont. Kriskov asked a few people."

"Conclusions?" asked Rostnikov.

"Someone is trying to make it look as if Svetlana is the thief," said Elena.

"And I would guess that this note was written on her typewriter, if she has one," added Sasha.

"Our thief thinks he is very clever," said Elena.

"Playing a game," said Sasha.

"More chips?"

"No, thank you," said Sasha.

Rostnikov shrugged and finished off the last few salty pieces.

"I'll take a few," said Elena.

Why was the sight of the chips making her feel suddenly fat? Why was she worrying about her weight? Before Iosef had besieged her, Elena had lived in relative culinary contentment, aware of her weight and mildly cautious, exercising each morning till she worked up a sweat, checking the scale in the corner of her aunt's bedroom. But now . . .

"Do you agree, Elena Timofeyeva?" Rostnikov asked.

She had been aware that Rostnikov had said something after he finished his final bite of sandwich but she wasn't quite sure of what it had been. Her mind had wandered to her waistline.

"I'm sorry, I . . ."

"If the thief is someone trying to put the blame on Svetlana Gorchinova, then he or she is someone inside the company. The thief would very likely know that Kriskov cannot raise two million American dollars in one day."

"Then why? . . ." Sasha began.

"Ah, yes, a puzzle, a conundrum," said Porfiry Petrovich, handing the note to Sasha. "Work on it. I think the solution may lead you to a thief with an agenda we do not yet know. And now I must clean my desk and turn my thoughts to outer space and distant villages."

Elena and Sasha went into the hall. They stood silently for a moment and then looked at each other and the note in Sasha's hand.

"You know what we must do," he said.

"Yes."

The trip was brief, four flights down to the ground and two below that to Paulinin's den. Neither of them looked forward to it, but it was the quickest way to get an answer.

Sasha knocked. They thought they heard someone behind the door and in the distance answer, but the words were unclear. Sasha opened the door. At the end of the room, Paulinin looked up over the naked male body before him. The dead man was an almost bleached white, young, handsome.

The two detectives wended their way through the maze of tables, benches, specimens, debris, and books. Paulinin was wearing rubber gloves. His hair was in desperate need of attention.

"What?" he asked impatiently, eyeing Elena. Paulinin did not welcome living women visitors. "I'm busy. Two corpses. Seven boxes of shoes to examine. I'm busy."

Sasha had dealt with Paulinin before, had watched Rostnikov deal with him. "This should take you but a minute, perhaps a few seconds," said Sasha with his best smile. "You are the only one who can help us."

"Quick then," Paulinin said. "Quick, quick, people are waiting. Shoes are waiting, and I haven't had my lunch."

Sasha reached across the corpse and handed Paulinin the note. Paulinin looked at it and placed it on the chest of the corpse of Vladimir Kinotskin.

"What about it?" he asked.

"How long ago was it written?"

"Weeks, maybe months," said Paulinin. "One need only look at the absorption of the ink, the small flecking, the . . . This does not even require magnification. Is that all?"

"That is all," said Sasha. "Thank you."

Elena and Sasha exchanged a look which made it clear that both now knew the theft of the negative had been planned long ago.

Paulinin returned the note and, ignoring his visitors, whispered something to the corpse.

Sasha and Elena left quickly.

On the way out, they had to avoid the seven cartons of shoes Paulinin had mentioned.

Vera Kriskov would be thirty-seven years old next month. She was looking forward to the day. She felt like celebrating. Her mirror told her she was still capable, if she chose, of returning to modeling for catalogues, magazines, perhaps even on television, but she really didn't wish to do so and Yuri would not have permitted it. The bedroom mirror, in front of which she stood quite naked, told her clearly once again that having children had not destroyed her figure, though it had taken enormous exercise and diet restraint to remain the way she looked now. Her trademark long, soft, natural amber hair was as flowing and bright as ever.

Yuri wasn't quite rich, but they lived comfortably in a dacha with three bedrooms just beyond the Outer Ring. She had her own car, a cream-colored Lada, and plenty of time and spending money.

She also had a husband who hadn't made love to her in four months, a fact that only bothered her because she wanted to be wanted. Actually, she had no desire to spend time with her husband grunting and moaning in bed and smelling of stale cigarettes. He was, at his best, a conventional lover and certainly a frightened and indifferent one. His absence from bed was matched only by his absence from home. That absence too was not unwelcome.

She began to dress, nothing striking, nothing that would draw special attention, but something that would show her figure and draw attention to her face and hair. She moved, now wearing underpants and a bra, to the bathroom to put on her makeup. Even up close and with magnification her skin was smooth.

Vera had seen her husband's new mistress, an actress, very young and definitely not as pretty as the face in the mirror before her. The girl was part of the act, Yuri's pose as a creative, virile, philandering movie producer.

When she was satisfied with the face in the mirror, she got down a simple blue dress of cotton and put on comfortable white shoes with very low heels. Vera was tall, five-feet nine-inches tall, as tall as her husband when she wore even moderate heels.

She was ready. She would meet Yuri for dinner, as he had asked. She would listen to him bemoan his fate. She would be sympathetic, might even pat his hand. She would watch him smoke and eat and fret.

She would be a good wife, but she would also be a good actress, showing deep sympathy and close to tears, while she enjoyed his torment. She had married him because of his energy, money, connections to vibrant people, and the opportunity to become an actress.

Vera had appeared in a secondary role in one of Yuri's low-budget comedies about a Bulgarian who becomes a Moscow taxi driver and can't find any address. In addition, the other cab drivers make the Bulgarian's life a nightmare. Vera played a model who has to get to a photo session. The part was small, but Yuri had told her she had been very good though the director was drunk during Vera's three scenes.

Then Vera had gotten pregnant. Yuri wanted children. Yuri forced himself to work at it. Yuri worried that he could not create babies. Doctors helped. They worked out a schedule. There was no joy in the process. But Vera did find pleasure in her children. Ivan was almost ten and she prayed that he would not grow up to look like his father. He was a good-looking boy hovering between the image of his mother and father. Even if he grew to look like Yuri, she would love him. And Alla, Alla was four, beautiful, happy, definitely her mother's child.

Though the children spent most of their time with friends or being watched by a frail young nanny from Odessa, Vera saw to it that she was with them most nights, read to them, bought them clothes and ice cream, took them to the circus and movies.

Yuri, on the other hand, spent no time with their children and was usually thinking of something else when Ivan tried to talk to him or Alla climbed into his lap.

Vera was ready now. She examined herself one last time in the mirror. Her mouth could, possibly, stand a bit more moisture, a bit more sympathetic red, but there was no time.

This was to be the first sequence in a dramatic unfilmed movie called *The Death of Yuri Kriskov.* It was arranged. She would see to it that it was done. Valery would play out the game they had planned and then, with the promise of having Vera, Valery would kill Yuri.

When Yuri was dead, his widow would inherit. The negative would be returned. The film would go to Cannes and make money. With luck Vera would be wealthy.

Valery was a very different lover from Yuri, but in his way almost as bad. Four inches shorter than she, homely and hairy as a bear, he would make wild sounds, cling to her till welts formed, lick her body in a way that both excited and repulsed her. He had tremendous staying power and was still many minutes away when she had long finished. And when it was over, he did not want her to leave whatever hotel room they were in. He usually wanted to talk about chess, about how life was a game of chess, a Russian game.

Yuri was a weakling. Valery was a bore.

Vera would gently get rid of Valery when all was over. She would see to it that he became an editor on a small picture and then she would set him up as a producer with his own very small independent company. She would invest heavily in the company and live up to her agreement to share in the profit and estate. She would guide Valery to other women, girls, and she would wait for him to break off their relationship. Before that, however, she could keep him at a distance, claiming that they could not do anything to draw suspicion. And then she would produce a movie of her own, a big movie, in which she would star.

Yes, she was ready for Yuri. She could stand her husband for another day.

The Yak was seated at the conference table when Porfiry Petrovich entered the office. Yaklovev waited while the chief inspector sat, opened his pad, and took out a pencil.

"Porfiry Petrovich, you are trying to find a missing cosmonaut."

Rostnikov nodded, head down, examining the blank page before him, a bit curious about what images his pencil might find on the pale whiteness.

"You are not to pursue the unfortunate death of another cosmonaut this afternoon."

"Murder. The two are connected," said Rostnikov, drawing a straight line. "We began our investigation, requested a meeting with Vladimir Kinotskin, and hours later he is murdered." Rostnikov began to draw something, a straight line.

"The murder is not ours, Porfiry Petrovich."

There were many things Rostnikov wanted to say, but the director would know all of them. Something else was going on, and Rostnikov had no choice but to say yes.

"Then your pursuit of this death will not continue?"

"It will not," said Rostnikov, seeing something come to meaning in the drawing.

"The newspapers, as you may know, and the television are being told that Vladimir Kinotskin appears to have suffered a stroke while standing before the boyhood home of his favorite poet and artist. The media has been told that his body will be handled with dignity and that there is no connection with his time in space and the tragedy. It seems there is a history of stroke in his family. It has been noted in his records."

"The inescapability of revised genetic history," said Rostnikov.

The Yak looked at him for a sign of sarcasm. There was none. Perhaps resignation, but not sarcasm.

"What is your next step?" asked Yaklovev.

The drawing was now clearly that of a man walking a tightrope, pole in hand to maintain his balance. The man had no face and was wearing a bathing suit. The task of the imaginary man was rendered impossible by the fact that he had only one leg.

"We would like to interview the three cosmonauts who brought Vladovka, Kinotskin, and Baklunov back from *Mir*," said Rostnikov.

"You think they confided in each other on a brief shuttle to the earth?" asked Yaklovev.

"No, perhaps, but something took place on *Mir*, something that probably accounts for this afternoon's death, the disappearance of Tsimion Vladovka, and quite possibly the death of the third cosmonaut, Rodya Baklunov."

"You think Vladovka is dead?"

Rostnikov shrugged. The drawing lacked something, something essential. "Iosef has made inquiries," said Rostnikov, drawing wings on the one-legged man, large wings, the fingerlike black wings of a predatory bird. "Two of the cosmonauts on the rescue mission are in America learning English, preparing for a flight to the new space station when it is built and some shuttle missions in the meantime. They will not be back in Russia for at least a year."

"You will interview the third cosmonaut," said the Yak.

"I cannot," said Rostnikov. "He is dead. An accident. He was visiting the small farm he had purchased for his father. While out alone in the nearby city of Vologda, he had a heart attack. He was thirty-two years old."

"The Russian death rate is among the highest in the world," said the Yak.

"Primarily resulting from smoking, drinking, poor diet, and family rage," answered Rostnikov. "It seems the mortality rate for this group of cosmonauts exceeds the national average and that their demise came not in space but on the earth. But, I will cease to follow leads in the space program."

"And so?"

"And so," said Rostnikov. "I have read through our missing hero's file and come to the conclusion that Iosef and I should go to Kiro-Stovitsk."

"Kiro-Stovitsk?"

"The town near Pikolovo not far from St. Petersburg where our missing cosmonaut was raised, where his parents, brother, cousins still live, farm, work."

"You think he is there?"

"Perhaps, perhaps not. It is probably where I would go if I wanted to be with people I trusted, if only for a little while before continuing to run, continuing to find a place to hide."

The drawing was complete. The one-legged man would surely fall, but his wings were strong. Rostnikov wondered if the winged man were Vladovka, Porfiry Petrovich, or a combination of both. He closed the notebook.

"Then," said Yaklovev, "go to Kiro-Stovitsk, find him and find him quickly. And remember, no interrogation. You simply and quietly bring him to me. You will probably be followed by State Security, Military Intelligence, and others."

"Strangers will stand out in Kiro-Stovitsk. The town, I understand, is very small and there are no hotels."

"Good, go quickly and succeed," said the Yak, rising. "Pankov will see to an advance for your expenses. Take what you need. I know I need not worry about your spending more than is necessary."

"There is a flight to St. Petersburg early in the morning," said

Rostnikov, getting up. What remained of his left leg had fallen asleep. He could feel nothing but tingling. He almost fell. He steadied himself on the table and the Yak moved away, pretending not to have seen.

When Rostnikov was out the door, Yaklovev went over the reports on the other two cases now underway by the Office of Special Investigation. The missing film negative had not yet been found. It was of great importance to the government. Yaklovev had the power, with a phone call, to obtain the two million American dollars for the return of the negatives. The problem, however, was that if he did so, he would be obligated to the powerful advisor to the president. As it stood now, the powerful advisor was deeply obligated to Igor Yaklovev. A time would come when the Yak would pick up the phone and arrange a meeting with the powerful advisor, a member of the duma. That time would have to come soon and the favor asked would have to justify itself. Timing was everything. The powerful advisor might become president in the not-distant future, but then again, Russia being as dourly manic as it was, the advisor might be just another citizen within the historical change of a single day. And what if Yaklovev did ask for a two-million-dollar favor and the negative was not returned or was destroyed? No, in that direction lay a greater danger. Elena Timofeyeva and Sasha Tkach would have to succeed without the money. If they failed, Yaklovev would accept responsibility for the failure. There were more successes than failures. He could weather a few such failures and tolerate the gloating satisfaction of his enemies. While his enemies gloated with self-satisfaction, Igor Yaklovev would find a way to leap ahead of them.

The second case underway was less clear but more likely to come to a satisfying conclusion. Psychic research was an up-and-down issue. With money short, a murder could cause a shock to the system, could be disastrous. Yaklovev did not believe in ghosts, telepathy, telekinesis, or anything else that these scientists were

wasting time and money on. On the other hand, he didn't dis-
believe. He simply didn't care. What he did care about was the
good will of the wealthy, very wealthy businessmen who were
funding such research and wanted it to continue. Such men had
arranged for the case to go to the Office of Special Investigation.

Yaklovev read the preliminary autopsy report and the trail to
the shoes. There was nothing in Emil Karpo's report about the
supposed psychic powers of Akardy Zelach.

The investigation, Yaklovev decided, was going well.

He looked at the plain, white-faced clock with large numerals
on the wall. He sat at his desk and touched a button that opened
the line to the microphone in the outer office. There was no
sound, a sign that Rostnikov had made his arrangements with
Pankov for the trip.

The Yak flipped the switch off, rose, and moved to the outer
office where Pankov sat, suddenly at sweating attention.

"Pankov," the Yak said. "You know the notebook Chief Inspector Rostnikov carries?"

"The larger one or the one in his pocket?" asked Pankov, to
show that he was indeed observant.

"The larger one. You know where the chief inspector keeps it
when he goes out?"

"In his drawer, the middle one, or he just leaves it on his desk,"
said Pankov, trying mightily not to show any curiosity about the
curious questions from the director.

"In five minutes, you will call the chief inspector and tell him
he is to go down to Section Seven to sign papers for his trip.
You will then call our friend in Section Seven and tell him to
keep Inspector Rostnikov busy signing papers for fifteen minutes," said Yaklovev. "When he is signing papers, I want you to
enter the chief inspector's office, find his notebook, copy every
page quickly on our machine, and return the notebook to the
exact place where you took it from."

Pankov wanted to plead, weep, beg. Rostnikov might come back, find him, break him to pieces. And what of the others across the hall? What if the Vampire caught him?

"I understand," said Pankov.

"Good."

And with that the Yak went back into his office, leaving Pankov to wonder what might be of interest or importance enough to merit this errand, an errand filled with danger for the frightened assistant.

Had he been able to ask the director, and had the director been willing to give an honest answer, that answer would have been "I don't know." But at a deeper level, the real answer the Yak barely acknowledged was "I want to know this man in whom I put so much trust."

The sky was clear and the day warm as Maya Tkach crossed the Paton Bridge over the Dnieper River. She walked without thinking about where she was going, letting her body take her as it had more than a decade earlier when she had been a very young woman in Kiev.

People, cars, and buses passed her in both directions. She looked neither at them nor at the water to her right. She knew she was heading for the heart of the city, where she would probably wind up on Kreschatik, the busiest street in Kiev, where she would go into the Kreschatik metro station and head for the house of her brother and her sister-in-law.

Young men and old men glanced at the pretty, dark woman who appeared to be lost in thought or grief. Maya was vaguely aware of the glances, as she had been since she was a girl of fifteen.

Her sister-in-law would watch the children and her own till three. If Maya was back by then, there would be no problem. In truth, Rita would probably not grumble even if she were quite late. Rita had welcomed Maya and the children and refrained from commenting on her situation or making negative comments about Sasha, though Maya's brother had told her at least something of Sasha's behavior and the reasons for Maya's coming to Kiev.

Maya had said she was going to an afternoon concert and she had fully intended to do just that, but as she had approached Philharmonia Hall, she knew she could not possibly sit through even a short afternoon concert of light baroque works.

Instead she had wandered.

Maya was the only one who really knew why she had left her husband in Moscow. Yes, he had betrayed her with other women at least five times since their marriage, but she also knew that Sasha was very vulnerable. It was his prolonged depressions that were more responsible for her decision to leave him than were his indiscretions.

Those were the reasons for which he himself was responsible.

Her own responsibility was the real secret. He had entered into his encounters with women impulsively. Maya had entered into her one affair with calculation and determination. She had first told herself that she had begun the affair with the Japanese executive who dealt with her office to get even with Sasha. Then she had told herself that she had done so because she was lonely and beginning to feel unwanted. Then she told herself that she had begun the relationship to escape from the deadening blanket of Sasha's depression. Finally she had concluded that it was all these things and a simple desire to be desired. It had gone on for a long time, far longer than all of Sasha's encounters put together.

So, one important reason for her fleeting was a deep sense of guilt.

But something now had to be done, had to be decided. Sasha had called. She had chosen not to carry on a conversation. Lydia Tkach had called. Maya had been polite and let her talk to the children, though the baby knew nothing of what was going on and had no more than a few words to say, prompted by Maya's mother and sister.

A decision had to be made soon. Maya would have to get work or consider returning to Sasha. If she returned, should she confess? No, she decided, no. She would live with her guilt. But returning to Sasha would require more than her willingness to try. For her sake, for the sake of the children, she would need to truly believe that Sasha would and could change, that he had made a beginning.

Time was running out. Maya had heard quiet conversations in Moscow about Kiev and Chernobyl, which was a short ride away. Kiev, she had been told officially, was a safe city to visit for as much as four months or even longer. Unofficially, she had been told that it would take a century for the entire region to be safe.

Stories had come from her brother about sickness in the family, aunts, uncles, cousins with cancers and other illnesses. All were explained away, but now Maya had seen with her own eyes. More than a decade after the nuclear disaster there were sick people on the streets, sickness that could not simply be explained by heavy smoking and alcoholism that matched that of Russia and caused a death rate equal to that of the poorest African countries.

She had to get her children someplace safer. She knew of no other place but Moscow.

As she crossed Leipzig Street, she willed her husband to call tonight. She willed him to sound genuinely different, not just guilty and contrite. She was no longer really interested in guilt. They had more than enough between them to last a lifetime.

He will call, she thought. Sasha will call. If not tonight, tomorrow. And then what will I say? She really had no idea.

She remembered that there was something she had to do before she went back to the apartment. Something . . . oh, yes. She would stop at the sweet shop near the Tchaikovsky Conservatory and bring something back for her children and her brother.

*   *   *

"A great chain of being," Mikhail Stoltz said, sitting in his small office behind his desk. "An action begets another action which begets two reactions and . . ."

He leaned forward and looked around his office. There were photographs of him with astronauts, cosmonauts, visiting dignitaries, and members of the current government. He had other photographs with now-discredited leaders. They were in a drawer in the desk behind which he sat looking at the man across from him.

The man sat back, his umbrella between his legs. The umbrella was upright on the floor. The man had both hands on the curved handle. He said nothing. Stoltz would say what he had to say and the man with the umbrella would do what he had to do.

Stoltz sighed. "How many will we have to eliminate before this is ended?" he asked.

Since the question was not really being asked to the man with the umbrella, he did not answer.

"There are some secrets too big to conceal forever," said Stoltz. "For such secrets there is only the possibility of delay."

The man with the umbrella nodded in agreement.

"The two in America?" Stoltz asked.

"It is being taken care of," said the umbrella man.

"The one in China?"

"Done," said the umbrella man.

"Then . . ."

"There is just Vladovka," said the man with the umbrella. "And I will find him."

"Rostnikov."

"Rostnikov."

Chapter Six
★ ★ ★ ★ ★ ★ ★ ★ ★ ★ ★ ★ ★

It flew through the air?" asked Laura with the skepticism of both a twelve year old and a Russian.

"Yes," said Rostnikov, examining the weights he had laid out for the nightly ritual.

"A green bench?" said Nina with the desire of an eight year old to fix on a fact.

"Green," said Rostnikov. "It flew down Petrovka Street about three feet higher than a car, flew like a spaceship, zing-zing-zip." He reached over to turn on the Dinah Washington tape he had set up.

"Why didn't you fly?" asked Nina.

"I clung to a tree," he said as Dinah Washington began to sing "Nothing Ever Changes My Love for You."

"Did you stick straight out like in cartoons?" asked Nina.

"Straight out," said Rostnikov, sitting on the bench which he kept stored in the cabinet in the corner of the living room along with his bars and weights.

"And you didn't fly away?" said Nina.

"Porfiry Petrovich is very strong," said Laura.

Sarah was in the bedroom, reading and listening to her own music. She preferred Mozart, chamber music. Porfiry Petrovich was not fond of chamber music, though he now took them all regularly to the concerts put on by Sarah's cousin Leon and three of his friends. Leon was a doctor who catered to the well-to-do and well connected and was probably quite wealthy, but his passion was the piano.

Rostnikov began to do curls with his fifty-pound dumbbells. He did twelve with each hand and then twelve more with each hand and then a final dozen with each hand while the girls stood watching and, perhaps, listening to the sadness of Dinah Washington.

"Porfiry Petrovich," Laura said, and then puffed out her cheeks like a balloon. "Nina and I took one of those out yesterday. It took both of us to lift it just a little."

Rostnikov adjusted the weights on the bar, tightening the lock, being sure that all three hundred pounds were secure. "I know," he said.

"How?" asked Laura. "We put it back exactly."

"I'm a detective," he said, lying down awkwardly, his gray sweat suit already showing patches of perspiration under the arms and at the stomach. "I'm obsessive about details."

"What is *obsessive*?" Nina asked.

"It means," said Laura to her sister, "that he weighs too much and it makes him watch his stomach and other things carefully."

Rostnikov dried his hands on the towel beside him on the floor and reached up to grip the weight. Since he had no spotters, he could not push himself to the maximum, but he came close, very close, painfully close. The senior competitions were coming up in less than two months. Rostnikov was looking forward to them. He imagined Mikhail Stoltz in some gym at this very moment with five pounds more on each end of the bar or maybe even working on five hundred pounds.

"That's not right," said Nina. "About *obsessive*."

Rostnikov had learned to count on his new leg in a way he had been unable to count on the sickly old one. If he managed to place the leg just so, it could actually help him lift, but he still had much to learn about adjusting the leg. He was concerned that there would be some protest this year, claims that the leg was helping him. Rostnikov was prepared for that. He would simply volunteer to participate in all the events for which he had registered on one leg. Since he was only doing what he could with his arms and lying on his back, it might cost him a few pounds, but he would still be very competitive.

"Sarah says that lifting weights is your only vice," said Laura.

Porfiry Petrovich could not talk. His face was red and he was doing his breathing as he went to five presses with the enormous weight.

"What's a *vice*?" asked Nina.

"A bad thing. Like sucking your thumb or taking drugs," Laura explained.

"What's wrong with lifting weights?" asked Nina, who had only recently stopped sucking her thumb.

"I don't know everything," said Laura.

For the first two months the girls had lived with them, they had said almost nothing, trusted no one, and never asked to watch anything on television or go anywhere. Only gradually had they taken to watching Rostnikov lift his weights and listen to American music. And little by little they had come closer and begun to talk.

The girls' grandmother was still at work at the bakery but would be home soon. She spent all her free time with her grandchildren, listening to their day's adventures, telling what she had done. Every night she came home with something for each of them, an éclair they could share, their own cookies in the shape of stars, different things.

The girls' parents had long since left the scene. And it was very likely, though they did not know it, that each girl had a different father. They did look somewhat alike, thin of face and body with clear skin, a small nose, short brown hair, and pink cheeks. They might well turn out to be pretty.

The time when their grandmother had been in prison had been the worst, but they had taken it as just another blow that was their lot in life.

But things were getting better now.

One more, Rostnikov thought, just one more.

The phone was ringing. Laura hurried across the room to where it sat on a table near the sofa.

Rostnikov and Dinah Washington finished at the same time. The weight went back on the rack over Rostnikov's head. He lay there exhausted, breathing deeply.

"When you breathe like that, it looks like there is a melon in your belly," said Nina, pointing to Rostnikov's abdomen. "And your face turns red like a crayon."

"I'm pleased that the display provokes your imagination," said Rostnikov, sitting up and reaching for his towel. His hands were wet now. His palms were red. He still had more to do, and Dinah Washington was well ahead of him.

"It's Iosef," said the older girl, holding the phone out. "He says lots of things were flying today, like horses and pots of flowers and balloons."

"Balloons fly every day," said Nina.

"Iosef Rostnikov was making a joke," Laura said with an exaggerated sigh.

Rostnikov reached out his hand for the phone. He had a fifteen-foot extension that could reach anywhere in the room and just far enough into the bedroom so that one could close the door for some privacy.

"Iosef," he said, taking the phone. "You called me to say that you are packed, ready, and will meet me at Sherametyevo Airport at seven in the morning. Correct?"

"Yes, but . . ." Iosef began.

"Then there is nothing more to say," Rostnikov said pleasantly. "I am busy getting ready. We can talk tomorrow."

He hung up, knowing that his son had understood, that whatever he was going to say, and Rostnikov thought he knew what it was, would be best not spoken on the phone.

Rostnikov had been followed home from Petrovka. He had been followed, in fact, by the same man he had seen in the crowd at Lermontov's house. The man had been carrying an umbrella. When he had come home, Rostnikov had looked out the window in the kitchen alcove. Another man, also with an umbrella, was standing across the street in the shadow of a doorway.

Sarah appeared at the door of the bedroom, a book in her hand. She was still dressed, but in one of her loose-fitting, comfortable dresses, the orange one with white flowers.

"Who called?" she asked.

"Iosef," said Nina. "He says horses can fly."

"But I would advise them not to do so," said Rostnikov.

Sarah was still well built, red haired and beautiful, with pale unblemished skin. Since her brain surgery five years earlier, she had lost some of the weight it had taken her years to nurture, weight Rostnikov had loved. She had gained back her hair and taken on a knowing smile. Rostnikov once told her that she looked as if she had had a long talk with death and that he had told her that she had too much life in her for him, and so he sent her back to Moscow and her husband.

"I wanted to talk to him," Sarah said.

"Nina, you know the number?" asked Rostnikov.

"Yes," she said.

"It is my turn," said Laura.

"No," said Rostnikov, wiping his neck with his now sweat-drenched towel. "I remember precisely. On Tuesday, just after dinner, I asked you to call Sasha Tkach for me. You were sitting on the chair at the table doing homework. You were wearing your jeans and a blue T-shirt. Nina was sitting on the sofa, looking at the dinosaur book. She was wearing . . ."

"It is difficult living with a detective," said Laura.

"Very," Sarah confirmed with a smile. "But it has its rewards."

Rostnikov smiled and moved back to his bench. Dinah Washington had not waited for him. She was selling more love.

Nina dialed.

Rostnikov reset the weights on the bar and wondered briefly if the first man with the umbrella had been the one who murdered Vladimir Kinotskin. He probably had.

The two men, both bachelors, both in their mid-thirties, stood in front of the bar in the town of Brevard, North Carolina, hoping for quite different encounters.

Both men were Russians. Both spoke passable but not fluent English. The move had come abruptly. They had been summoned to the office of their commander at Star City, where they had been assigned since returning to earth from their mission on *Mir.*

They were not celebrities, though their names were known within the space community. Their jobs were simply to keep up with their technology studies and training in preparation for their next mission.

When they had been summoned, the two men, Misha Sorokin and Ivan Pkhalaze, who had been kept apart since their return to earth, both wondered if this was the moment when the secret they held would end their careers if not their lives.

But the meeting had gone quickly and much to their satisfaction. They were being sent to the United States, immediately, to serve as liaisons with a space-study program at the University of North Carolina, a satellite program near a town called Brevard.

Misha and Ivan had been given a crash course in English and told that the assignment was open-ended. Its conclusion would be determined by consultation with the Americans. Both men were told to be cooperative. American support and money were needed for the construction of the new space station. No mention was made of the secret the men shared. Perhaps, both thought, it has been forgotten, put away, no longer meaningful.

They were, of course, quite wrong.

Within two weeks Misha and Ivan were sharing a house near a waterfall near the small town in North Carolina. Their input, services, and expertise were seldom drawn on by the quartet of three men and a woman who came occasionally to meet with them and even more infrequently to drive them to Asheville or even as far as Chapel Hill for discussions with professors and students.

Eventually, they had been assigned a 1995 Chevrolet Celebrity, white, with a blue cloth top.

It was in Brevard that night that they first discussed what they had not discussed before.

Misha, tall, with light-brown hair and looks that often resulted in his being compared to Liam Neeson, was acknowledged to be the leader of the duo, a degreed aeronautical engineer, a voracious reader, and a man who perhaps thought too much but kept most of what he thought to himself, his primary goal in life being to survive in safety and to continue to hide his homosexuality, a homosexuality he had not engaged in for the past six years since becoming a cosmonaut. Ivan knew nothing of his fellow cosmonaut's sexual orientation. Misha was certain, however, that Mikhail Stoltz was very well aware of it. Soon after their return from space, Stoltz had a meeting with Misha in which he made it clear without really saying so that he knew. He also made it clear that secrets could be kept for those who could keep secrets. Misha had understood and agreed.

Ivan's solid body and dark face suggested an intellectualism which was not there but which he had learned to feign. In contrast to his fellow cosmonaut, who was now his friend, Ivan's sexual urges were decidedly heterosexual and open. Women, however, were in short supply where the two of them had been sent, and their lack of ease with the English language did not help his pursuits.

Coltan's Bar just outside of Brevard had a reputation that had eventually made its way to the two Russians. The reputation was that people could be met there for friendly encounters, possibly free, possibly for money. Ivan and Misha had money, a more-than-adequate amount for their needs.

Both men hoped to make contact. Both men hoped that they could do so separately and move on with discretion.

The bar was crowded and since they were wearing American casual clothes no one seemed to pay attention to the men who made their way through the noise, past a few tables, and into a booth. Both men knew they were here for sex. Ivan did not know that Misha's idea of what that might be was quite different from his own.

"I suggest we separate," said Misha, scanning the room as a waitress made her way to their table and a woman's voice, over two badly balanced speakers, sang plaintively, "if you loved me half as much as I love you . . ."

"Name it," said the heavyset woman with clear skin and a body that very much suited Ivan.

She wore no uniform, just a pair of jeans and a flannel shirt with an order pad and pencil in one pocket in case she needed it.

"Name? . . ." asked Ivan.

"What are you drinking, eating, buying?" she said, shifting her weight to her left foot.

"Beers," Misha said.

"Germans?" she asked.

"Germans," Misha said.

"My name's Hoffer," she said. "Helga Hoffer, German."

"A pleasant coincidence," said Ivan. "You are married?"

"I am not," she said, turning her eyes from the handsome one to the intense dark one, who was cute in his own way.

"You accept invitations to drink from German customers?" Ivan said.

She smiled now. Her smile was good. Her body was better.

"We don't get Germans in here," she said, leaning over and

showing her ample breasts as she lowered her voice. "No young, good-looking ones."

"Then it might be possible to? . . ." Ivan asked.

"You're in luck," she said. "I get off in half an hour. You have a car?"

"I do," said Ivan.

"Then maybe we can go somewhere and talk," she said. "Two beers."

She turned and walked back toward the bar.

"I can't believe it," said Ivan.

"It is probably that touch of French blood in you left over from Napoleon's short-lived vacation in Rostov," said Misha.

"I don't care," said Ivan with a grin.

"She is not young," said Misha. "Perhaps forty-five."

"Age means nothing," said Ivan. "She is my kind of woman and I am very, very much in need."

"I understand," said Misha, looking toward the bar where two men in their twenties were looking at the two cosmonauts. One of the men caught Misha's eye and the two men exchanged a look that Misha well understood.

"Shall I ask her if she has a friend?" asked Ivan.

"No, thank you," said Misha with a smile. "I will see what I can do on my own. You go off with Miss Hoffer. I'll make my way back to the house. If worse comes to worse, I'll get a cab."

They listened to music and drank two beers each.

Misha and the young man at the bar glanced at each other from time to time, and eventually Helga Hoffer, minus pencil and pad, made her way to the booth and wedged in next to Ivan, who enjoyed the touch of her hip against his.

"I think I'll leave you two," said Misha, standing and placing a ten-dollar bill on the table.

"We're gonna leave too, aren't we?" Helga asked, looking at Ivan. Their faces were no more than six inches apart.

"We are certainly leaving," Ivan said, letting his nose touch hers, feeling her breath against his mouth.

Misha waited till Ivan and the woman had left and then he sat back down and waited. It was probably no different here than it had been in Moscow, but it had been a long time. Misha was definitely nervous, but he did his best not to show it. He had purposely nursed his second beer and now reached for it. Both of the young men approached the table and the one whose eyes had met Misha's asked, "May we join you?"

Misha showed his best smile to the young men and said yes.

It was more than twenty minutes later and Ivan was still no more than fifty yards from the bar. He was now parked at the dark, far end of the gravel-covered parking lot. The nearest car was about twenty-five feet away. He would have preferred to be someplace more private, possibly even their house, but Helga had reached down the front of his pants and between his legs before he could ask her where she suggested they go.

The experience had been wonderful. She had proved to be experienced and he had been quite durable and willing. Now he was spent from her hands, her mouth, and, finally, from her surprisingly firm body in the back seat.

She sat up and began to dress. She turned her head toward the entrance to the club as he sat up.

"You wish to continue elsewhere?" he said, quite naked except for his shoes.

"Not tonight, honey," Helga said, leaning over to give him a moist, open-mouth kiss that tasted of her, of him, and of something quite sweet.

"Then I can see you? . . ." he began.

The door on his side suddenly opened. Helga, not yet fully dressed, opened her door and hurried out, saying, "Sorry, honey. I had fun."

The two men pulled the naked Ivan from the car. One of them kicked the door closed.

"*Bi'str iy*, 'quick,' " said one man to the other in Russian as they pulled Ivan toward the nearby trees, shredding his bottom on the gravel.

Ivan struggled, but the men were strong and his leverage poor.

A few seconds later Ivan lay in pain, naked, on his back, and the two men over him, behind a wall of bushes and trees.

"What is this?" Ivan demanded.

"You've talked," one dark figure over him said.

"Talked? About what? To who?" Ivan demanded, wishing he had something to cover himself.

"You know," said the second man.

"I . . . you mean? No, I have not."

"But what is there to stop you?" asked the first man.

"I wouldn't," said Ivan.

"Why are we talking?" asked the second man. "Let's do it and get out."

"You are going to kill me?" asked Ivan.

The first man reached under his jacket for something. Ivan knew what it was.

"No . . . I . . ." he said, trying to back away, holding his hand up.

What happened next was a blur of imagination and confusion.

The man with the gun grunted and staggered forward. The other man turned toward the first and Ivan could see something heavy, a rock, crash into his face. The second man fell next to Ivan, soundlessly bleeding, his nose broken. Ivan tried to sit up.

The first man tried to level his gun but someone stepped forward and seemed to punch him in the stomach. The first man let out an "Ohh" that faded like the air from a flat tire.

"Are you badly injured?" Misha asked, helping Ivan to his feet.

"Badly? . . . No, I don't think so. They tried to kill me. They are Russians," said Ivan, bewildered.

"We heard," said Misha.

Ivan looked at the two men who were with Misha. They seemed familiar. Yes, they had been in the bar.

"How did you know? How did you find me?" asked Ivan, now on his feet.

One of the two young men took off his jacket and handed it to Ivan, who tied it around his waist.

"My friends told me that this was a place where people come to get together. We saw them dragging you from the car."

"You make friends quickly," said Ivan.

One of the two young men said, "Maybe another time."

The evening had already been a nightmare by the time Sasha and his mother had arrived at the movie theater.

They had gone out for dinner. Lydia had insisted. This was a special occasion. She would pay. They had eaten at the Yerevan, with Lydia, who had picked out the restaurant, grumbling rather loudly that she was not terribly fond of Armenian food.

"Then," Sasha had said, loud enough for his mother and the people at the tables on both sides of them to hear, "why are we here?"

"Because you love Armenian food," she said.

Sasha did not love Armenian food. He liked it reasonably well, but it was certainly not a culinary love. The *bozbash*—'lamb and potato soup'—which seemed just fine to Sasha, was "too full of spices" for Lydia, who drank it all anyway. The *chebureki*—'deep-fried meat pies'—which Sasha found delicious, were, according to Lydia, "filled with things that would block your heart and kill you." She ate her entire plateful and drank a large glass of Armenian brandy.

The waiter had refused to acknowledge Sasha's shrug and search for sympathy in a conspiratorial glance.

"What are you smiling about?" Lydia had said over brandy.

"Nothing. I don't know."

"You look content," she said suspiciously. "You've found some woman."

"No," he said, loud enough for her to hear. "But I was asked to be a movie star today."

Lydia shook her head. She did not understand her son's jokes.

"You should look terrible," she said. "Your wife and children are gone. You should go get them. You could be in Kiev by train in half a day. I would pay. I want my grandchildren back."

Now the entire restaurant, Sasha was sure, knew the history of the Tkach family. He doubted if that history interested them.

Lydia had paid the check, saying, "My son loves Armenian food. It doesn't suit my stomach. He's taking me to a movie."

The waiter had said nothing. He didn't have to be particularly polite. His tip was built into the check.

"*Shto ehtah zah feel'm,* 'what kind of movie is this?' " she asked.

"I told you," Sasha said, "a *kahmyehdyeeyoo,* 'a comedy.' "

"It is Japanese?" she asked. "I don't like Japanese. Your great-grandfather died fighting the Japanese, and for what, Vladivostok."

"It isn't Japanese," said Sasha, ushering his mother out of the restaurant. "It is English."

And then they were in the movie. It was crowded. Before it began, Sasha begged his mother to turn on her hearing aid. He still had daymares of the last time he had taken his mother to a movie.

They sat.

"I can hear perfectly," she said, loud enough for a thin young man with glasses in front of her to turn and give a look designed as warning against such outbursts during the film.

There were few empty seats in the theater. The murmur of the crowd was loud. Then Sasha Tkach's nightmare in darkness began. The movie had started.

The subtitles seemed too long for what the English actors were saying on the screen.

"Which one is Monty?" Lydia asked aloud.

How, Sasha thought, could one explain. "The skinny one with the bad teeth," said Sasha. "It's his nickname."

"Look, what? I thought those were women," she said a little later. "One of them is standing by that urinal, peeing. It's a man dressed like a woman."

"It is a woman making a joke about men peeing," said Sasha.

"Be quiet, please," said the young man with glasses, turning to them.

"What is funny about women pretending to pee like men?"

"I don't know," said Sasha, sinking down in his seat, barely watching the movie, hoping for the end to come soon.

"What is . . . why are those men taking off their clothes?"

"They want to make money stripping," Sasha explained. "They're out of work."

"I know that," she said. "I can read, but who would want to see those men take off their clothes? Well, maybe that nice-looking one. Ah, I knew it, he's a sissy boy."

The young man with glasses turned around in his seat and said, "He is gay and you are loud and I think you should leave so that the rest of us in this theater can salvage some sense of satisfaction from this so-far intolerable situation."

"I'm a police officer," Sasha said, sitting up and reaching into his pocket to pull out his badge. "This is my mother. If you think you are having a bad time, try, if you have the imagination, to think of how I am feeling. You will go home alone. I will go home with my mother."

"You have my sympathy," said the young man with glasses, "but . . ."

"Right," said Sasha. "Mother, let's go."

Sasha started to get up.

"I like this movie," she said, refusing to budge.

"Listen to your son," came a voice from behind.

"Why are they breaking those beautiful little gnomes?" asked Lydia.

"Sometimes, my mother, people get the uncontrollable impulse to break things. Let's go."

"You don't like the movie. We will go," said Lydia. "He invites me to a movie and then we leave before we know what's going to happen."

Sasha guided his mother up the aisle. Several people applauded their departure.

Once outside, Sasha took a deep breath of relief.

"I don't understand why you didn't like the movie," Lydia said.

"You didn't laugh once," he said as they walked down the Arbat toward the metro station.

"It wasn't a comedy," she said. "You didn't understand. That was the problem, why you didn't like it. It was sad. They were out of work."

"Mother, you are absolutely right," he said.

"When are you going to Kiev?"

Akardy Zelach sat at the small kitchen table, turning a chicken bone over with his fork. His mother shifted her position in the next room. He could see her. She, like him, was a bit heavy and awkward, but she had a confidence and dignity, a certainty about everything, that he would never possess.

She was watching some game show on television. Akardy could see that it involved a big wheel with numbers that made no sense to him. Contestants spun the wheel and the audience shouted as it turned. His mother, fist clenched, urged the wheel on, turned sideways to will it another notch or turn.

"Then," he said. "I should refuse."

"If you can," his mother said. "If you cannot..."

She shrugged and reached for the glass of tepid tea on the table in front of her.

Akardy adjusted his glasses and looked at the bone.

"Then shall I lie?" he asked.

"Will they pay you if you tell the truth?" she asked. "Look, look, if she just . . . she can win a car. She can . . . oh, no."

"I don't know if they'll pay," he repeated. "I don't know if I'm allowed to take it even if they do pay."

Akardy's mother stood up, reached over, and turned off the television set.

"Your grandmother, my mother, read tea leaves, palms, bumps on the head, cards," she said, looking at her son.

"I know," he answered glumly.

"And you know what? It was all for show. She didn't know how she knew what she knew. It was just there. People want the show. That's what my sister and I did when we learned we had the gift or curse. And you don't know either."

"I didn't . . . I just said whatever came into my head," said Akardy. "I'm not even sure how to lie about it. Do I let something come into my head and then lie about it? And where does the new lie come from? Perhaps it is really the truth. How do I know? How am I to know? I don't want to be studied."

His mother walked over to join him at the table and picked at the crumbs of the flat cake she had baked earlier that day. Akardy didn't like when she picked at crumbs and then licked her fingers and picked again. He had never told her. She loved him, had taken care of him when he had been injured and almost died. That was when the gift or curse had come, after he had been beaten, after his skull had been cracked. It didn't come often and he had always been able to ignore it before, but that dark woman with the glasses at the psychic center, Nadia Spectorski, she had been like a . . . a jumping dog, all over him, demanding, excited. He did not want to see her again, but he had no choice. Perhaps he could call in and say he was ill or that his mother was ill? She really wasn't well. No, he would have to go. He would have to face Emil Karpo's doubting eyes.

He decided that he would try to lie. Perhaps the Nadia Spectorski woman would turn out to be the murderer. That would save him. He wished there were more cake.

"What are you doing?" asked Elena.

The night was relatively warm though there was a smell of the possibility of more rain in the clouds that covered the sky. They sat on a bench in the concrete courtyard just outside the window of the apartment Elena shared with her aunt, Anna Timofeyeva.

Had she been home, Lydia Tkach could have looked out the window and seen them from her apartment in the far corner of the one-story building, but she was staying with Sasha.

Anna Timofeyeva regretted the day she had agreed to help Lydia Tkach find an apartment in the building. As a former procurator, Anna still had friends or friends who had friends. She had misgivings when she agreed to help Sasha's mother. To protect herself and Elena, Anna had set down clear rules by which Lydia was to abide. These rules regarded when Lydia could visit and under what conditions. Lydia had begun violating the rules the day after she moved in.

The day before, Anna Timofeyeva had sat petting her cat, Bakunin, in the window and had said to Elena, "Perhaps we will be lucky. Perhaps Sasha's wife will never return."

"You mean that?" Elena had asked.

"I don't know," said Anna. "Maybe I do."

And now, Elena and Iosef sat in the dark and empty courtyard surrounded by dimly lit windows, possibly being watched by Aunt Anna.

"What are you doing?" Elena asked, putting her hand on the shoulder of Iosef, who leaned forward, his elbows on his knees, his head in his hands.

"Brooding," he said.

"Are you going to stop brooding sometime tonight? I have to get up early and catch a thief."

"I'll stop," he said. "It will take great effort. You can help by setting a clear date for our marriage, a date when you will be moving into my apartment."

"Which," she said, "will then be 'our apartment' and which, you have agreed, will be redecorated to our mutual satisfaction."

He sat up and looked at her.

"I thought you liked the way my apartment looks."

"Iosef, we've talked about this. I like it for you. For us, I want more of us, or me, to be there, which is why I want to pay half the rent. And please, don't talk about how all of our money will be together. I don't want to bicker about tables and chairs and . . . Iosef, tell me truthfully, am I fat?"

He leaned back a bit to examine her as if for the first time, from foot to head.

"Stop," she said. "This is not a joke."

"You are not fat," he said. "You are voluptuous. You are perfect. If you lose a pound, one pound, I will call off the marriage. If after we are married, you lose one pound, I will seek a divorce."

"You mean it?"

"Yes."

"Good. If you want to brood some more, you have my permission," she said.

"No, you've taken the pain out of it."

"What were you brooding about?"

"Dead poets. Dead cosmonauts. Did you know that Mikhail Lermontov was only twenty-seven when he died?"

"Yes," Elena said, tugging at his ear. "He died in 1841. Did you know he was descended from a Scottish family that came to Russia in the seventeenth century? And that Lermontov was a military officer transferred to the Caucasus for writing poetry attacking the royal court?"

"No," said Iosef. "You are fond of Lermontov's work?"

"Not particularly," she said. "He is too brooding."

"Your point is taken," said Iosef, leaning over to kiss her. She liked his kisses. His lips were ample, his mouth and tongue passionate. She had taught herself to be careful with men, but with Iosef she felt she could let herself float without flying away.

When the first kiss had ended, she said, "I will have to get some sleep and you have to be up early to get to the airport."

"I'm packed," he said, leaning toward her again.

"We're being watched from many windows," she said with a smile.

"I would hope so," he said. "I have never completely lost my desire for an audience."

"And I have never lost my desire for privacy," she said.

"A perfect match," he said, placing her hand gently between his legs.

"Perfect," she said.

Emil Karpo continued to believe that Communism was a nearly ideal social-political system. The problem, he had come to believe, was that humanity could not abide an ideal system. People were self-serving, animalistic, and were capable of destroying anything that required total cooperation. There were many individuals of worth who cared about others, who had, he knew not why, cared about him. Porfiry Petrovich and his wife clearly cared. Mathilde had cared.

Emil Karpo sat at the table in his room, facing the floor-to-ceiling bookcase filled with files and notes of unresolved cases. Emil Karpo sat in the light of a single lamp behind him and the glow of his computer screen. He wore a white T-shirt over a pair of white shorts. In his room, alone, he wore white. Outside, he wore black.

Barefoot, Karpo looked at the screen.

When he had become a policeman, his goal had been clear, his task certain. He would find and help punish those who broke the law, those who were not fit for a Communist state. He knew that he would never stop all crime, not alone, not with the help of thousands, because people did not live for an ideal. They lived for themselves, for their families sometimes, for a few others or one other for whom they had often-fleeting feelings. But he could keep to a minimum the numbers of those who did not conform.

He quickly discovered, however, that the task was beyond monumental. The people who ruled were corrupt. The people who were supposed to contain crime and prosecute criminals were corrupt. Soviet Communism had turned into a grotesque distortion of what his father, his readings, and the speeches of many had promised, but it had been replaced by an even more corrupt system.

Emil Karpo was still a Communist, not a member of the party any longer. Those who said they were Communists now were opportunists preying on the memories of the poor who had forgotten the corruption and remembered only safe streets and having just enough to eat without worrying about making a living. Perhaps there was only one true Communist and his name was Emil Karpo.

He moved the cursor and found the file he sought on the computer screen.

Outside of the table, bookshelves, and chair, Emil Karpo's room was, intentionally, as bare as a prison cell or a monk's chamber. The wooden floor was dark and uncovered. There was a cot in the corner near the single window covered by a shade. Next to the cot was a small square table with a telephone, a clock, and a lamp on it. Under the single drawer of the table was space for about a dozen books. The space was filled. There was a wardrobe, a tall rectangle in a corner that could have been a large standing coffin. Next to the wardrobe was a modest, dark chest of drawers upon which stood nothing. Above the chest of drawers was a painting, a painting of a smiling red-haired woman in a field with a barn in the distance behind her. The painting was of the dead Mathilde Verson. It was the only sign of life in the room.

Emil Karpo kept his room scrubbed and clean. Each morning, before dawn, he awoke without needing to check the small electric clock. It took him exactly twenty-eight minutes to exercise by the light of his lamp. His motions were without sound and without the accompaniment of music or the news. He owned no television set.

After he exercised, Karpo would don a robe, a blue one Mathilde had given him for a birthday, and he would go down the hall with a towel to take a shower in the bathroom he shared with the other tenants on the floor. Everyone knew when the ghost got up to take a shower. No one left his apartment till he had finished.

Karpo could have afforded much better. He spent almost no money and ate little. He cut his own thin hair the infrequent times that it was necessary, and he did not use a bank. His room was a vault, rigged to shock an intruder and detect any attempt to enter without the specially machined two keys of which only he and Porfiry Petrovich had a set.

Now Emil Karpo worked not for a cause but to punish. The law was under siege, had always been. The law was ridiculous, but it was law. Those who challenged it had to be stopped if even the semblance of sanity was to be maintained.

Karpo was relentless. To be otherwise was to invite madness. Karpo, who had decades earlier accepted that he was devoid of emotion, had discovered when he was past the age of forty—with the help of Mathilde—that he did have emotions, had covered and protected them. When she had gotten him to let some of those emotions out, she had left a hole big enough for madness to slink in.

Mathilde had given him a gift and a curse.

Very early that evening, Karpo had talked to Porfiry Petrovich by phone. The conversation had been brief.

"Paulinin is examining all of the shoes tonight," Karpo had

said. "He will work through the night if necessary, and he believes it will be necessary."

"So?" asked Porfiry Petrovich.

"We may know by morning who killed Sergei Bolskanov."

"And your thoughts about psychic happenings?" asked Rostnikov.

"I have brought some books to my room," said Karpo. "I will read. However, I believe some psychic phenomena may well exist. They are not mysterious in any way other than that we do not yet understand them scientifically."

"Then," Porfiry Petrovich had said, "they do not lead us to gods, demons, or ghosts?"

"No," said Karpo.

"But perhaps people can move objects with their thoughts, and dreams can tell us of the past and the future, and unidentified flying objects may exist?"

"You are being provocative, Porfiry Petrovich Rostnikov."

"Yes."

"It is likely at some point in the future there will be only identified flying objects, as there may be dreams which contain the possibility of alternative future events," said Karpo. "The dreamer remembers only those aspects of the dream which prove to be more-or-less prophetic and forgets those which are not."

"Emil, it might help if you tried using your imagination."

"You have suggested this frequently in the past. I have little or no imagination. I do not wish one. I am reading books and examining theories," said Karpo. "I continue to believe that there is but one life, that magic does not exist, and that which we have called magic is simply phenomena not yet explained by science."

"I don't believe you are as dispassionate as you claim," said Rostnikov. "I have seen you when . . . but that is yours to do with as you will. Iosef and I will be gone a day or two or three, no more than that. Pankov will know how to reach me."

"Very good," said Karpo.

"And, Emil, I think that if you could allow yourself to do so, you should find someone you could trust with your secrets."

"I have no secrets."

"You have secrets, Emil Karpo. I have known no one without secrets. Even apes, even dogs and crows have secrets, places where they have things. We have places like that within ourselves."

"And the person I could trust is you?"

"No, Emil, the person you can trust is you."

"You are feeling very philosophical tonight."

"Yes, I think it is storms that make buses and benches fly and the vastness of the universe in which tiny machines carry men beyond our sight that has put me in this mood. When we come back, you will come to dinner. I will be less pensive. The girls miss you. Laura thinks you are cute."

"I am not cute," said Karpo.

"You can explain that to Laura. She doesn't believe me. Be good to yourself, Emil Karpo."

And then the conversation had ended.

Emil Karpo had gone to see Mathilde regularly once a week for years. He had paid her the price she asked till the last year or so when she had refused to take his money. He had told himself that going to a prostitute was essential, that he was a man, that man was an animal. He was satisfying a need. But his relationship had changed and he had been about to give that change a name when Mathilde had been murdered in the crossfire of a Mafia war. Her death had given him a determination, a new meaning, to destroy the gangs, the gangs that slaughtered the innocent and destroyed hope. He had made clear to Rostnikov that he wished to be assigned to Mafia-related crimes that came to the Office of Special Investigation. Sometimes Rostnikov listened to his wishes. Sometimes he did not.

Karpo had not wished to go to a prostitute since Mathilde had died. He had briefly thought that Mathilde's sister, who had come to Moscow from Odessa for the funeral, might . . . but she had left. It was better to be alone. Feeling was less likely to enter the portal Mathilde had created in him if he was alone.

Enough. He knew it was two in the morning. He required a full four hours' sleep. He turned off the computer, rose, moved to the cot, turned off the light, and was asleep in less than thirty seconds.

Chapter Seven

★ ★ ★ ★ ★ ★ ★ ★ ★ ★ ★ ★

A sleepy dawn of dark clouds was just coming when the phone in Yuri Kriskov's living room rattled. It was sitting on a table before the three of them—Kriskov, his wife, Vera, and Elena Timofeyeva—who had been drinking coffee and waiting with little to say.

The house was large, not a mansion but complete with large living room, three bedrooms, two baths, full kitchen, separate dining room, and a garage. The view from the front windows was of other recently built houses that looked much the same.

"Wait," said Elena, touching Yuri's hand as he reached for it.

The line had been tapped, and in the small blue van parked outside two men were going to record the conversation and find the location where the call was coming from. Elena knew that the new technology was such that they needed less than a minute to locate the caller. A few extra rings would give the men in the van more time to trace the call.

After three rings, Elena said, "Now."

Yuri Kriskov was fully if casually dressed, dark slacks, light-blue silk shirt open at the collar. Vera Kriskov wore only a robe and slippers, though she had taken time to brush her hair and put on makeup. Elena and Yuri Kriskov sat next to each other on a white sofa. Vera Kriskov sat across from them, legs crossed, on a matching chair.

Just before the call came, Yuri had lit his fourth cigarette of the brief morning.

"Yes," he said, after Elena nodded to him to pick up the phone.

Elena had told him not to drag out the call, not to cause suspicion. In fact, if he could, he was to ask reasonable questions of clarification, ask them quickly, and not provoke the caller.

"You have the money?" Valery Grachev said in the high-pitched voice he had been practicing with Vera's coaching.

"I have it. It wasn't easy to . . ."

Elena shook her head *no*.

"I have it," he said. "In a large gymnasium bag, blue."

"American dollars? No rubles. Rubles are worth shit."

"American dollars."

"When we hang up," Valery said, "you get in your car and drive as quickly as you can to Timiryazevsky Park."

"I can't," said Yuri, looking at Elena, who was now nodding *yes*.

"What?" asked Valery, sounding suspicious, though Vera had told him exactly what to expect.

"I broke my leg," said Yuri. "Actually, you broke it."

Yuri was improvising now and Elena shook her head *no* quite decisively, but Yuri turned away from her.

"You broke it because you made me so nervous with your threats and the horror you are committing that I fell and broke my leg. I have a wife, children. If you do this . . ."

"Stop, now," shouted Valery, checking his watch. "Who is coming with the money? Your wife?"

"No," said Yuri. "She is too frightened. My niece, Elena, will bring it."

"No, hobble to your car," Valery said. "Or I destroy the negative and kill you as I promised."

"I can't," said Yuri mournfully. "I . . ."

"Stop," shouted Valery. "All right, have your niece bring the bag to Timiryazevsky Park. You know where the chess tables are?"

"The chess tables in Timiryazevsky Park," Yuri repeated for Elena's benefit.

Now Elena was nodding *yes*.

"I know where they are," Yuri went on.

"Have her go now," said Valery. "Have her go quickly. She should stand by the chess tables with the bag. If she hurries, she will get there before any players arrive."

"And what? . . ." Yuri began, but Valery Grachev had already hung up the phone.

Yuri did the same.

The unlocked front door suddenly opened. A large man in blue jeans and a denim shirt stepped in.

"Stop," shouted Vera Kriskov, rising.

The man stopped suddenly.

"If you are coming in here," Vera said, "take off your shoes. You have mud on your shoes."

The large man looked at Vera and then at Elena. He did not move.

Yuri was up now. Vera had moved to his side and taken his hand reassuringly.

"A public phone near the entrance of the Kuznetski Most metro station," the big man said. "Two teams will be there within a minute."

Elena nodded and reached for the gym bag filled with rectangles of cut-up newspaper.

Within the coming minute, she was sure, the caller, along with thousands of people going to work, would be on a crowded metro train, going in any of eight directions. The man had chosen wisely. The metro station was at the center of the train system.

"Be careful with my negatives," said Yuri as Elena went to join the big man with the muddy shoes, who seemed nailed to the floor.

"Be careful," Vera Kriskov said with concern, taking her husband's left hand in both of hers.

"We will be careful," said Elena.

Elena picked up the bag and nodded to Sasha, who rose. There was something about Vera Kriskov that Elena didn't like. She had been watching the woman who looked with loving concern at her husband and touched him frequently. Elena sensed the woman was acting. It probably meant nothing. Perhaps she didn't really love or even like her husband. There was nothing unusual in that. Perhaps it was what happened to people when they were married, most people. She tried to banish such thoughts and concentrate on what she now had to do.

The big policeman with the muddy shoes followed Elena and Sasha into the dark dawn, closing the door behind him. Sasha moved to the small truck. Elena got into the car.

Elena was not used to the Volga she had been given. The car had almost eighty thousand miles on it and handled sluggishly, with a willful tendency to veer to the left. There was also a stale smell on the seats, probably years of food eaten by detectives on stakeouts.

Traffic was worse than she had expected, but she was a good driver who gauged well just how much space she needed to make a move. In twenty minutes she was at the park. Even at this hour she would have had trouble finding a place to park had she been a civilian. She parked quite illegally on a concrete driveway expressly labeled for use by park personnel only.

Elena slung her pouch-purse over her shoulder. Inside the purse was her pistol, in a pocket that came close to being a holster. She grabbed the blue gymnasium bag, got out of the car, and walked to a path that would lead her through the trees to the chess tables.

There was a wind this morning. It played a leafy morning song through the leaves as she walked. It would rain again. The full gym bag was heavy. It had to look as if it contained two million dollars.

When she reached the clearing she sought, there were already two men seated at one of the chessboards. They were at one end of three boards on a table. The men sat on opposite sides of the board, examining the pieces before them. Both men were over seventy. One of the men looked up as Elena approached. He watched as she moved to the end of the table away from them and placed the blue bag on the bench.

"Play," said the man who had not looked up.

"Look," said the man watching Elena.

"I see her. Look at the board. You'll see that you are already in enough trouble."

The man reluctantly turned his eyes from Elena to the problem before him.

She stood holding the strap of her purse, knowing that somewhere Sasha Tkach was watching her through binoculars and scanning the places where someone could hide.

Elena checked her watch and waited. Almost fifteen minutes later, two burly men moved through the trees and headed directly toward her. They looked determined. Both wore lightweight jackets. Both had their hands plunged into the pockets of their jackets. When they were close enough, Elena could see that they had the tough, lined faces of Russian males who had not gone through life lightly.

Elena felt with her fingers through the unzipped top of her purse. Her hand moved toward the gun.

The men came toward her, one on each side. They looked directly at her as she put her hand on the gun. The man on her right looked at the blue gym bag and then at Elena.

"The bag," he said.

His voice was as lined as his pink-white face.

"Yes," she said.

He picked up the bag and faced her.

"Move it," he said. "This is our place."

The other man, almost a twin of the man who had spoken, moved past Elena and sat on the bench. Elena took the gym bag, and the first man sat where it had rested.

Elena moved away from the table with the bag. The first man to sit removed a bag from his pocket, opened it, and began to set up the chess pieces. Elena placed the blue bag on a more-or-less dry patch of grass before her.

About two minutes later a boy of about twelve came through the trees not far from where the two new players had come. He wore dark pants, an oversized orange T-shirt, and a school bag over his shoulders. When he was closer, Elena could see that the boy had a smooth, pink face, dark straight hair, and an angry, defensive scowl. He was thin and short and in a hurry.

He came directly at Elena but did not look at her. His eyes were on the bag. Without a word or acknowledgment of her presence, the boy unzipped the bag and looked inside. He moved the newspaper pieces around and then stood up and turned away from Elena. The boy began crossing his arms in front of him and shaking his head *no*.

Elena moved next to the boy to see where he was looking, but the boy's eyes were looking upward, over the trees, toward the sky. Elena scanned the path, the trees on all sides, even looked back at the men playing chess. The first old man at the far end of the bench, the one who had watched Elena, now watched the boy.

"Stop," said Elena to the boy.

He didn't stop.

"I am a police officer," she said. "Stop now."

She reached into her purse and removed the stiff leather square that held her identification. She held it in front of the boy with one hand and stayed one of his arms with the other. The boy stopped and looked at her.

"Who are you signaling?"

"The man," he said.

"Quickly, tell me what man and what he told you to do. I am the police," she said, knowing that Sasha had seen the boy, watched him signal, and was now scurrying to find someone else who might be watching and waiting. But Sasha would have no idea of the direction in which he should look. There were two uniformed police with Sasha. They would spread out as best they could, but Elena knew the task was close to hopeless.

"He gave me this," the boy said, reaching into his pocket. "One hundred new rubles. You're not going to take it away, are you?"

"No," said Elena, looking at the bills, which, in exchange, would have brought about five American dollars, probably less in a day or two. "You can keep the money."

The boy relaxed.

"I was on the way to school," he said. "The man came up to me. I looked around. There were other people. Not many, but a few. I thought he might be one of those dirty men. There are some who come here. My friend Gregor kicked one of them in the balls only two weeks ago."

"The man," Elena said. "What did he look like?"

"Not big. Wide like . . ." The boy opened his arms to indicate the width of the man's body. "His face . . . he wore a cap pulled down to his ears. A cap like the men on the riverboats wear. And he had a short beard, black. And a Band-Aid on his nose."

"What was he wearing?"

"Wearing? I don't remember. Pants. A shirt. I think they were dark or something."

Elena knew the beard, the Band-Aid, and hat were probably gone by now. Even if he had the description from the boy, Sasha could walk right past the man.

"And he told you to do what?" Elena said.

The boy pursed his lips and paused. "Will you give me thirty rubles if I tell you?"

"If you don't tell me, and quickly, I will give you the day to think about the consequences of not telling a police officer what you know. The day will be spent in a cell. If you are lucky, you will be alone."

"He told me to come here, to the lady with the blue bag. That I should open the bag, and if there was anything but money in it I was to make that signal with my hands and shake my head."

"Be quiet," grumbled one of the two big men playing chess behind them.

"Did he tell you what this was supposed to be about?" Elena asked, ignoring the men.

"He said you and he were playing a game."

"You believed him?"

The boy turned away. "He gave me one hundred rubles."

"Would you recognize him again if you saw him without the cap, without the Band-Aid, without the beard?"

The boy shrugged and said, "Maybe, no. No, I don't think so."

"Even if I gave you another hundred rubles?"

"No," said the boy. "I know what police do. You would have a lineup, and if I identified some policeman as the man, you would put me in children's detention."

"Go to school," said Elena. "Now, fast."

The boy ran, back in the direction from which he had come.

Elena suddenly felt a presence behind her. A hand touched her shoulder. She drew her pistol from her purse and turned, backing away a step.

One of the two big men who had been playing chess behind her stood looking at her and the gun. There was a look of surprise on his face, which quickly turned to resignation. He shook his head.

"Am I to die at the hand of a pretty young lady in the park just because I want to have a quiet chess game?" he said. "Yevgeny Savidov, this was a day to make deliveries, not to die."

Elena put the gun away and said, "I'm sorry. Finish your game. I'm going."

The man with the tough face nodded and moved back to the table.

Elena picked up the blue bag and began to walk back to the car. Sasha appeared before her, out of breath.

"Nothing," he said.

Elena nodded and kept walking. "Something is wrong," she said.

Sasha walked at her side. He had not exercised in weeks and he had a slight pain in his side.

"What do you mean?"

"Why didn't he do this at night?" she asked.

"Who knows? Maybe he works at night or has a wife who knows nothing about his extortion."

"Maybe," said Elena. "But he sent the boy and told him to signal if there was no money in the bag."

"So?" asked Sasha.

"Would it not have made more sense for the boy to nod or bow to indicate if the money was there?"

They were almost at the street now.

"It could go either way," said Sasha.

The pain in his side was gone and he could breathe normally now. He would have to start exercising again. He was the youngest member of the Office of Special Investigation, and everyone, with the possible exception of Pankov and the Yak, was in better condition than he was.

"What if he expected the bag would not contain the money?" she asked him. "He gave Kriskov a little over a day to raise two million American dollars in cash. Why didn't he give him more time? Raising that much would be difficult, if not impossible."

"Our man didn't know that," said Sasha. "He just thought Kriskov was a millionaire movie producer with big backers. Why would he want Kriskov to fail to raise the money?"

"I don't know," she said, facing Sasha. "Maybe he just wants an excuse for killing our movie producer."

"And the negatives?" asked Sasha.

"I don't know," said Elena. "I think we should talk to Porfiry Petrovich."

When the boy was waving his arms in Timiryazevsky Park, Porfiry Petrovich Rostnikov was in an aisle seat near the front of the airplane. He was reading a tattered paperback of Ed McBain's *Sadie When She Died.* The book was in English.

Rostnikov was aware of several things on the airplane as they headed for St. Petersburg, but these things did not stop him from enjoying the book, though it was the third time he had read it.

He was aware of his son, Iosef, seated next to him at the window, looking out at dark clouds below, chin resting on one hand, thinking of something important, something about which he had to make a decision. Porfiry Petrovich was aware of the vibrations of the plane and the hum of the jet engines. He was aware of conversation among the hundred or so other passengers behind them. But foremost in his awareness was the man seated fourteen rows back, on the aisle. It was the same man who had been in the crowd looking at the body of the murdered cosmonaut. The man was even carrying an umbrella, probably the same one he had when he looked up at Rostnikov's window the night before.

"Iosef," he said, putting the book in his lap and using his hands to move his leg.

His son turned to him and pulled slowly out of his musing. "Yes."

"I have a game I wish to play with you. A game I played with the same Elena Timofeyeva about whom you were thinking just now. We played it when we were on a plane to Cuba."

Iosef nodded and shifted to face his father. The young man's handsome face, the male version of his mother, was now focused.

"What is the single most interesting thing about the people on this flight?"

Iosef smiled. "The lady, the one with the wig, four rows behind us at the window. She keeps looking back through the window, back toward Moscow, as if something or someone is following her. I would guess that she is right. Since she is no beauty, I would guess that it is not a lover. I would guess that she is running away with something of value. It would be interesting to talk to her."

"Very interesting to talk to her," agreed Porfiry Petrovich. "Anything else?"

Iosef's smile broadened. "The man with the umbrella who is following us," said Iosef. "The one in the crowd at Lermontov's house. Do I pass the test?"

"Tell me more about the man."

"Well," said Iosef. "He is almost as tall as I am, not as heavy. His clothes are adequate but not expensive. His face is the face of hundreds we pass in the street every day. He is bland, not the least bit sinister. A quick glance would lead one to the conclusion that he worked in a bank or office, low-level, a dull man."

"In short?" asked Porfiry Petrovich.

"In short," Iosef continued, "a good appearance for an assassin. A young woman with a baby, a very old man who needed a cane to walk, an overweight babushka with pink cheeks carrying a string shopping bag, they would be even better for the task, but he will do."

Rostnikov reached over and patted his son's cheek. "And what shall we do with him?" he asked.

"For now? Nothing, but when you do decide to confront him, I would like very much to squeeze fear and a groan of agony from him."

"That may be possible, but I don't think it will be a good idea."

"I know," said Iosef. "It is a fantasy. I am learning to live with my fantasies."

"Have you read this book?"

Iosef looked at the paperback. His English was not as good as his father's but it was adequate.

"No."

"Here, try it," said Rostnikov.

"You are reading it."

"I have read it. Besides, I have work to do."

Iosef was not particularly fond of mystery stories, but he had brought nothing with him to read. He accepted the offer, and his father shifted and awkwardly removed his pad of paper from his inner jacket pocket.

Iosef began to read and Porfiry Petrovich began to draw.

There was a mischief in Rostnikov. It had come before. On occasion, it had yielded interesting results for him and others. On other occasions, it had gotten him into trouble. But it was an urge he had trouble resisting.

He got out his mechanical pencil with the eraser, clicked once to make the lead come out just a bit more, and began to draw.

"Boris Adamovskovich, you are under arrest," said Emil Karpo.

"What?" asked the scientist, looking up, mouth open, at the two unsmiling inspectors.

"On suspicion of murder in the death of Sergei Bolskanov," Karpo continued.

The office was not large. Adamovskovich rose from behind his desk, computer screen alive with numbers behind him. He looked from Zelach to Karpo with disbelief.

"I did not kill him," Adamovskovich said with his right hand on his heart.

"There is blood on your shoes, the blood of the victim."

"On my shoes? Blood? Sergei Bolskanov's blood? No. No. That

isn't possible. Someone put it there. People here are jealous of my success."

"We have heard that you were jealous of Bolskanov's success," said Karpo flatly.

"No, nonsense . . . well, maybe a slight bit of envy, but we all . . . I didn't kill him. We weren't even interested in the same research."

"We shall see," said Karpo. "Please come with us. If we are in error, you will be given a letter of apology."

"I need to finish what . . . I am in the middle. I'll save it and turn off my computer."

Nothing else was said inside the office. Adamovskovich turned off the computer, looked around, patted his pockets to see if he might be forgetting something, and followed Zelach and Karpo into the bright white corridor.

Nadia Spectorski was the only one in the hall.

"I didn't do this, Nadia," Adamovskovich said.

She looked at him and smiled knowingly.

"Someone is making me take the blame," he said, following Karpo and Zelach.

About halfway down the hall, Nadia called, "Wait. Please. Inspector Zelach, can you give me just half an hour?"

"No," he said.

"The director has called your director, Yaklovev," she said. "Director Yaklovev said that you are to cooperate with us, cooperate fully."

Karpo had stopped and so had the bewildered Adamovskovich. Zelach adjusted his glasses and looked to Karpo for help.

"I have to help take the suspect in," he said.

"I expect no trouble," said Karpo. "Stay, then join me at Petrovka."

Karpo led the scientist down the hall, and Zelach stood facing the diminutive Nadia Spectorski. He wondered if he could possibly outwit her. He very much doubted it.

*   *   *

Kiro-Stovitsk, eighty miles west of St. Petersburg, was little more than a village. It lay in a vast plain of bleak cold winters and summers that were either too dry or too wet. The two hundred and forty people of the town were either potato farmers or made a meager living selling to or working for farmers.

For more than a thousand years, Kiro-Stovitsk had been relatively undisturbed by the outside world. During World War II, the Germans had not bothered with the town or not known it was there. That did not mean that the people of Kiro-Stovitsk had not fought and died. Half of the men, all between the ages of sixteen and fifty-five, had gone off to fight. All but six of the eighty-seven men had died. There was a cemetery a short walk from the edge of town. It was marked by small headstones. Some of the headstones were for those who died in the war, though their bodies were not here below the ground.

Food had always been scarce. The people of Kiro-Stovitsk had lived mainly on their own potatoes and what little they could get for trading those potatoes. Cash was almost nonexistent. It had been a barter economy, even with Alexander Podgorny, who ran the store and the tractor-repair shop behind it. Podgorny, his father before him, and generations before that of the family, had owned the store, which stocked meager supplies of clothing, food, tools, a few items of furniture, and Pepsi-Cola in a large blue cooler. The Russian Orthodox church, the tallest building in the town, a solid structure of red stone built by farmers more than a century ago, had served as the town meeting hall in the years of the revolution. Five years ago, a pair of priests with a small group of servants and a single nun had come to the town to reclaim the church, but the people had no heart for the enterprise. The men, women, and children did not wish to give up their town hall, which had become not only the meeting center but the communal gathering place where people came to gossip, drink tea and coffee, play chess, make plans.

Only a small handful of people had come to the services and none had volunteered to bring the church back to its former state. An attempt was made by the priests and the nun to gather donations to buy icons, but it failed. After almost two years, the priests had declared that the town was not ready for God, and they had left vowing to return when the mother church told them the time was right and God had entered the hearts of the ignorant farmers who had for too long been under the oppressive spell of Communism.

Boris Vladovka and the people of the town of Kiro-Stovitsk knew the priests were wrong. Whether it was the church or government or a political party, the people of the town wanted no part of it. The church might well return. The government would grow increasingly corrupt and, if they felt it was profitable, appointed officials would set up an office and try to take a piece of the town's small profits. Something calling itself Communism might even return, but the people were determined to survive. History had long since proved that they could.

When the commune farms had been disbanded and the land given to the people who had been tenants of nobles, kulaks, small landlords, and corrupt Communist commissars, most of the people had been frightened. They had no experience selling potato crops. They could not afford their own machinery. They prepared themselves for starvation.

But Boris Vladovka had reluctantly stepped forward. Boris, father of Konstantin the farmer and Tsimion the cosmonaut, had suggested that the farmers of Kiro-Stovitsk enter into a partnership, pool their meager money, buy two ancient trucks, and have Boris and Konstantin drive to the markets of St. Petersburg and sell the crops to one of the new dealers who had stepped in to serve as brokers for restaurants, the new supermarkets, and the growing number of hotels and clubs throughout Russia and beyond its borders.

Boris did not make the town wealthy, but as long as the weather did not destroy an annual crop, he did bring in enough for the people to live without fear of starvation or even hunger.

Boris was the unofficial mayor of Kiro-Stovitsk, a sixty-year-old patriarch of the entire grateful town, a town that had little to be proud of outside of Boris's cosmonaut son.

In the center of the town's only street there was a war memorial, a simple, six-foot-high weather-pocked concrete obelisk with the names of the eighty-one who had died fighting the Germans chiseled carefully into its surface. Many of the names on the obelisk were Vladovka, Dersknikov, and Laminski. The town, like hundreds across Russia, had been inbred for as far back as anyone could remember and farther back than that.

Kiro-Stovitsk was now a town of the very young and the very old. The young left, most of them as soon as they were able. They left with dreams of becoming business successes or cosmonauts like their most famous citizen. A few of them had returned, disillusioned, carrying a wisdom of the outer world that had drained a bit of life from them.

Most of the people of the town lived in the small farms well beyond the edge of the wooden buildings on the main street. Over the centuries, the farms and village buildings had been propped up, rebuilt, and reinforced so many times that there was no real sense of what they had been originally.

The wind blew hard enough in winter to knock a man from a tractor or lift a child into the air. But this was summer. It was hot and humid and the heavy clouds brought rain. It was a good season.

Into this town drove Porfiry Petrovich Rostnikov and Iosef Rostnikov in a ten-year-old tan Ford Mustang provided by the security staff by order of General Snitkonoy, head of Hermitage security and former director of the Office of Special Investigation. The general had not forgotten his debt to Inspector Rostnikov for helping to make his reputation. Not only had he provided a car but a driver too, a driver who had been born in the town to which they were going.

The driver, a very thin, talkative young man with a red face, named Ivan Laminski, wore a blue summer uniform and cap. The uniform was clean and the buttons polished. Ivan occasionally returned to Kiro-Stovitsk to show off his uniform and talk of his responsibilities in the city. Ivan was close to having saved enough money to buy his own car so he could return more often to his brothers, sisters, father and mother, and friends.

Ivan told the two detectives from Moscow about the town, its past and present.

"I don't think Tsimion Vladovka has come back here more than once or twice," said Ivan, looking at the two detectives in his rearview mirror. "Once, when his mother was sick with some problem, liver, gallbladder, he took her into town and used his influence to get her an operation. I think he came again but I don't know if there was a reason. That was a few years back. I doubt if anyone in town knows where he is if he is missing."

The road was not paved, but it was not particularly bumpy.

In his rearview mirror, Ivan watched the older policeman, the one built like a block of stone, listen and look out of the window. There was little to see but open fields of weeds and an occasional farm. The other policeman, the younger one, listened to Ivan, nodded at appropriate times, knowing he could be seen in the mirror, and occasionally asked a question.

"There it is," said Ivan, pointing a little off to the right.

"Your great-grandfather came from a town like this one," said the older policeman to the younger.

The younger policeman looked through the front window at the cluster of small buildings ahead of them.

"You are sure they are not expecting us?" Rostnikov asked the driver.

"They are not," said Ivan.

"You are certain?" asked Rostnikov.

"I . . . well, who knows?" said Ivan. "But I don't think so."

Ivan was soon proved wrong.

When they drove down the street, a few dozen people stood in front of the stores and former church. There were five cars and two pickup trucks parked on the concrete street, which had no sidewalk. Ivan pulled the car to a stop next to the general store and beside the memorial obelisk.

The day was dark and damp as the Rostnikovs got out of the car. Ivan got out quickly and moved to a group of people, hugging first a narrow woman of about fifty and then some other men and women. Porfiry Petrovich and Iosef stood waiting while Ivan completed his greetings and basked briefly in the admiration of his family and friends. He was probably the second most successful of the sons who had left the town.

"Inspector Rostnikov, this is Alexander Podgorny."

A heavy man took a step forward and extended his hand. The man had a large belly, a knowing smile, and a crop of white hair brushed straight back and whispered by the slight wind.

"And," said Rostnikov, "this is my son, Inspector Iosef Rostnikov."

Podgorny shook Iosef's hand and stepped back.

The small crowd was silent, watching.

"Our meeting hall is inside," said Podgorny. "We can go in and talk, or go to my home."

"The meeting hall will be fine," said Rostnikov, following Podgorny, trying to remain steady on his insensate leg.

Behind them the people who had stood on the street waiting for the arrival of the important visitors filed in after them. A table and chairs had been set up on the small platform where priests and party officials had once stood. Podgorny ushered the Moscow detectives to the table, where they sat.

An audience began filling the folding chairs facing the platform. Ivan the driver was not sure whether he should be on the platform at the table or in the audience. He opted for the audience and sat between the man and woman who Porfiry Petrovich assumed were his parents.

"You are looking for Tsimion," said the fat man, whose eyes were very dark and moving from one to the other of the detectives.

"We are looking for information on where we might find him. We believe that he may be in great danger," said Rostnikov, folding his hands. He had done his best to sit without looking awkward. He had done well but not perfectly.

Podgorny sat on one end of the table. Iosef and his father sat behind it, facing the audience. Iosef expected that when Podgorny was finished, the people before them would begin asking questions.

"You have made a long trip for nothing," Podgorny said sadly. "We know nothing of Tsimion or where he might be. We wish that we did. If he is in danger, we would like to help him. But . . . we know nothing."

"He has a father, a brother, and a mother," said Rostnikov. "We would like to talk to them."

Podgorny shook his head sadly. "Unfortunately, they are working today," he said. "And as I said, they have heard nothing from Tsimion. We would like to offer you a meal, show you what little there is to see of our town, and then have Ivan drive you back to St. Petersburg."

"That is very kind of you," said Rostnikov. "We will accept the meal and the tour, but since we have come this far, I would like to talk to Tsimion Vladovka's family. I am sure Ivan Laminski knows the way to their farm."

"That will not be necessary," said a man about Rostnikov's age, rising from the back of the small hall. "I am Boris Vladovka."

The man was wearing a dark-green shirt with the sleeves rolled up. His work pants were dark with stains of white potato dust. He was average in height, lean, with tightly muscled, veined arms. He was dark from years of the sun.

Next to Vladovka sat a younger man with a beard.

"This is my son Konstantin, Tsimion's brother."

His son, arms folded across his chest, was dressed like his father, though his face was not as dark. Konstantin nodded, his face serious. He did not rise. An older woman, who looked frightened, took Konstantin's hand. The conclusion was simple. This was the wife of Boris and the mother of Vladimir and Konstantin.

"Shall we talk here or somewhere? . . ." Rostnikov began.

"Here," interrupted Boris emphatically. "We are a family, all of us. The entire town. We have no secrets from each other."

"I believe that," said Rostnikov, "but do you have secrets from the rest of the world?"

Something touched the rugged face of Boris Vladovka, but just for an instant.

"All families have secrets," said Boris. "They are no business of those outside. They are of no interest to those outside. If you have questions, ask. We will do our best to answer. And then we will ask you to leave."

"Perhaps we will leave after we eat and have a tour of your town," said Rostnikov. "Perhaps we will remain till tomorrow. We've had a long trip."

"Yes," said Boris, still standing.

"Do you know where your son Tsimion is?" asked Rostnikov.

"No," said Boris.

"Do you know where he might be?" asked Rostnikov.

"No," said Boris.

"I wish to ask the same question of your wife and son," said Rostnikov.

"They will tell you the same thing," said Boris.

"I expect so," said Rostnikov with a smile. "It is not a matter of what they say, but how they say it. So . . ."

The bearded man seated next to Boris Vladovka gently removed the hand of the older woman from his and stood up. He was as tall as his father, a bit fuller of body.

"My brother is dead," the man said.

The older woman began to cry. She was comforted by a pleasant-looking woman at her side.

"You are certain?" asked Rostnikov.

"We talked on the phone last week. I spoke to my brother," the man said. "He said he was dying. I asked for information. He gave me none. He asked me to take care of our parents, our family. I told him I would. My brother is dead."

There was a certainty and sadness in the voice of the bearded man that convinced Rostnikov of his sincerity. But though Tsimion Vladovka may have been convincing on the telephone, he may not have been telling the truth.

Rostnikov looked at the faces of those before him. They sat in clear anticipation, waiting to be questioned, waiting for the eyes of the detectives from Moscow to fall on them. Rostnikov looked at his son and it was clear that Iosef had seen the same look.

"I must do my job," said Rostnikov with a sigh. "Boris Vladovka, if we can have a few minutes with you and your family, and perhaps a word or two with some of your neighbors, I think we will be able to leave quickly and file our report. My mission, however, is to find your son, to find him alive or dead. You understand?"

"I understand," said Boris, looking down.

Rostnikov turned his eyes to Boris's surviving son.

"I understand," said Konstantin.

Podgorny rose now, not sure of what he should say or do.

"A meal has been prepared in my house," he said. "If the Vladovkas would join us . . ."

"We will," said Konstantin, putting his hand on his father's shoulder.

"Then . . ." Podgorny began as the door at the back of the

room opened and a small boy came in, looking around. He spotted Boris and ran to him. Everyone in the room waited while the boy whispered to the farmer, who bent over to listen. The boy stopped and Boris stood and said, "We have another visitor."

"A man with an umbrella," said Rostnikov.

"Yes," said Boris suspiciously.

"Perhaps we should all go out and give him the greeting you were all kind enough to give to me and my son," said Rostnikov, getting up a bit awkwardly.

Iosef had not strapped on his holster. His gun lay in the suitcase in the back of the Mustang. He expected no trouble, but he would cut short the greeting and get Ivan to open the trunk as soon as possible.

Chapter Eight

★ ★ ★ ★ ★ ★ ★ ★ ★ ★ ★ ★

Valery Grachev was halfway home when the boy in the park began to signal that there was no money in the gym bag in front of Elena Timofeyeva. He knew the bag contained paper and nothing else. Vera had confirmed it. The wooded areas, he was sure, were streaming with police moments after the boy signaled. While Sasha Tkach was rushing madly through the park searching for him, Valery was on the metro going to work, where he had parked his motor scooter very early in the morning. Valery smiled at a woman across from him. She was well dressed, a black suit, short hair, made-up, and carrying a black handbag. She was reasonably pretty but not nearly a match for Vera Kriskov.

Valery was under no illusions. Well, perhaps he was under one illusion. He knew Vera did not love him for his looks, but he thought she did because he was both smart and a satisfying lover who was eager to do what she wished done.

What she wished done now was to have him kill her husband, a task he had been quite willing to accept. He had even purchased a weapon through someone he had met in the same park from which he was now traveling. The man, a very bad chess player with very bad teeth and a smoker's cough, though he was no more than thirty, had bragged that he "had connections." He knew Valery only by his nickname, Kon, and when Kon had expressed an interest in purchasing a particular kind of weapon, a rifle he could fire accurately from a distance of two hundred yards, the man with bad teeth had confidently and confidentially said that it could be arranged for the right price.

Valery, with money given to him by Vera, had paid that price, and the weapon was now in the rented closet of a bicycle shop, alongside the two sets of negatives he had taken, plus a pistol he had also purchased from the man in the park with bad teeth. The pistol was clean but it looked a bit old to Valery, who knew little about firearms.

"It's a classic," the man had confided, using his back to shield the weapon from the view of anyone who might be approaching. "Put it in your pocket. Here's a box of ammunition. It's a nine-millimeter Makarov. Powerful. Simple to fire. Effective. I won't lie to you. It is not the perfect weapon for long distance, but you have the rifle for that, complete with the best scope that can be had."

Valery had learned to distrust anyone who said, "I won't lie to you" or "trust me."

The train was full. It was rush hour, but through the standing bodies, Valery's eyes met those of the woman in black. She glared at him. He smiled back.

Vera had left to him how Yuri Kriskov was to be killed. She didn't care, as long as it was soon.

She had urged him to be careful. He wanted to think that she was concerned about him. He knew that, at least in part, she was afraid that if he were caught, she too would be caught. It was understandable. The queen had to be protected. The game would end when the black king was dead.

It was hot in the metro car. Valery was standing, holding a metal pole, crunched between people. An old man with bad breath was almost staring him in the face. A woman pressing into his side made grunting sounds whenever the train jostled or stopped.

He felt warm, very warm. Perhaps he was coming down with a fever.

He suddenly decided to get off at the next stop and forced his way through the crowd. He was short and powerful and well equipped for entrance to and from train cars.

On the platform of the Novoslobodskaya station he stood on the floor of black-and-green marble rectangles, breathing deeply. It was cool deep underground on the platform, but he was perspiring. People jostled past him as he stood looking without seeing at the familiar stained-glass illuminated panels depicting traditional themes and life rather than the revolutionary artwork that decorated many of the other familiar platforms. He didn't know quite why but he felt an impulse to run up the stairs. He paused for an instant in front of the panels where a stained-glass man in a stained-glass black suit, wearing a red tie, sat at a desk looking at a large document in his hands. A globe with Russia in the center stood on the man's desk. Rows of books faced him. The man's stained-glass brown wooden chair supported him, and squares of windows floated in an eerie green-white light. The man's office was neat, permanent. Valery was fascinated. The man reminded him of Kriskov. In fact, Kriskov could have been the model for this encircled depiction.

It was like being in a church.

Valery had to get somewhere, do something. Was he doubting his enterprise? Was the promise of Vera Kriskov an illusion? No. He turned from the panel. A feeling of power, almost of flight, ran through him. He pushed past people, slowed, still moving, to drop a few kopeks into the hand of a begging old woman sitting cross-legged at the entrance, and then ran to the phone.

He dropped in a coin and dialed.

"Yes?" answered Yuri Kriskov tentatively.

"You made a wrong move," said Valery in his disguised voice. "You are now in check. End game."

"Look," said Yuri. "I can . . ."

"Say nothing or I call checkmate," said Valery, hanging up.

He didn't run, but he did move quickly past people heading away from the metro entrance. The police would be converging on the phone within a few minutes. He wanted to draw no attention by hurrying. He walked past the begging woman and reentered the station, now able to breathe. He got on the first train and by the time he got to work he was ten minutes late.

"Do we have the negative back?" he asked Nikita Kolodny as he entered the door of the editing room and breathed in the celluloid smell.

"I don't know," said Nikita. "Svetlana Gorchinova is looking for you. She is more crazy than usual. Be careful."

With that, Svetlana entered the room, looked at him and glared. "You are late," she said.

Valery smiled and Nikita stepped back in near terror. No one smiled at Svetlana Gorchinova when she chastised, not even Levich or Kriskov.

"I have a fever," said Valery, still smiling.

Svetlana looked at his pink face and the drops of moisture on his upper lip.

"Then why are you grinning like a fool?" she said.

"Am I grinning? I didn't know. Perhaps I have a secret," he said.

"Perhaps you are delirious," she said, moving to her chair in front of the Avid editing machine.

"Perhaps," he agreed. "You know, you look like the pilot of a Klingon warship, sitting in front of the editor. The light hits your face eerily. You look determined and formidable."

She turned in her chair and looked at him. "Go home," she said. "You are sick. You are talking like an idiot."

"I'm perfectly fine," he responded.

Nikita had turned his back and moved to a corner, where he pretended to examine a long-nosed pliers.

"Well," she said. "I am not perfectly fine having you here.

There isn't that much to do until . . . there isn't that much and I don't want to go through the day with you acting like a maniac."

"I am perfectly sane," he said. "A bit feverish perhaps, but . . ."

"Go home," she shouted. "Or don't go home. But go."

Valery shook his head knowingly and said, "I'll go."

"Then go, you fool, and don't return until and unless you can behave, be quiet, and take orders."

Valery shrugged and moved to the door. "When I return," he said, "it will not be as a pawn to take orders, but as a king."

And out the door he went.

Svetlana muttered something and ignored Valery's parting words.

Nikita Kolodny did not. Nikita suspected that Valery Grachev had taken the negatives. This behavior had made him more than suspicious. But Nikita was a coward. He had come from a long, long line of cowards who rose no higher than their intelligence or lack of it and their desire for safe anonymity would permit. There was no way Nikita would risk his safety and job by reporting what he believed. There were no rewards to be gained and, even if there were, risking Valery's wrath would not be worth stepping forward. No, Nikita would stand back in the corners of his life, watching, listening. Perhaps if Valery were caught, Nikita might move up to first assistant. That was as far as he aspired to. It would be enough.

Vera Kriskov comforted her husband with no success while the two policemen made calls and tried to trace the man who had just telephoned. The children were at school and, thank God, she thought, they didn't have to see their father nearly hysterical.

"He's mad," said Kriskov, reaching for a cigarette, unable to light it with his shaking hands. Vera helped. "What was he talking about? Chess games? This isn't a chess game. That bastard is going to destroy my negatives, destroy me. He is going to kill me."

"He is not going to kill you," Vera said, knowing that the younger of the two policemen in the room had been admiring her since he came into the house. "He will stay away. The police will not let him get close."

"Like they were going to catch him with the bag of strips of paper," Yuri said, leaning over to put his head in his hands. "He's probably burning the negatives now, right now."

"Why would he do that?" she said. "He'd have to be mad. The negatives are worth money to him. He will call back. He will make a deal."

"He is mad, Vera," said Yuri, looking up. "Crazy, crazy mad." He pounded the sides of his head with the heels of his hands. "A lunatic."

Vera thought her husband might well be right. Valery Grachev had not done what they had agreed upon. The second call was not just a mistake, it was an act of madness. There was no point to it. Perhaps she should cut her losses, kill Valery, let the police discover the negative, drop the whole idea.

But there were two reasons why she could not seriously consider this. First, she could not imagine killing Valery or anyone else. What would she use? A gun? There were two in the house, but she couldn't. And then there was Yuri sniveling next to her. She put her arm around him soothingly under the eye of the envious young policeman.

"Shh," she said. "It will work out."

Yuri simply shook his head.

He had to die. She could not live with this lying, worthless thing next to her for another week. Valery would have to kill him and kill him soon. She would have to find a way to get in touch with him, to urge him to move quickly. Maybe she would threaten him, tell him that he would lose her if he didn't act, tell him that his mad phone call was giving her second thoughts about him and the whole plan.

"Can I get you anything?" the young policeman asked.

"No, thank you," said Vera with a sad smile.

"A drink," said Yuri. "I'll die if I don't have a drink."

You will die with or without a drink if Valery Grachev keeps from going completely insane, Vera thought. "Brandy, in the cabinet over there," she told the policeman, nodding toward the large wooden antique in the corner.

"They've traced the second call and a car was there in less than two minutes," said the older policeman from the phone. "A public phone just outside a metro station."

"And?" asked Yuri hopefully.

"Nothing," said the older policeman. "They're asking questions. Trying to find if someone saw . . ."

The front door opened. Sasha and Elena came in.

"Doesn't anyone knock?" Yuri shouted, accepting an overly large and welcome brandy snifter from the young policeman. "Knock. Knock. Knock. That lunatic could walk right in here with a . . . an automatic weapon and kill me. You failed."

"Not completely," said Elena, looking at him and then at Vera.

"Not? . . ." Yuri said, looking up from the drink he held in two hands.

"The second call," said Sasha. "The chess allusion."

"He sent us to a chess table in the park," Elena went on. "It is possible he has played at that table."

"Thousands of people must have played at that table," groaned Yuri.

"We have officers talking to people at the metro stop and near the telephone," said Elena. "Perhaps we can get a description of whoever used the phone."

"But people just rush by," said Vera. "Anyone who might have seen him has long gone."

"No, perhaps," said Sasha. "Someone running a kiosk or some pensioner who might have been strolling by with nothing to do or walking his dog, or . . . maybe someone will be able to come up with a description we can take to the regular chess players in the park."

"No," said Yuri. "He will kill me. That is that."

"He won't kill you, Yuri," Vera said soothingly, beginning to worry now that Valery might, in fact, fail, and deciding that she would have to find a way to get rid of Valery when Yuri was gone.

Elena watched the beautiful woman soothe her frantic husband. She watched and she felt that it was not love she was seeing. But what of it? Many women did not love the men to whom they had found themselves married. And, besides, perhaps it was the woman's beauty to which Elena was reacting. It made no difference. What was important was the tugging feeling that the man with the negatives somehow knew that the money would not be delivered.

Elena was more and more certain that the real goal in this was not ransom but an excuse to kill Yuri Kriskov. But who would want Kriskov dead? She had no intention of sharing this intuition with Sasha Tkach, who would, in his present state, humor her. Had he been as he had before this inexplicable euphoria, he would have ridiculed her feelings and they would have fought. Elena would have to talk to Porfiry Petrovich.

At the same moment Elena was deciding that she had to talk to Rostnikov, a twenty-four-year-old uniformed policeman named Yakov Pierta, his second week on the force, was talking to a beggar woman just inside the entrance of the Novoslobodskaya metro station, within sight of the phone from which Valery had made his call to Yuri Kriskov. He leaned in front of her, gave her some coins, and asked her if she had seen anyone making a call on the phone to which he now pointed. She looked at the coins and then at the phone. Then she looked at the policeman and said, "Ten rubles."

*   *   *

Emil Karpo patiently questioned Boris Adamovskovich in a small, white-walled, windowless room on the fourth floor of Petrovka. There was a table in the room with four chairs. Adamovskovich had been directed to sit in one of the chairs. Zelach had taken a position behind the scientist. Karpo stood across the table before the man they were questioning. It was routine procedure. Zelach did his best to pay attention, but it was still early and much had already happened.

Less than an hour earlier he had walked behind Nadia Spectorski down the hall of the psychic research center and into the same room where she had tortured him with playing cards. He had little hope of outwitting the scientist, so he had a battle plan to name the cards based on a simple pattern he had worked out the night before with his mother.

Eagerly, Nadia Spectorski had sat him at the table and said, "We are going to do something different today, Inspector Zelach. Here is a pad of paper and a pencil."

He adjusted his glasses and looked at the pad and pencil.

"I am going to draw six things on the pad before me," she said. "This screen will prevent you from seeing what I am drawing."

The screen was simple, a tall brown piece of plastic with two hinged sides.

"I will draw first, nod to you, and you will draw," she said.

"What will I draw?" he asked.

"Whatever you wish to draw," she answered. "Simple drawings."

"I can't draw," he said.

"Keep it very simple," she said. "This isn't an art class. It won't take long. Trust me. There are no grades. Just draw."

Ten minutes later Zelach was breathing hard. The experiment was over. He put down his pencil. Nadia Spectorski reached for his pad and took it behind her screen.

Zelach watched her eyes compare what she had done with what he had drawn. She made a sound, made some notes on a separate pad, and looked up at him.

"Would you like to see?" she said.

"See?"

"What you did."

"No," he said. "I would like to go now."

"Look," she said, folding the screen and turning the pads toward him. "This is my first drawing and this is yours."

Nadia Spectorski's drawing was a circle with a small square inside it. Zelach's drawing was a circle with a squiggle inside it. She went through the six drawings. Her number-two drawing was a crude man. His was a stick figure of a man. Her third drawing was an automobile. His third drawing was a cart with wheels. Her fourth drawing was the letter *L*. His fourth drawing was a right angle with both sides equal. Her fifth drawing was a vertical pencil. His fifth drawing was a simple vertical straight line. Her sixth drawing was a five-sided star. His sixth drawing looked like an asterisk.

"Nothing alike," he said, peering at the pads through his glasses.

"On the contrary," she said. "The match is remarkable. Another test."

"No," he said, rising.

"I understood that you were asked to cooperate, Akardy Zelach."

"Another time," he said. "I cannot . . ."

"Yes, I understand," she said. "Talk to your mother."

"My mother?"

"The woman at the table last night. That is your mother?"

"Yes," he said.

"Don't worry. Tell her not to worry. I won't make trouble for you. I'll keep it to myself."

That was no more than an hour ago. Now he stood behind

the big scientist named Boris, who was being questioned by Emil Karpo.

". . . the blood of Sergei Bolskanov," Karpo said.

"I don't know," said Adamovskovich, shaking his head.

"You were there," said Karpo.

"In the center, yes. I was there, but I didn't kill Bolskanov. I was in my office and then in my sleep laboratory, working."

"Your shoes," said Karpo.

Boris looked up, clearly unnerved by the situation and the pale, unemotional man before him.

"My shoes," Boris said almost to himself. "I don't . . . I took them off for a while. I slept. Sometimes I work for two, three days without sleep and then I nap for an hour or two. I must have been asleep when Sergei was murdered."

"In your laboratory?"

"Yes, asleep."

"You took your shoes off?"

"When I sleep, yes. I took my shoes off. Put them on the floor next to the bed."

Karpo looked down at him for what may have been a minute. Zelach stood quietly. Boris turned to look at Zelach for sympathy. Zelach did not return his look.

"You are suggesting that someone came into the sleep laboratory while you were napping, took your shoes, put them on, murdered Sergei Bolskanov, made an attempt to clean the shoes, and then put them back where you had left them," said Karpo.

"I . . . I suppose. Yes, that is what I must be saying. Though I don't . . ."

"That someone took your shoes, wore them, murdered, and returned them," said Karpo.

"I don't . . . yes, that must be."

"Perhaps you walked in your sleep and killed Sergei Bolskanov without knowing it," said Karpo.

"No," said Boris. "That is not possible. I do not walk in my sleep."

"It would explain the blood," said Karpo. "Possibly give you an excuse for what took place."

"I did not commit murder while asleep. I did not commit murder while awake. If there is blood on those shoes, someone else wore them."

"Why?" asked Karpo.

"I do not know," said Adamovskovich, pounding the table with both fists. "I do not know."

"I am sorry I'm late," said the man with the umbrella, standing in the middle of the muddy street of Kiro-Stovitsk. "I was fortunate in having the opportunity to attend the annual services for the burial of Czar Nicholas and his family in St. Petersburg."

The people of the town were lined up as the lean man in a business suit, umbrella tucked under his left arm, walked directly up to Rostnikov and held out his right hand.

"Primazon," he said. "Anatoli Ivanovich Primazon."

"Porfiry Petrovich Rostnikov," Rostnikov replied, taking the man's hand.

Primazon's face was pink and smooth, his hair freshly barbered and white. His smile was of a man hoping for a reaction. "And this," said Primazon, "is your son, Iosef."

Primazon's hand went out again. Iosef took it.

Rostnikov did not ask how the man with the umbrella knew his son's name. He did not have to ask.

"And . . ." Primazon went on looking around at the small gathering. "Which one is Vladovka's father?"

Boris stepped forward. He did not extend his hand, but he did introduce his son and Alexander Podgorny.

Primazon nodded politely and said, "Porfiry Petrovich, is there somewhere we can talk?"

Rostnikov looked at Boris Vladovka, who nodded toward the meeting hall they had just left.

"Thank you," Primazon said with sincerity to Vladovka. "Official business. It shouldn't take long."

The man with the umbrella led the way into the former church, and the Rostnikovs followed. Iosef closed the doors and there immediately came the sound of people outside talking. It was likely, thought Iosef, that this was the singularly most interesting event they had witnessed in years, possibly in their lifetimes.

Primazon looked around with approval.

"They probably show movies here," he said. "Old movies. I love old movies. I collect videotapes. Mostly American, but I like the Russian biographies. The admirals, scientists. All long, ponderous. You can live a lifetime watching one of those old biographies. Shall we sit?"

Primazon had taken over, serving as host, smiling genially.

Porfiry Petrovich moved back to the table where they had sat and joined Anatoli Primazon, who had already sat and placed his umbrella on the table. Iosef chose to stand.

"I must thank you, Porfiry Petrovich," he said, leaning forward and, for no reason Iosef could discern, speaking in a whisper. "If you had not come to St. Petersburg, I would not have had the opportunity to attend the burial services. You know Putin was there? He spoke, apologized for the murders, more than eighty years ago, all murdered. Official Russian Orthodox service. Priests with those tall white hats with the crosses pinned in the center. Everyone stood. The service was, as you may have guessed, long. Have you ever been inside St. Peter and Paul Cathedral?"

"No," said Rostnikov.

"No? You should stop on your way back. Beautiful. Glass chandeliers. High-domed ceilings. Pink-and-blue walls. And pomp? Gold-robed priests, black-suited descendants of the Romanovs, all holding the thin candles. A choir sang the Orthodox requiem for the dead, priests filled the air with incense. At the original burial several years ago, royalty from all over the world, the English sent the Prince of Kent. And the nineteen-gun salute when they lowered Nicholas's coffin. Only nineteen instead of twenty because he had abdicated. An irony there? We force him to abdicate and then when we repent we fire only nineteen shots. The shots echoed off the buildings, frightened birds flew, thousands watched. The Neva wept. I exaggerate, but it was a scene to remember, to tell one's grandchildren. Unfortunately, I have no grandchildren, but I do have a son, a teacher in Minsk."

"It sounds as if it was a moving experience," said Rostnikov, adjusting his leg.

"I did not kill Vladimir Kinotskin," Primazon said, suddenly quite serious. "As you can tell, I have great reverence for history, for the past. History is my passion. What else is there but family and history? I would not kill a man before the house of Lermontov."

"Would the lobby of the Russia Hotel be an acceptable location for murder?" asked Rostnikov.

"Oh yes, certainly. It has no history, not yet. We will all be long gone like the czar and his family before it deserves such reverence," said Primazon.

"But you know who did kill Kinotskin?" asked Rostnikov.

"I know why," the man said with a smile, "and I am waiting for you to find out *who*."

"Then," said Rostnikov, "let us now ask *why*."

"Splendid," said Primazon, sitting back, still whispering. "Then that will leave us only *who*. Perhaps I should tell you who I am and what I do."

"Perhaps," agreed Rostnikov.

"My task is not to kill cosmonauts but to protect them," he said. "My small group is part of the Space Security Organization. We protect the launch sites and villages where cosmonauts and visiting astronauts and others are trained and housed. My small group is assigned to the present and past cosmonauts."

"Who would want to harm cosmonauts?" asked Iosef.

Primazon looked up as if he had forgotten the younger Rostnikov's presence.

"Who? I think we have ample evidence that someone would, don't we? We have a murdered cosmonaut and others who have died under some suspicion. Why would one want to harm cosmonauts? Terrorism? Insanity? Revenge?"

"Revenge for what?" asked Iosef.

Primazon shrugged. "We have a list of hundreds in the space-exploration program, a list that goes back before 1957. Hundreds have been terminated for incompetence, mental illness, as scapegoats for missions or experiments that went wrong. See, I am being honest with you."

"I appreciate that, Anatoli Ivanovich," said Rostnikov.

"Then I will be even more honest," the umbrella man said, still whispering. "I have not done a particularly good job in the current situation. Only one cosmonaut remains in Russia of the six involved in that troubled mission. The two who are out of the country are being protected by my colleagues."

With this, Primazon reached into his jacket pocket and dramatically pulled out a photograph, which he turned toward Porfiry Petrovich.

"Tsimion Vladovka," said Primazon.

Rostnikov had the same photograph in his small suitcase. He had looked at it, memorized each feature and detail. Primazon turned the photo to look at it himself as if for the first time and said, examining the picture, "I must save him, you must find him. There is none better than you for such a task, or so I have heard. I'll be honest again. If something were to happen to Tsimion Vladovka, I might well end my career by cleaning the statues of poets and authors in the squares of Moscow."

"And since you could not hide in such a small village as Kiro-Stovitsk . . ." Rostnikov began.

". . . I decided to face you honestly," finished Primazon, patting his umbrella.

"And at some time, if we find Vladovka and he is safely back in Moscow and under your protection, and I tell you who killed Vladimir Kinotskin? . . ." Rostnikov tried again.

"Then perhaps I will be in a position to tell you *why* someone does not want these cosmonauts to live," said Primazon. "I must ask. Why have you come here?"

"Instinct," said Rostnikov.

Primazon nodded in understanding.

"Instinct and a belief that Vladovka would not disappear forever, if the choice of disappearance were his own, without making some contact with his family," said Rostnikov.

"Yes, yes," said the umbrella man, nodding his head. "He is such a man. I understand. It might be dangerous to see them in person, but such a man . . . Well, is there some place we can spend the night here? It's getting late and you have work to do."

"I don't know," said Rostnikov. "Perhaps Iosef could . . ."

"No, no," said Primazon, rising and holding out his hand, palm open and facing down to keep father and son in place. "I will take that responsibility. I am, after all, the intruder, and I owe them some explanation."

"And what will that be?" asked Rostnikov.

"Something novel, unexpected," the man said, tucking his umbrella under his arm. "I shall tell them the truth. Are you coming?"

"We will be there in a moment," said Rostnikov. "My leg is causing me a bit of difficulty. Iosef can help."

"Your leg? Oh, yes, I had forgotten. War injury. You have medals?"

"I have medals," said Rostnikov. "Everyone has medals."

Primazon nodded again and went down the short aisle and out the doors, closing them behind him.

"There is nothing wrong with your leg?" said Iosef.

"Nothing," said Rostnikov, still sitting.

"Then? . . ."

"I wanted to talk to you briefly before we join our new friend on the street as he charms the populace."

"You have some idea of where Tsimion Vladovka might be?"

"Yes."

"And," Iosef continued, looking at his father, who was now rising, "you know who killed Vladimir Kinotskin?"

"Oh, yes," said Rostnikov, patting his son on the cheek. "The killer just walked out of here with a smile on his face and an umbrella under his arm."

Chapter Nine

★ ★ ★ ★ ★ ★ ★ ★ ★ ★ ★ ★

There were three rooms for guests above the shop of Alexander Podgorny. They were all small bedrooms that had belonged to the Podgorny children, who had moved to St. Petersburg and Moscow years before. In one room, the man who called himself Anatoli Ivanovich Primazon was supposedly sleeping. In the center room, Iosef lay in bed, reading the mystery his father had given him. He was not particularly enjoying it, not because he thought it bad, but because his thoughts were with Elena and the man who his father had labeled a murderer, the man in the room next to his. Iosef's gun was on the small table next to the bed. The light was too dim and the bed too soft.

Porfiry Petrovich was not in the third room. He had quietly asked if Podgorny had a telephone. The storekeeper had said that there was one in the shop, right outside the two rooms behind the shop area where Podgorny lived with his wife.

Rostnikov paid him generously in advance for the call and volunteered to pay now for the room.

"For the phone, yes," said Podgorny. "For the room, no. You are our guests."

Rostnikov asked for a receipt that he could hand to Pankov for reimbursement, which might take weeks and might never come.

It took him ten minutes to complete the call to Elena and

Sasha, who were in her cubicle at Petrovka. Neither had reason to go home. For Elena, Iosef was eighty miles outside of St. Petersburg. For Sasha, his family was in the Ukraine. They spoke, knowing the conversation was being recorded for later listening by the Yak.

ROSTNIKOV: I have a window in my room. There is a moon and nothing as far as I can see but flat fields and a single tractor. Melancholy and quite beautiful. And Iosef is fine.

ELENA: We did not get the negatives back. I—we, Sasha and I—think that the thief expected a trap. But he did make a mistake. He made a strange call, talked about chess. We questioned some of the players in the park by the chess bench where the exchange was to take place.

ROSTNIKOV: —A name? Description?

ELENA: Perhaps from a beggar at the metro station. An agitated man gave her some coins, the most she has ever been given. He did not wait for thanks but hurried away. Normally, she would have gone back to the business of begging, but the amount had been so much that she watched him hurry to the phone. Her description of him is quite good. That is the description we gave to the chess players in the park. Most did not want to talk. A few said they thought it was a young man they knew only as Kon, who sometimes plays in the park. They said he is a nervous type, good player but impatient. The way to beat him is to wait him out, take your time until he makes a mistake.

ROSTNIKOV: Then that is what you should do. Have you given the description to Kriskov?

ELENA: Yes. He had no idea of who it might be. Nor, apparently, does his wife.

SASHA: Porfiry Petrovich, our Elena has a few other ideas, one of which makes sense, the other . . . I leave to you.

ROSTNIKOV: Have you? . . .

SASHA: I'll call Maya and the children tonight, when I get home. I shall probably wake them and she will probably comment on my bad timing and insensitivity.

ROSTNIKOV: You do not sound concerned, Sasha.

ELENA (*in English*): He is in a state of inexplicable euphoria. I don't know which is worse. This near-Buddhist placidity or the old morose and sullen Sasha.

ROSTNIKOV (*in English*): This too shall pass.

SASHA: You are talking about me.

ROSTNIKOV: Yes, but it is with concern. I have learned that one can be manic and depressive at the same time. It is a paradox, but it is true. The problem is that one will eventually dominate if you do not deal with Maya.

SASHA: Perhaps Elena will tell you now, in Russian, what she feels intuitively.

ELENA: I think it possible that the money was just a ruse to deter us from the real purpose of this theft. I think it possible that the real goal was to find an excuse for murdering Yuri Kriskov and make it look as if it were being done because he failed to deliver the demanded money. The threat was always there.

ROSTNIKOV: And why would our thief want to kill Kriskov and make it look like retaliation?

ELENA: Possibly, and I add that it is only possible, to conceal the real reason for killing him.

ROSTNIKOV: And what might that be?

ELENA (*after a very long pause*): Yuri Kriskov is not a very pleasant man. He abuses those who work for him and keeps a mistress, about whom everyone around him knows. His wife has been at his side, consoling, attentive, holding his hand, touching his shoulder, bringing him tea. She is nearly a saint.

ROSTNIKOV: And so?

ELENA: I think she is acting. She was an actress. I don't see love and concern in her eyes. I see someone acting.

ROSTNIKOV: You believe she is conspiring to kill her husband.

ELENA: I believe it is one possibility that should not be overlooked. I could well be wrong. I am probably wrong, but it is what I . . .

SASHA: If you could speak French, Porfiry Petrovich, I would say this in French so that Elena Timofeyeva would not understand, but I say it in Russian, knowing the consequences when we hang up. Vera Kriskov is a very beautiful woman. Perhaps Elena is suspicious of Kriskov's wife because she is a bit—

ELENA: No. And, I repeat, no. I may be wrong, but it is not—

ROSTNIKOV: It will not hurt to follow her. See what happens. You are getting an artist's sketch of the chess player, Kon?

SASHA: It is being done. I saw the first crude sketch. It is a bit, I don't know, generic. It could be almost anyone we see on the street. He looks like a Russian. We know he is short, young, built, as the beggar put it, like a small bear.

ROSTNIKOV: Find him. Hope that he has not destroyed the negatives. It is unlikely that he will give up that possibility of wealth even if his plan is murder, but one never knows. Now, hang up, have your inevitable argument, and go home to bed.

ELENA: And how does it go with you?

ROSTNIKOV: The czar and his family were buried today in St.
        Petersburg. I have been told that it was a moving cer-
        emony. I should like to have seen it. I was told that
        it was something to tell one's grandchildren. Iosef is
        well. He may be sleeping or reading or thinking.
SASHA: I believe Inspector Timofeyeva is blushing.
ROSTNIKOV: Hang up. Fight. It will do you good, Sasha.
SASHA: I don't feel like fighting.
ROSTNIKOV: Try it.

They hung up.

There was no problem finding Emil Karpo. Rostnikov could
imagine him in his room, a room he had seen only twice, sitting
in front of his computer, notebooks behind it, a single light over
his shoulder.

ROSTNIKOV: Emil Karpo, how was your day?
KARPO: We have a suspect. We have evidence.
ROSTNIKOV: A suspect?
KARPO: A scientist, a specialist in dreams: Boris Adam-
        ovskovich.
ROSTNIKOV: And you have discovered why he committed this
        murder? Was he walking in his sleep? Did he use one
        of his experimental subjects to move in a somnam-
        bulistic state to commit murder, like Cesare in *The
        Cabinet of Dr. Caligari?*
KARPO: Am I to take that as one of your humorous attempts?
ROSTNIKOV: No, only a flight of fancy and fantasy. The full
        moon brings it out in me. Sometimes you remind me
        of that somnambulist, the one in the German movie.
        You even look a bit like him.
KARPO: I gather that is not a compliment.

ROSTNIKOV: It is an observation. Did you do anything you enjoyed today? What about tomorrow?

KARPO: I am having lunch with Paulinin.

ROSTNIKOV: The epitome of a good time. Will you do something for me, Emil?

KARPO: Whatever you wish.

ROSTNIKOV: Turn your head to the left and look at the painting of Mathilde Verson.

KARPO: I would prefer to discuss the case at hand.

ROSTNIKOV: I asked. You said you would do as I asked.

KARPO: I am looking at the painting.

ROSTNIKOV: What are you feeling?

KARPO: I don't understand.

ROSTNIKOV: When I hang up, look at the painting as if it were just placed on the wall.

KARPO: I look at it frequently.

ROSTNIKOV: I know, but this time with fresh eyes. Let her teach you. Don't lose the lesson of life, the gift she gave you.

KARPO: You are being especially whimsical tonight.

ROSTNIKOV: Yes, I have learned that I cannot and do not wish to deny my sentimental nature. I think it is this wilderness that brings it out in me.

KARPO: Adamovskovich denies his guilt.

ROSTNIKOV: And?

KARPO: The evidence condemns him, but I think he may be innocent.

ROSTNIKOV: Intuition?

KARPO: Intuition is simply a conclusion drawn from experience, both environmental and genetically guided. His shoes had the victim's blood on them. He disliked the victim, but then almost everyone at the center disliked him. He suggests that someone came into his laboratory when he was in a deep sleep and wore his shoes to commit the murder.

ROSTNIKOV: And you find that plausible?

KARPO: I find it possible. We have both seen far stranger things, and the people who work in that center are quite strange.

ROSTNIKOV: And that, Emil Karpo, is why I gave you this assignment. You recognize the strange. You are not taken in by it. Imagination does not get in your way. That is your strength and weakness.

KARPO: You have more than sufficient imagination for both of us.

ROSTNIKOV: Humor, Emil. A touch of irony?

KARPO: An observation.

ROSTNIKOV: Is Zelach of any help?

KARPO: Zelach has become an object of great interest on the part of one whom I consider a suspect, a Nadia Spectorski. She believes Akardy Zelach has psychic powers.

ROSTNIKOV: Our Zelach has abilities that lie below the surface. Iosef tells me that he can also kick a soccer ball seventy yards. Perhaps he missed his calling. The Russian national team might well use a psychic fullback.

KARPO: Another joke? They are wasted on me, Porfiry Petrovich.

ROSTNIKOV: I don't think so. Allow me to keep trying.

KARPO: You do not need my permission.

ROSTNIKOV: Good night, Emil. I'm going to call my wife now. Is there anything you want me to say?

KARPO (*after a long pause*): Please tell the young girls that I wish them a good night.

ROSTNIKOV: I will do so. You know I like you, Emil Karpo.

KARPO: I do not understand why. I am not a likable person.

ROSTNIKOV: You sell yourself short. Good night again.

Getting through to home was relatively easy. Sarah answered the phone.

SARAH: Porfiry.

ROSTNIKOV: You are psychic, like Zelach?

SARAH: Who else would be calling at this hour? I've been expecting the phone to ring. What about Zelach being psychic?

ROSTNIKOV: I'll explain when I am back in Moscow. Before I forget, Emil Karpo and I say good night to Laura, Nina, and Galina Paniskoya.

SARAH: They are already asleep.

ROSTNIKOV: Then tell them we say good morning when you see them. You are well?

SARAH: I am well. Iosef?

ROSTNIKOV: Well. I have been thinking about grandchildren.

SARAH: As have I.

ROSTNIKOV: It would be best if they looked like you and Iosef.

SARAH: I would be happy if they looked like you.

ROSTNIKOV: But you would be happier if they looked like you and Iosef.

SARAH: Perhaps, but it is also possible that they will resemble Elena.

ROSTNIKOV: I think that would be an acceptable compromise.

SARAH: What will happen, will happen. Will you be back tomorrow?

ROSTNIKOV: Or the next day. There was a service for Nicholas and his family, or at least what remains of their bones.

SARAH: I know.

ROSTNIKOV: They were murdered only miles from where I am now standing. History has power for Russians, does it not?

SARAH: Yes.

ROSTNIKOV: And your day?

SARAH: I worked. One customer wanted an old Beatles album we had on display. He was an Englishman. He paid in dollars. Six hundred. I did nothing but make the transaction. Bulnanova praised me, promised a bonus at the end of the month. She will forget.

ROSTNIKOV: You had a headache today?

SARAH: No. Get some sleep, Porfiry Petrovich. And come home to me soon. Good night.

ROSTNIKOV: Good night. Look at the moon if you can before you go to bed. It is full and clear where we are.

SARAH: It is obscured by the pollution of Moscow, but I see it. Good night.

They both hung up. Porfiry Petrovich knew she had lied about the headache and she knew that he knew. Perhaps he should not have asked her so that she would have had no need to lie. Her cousin Leon the doctor had said that she was doing well, that she did not need more surgery, but the surgeon who operated on Sarah for the tumor five years ago predicted that she would continue to have painful headaches, probably for the rest of her life, and the headaches might well get worse. They would watch her. Leon, who was in love with Sarah and had been all of their lives, would take special care of her.

Rostnikov hung up the phone. Podgorny had left him alone in the shop to make his calls. Porfiry Petrovich made his way up the narrow wooden stairs. He moved slowly, not relying on his alien leg. There was no light under the door of the man who called himself Primazon and who Rostnikov had recognized as a former KGB agent whose name was something like Disiverski. The name would come. Porfiry Petrovich and Iosef were safe from him. He wanted them to lead him to Tsimion Vladovka, almost certainly to kill him and preserve whatever the secret was.

There was a light under Iosef's door. Rostnikov hoped that

his son would soon turn out his light and move to his window. He imagined that father and son would be looking at the moon at the same time, thinking of dead czars, of Ivan the Terrible, of Catherine the Great, of men who rode in small spheres circling the earth and looking at that full moon. He could not see *Mir,* but there was a secret about it that he would like to know. Perhaps a cosmonaut or two were now circling in the sky, looking at the same full moon, thinking about dead royalty.

The murderer of Sergei Bolskanov was Andrei Vanga, the director of the Center for Technical Parapsychology. He acted in rage, out of jealousy of Bolskanov, who had come into his office to tell the director of the lengthy article he had just completed. Bolskanov had been ecstatic, jubilant—perhaps, Vanga had thought, he had been gloating a bit, because the director, who worked in the same area, had published nothing for over a decade. There was an implication that the director lacked the imagination to make such a research breakthrough.

Oh, yes, Vanga, as director, would get some of the credit. He could use the findings to raise more money, but his success would come as an administrator, not as a scientist. It would be the insufferable Bolskanov, whom no one liked and many hated, who would be quoted, mentioned in the literature, go down in the history of psychic research for his findings.

It was at this point that Bolskanov had said that Vanga was the first to know, that he did not plan to tell anyone else till the next morning.

If it were done when it is done, thought Vanga at that very moment, then better it were done quickly.

The murder had not been planned, but in executing it Vanga had demonstrated, if only to himself, that he had imagination. It might be an imagination better suited to murder than to scientific research, but an imagination of no small proportion nevertheless.

He had worn an old lab coat that he had disposed of after the murder, in the small incinerator on the research floor. It existed to dispose of items of clothing or papers that might contain evidence or information about ongoing research which should not get into the hands of those who could use it—the Bulgarians, the Latvians, the Japanese, the English, the Americans.

But Andrei Vanga's triumph was the shoes. He had carefully crept into the sleep-research lab where Adamovskovich was napping. The instruments glowed with the information that the man was in deep REM sleep. Andrei did not have to be particularly quiet, but he was. Adamovskovich, the sarcastic bastard, the smug, superior bastard who was no better than the man he was about to kill, would remain asleep long enough, if Vanga hurried.

The shoes were too large but not so much that he could not walk in them. The murder had gone quite well. Andrei Vanga, who had never harmed another human in his life, found the act particularly satisfying. As a scientist, he found the release of violence surprising, leading to the conclusion, even as he searched for the paper Bolskanov had written, that everyone probably had great power within him, that there existed a core, perhaps even a spiritual core, which did not reside in the brain, that accounted for psychic powers.

He had found the printed copy of the paper quickly, on the chair next to the murdered man. There were a few drops of blood on the cover page, but that didn't matter. He would, and did, incinerate that page along with the lab coat. But before he did that he found on the dead man's computer the file which contained the paper he now possessed. He also found the backup disk. He erased the file on the hard disk, put the shoes back near the sleeping Adamovskovich, went back to his office after retrieving his own shoes from his laboratory. He transferred the file on the disk to the hard drive of his own office computer, making the necessary changes to erase any sign that the paper belonged to Sergei Bolskanov, the dead, gloating son of a bitch. Only then did he incinerate the lab coat, cover page of the paper, and the backup disk.

When he had closed the door of the incinerator, he had a sudden thought. What if Bolskanov had printed more copies? He had been careful, had seen no one else, though he was sure others were in the building. There had been a risk, but it had been slight. He could have run into someone, but what of it? He had taken the bloody lab coat off before leaving the lab. With shaking hands he had folded the thin coat and plunged it under his shirt. It showed only as a bulge. He had put his own shoes on immediately after the murder.

But now he would have to take the chance. His mind had worked quickly. If he heard someone coming to Bolskanov's laboratory, he could shout out for help and claim to be discovering the corpse.

His luck had remained. There was no other copy in the laboratory. He looked carefully, thoroughly. He was certain. He moved downstairs to the dead man's office. Drawers, files, top of the desk, nothing. He was sure. He even checked to see if there was a second backup disk. This had been the most dangerous part of the evolving plan. If he were found in the dead man's office he would make an excuse, but his presence would be noted. He would surely be a suspect, a secondary one to be sure, but a suspect. Again he was certain. Nothing there.

He went back to his office, checked everything, put the report in his briefcase, signed out, and went home.

That night, at home, in bed, certain that he would sleep well and be ready for the chaos that would come during the night or in the morning when the body was discovered, a new thought came and Vanga suddenly realized that he was a fool.

He sat up in panic. What if Bolskanov had a copy of the research in his home? On a home computer? A hard copy? Maybe several copies, just lying in the open? Vanga had never been to Bolskanov's apartment, didn't know where it was, though he could have found out simply by looking at the . . . wait, he had a copy of the two-sheet directory in the top drawer of his desk, which stood in a corner of his bedroom. He rose quickly, found the address, and stood thinking.

He rejected the idea of dressing, going to the man's apartment, breaking in, searching. Far too dangerous, even more dangerous than going back to the lab, finding the dead man's keys and attempting to sneak into the apartment, search, and get the keys back before the body was discovered, if it had not already been discovered.

No, he would not reveal the paper as his own till he was certain. He would suggest that he go with the police to search Bolskanov's apartment for anything that might shed light on his murder. If they said no, he might suggest that when the investigation was done he would like to look for some notes he and Bolskanov had been working on. He had to remain calm. There would be no reason for the police to bring anyone else to the dead scientist's apartment, and the police would not understand what the paper meant even if they found a copy. Vanga would work that out.

The shoes, the shoes. What if they were too stupid to check the shoes? Then, somehow, he would have to suggest it to them, subtly. He hoped that would not be necessary. As it had turned out, it wasn't.

But hours after he had committed murder, Andrei Vanga could not sleep. His mind was racing. He had to slow it down.

He got back in bed and picked up the copy of *War and Peace* that rested on his night table. Perhaps once every month or so he would read a bit of it. He had never actually finished the book and felt guilty about it. Tonight he would read. He would read till he fell asleep.

He remembered reading somewhere or hearing on the radio or the television that a movie was being made about the life of Tolstoy. Though he seldom went to the movies, he would make it a point to see this one.

He read: "The day after his initiation into the lodge Pierre was sitting at home reading a book and trying to fathom the significance of the square . . ."

It was after midnight. Lydia was snoring in the bedroom and Sasha sat at the table in the tiny kitchen, cutting slices from the block of yellow cheese his mother had left out for him along with a small loaf of bread. He sat in his shorts, not wanting to get into the bed on the floor. He continued to feel free, able to do anything, full of good will, and, at the same time, wanting desperately for Maya and the children to come back. It was a contradiction Porfiry Petrovich had pointed out and that Sasha could not comprehend and was not certain that he wished to, though he knew the contradiction would haunt him.

The television, a small black-and-white on the table before him, was tuned to a station showing a documentary about bears in the Ural Mountains. He had the sound turned down very low so that Lydia would not wake up, come in, and complain. She was almost deaf, yet she could hear a television through a door even if the sound was nearly off. It was a gift granted only to mothers who in spite of failed eyesight could see the hint of a frown on a child's face, or despite deafness hear the whisper of an aside across a room full of people, providing the aside was made by their son or daughter.

The table was cluttered. Sasha decided that it was time to clean up, which meant putting the bread back in the bag, covering the cheese with plastic wrap, putting them in the refrigerator, and consolidating the papers he had spread out to look at. He would brush his teeth in the small kitchen sink so he wouldn't have to go past Lydia to the bathroom. That meant he would have to go down the hall to use the community toilet for the three apartments on the floor which had no private toilets. It was worth it.

A bear was standing tall on its rear legs in front of a woman with a very wide-brimmed hat. She looked skinny, English or American, but she could have been Russian. Russian women with a bit of money had learned how to look like people who spoke English or French. She was very pretty in a healthy kind of way. Sasha paused, cheese in one hand, bread in the other.

The woman was smiling at the bear. The bear was showing its teeth. The woman reached over and scratched the bear's chest. Sasha was fascinated. The documentary was on film, so he knew the woman would not be torn apart on television. And yet there was a tension. If he could not have Maya in bed tonight, the woman with the hat... The bear turned its head sideways in ecstasy. It would have been nice to be that bear instead of a tired policeman whose wife had left him, and who stood holding a plate of cheese.

The scene changed. A sincere, thin man with white hair, wearing a suit, was sitting behind a desk. Behind him was a map of the Ural region. Sasha looked at the pile of papers he had to put away. If he didn't organize anything, and he didn't plan to do so, he could simply push it all together, shove it in his briefcase, and worry about it in the morning.

His eyes fell once again on his copy of the artist's sketch of the man the beggar had described and the chess players had identified. Kon. It looked like many sketches, but something... the description—stocky, homely—and the drawing. Sasha, for just a moment, felt that he may have seen the man somewhere. He stood dreamily trying to put a living face to the drawing. His memory was normally very good, not as good as Emil Karpo's but better than Elena's.

No, it didn't come. He turned off the television set, felt the stubble on his chin, put the food away, and gathered the papers into a pile with the sketch on top.

Then he went to bed.

In the dark, the baby did not turn restlessly or cry, Pulcharia did not come in and ask for water or to climb into bed with her parents. Maya did not reach over in her sleep to touch his bare bottom.

As he went to sleep, he felt the inexplicable euphoria of the past days begin to slip away.

Chapter Ten

★ ★ ★ ★ ★ ★ ★ ★ ★ ★ ★ ★

In the morning, Nadia Spectorski awoke to a fresh, vivid, and inexplicable vision that seemed to mean absolutely nothing. It was another overcast day. Somewhere north of the city clouds were rumbling. Her room was small, brightly decorated, small computer desk in the corner with a flowerpot and cactus next to the Compaq Presario 2240. Next to the cactus was a kaleidoscope that she looked through every morning for a few minutes, losing herself in the never-repeating meditation of changing colors.

The vision was just as vivid as the one in which she had seen the murder of Sergei Bolskanov through the eyes of the killer. Nadia had feared that she had simply remembered what she herself had done and that she was the killer, but there were too many details, little things that convinced her she had not done this thing.

This morning she was as sure that she had not done it as she was that Boris Adamovskovich had not committed the murder. She had looked down through the killer's eyes at the shoes and remembered now that the shoes had not fit, had been too large. Yes, Adamoskovich's shoes would have been too large for her, but the leg was not that of a woman. Nadia reached for her glasses. She needed them to think.

The vision had been brief, mundane.

In the vision a book lay in her lap. The book was thick and open, facedown. It was *War and Peace*. Had the person in her vision turned the book over, she was certain she would have been able to read the words before her.

Such things happened to Nadia less frequently than they had when she was younger. When she was a young teen, the visions had come so frequently that they disrupted her life, set her trembling, caused her parents, who were both physicians, to send her for medication and treatment. Almost none of the visions had any meaning. She had seen unfamiliar couples screaming at each other, a cat dying in a doorway, screaming in pain, a boy writing something obscene on the wall of a school or church, a woman with an enormous head smiling at her. Medication and hundreds of hours in therapy, coupled with the passing of time, had kept the visions from lining up and leaping out. Her experiences and her curiosity had led her to her lifetime career and the hope, so far unrealized, that such phenomena could be understood in a scientific context.

Yes, Jung, Freud, and others had noted that what they called hysteria seemed particularly powerful in young girls reaching puberty. Witches, who were probably hysterical girls, began their calling early. She herself had concentrated much of her research on girls in their teens, many of whom had been considered extreme neurotics and borderline psychotics. She had taken them off of drugs and also taken them seriously. She had been one of them.

Occasionally, a man would turn up who had some of the psychic characteristics, someone like the not-too-bright, gentle slouching policeman who was afraid of his ability, wanted to deny it.

Nadia, wearing an extra-large plain-white T-shirt, got out of bed, deciding to get a copy of *War and Peace*. She had read it only once, when she was a brilliant, nearsighted girl who was being given drugs to help control her supposed deliriums. The book

had absorbed her, helped calm her. She had been particularly fascinated by Tolstoy's Napoleon, a tormented, overly confident creature moved more by chance and the inevitability of history than
by his own design. But she had soon moved from fiction and for
more than a decade now had read none at all.

But now . . . she suddenly felt weak. Her knees threatened to
abandon her. A vision. Brief. A computer monitor with a file
open on the screen. The file had a name. She could read the
name. Sergei Bolskanov. The name was suddenly deleted. The vision was gone.

Nadia put one hand on the bed, adjusted her glasses with the
other, and moved to the window to whisper to her cactus and
look through her kaleidoscope.

In the morning, Iosef awakened and looked at his watch. It
was after seven. He had stayed up late, reading. When he had
been a soldier, for three years Iosef had gone to bed early and
been awakened early. When he had left the army and become a
self-employed and not-successful playwright and actor, he had
gone to bed late and awakened well after eleven. And now he
found himself caught between two routines. He went to bed late
and got up early.

The sun was up. The day was slightly overcast.

He got out of bed, rubbed his stomach to be sure it hadn't
ballooned to a grotesque size, and walked across the small room
in his underpants to put on his trousers. On top of his trousers,
someone had placed a towel and a very small bar of soap. He
picked them up and went in search of somewhere to shave.

On the narrow landing he saw that the door to his father's
room and that of the man who called himself Primazon were
open. Iosef looked into both rooms. They were empty. A woman
was in Porfiry Petrovich's room making the bed. He had noticed
her the day before. With the sun behind her through the window, she reminded Iosef of a painting by Vermeer. The illusion

was shattered when she sensed him watching her and turned to face him with a smile. It was a good smile but one in need of serious orthodontia.

He smiled back as she brushed her hair from her eyes and examined his bare upper body.

"*Gdyeh tooahlyeht?* 'Toilet?' 'Wash room?' " he asked.

"Downstairs," she said.

He nodded, took his towel, soap, toothbrush, and razor and walked barefoot down the wooden stairs, following now the sound of voices. The shop was empty. The voices came from behind a curtain. Iosef followed them and found himself in a large room, surrounded by cabinets containing dishes, pots, books, candlesticks, and children's board games.

In the center of the room was a round table with six chairs. Only three of the chairs were occupied. Porfiry Petrovich, fully dressed and shaved, sat in one chair, drinking tea. In another chair, also fully dressed, sat Anatoli Primazon, tearing pieces of bread from a loaf in the center of the table and popping them into his mouth. The third person at the table was Boris Vladovka, who looked somber and pale and was neither eating nor drinking.

"Bathroom?" asked Iosef.

Primazon pointed deeper into the room to another curtain.

Whatever they had been talking about, they had stopped when Iosef entered.

Iosef looked at his father, who turned his head to face his son.

"There is a pot of tea in the other room," Rostnikov said. "And a refrigerator. Alexander Podgorny's wife has been kind enough to also make some noodle soup."

"From a can," the umbrella man, who did not have his umbrella at the moment, said with a smile. "A bit too salty for me. High blood pressure. I take pills. Little round brown pills."

Iosef nodded. "Then I better . . ." he began.

"Boris Vladovka has just told us something of great importance," said Porfiry Petrovich.

Iosef looked at the large man and understood that the expression on his face was not simply somber but one of grief.

"Something about Tsimion Vladovka," said Primazon, looking at the somber man.

"My son," said Vladovka, holding back tears, "is dead."

"Dead?" asked Iosef, glancing at his father and then at Primazon.

"Natural causes," said the umbrella man.

"When?" asked Iosef.

"A week ago," said Vladovka. "He had been ill for a long time. Liver disease. He had kept it a secret. He wanted to die at home. We buried him four days ago."

"Why didn't you tell us?" asked Iosef, looking to his father for help and receiving none.

"Before he died, he asked us not to," said Boris. "He was afraid someone would be coming from Moscow and want to dig him up."

Iosef was confused. He felt suddenly naked. He draped the towel over his shoulder.

"Why would anyone want to dig him up?"

"Tsimion had been in outer space. He had heard that other cosmonauts had been cut open when they died, cut open to see what, if anything, flying around the earth had done to their bodies."

"And so . . ." Iosef tried.

"And so," Boris went on, "here you are, from Moscow."

"I am afraid we will have to see the body," said Primazon, chewing on a piece of bread. "It will take only a few moments. We need identification."

"Identification?" asked Boris, looking at the umbrella man.

"Verification," Primazon said. "That he is dead."

"Doctor Verushkin from Yerkistanitza gave me this," Boris said, reaching into his pocket. "I'm sure you can talk to him. He is new in the area. We don't really know him, but the old doctor, Feydov, he died. Feydov delivered both my sons and . . ."

Boris Vladovka's voice trailed off. He started to raise his hands as if in a prelude to a new thought, but none came.

Primazon wiped his hands on the napkin in his lap and looked at the death certificate witnessed by a nurse and a deputy mayor.

"Liver disease," Primazon confirmed. "Still . . ."

"I anticipated someone like you. My remaining son and his friends have dug up the coffin. It is next to the grave. The sky is clear but it has been raining. The clouds rush in from the east and . . ."

"We're coming," said Primazon. "Inspector Rostnikov?"

Rostnikov nodded, put down his tea, and got up along with Boris Vladovka.

"I'll hurry," said Iosef. "I can wash and shave later."

"You saw the cemetery when you came in?" asked Boris.

"Yes," said Iosef.

"We will be there."

Iosef ran up the stairs, listening to the three men below him heading through the shop toward the front door. There was no mistaking his father's footsteps, the sound of the slight limp.

The young woman was still in his room, making up his bed. She looked up at him and smiled again as he pulled a fresh shirt from his bag, put it on quickly, slipped on his socks and shoes, and grabbed his blue zipper jacket.

He found the driver, Ivan Laminski, standing next to the Mustang, reading a St. Petersburg newspaper. Laminski was still wearing his blue uniform, but Iosef noticed that the shirt under his open jacket was definitely wrinkled. Laminski looked up and nodded soberly.

Iosef trotted toward the cemetery just outside of town. He could see a very small group: his father, Boris, Primazon, Konstantin Vladovka, and another man holding a shovel.

Iosef slowed down and walked up to the open coffin in time to hear Porfiry Petrovich say, "It is him."

Primazon looked at the dead man and then at Boris and said, "Yes, but I have a request. I would rather not make it, but it is essential. I was supposed to protect your son from harm. Now I would like to protect myself from the censure of my superiors. I would like a copy of the death certificate and I would like to take a photograph of your son."

Boris Vladovka took a step toward Primazon, who was now carrying his umbrella, but his son stepped between them.

"It can do no harm, Father."

"Take your photograph," said Boris, turning away and heading back to the village.

Primazon tucked the umbrella under his arm and awkwardly reached into his pocket to produce a very small camera.

"Important in my work," he explained.

They stood watching as Primazon took three photographs, zooming in for one head shot. Iosef, for the first time, looked at the dead man. His hands were folded. He was the pale white of death and wore a suit and tie. His hair was brushed back. The dead man looked like a ghastly version of the cosmonaut in the photograph in Porfiry Petrovich's file. The quest for Tsimion Vladovka was over.

"Enough," said Primazon, pocketing the camera. "I am sorry, but . . ."

"Let us leave so that—" Rostnikov began.

"Of course," said Primazon with a sad smile, looking at the bearded brother of the dead man and at the man with the shovel. "It's time to leave."

When they got back, Podgorny's shop was open and the shopkeeper was reaching up to take something from a shelf. "You'll be leaving now?" he asked.

"Shortly," said Rostnikov. "You knew about—"

"We all knew," said Podgorny, carefully lifting a carton with a slight grunt. "The whole village. We did as Boris asked us."

"I am leaving, Inspector Rostnikov," said Primazon with a sigh, as the three headed up the stairs.

"No point in remaining," said Rostnikov. "Perhaps we will encounter each other in Moscow."

"It is possible," said Primazon. "It is possible."

Porfiry Petrovich was moving slowly, more slowly than usual. Primazon went into his room and closed the door. Iosef was about to do the same but his father motioned to him and Iosef followed Porfiry Petrovich into his room, where Rostnikov closed the door behind them.

"Pack quickly and then meet me in the hall when you hear our umbrella man coming out of his room," Rostnikov whispered. "I will be waiting. I am already packed. In his presence, you will ask me if we have time to visit a farm before we leave. You have never seen a real farm."

"I haven't?" Iosef whispered back.

"You have not. I will say that it is all right to visit a farm, but we should do so quickly because we must get back to Moscow. You understand?"

"Not in the least," said Iosef, "but I will certainly do it."

"You were an actor."

"I was a mediocre actor."

"Mediocrity is all that is necessary in this situation."

"May I ask why?" said Iosef.

"Because while I do know who killed the cosmonauts, I do not yet know why."

"Primazon killed Vladovka?"

"No, I am convinced that Vladovka died of liver disease."

"And you think you will find in this village the reason why the others were killed?"

"I am certain of it," said Rostnikov.

* * *

In the morning Sasha Tkach sat up suddenly.

"I know who it is," he said aloud.

"American cereal," said Lydia, who was fully dressed and standing next to the kitchen table across the room with a box of Froot Loops in her hand.

"I've got to go," said Sasha, getting up quickly and reaching for his pants. "No, maybe I should phone Elena."

"You should eat your American cereal," Lydia said. "There are all kinds of things about how healthy it is for you on the side of the box. That's what the man I got it from said. All I can see are numbers. Take a look."

"I can't read English," he said, looking for his socks.

"Then just eat them. I opened the box. Very pretty colors. Look. A red one."

"Mother, I am thirty-four years old," Sasha said, finding his socks. "You can talk to me like an adult."

"You are thirty-four years old, which is why you need a shave before you go anywhere."

"Yes," he said.

"And some American cereal. I have milk. It's sweet like candy. How can something sweet like candy be good for you?"

"A miracle of American technology and artificial ingredients," said Sasha.

"Do not be sarcastic, Sasha."

"I apologize. I must go."

"What is the hurry?" she asked, looking at the picture of a big-billed bird on the front of the box.

"I have to prevent a murder," he said.

"Then go," she said. "Why is there a bird on the box? Do they put chicken or something in the cereal? I prefer kasha."

"Then why did you get American cereal?" he asked, regretting it even before the question was finished.

"I thought you would like it," she said. "I know our little Pulcharia would like it."

Sasha nodded and looked again at the drawing lying on the table. Yes, it was him. Sasha scooped his papers into the briefcase, reached over and took a handful of Froot Loops from the box his mother was holding, and began putting them into his mouth as he moved to the door.

"Very good," he said.

"Shave," she said.

"When I get where I'm going. I have one of those disposable razors in my briefcase."

He had the door open.

"Sasha," she commanded. "I want to see the rest of that movie, the one where the men were taking off their clothes."

"Mother . . ."

"You made me leave. You are an adult. I am an adult."

"Yes, all right. We will see it again. Under one condition. You may not talk during the movie."

"I will be quiet as death," she said, arms folded. "As quiet as I will soon be when I am dead."

He didn't believe it for a moment. "You are only sixty years old. You are, with the exception of your hearing, in perfect health."

"All I want to do is live long enough to see my grandchildren again, just one more time."

"I am confident that you will see them again. I have an idea. You go to Kiev."

"Maybe I will. And I'll bring with me boxes of sweet American cereal."

He closed the door. If he moved quickly, they might still be able to recover the negative and keep Yuri Kriskov from being murdered. At least that is what he thought.

Sasha Tkach was wrong.

In the morning, very early in the morning, after little sleep, Valery Grachev awoke covered in sweat. There was no doubt. He was feverish, some virus or flu. He should spend the day in bed.

Maybe tomorrow if everything went well. He dressed, was out of the apartment before he had to talk to his uncle. The sun was battling the cloud cover as he walked past a street-cleaning truck that was noisily brushing away the filth of the night before.

The apartment of Valery's uncle was on the fifth floor, a block of concrete with thin walls, rusted radiators, peopled by pensioners with nothing to do but complain about the landlady, who made excuses and no repairs.

In less than an hour, the men with caps, cigarettes, and the weary faces of resignation would congregate in the doorway of the building. The doorway reeked of years of tobacco smoke. Valery's uncle would trudge off to work, nodding to Yakov, Panushkin, and the others, trudge off to a day of scrubbing subway stations and counting himself lucky to have a job.

When Valery had money, he would give his uncle a job. Valery did not particularly like his uncle, who spoke little, provided meager food in the apartment, and played such awful chess that his nephew had long given up wasting his time in front of the board with the grizzled, grunting man who had no passion for the game. Where was the satisfaction of defeating an opponent who did not care?

The key in Valery's pocket was small. He checked again to be sure it hadn't fallen through a forgotten hole or been flung onto the street when Valery had taken out his other keys or change for the bus. Since he'd gotten the key, he had checked to be sure it was there at least a hundred times a day. He had considered taking his scooter, but he decided to come back for it later, to leave as much of the morning as he could to concentrating on what he had to do, and not on traffic.

The walk was long, the summer morning hot. Valery felt dizzy with anticipation and possibly with fever. He wiped his damp forehead with his sleeve. Others walking with and past him were not yet affected by the heat. They walked as they always walked unless they were with someone. They walked, heads down, clutching the bag, briefcase, book, or whatever they were carrying.

Valery walked with his head up this day. He was Kon. He was not afraid of beggars or of the mad woman who spent her mornings and most of the day in front of the Sokol metro station. Her hair was as wild as her words. She wore a series of solid-colored dresses—blue, green, black, but never red—and could have been any age. A fire raged in her eyes. She never seemed to grow tired of berating the passersby, who pretended that she did not exist. On the sidewalk each morning, in white chalk, she wrote a new message. Today's was "You are destroying the air we breathe."

For the first time Valery paused in front of the woman, who looked him in the eyes and lowered her voice to say, "You are destroying the air we breathe." Her face was red from months of shouting and the summer sun.

"You should wear a hat," he said.

"You are destroying the air we breathe," she said again, her voice a bit louder.

"We are all destroying the air we breathe. What would you have me do about it?" he asked.

"Stop," she said.

"Stop what?"

"Creating filth, smoking, driving cars, running factories, making bombs and biological weapons."

A few passersby glanced at the odd pair, the thin ranting woman and the short block of a hairy young man, standing face to face.

"I do none of those things," Valery said.

"You allow others to do them."

"And what am I to do?"

"Stop them," she said, pointing down the street at some vague them.

"Are you trying to stop them?"

"Yes, by being here each day."

"You think you are successful?"

"No," she said. "But that is no reason not to try."

"People think you are crazy," Valery said. "They don't listen to you because you rant and scream your messages."

"I tried to be more reasonable," she said, suddenly transformed and calm. "I tried. I dressed well, talked reasonably, went to meetings protesting this, that, everything, was even elected to committees to lead marches. Nothing was accomplished. And so I began to scream. My husband left me. My mother will not let me come to her house. I have nothing left but to try, to scream."

"And to fail?" Valery asked.

"Possibly, probably, but I cannot live without trying," she said. "Do you understand?"

"Yes," he said, "but that means little. I am in a fever and I fear that I may be going mad."

"You too have a mission?"

"I have a mission."

"Then do it," she said, touching his shoulder. "Do it and fight the taxes, the people who kill animals and wear them, the Nazis who have infiltrated our economy and our government, the people who make artificial sugar that is killing us. Don't eat artificial sugars. Don't let your children eat them."

"I won't," Valery said. "And I will complete my mission."

He walked on. Behind him the woman resumed her screaming. Valery wiped his damp hands on his trousers.

When he arrived at the bicycle-repair shop on a small street just off Gorky, the owner, a man who resembled a long-necked chicken, was just opening for business. He looked over at Valery, who nodded to him, and Valery followed the man into the shop where the chicken man turned on the lights.

"You do not look well," the man said.

"I am well," Valery answered.

The chicken man who sold and repaired bicycles shrugged. It was not his business.

Valery walked past the racks of bicycles and through the smell of oil and grease to the back of the shop where he had rented a closet.

Valery paused to be sure the owner was not watching him. He heard the man in the front of the store. Valery opened the closet door. In the dark closet were the cans containing the negatives, the case containing the rifle, and the small pouch containing the pistol. The cans were in a sealed cardboard box. He knew that they would have to be stored somewhere reasonably cool within the next few days. The rifle was inside a separate long cardboard box, which had once held curtain rods. He took the box with the rifle, locked the closet, and tucked the box under his arm. It was not particularly heavy. Valery thought of it as a black rook. He was going to move this rook into checkmate position within the hour.

In the morning, well before dawn, Igor Yaklovev sat in his living room drinking coffee, being very careful not to drop any of the thick dark liquid on the notes neatly arranged before him on the square work table.

The Yak had few indulgences but he took great pleasure in his coffee, which he prepared each morning by selecting an appropriate bean from the collection of eighteen that sat in glass containers on the counter in his kitchen. The appropriate coffee for each day depended on his mood. Sometimes he wanted a coffee that was thick, dark, and even somewhat bitter, a Sumatra. Other times he went for a lighter Colombian or African blend. He ground his own beans and kept his coffeepot spotless.

The Yak lived alone in an apartment building on Kalinin that had once been reserved for Party officials. It was more space than he really needed, but it was conveniently located. He could and did walk to Petrovka almost every morning for exercise, uninterrupted thought, and scheming. He was a solitary, pensive figure with a determined, marchlike step. He was lean, dark haired, and had only one really distinctive feature, his bushy eyebrows.

Once he had a wife. She had conveniently died. He had not disliked her. On the contrary, she was decent company, but she wanted more of him than he was willing to give. He was willing to give nothing.

Now he was fifty years old, director of the Office of Special Investigation, preparing for his next move upward. To do so required careful planning and all of his time. Idle conversation, music, theater, movies, restaurants, were a distraction. There were risks. A need to be constantly alert, prepared. There were always risks when one chose to make use of the mistakes and secrets of others. The papers before him and the documents and tapes he had safely stored were going to be used with great care, if at all.

Igor Yaklovev was ambitious. He lived for power, intrigue. He did not question his need. He had a few theories about why this was so, but he didn't waste his time thinking about his father's fall from grace in the Party and his eventual suicide. His father had been weak. His father had not planned, as his son was doing. His father did not gather evidence and secrets that could have not only kept him in his position but allowed him to move up and keep his family in comfort and prestige. So, perhaps the lesson of his father's failure had been a factor in the decision of Igor Yaklovev to become what he had become.

Igor had a brother and a sister. The brother was a low-level postal worker who had inherited the low intelligence of their mother. His sister was married to a relatively successful owner of a children's clothing store near the Kremlin. She had two children. Both were probably grown by now. Igor never saw or talked to his siblings, though his sister lived no more than five miles from the Yak's apartment. Their mother had died ten years earlier. He had not attended the funeral.

The papers were in five piles laid out neatly before him, three relating to current investigations and two relating to past investigations that had yielded information Yaklovev was deciding how to use.

A small blue stick-em note was pressed onto the document at the top of each pile.

The stick-em on pile one read: "Mikhail Stoltz. What is the secret of *Mir*?"

The stick-em on pile two read: "More than gratitude to be gained from duma for saving Tolstoy film?"

The stick-em on pile three read: "Who supports psychic research center? Is there a secret? Why the high priority to solving the murder of the scientist quickly?"

The other two piles carried only single names. The people named were powerful. Others would call what Yaklovev was going to do blackmail, but if nothing was openly said and no overt pressure took place, it was simply a matter of one person doing a favor for another whom he respects or who has done him a favor. One of the piles was urgent. The man named on the stick-em was quickly drinking himself to death and his chances of eventually succeeding Putin were all but gone. Igor had a great investment of his time in this well-meaning alcoholic. He had tapes, documents that demanded favors, but what good were obligations and favors if the man was dead? Still, if Igor Yaklovev moved quickly, there was possibly still something to be gained from him.

He sat back, looked at the five piles with satisfaction, and considered when he would make his move. This was his favorite time of each day. Coffee within reach, papers and files before him to be studied, considered, manipulated. He was satisfied for now serving as director of the Office of Special Investigation. Rostnikov was the ideal partner to serve Yaklovev's needs. Rostnikov was interested in solving crimes. In the process, he fed Yaklovev golden data. It was a perfect relationship, and Yaklovev showed his appreciation of his chief investigator by giving Rostnikov what he needed and providing protection for Rostnikov or his people when they were in trouble. Yaklovev was loyal to those who worked for and with him. He had never betrayed those who worked in his KGB unit and he would never betray his present investigators, but in a year or two, possibly three at the most, he would humbly accept a major promotion, possibly even to Minister of the Interior. He would see to it that Rostnikov and the others were in good hands. He wanted to leave no enemies behind him. He did not want to be liked. He wanted to be respected. Had his father learned this lesson . . . but that was in the past. The present and future lay before him in neat piles.

He finished his coffee, cleaned the cup and dried it, and then went back to gather the papers. They were all copies. The original documents and reports were well hidden in a well-protected, large steel safe-deposit box in a bank in Korov.

The director of the bank owed Igor Yaklovev a very large favor. The director owed Yaklovev his very life. He had learned that paranoia was essential to his survival. Still, these piles had to be returned to the wall safe in the bedroom. While there were ways of getting into the safe in the apartment other than by using the proper combination, there was no way someone could get into the safe without leaving clear signs that a theft or even attempted theft had taken place. Igor had been a KGB field director for fourteen years.

A fleeting, pleasant memory of his wife almost came to life, but, as was usually the case, it faded before it could take shape.

He had much to do.

When the papers had been tucked away in the large safe, Igor Yaklovev looked out the bedroom window at the sky. It might rain. He could always hail a cab on the way to Petrovka. He hoped the rain would hold off for an hour or so. He had much to think about. He would prefer the long walk.

Chapter Eleven
★ ★ ★ ★ ★ ★ ★ ★ ★ ★ ★ ★ ★

Yuri Kriskov had readily agreed to stay in his home and be
guarded for as long as was necessary. But the two policemen,
he decided, were too young and did not appear particularly interested, except for the younger of the two, who was definitely
interested in Vera.

Therefore, the night before, Yuri had made a decision and a
phone call. A little after midnight, four burly men heavily armed
with automatic weapons had appeared at the door. The confrontation with the two young policemen was brief and surly.
The policemen had called their chief at Petrovka, who said he
didn't give a shit about Kriskov. If he wanted to pay bodyguards,
let him. He ordered the two young policemen to end their vigil.
The two policemen departed.

The four armed men wore uniforms complete with badges and
stripes on their arms. The uniforms were decidedly more expensive and official-looking than those of the police. The bodyguards
quickly and politely checked the house and the view from each
window as soon as dawn broke.

In Russia there are forty-five hundred security firms, or *krysha*,
"roofs," with seventy thousand legally armed and very well paid
operatives, many of them former police, KGB, and soldiers. These
private armies, which protect businesses, banks, and wealthy in-

dividuals who have reason to believe their lives may be in danger, outnumber the police.

After several years with one of these security firms, hundreds of bodyguards leave to join the enemy, Mafias and bandit groups, which pay even better. The security guards are quickly replaced by policemen, who defect for the reality of hard cash.

"Is this really necessary? Do we really need these men in the house with guns?" Vera said softly in the kitchen to her husband.

Yuri had not ceased smoking and looking over his shoulder.

"They are better than the police," he said. "The police didn't tell me to cover the windows. The police didn't tell me to stay away from windows. The police didn't patrol the house and go down the streets and behind the other houses and knock at doors to ask questions. Let the police concentrate on finding this lunatic and my negative. This army will protect me till then."

"They will frighten the children," Vera said.

"The children are at school."

"What if this madman kidnaps our children?" she asked.

"What has that to do with these men guarding me? And why would he do that? Why would he take the children? Tell me. Why would he do something like that?"

"To get you to give him the money," she said.

"I have no money to give him," he answered between clenched teeth.

"You have enough to pay a private army. But you wouldn't have enough to save the lives of your children."

"No one is kidnapping the children," he said. "You want me to pay for more bodyguards to go to the school, fine. You want to go out, fine. Leave me alone. I will conduct business by phone. I will try to believe that I am safe and that there is a chance the negative will be returned and this lunatic found. Do you realize we could lose everything?"

Vera had taken extra time to select a proper dress and put on her makeup. She was now making an extra effort to continue to play the concerned and dutiful wife. She would keep up the show until Valery found a way to make his move. The big men with big guns complicated everything. Yuri was right. It would have been easier if the police were still in charge, but Yuri was not to be moved.

Her husband's behavior had kept her up during the night while Yuri, in spite of his fear, had managed a snoring sleep. She had even smoked a cigarette for the first time in two years. She wanted to call Valery, to make him come to his senses, to be careful, perhaps to wait a few days or even weeks. But she dared not go to the phone. She was beginning to think it possible that the police would find him, that he would fail to end Yuri Kriskov's life, and she would be denounced by this animal who loved her. And Yuri would live. No. She could not live another week with the reeking, unfaithful, lying coward whose existence made her feel dirty. Living a lie was something she no longer could do.

During the night she heard the security guards moving around the inside and outside of the house. She had moved to the room of each child, wondering how much of this they were absorbing. Neither child had asked many questions and both had seemingly been content to hear that a bad man was trying to get their father to give him money and the men with guns were going to find the man and put him in jail.

The truth now was that the men with guns would almost certainly kill Valery Grachev if they found him. The truth now was that this would suit Vera very well. It would be even better if it happened after Valery killed her husband. However, she now had little faith that Valery would have the skill, sanity, or patience to complete his part of the plan.

She looked at her husband, forced herself to touch his arm and try to act the concerned, loving wife. Yuri was showing definite signs of losing control.

"What have I done to deserve this?" he said. "Don't answer. I've done nothing. Absolutely . . ."

"Nothing," Vera confirmed.

"Nothing, exactly. I know it doesn't matter if I deserve this or don't deserve this. There is no justice. There is no God."

"And this you learned from your Tolstoy research," she said, drinking a very hot cup of tea, knowing that Yuri had done none of the research on the missing film, had read no Tolstoy biographies, none of Tolstoy's stories or novels. Yuri was a hypocrite. Yuri was a producer.

"Perhaps," he said. "From Tolstoy and from experience."

One of the armed security men, weapon cradled in his arms, entered the kitchen. The man's eyes were hooded like those of a boxer who had developed scar tissue from too many punches. He nodded and looked around.

"Would you like tea?" Vera asked.

The man said no and left the room.

"Prisoners," she said. "Yuri, we are prisoners in our own home."

"Yes, but not prisoners of these men," he answered. "We are prisoners of a madman. I'm going upstairs to make some calls. I need privacy."

You need, Vera thought, to call your mistress and explain why you aren't coming to see her today. Vera didn't care. She continued sitting and drinking and thinking as he left the room, pausing only to light yet another cigarette.

Yuri walked through his living room. One of the security guards followed him. The guard's name was Yevgeny. He was a former military policeman trained in weapons, martial arts, and surveillance. He knew he was good at his job, but he also knew what all bodyguards knew: that a capable, determined assassin cannot be stopped. He may fail to kill. He may be killed after his attack, but stopping him required great luck or a serious mistake on the part of the attacker. Yevgeny had been at the side of a publisher who was shot as they stepped out of the elevator in his office building. The killer, who stood no more than a dozen feet away, had dropped his weapon and run. Yevgeny recovered quickly and fired at the fleeing man in spite of the other five bystanders in the lobby. Yevgeny thought he hit him, but he never knew. The man got away.

Yuri stepped into his bedroom and indicated that he wanted Yevgeny to wait on the landing outside the room. Before the door closed on him, Yevgeny checked the room and adjusted the curtains over the window. Only then did he leave. Yuri locked the door and went for the white portable phone near the bed.

As he talked to Katya, who was very understanding, he wandered absentmindedly to the window and played with the curtains. "I cannot explain," he said. "And I cannot talk long. You must be patient."

"I will be patient," she said, actually quite pleased that she would be without his oppressive presence and massive ego for a few days. She was sure that when he did come he would bring a present of appeasement.

Yuri was, in some ways, a perfect lover. He didn't like sex and he came to see her infrequently. He talked, expected and received great but feigned sympathy, and demanded nothing more than to be seen with her at the proper clubs and restaurants. Katya was very young, a dark, slender beauty who had perfected her walk and voice. She exuded sexuality. She trafficked in it.

"It won't be long," he reassured her, opening the curtains just enough to look out onto the street.

The street was empty.

It then, very quickly, occurred to him that he had probably been leaning too hard against the window and that it had suddenly shattered. He let the curtains close.

"What was that?" Katya said.

"The window broke," he said.

He didn't move. A second bullet came through the now-shattered window. This one missed him as had the first. And yet Yuri simply stood talking on the phone, not believing what was happening.

"I think someone is shooting at me. He is shooting at me."

The bedroom door was kicked open. Yuri turned his head as Yevgeny rushed toward him, yelling, "Get down. Get down."

"Shooting at you?" asked Katya, hearing the noise.

Yuri didn't get down. He held the phone, fingers and knuckles turning white. The next two bullets tore through the curtains. The first hit him solidly in the chest. The second entered just below his right eye and exited through the top rear of his skull.

He went down, still clutching the phone.

Yevgeny crawled cautiously to the body, knew immediately that the man whom he was supposed to protect was quite dead, and very carefully made his way to the window. A fifth shot entered the room and shattered something against the far wall. The gunman could see nothing through the curtains. He fired once more. And then there was silence.

Yevgeny cursed his luck but did his job. He went to the window, peeked out carefully, and scanned the street. There were not many places to hide. There was no high ground, no real cover from trees, only houses which had been checked the night before.

A second guard entered the room and Yevgeny shouted, "He's dead."

"Shit," the man shouted back.

"Shot came from low, not close. Go."

When the man had rushed out of the room, Yevgeny pulled the small rectangular cell phone from his belt and pressed a button.

"No car," he said. "Nothing is moving. The houses across the street. There's a sight line from two houses on the street beyond, a gray house and a white one next to it."

He sensed someone in the doorway behind him and turned, aiming his weapon. It was Vera. She looked at her husband and began to shake. She did not have to act. It was one thing to wish him dead and quite another to see his head blown apart.

"Get down," Yevgeny shouted. "Now. Down."

Vera, her eyes fixed on Yuri, sank to her knees as if in prayer.

Yevgeny took another look out the window and moved to her, placing his weapon on the floor. He put his arm around her, knowing she was going into shock. He had trained for this but had never had to do it before.

She looked over her shoulder as he started to lead her from the room. His hand accidentally touched her breast. She didn't notice, but he felt a stir and damned himself.

"Wait," she said, pulling away from him and moving to the body of her husband. She took the phone from his reluctant fingers and spoke to the woman on the other end.

"He is dead," Vera said.

"Dead?" asked Katya. "You killed him?"

Vera hung up the phone. Yevgeny took it from her, put it down on the bed, and led her onto the landing and down the stairs.

The suggestion by Andrei Vanga that he accompany Karpo and Zelach to the apartment of Sergei Bolskanov was noted by Karpo with interest. Karpo had no belief in intuition and little faith in his own ability to detect the underlying feelings and motives of others. He tried to deal only in evidence based on a long career as a criminal investigator.

That experience reminded him of the many other instances in which people in major cases, often involving murder, had volunteered to assist in some aspect of the investigation. The morbid, the guilty, and occasionally the few who for emotional reasons wanted the crime solved and the guilty punished were the ones who volunteered. Occasionally, a person with a vested interest in the investigation would also cooperate. In Karpo's experience, there had been no other reasons.

The likely conclusion in this situation was that Vanga had a vested interest. It might simply be that he wanted to do what he could to find the killer and return the center to some level of

normalcy so that he could return to raising money and supporting research. Karpo entertained the other possibilities and
did not dismiss that Vanga might, in fact, be the murderer.

Karpo did not worry about motive. That would come if Vanga
was guilty.

The conversation had taken place at the Center for the Study
of Technical Parapsychology after Karpo and Zelach had returned
with a dour little man named Tikon Tayumvat, who could well
have been ninety years old. He grunted. He grumbled. Tayumvat
was a well-known name in the field of parapsychology. Vanga
had been impressed when he was introduced to the man, who
simply grunted. Not only was Tikon Tayumvat, who was no more
than five feet tall, an expert in the field, he also knew the technology and how to use computers. But what was of special interest to Karpo, who had found the man through Paulinin, was
that Tayumvat was a skeptic. His scrutiny of the research, according to Paulinin, was well known and much feared.

Vanga had shown the little man to Bolskanov's laboratory and
office and stood watching, offering suggestions, especially when
the little man had moved to the computer.

Tikon Tayumvat, in turn, had looked at the director, pursed
his lips, and said, "I will accomplish more if you take him away.
I am old and will die soon. I would like it to be sometime after
I complete this investigation."

And with that, Karpo and Zelach had accompanied the director back to his office.

"I thought Tikon Tayumvat was dead," said Vanga. "Everyone
thought he was dead."

"I believe his family, though he seems to be quite estranged
from them, are very aware that he is alive," said Karpo.

"Yes, of course. I meant in the profession. What has he been
doing for . . . what is it . . . what has he been doing for the past
thirty years?"

"He says he has been thinking," said Karpo.

"Well, what now? Has Boris Adamovskovich confessed? I mean, I can't believe he is guilty of anything, but someone did it and . . . Has he?"

"No," said Karpo.

"Then, what now?"

"We are going to Sergei Bolskanov's apartment again," said Karpo, standing next to Zelach, who would have liked very much to sit. "Dr. Tayumvat has agreed to see if there is anything there that might interest us."

"I can't imagine there would be," said Vanga, standing behind his desk and looking from one detective to the other.

"Why?" asked Karpo.

"Well . . . because . . . I don't know. This is all very, very difficult," said Vanga, starting to sit and then standing. "You know, Bolskanov and I were involved in the same area of research, sleep studies, dream states. Perhaps if I were to come with you, I might see something you would overlook."

"Dr. Tayumvat is knowledgeable," said Karpo.

"Of course, of course. He is a legend. Would you like some coffee, tea, Pepsi? He is a legend. But he is old. He might miss something important, very important. You want something to drink?"

"No, thank you," said Karpo for both of them, though Zelach would have loved a Pepsi.

Zelach kept listening for the door behind them to open. He wanted the ancient scientist to return so they could escape from the center before Nadia Spectorski found him.

"Yes, but this is new material, a new direction, don't you see," said Vanga. "And personal things. There might be some things of special interest that you and Tikon Tayumvat might miss."

"Such as?" asked Karpo.

"Such as? I don't know *such as* till I see it. It would hurt nothing if I joined you, and it might yield something," Vanga said earnestly. "I wish to help."

It was at that point Karpo had agreed. It was a moment later that Tayumvat entered the office and said, "Nothing in his office or his laboratory that will help you find a murderer. He appears to have been engaged in some interesting though probably flawed research. Some of his notes are in his computer, though they tell little. He was working on whatever it was for several years, though I see no evidence that he has written anything. I've read his other articles. He is not one to delay. I'd say he is, or was, one to publish a bit before it was prudent to do so. And yet . . . nothing."

"He had changed his way of thinking about publishing," said Vanga. "He didn't want to write anything till he was certain. He thought he might be two years from even beginning to write. He consulted me frequently. I assured him that support for his work would continue."

"He may have something written at his home," said Karpo. "You will accompany us to examine his papers?"

Tayumvat nodded and said, "Vanga . . . Andrei Vanga? You are Andrei Vanga."

"Yes," said Vanga.

"I read your article on dream states among the mentally ill. *Journal of Psychic Research.*"

Vanga smiled.

"That was twenty years ago at least," said the old man. "It stunk. You write stinking articles with flawed research and results, and they put you in charge of all this. What have you written since? Something better, I hope, or better nothing at all."

"I've been busy keeping this facility alive, raising money, finding . . ."

"You burned out," said Tayumvat.

"No," Vanga shot back. "In fact, I am almost ready to present a new and, I believe, major report on my research."

"I hope it's better than the last one," said Tayumvat.

"I believe it is," said Vanga. "Shall we go?"

"You are going?" asked the old man.

"He is going," said Karpo.

"Then see to it that he stays out of my way and touches nothing," said Tayumvat, turning toward the door. "Let's go. Time is something I, Tikon, will not knowingly waste."

They had barely opened the door when Nadia Spectorski appeared, arms folded over her white lab coat. "I would like a few minutes of Akardy's time," she said.

"I must . . ." Zelach began, feeling the panic he had anticipated.

"We have been told to cooperate with your research," Karpo said. "Zelach will stay, Nadia Spectorski."

Tayumvat, who had been walking slowly in front of them down the corridor, turned and looked at her. "Spectorski? Image projection?"

"Yes," she said.

"Don't trust the English," he said. "They find what they want to find. You find what you want to find. You rely too much on the English in your articles. To know someone can play card tricks is not to know how they play these tricks, and the real question is, When is a trick not a trick?"

"I agree," she said as Zelach stood listening, hoping that they would return with evidence from the dead man's apartment that Nadia was the murderer.

"Then write better articles," said Tayumvat, resuming his walk down the hall.

That had been an hour ago. They had been driven in the unmarked car Karpo had asked the Yak to sign for.

The first impression was that the dead scientist's apartment on Petro Street had been ransacked, but even a cursory examination by Karpo confirmed that the man had simply lived like a child. Papers were piled on the floor. Books were scattered about. Every chair was full of books and papers. The air was heavy with dust, and two open boxes of raisins sat on the table on which a computer rested.

"Stay out of my way," the old man said, surveying the chaos. "It will go faster."

"I would like to help," said Vanga.

"And I would like you not to help," said Tayumvat, pronouncing each word slowly and distinctly as if he were giving orders to a child who was being told what to do for the third time.

The old scientist started in one corner of the room, picking up books, examining them, riffling through the pages, and making comments to Karpo and Vanga.

"*Unidentified Flying Objects*," he said at one point, looking at a paperback book. "I wrote about this. Carl Jung wrote about this. Do you know what I wrote?"

"That the objects were not aliens but humans from the future," said Vanga.

Tayumvat paused and looked at Vanga. "Yes, yes," he said. "So, I am not completely forgotten. It is common sense. The ships come in two forms, saucers and cigar-shaped objects. My conclusion . . ."

". . . is that they come from two different periods in the future. The cigar-shaped ones are not as far advanced as the saucers," said Vanga.

"Correct. And why do these creatures have two arms, two legs, two eyes? Because they are evolved humans. Why would creatures from some distant galaxy look like us? Answer," he said, looking at a pile of papers, "they would not. And why do they abduct humans and examine them? Because they want to find out about their ancestors, us. And," he continued, going through more books, papers, and journals, "why do they avoid contact with humans?"

"Because they do not wish to alter history," said Vanga.

"No," said Tayumvat. "Don't you understand Einstein? Time is already determined. Even if they were to come back and destroy us all, the time that is already in motion would continue. The time they affect would go on separately. If I can figure this out, they can."

"You believe this?" asked Karpo, watching Vanga carefully.

"No, I do not believe we have visitors from the future," said Tayumvat. "I believe, however, that if these creatures do exist, my explanation is infinitely better than the theory of alien visitors. My great-grandson has one of those T-shirts, hideous, black with white letters. It says, Star Trek Is Right. What's this?"

The old man was examining a notebook with the spirals on top. Vanga took a step toward him. Karpo held out a hand to stop him. Vanga stopped.

"Notes about people whose dreams have been scientifically proved to foretell the future," said Tayumvat, flipping through the pages. "Interesting, the future foretold is not necessarily their own."

"Yes," said Vanga. "He was working with me on such a project."

"All anecdotal," said the old man, flipping quickly.

"We have hard research results," said Vanga.

"I'd be interesting in seeing it," said Tikon Tayumvat, with undisguised skepticism.

"I'll be ready to publish soon," he said.

"And the dead man? . . ."

"Bolskanov," Karpo supplied.

"Bolskanov," Tayumvat continued. "Your publication will include his name as co-author?"

Vanga had not considered this. He looked at the old man and then at Karpo. "He just did some of the research, under my direction. He has done none of the writing. Of course I will give him credit. I will dedicate the paper to him."

"Let's ask him for his side of this tale, which I have heard all too often," said the old man, turning his back on Vanga now and continuing his search. "Oh, yes. This Bolskanov is dead. He cannot speak for himself. But perhaps I can speak for him."

"What are you suggesting?" asked Vanga with great indignation.

"That it is convenient for you that the man is dead."

"And you are suggesting that I killed him because I wanted to steal his work?"

"I had not considered it quite that way," said the old man, turning again to face Vanga, "but it makes sense. It is a hypothesis. And what do you do with a reasonable hypothesis? You test it. We will test your hypothesis."

"Inspector, I do not wish to stand here and be insulted," Vanga said to Karpo, who stood close by his side.

"Then you may leave," said Karpo.

"Or," said Tayumvat, flipping through another book of notes which had been on top of a teetering pile, "you may sit."

"But I can't leave. I may be needed. I can check the computer."

Vanga moved to the computer. Leaning forward he slipped the disk he had brought with him into the hard drive, hoping neither of the other two men had seen him. It was a desperate act but one he could not avoid.

"Do not turn that on," Karpo commanded, taking Vanga's arm.

Vanga straightened up immediately. "Yes, if you wish. I won't turn it on. But . . . I just want to help."

Tayumvat dropped the notebook in his hand on the floor and wove through the debris toward the desk. "Yes," he said. "By all means. If this is so important to our friend, let us open it now."

Karpo guided Vanga a few steps back while the old man sat and turned on the computer. The black screen went blue and then a series of icons began to appear, but the appearance was brief. The icons began to lose their clarity and fade.

"A virus," said Tayumvat. "It is destroying all the information, all the files on the hard disk."

"Can you stop it?"

"No. What is this? What is this?"

He moved the mouse to the words *put away*, and the disk Vanga had inserted popped out. Tayumvat reached for it.

"Don't touch it," said Karpo.

The old man's hand stopped inches from the protruding disk.

"It's not a booby trap," Tayumvat said.

"But it may have fingerprints," said Karpo.

Vanga had not really considered that.

Ivan Laminski drove the tan Mustang down the bumpy dirt road in the direction he had been given by the shopkeeper Podgorny. Next to Ivan sat the younger Moscow detective. Ivan wanted to talk, but it was clear that the man next to him did not. There was nothing on the radio. They were too far from any station to be able to pick one up on the Mustang's radio.

In the back, the one-legged older Moscow detective sat looking out the window at the fields that extended back into forever.

"In the field is standing a birch tree," Rostnikov said. "You know that song? The birch tree song?"

"No," said Iosef.

"I think that's it," said Ivan, pointing to a house in a field in front of them and to the right.

Neither detective responded. Porfiry Petrovich was thinking of birch trees. Iosef was wondering what they were searching for and why.

Ivan found a smaller road to the right that seemed to head toward the house. He took it and drove slowly. When they pulled up next to the one-story wooden house, five people were standing in wait.

"Podgorny called to tell us you were coming," said Boris Vladovka as Iosef and Porfiry Petrovich got out of the car.

"You are friends," said Rostnikov. "I assumed he would do so if you had a telephone."

"There are only two telephones in our town. Podgorny has one. We have one. If people wish to call outside, they know they are welcome at either of our houses."

Rostnikov smiled at Boris Vladovka and his wife. A handsome dark woman, whose face showed the hard life she had lived, stood to the right, her hand clasping that of a small girl, no more than three, blond hair, clear skin. All were dressed cleanly but ready for a day's work.

"Your son?" asked Rostnikov.

"Konstantin is there," Boris said, pointing to a tractor in the distance. "We have work to do, but I understand you want to see a farm. We are happy to show you ours."

Ivan, the driver, got out of the car, said hello to the Vladovka family, and declined an invitation to see the farm. He had seen many farms. He had no need of another.

Iosef and Porfiry Petrovich followed the family into the house and politely moved into the large living room, which held surreal-looking paintings.

"Tsimion's work," explained Boris. "I don't understand what it means. Tsimion always said that it didn't have to be put into words, explanations. The paintings, his poems, were just there to be felt. What was it he said?"

"True meaning comes from feeling, not from words," Boris's wife said, looking at one small painting that suggested to Rostnikov a sky on fire.

The room was spare but comfortable, the furniture basic and wood with one old, patterned and upholstered sofa. There was a large radio on a table near the window but no television. Television stations were too far away.

They moved through the rooms and Boris explained that they had originally built two bedrooms. A third had been added. Everything was on one floor, so adding rooms was not a problem. Boris and his wife had one bedroom, which was small and neat with a free-standing wooden closet in one corner, the bed, covered by a colorful quilt, next to the window, and what Boris described as his wife's pride, a dresser with a mirror on top. The dresser was dark wood and elaborate, covered with carved flowers and leaves.

"It is an antique," Boris said. "Two, three hundred years old."

"Tsimion loved it," his wife said. "He liked to run his fingers over the flowers."

The room of Konstantin and his wife was the same size as the first bedroom. This room was furnished with a bed, closet, and a rocking chair. A trunk stood in the corner. It was open and filled with toys. On the walls were scribble drawings of a small child. The dresser was plain and large with six drawers. A small bookcase stood next to the dresser. It was filled with children's books.

The final bedroom was a duplicate of the other two except this had only a single-size bed. A desk stood at the window with a wooden chair before it. A dresser, almost a duplicate of the one in the last bedroom, stood in the corner. A large simple bookcase filled with books and magazines took up most of one wall.

"This was Tsimion's room," said Boris. "It was here if he ever wanted to return. Now it belongs to my granddaughter, Petya, my little one."

He reached down to touch the head of the little blond girl who was clinging to his leg.

"Now," Boris said, gently prying his granddaughter loose and guiding her toward his wife, "the barn and some of the fields. The tour, I'm afraid, is short because there really is not much to see."

"We can forgo the barn," said Rostnikov, "and I would like to look at the fields myself. I want to know what it feels like to be alone in such a vast sea of green and yellow."

"It feels . . . comforting," said Boris solemnly. "And when there is a breeze, the vines and leaves sound as if they are talking a soft, foreign tongue."

"I see where your son got his sense of poetry," said Rostnikov.

"No," said Boris. "He listened to his own silence in the darkness of the skies."

Outside the house in which they left the family, Iosef said, "You want to go for a walk in a potato field?"

"I must," Rostnikov said, looking around. "Wait here. I won't be long."

"I thought we were here to get some answers," said Iosef, following his father's gaze.

"We are," said Rostnikov. "Go back inside. Ask about farming. Tell them of your life and mine, of your engagement to Elena. Talk to them of dead czars and dark, silent skies."

"Now you are trying to be a poet."

"It's an infection," said Rostnikov. "Highly communicable."

With that, Porfiry Petrovich set off into the field.

The rows were even, but navigating them with one healthy and one independent leg was difficult. After a hundred yards, Rostnikov knew that what Boris had told him of the fields was true. There was a rustling calm. But growing potatoes was certainly not always romantic. In fact, Rostnikov was sure, such idyllic moments were probably reserved for visitors who did not have to work the fields, or men like Boris Vladovka who held on to their dreams and passed them on to their children and grandchildren.

It took Porfiry Petrovich twelve minutes to catch up to the tractor. The bearded driver saw him coming, turned off the engine, and waited as Rostnikov approached.

"Vladovka, when we have finished talking I would be very grateful for a ride back to the car."

Rostnikov looked up at the man and shielded his eyes from the sun.

"You have a question for me?"

"Yes, several. First, I would like to know what it feels like to be weightless and alone in the darkness of outer space."

"How would I know?" he said with a shrug, wiping his forehead with his sleeve.

"Because," said Rostnikov, "you are not Konstantin Vladovka. He is dead and buried. You are his brother, Tsimion."

Chapter Twelve

★ ★ ★ ★ ★ ★ ★ ★ ★ ★ ★ ★ ★

Valery Grachev had not arrived at work today. And, Sasha and Elena quickly discovered, he was not at home. No one was at home. They had gotten the landlady to open the door to the apartment where Valery lived with his uncle. They found no film negative, but they did find books on chess, eight of them.

"You are sure this is the man?" Elena asked as they stood outside the door of the apartment.

"I don't have to be sure," said Sasha. "We find him, bring him in, and let the beggar woman identify him. The man in the drawing is one of the assistant editors who works for Yuri Kriskov. I saw him when I posed as the French producer."

The only question for Sasha now was whether they would find Grachev before he decided to destroy the negative.

At this point, they did not know that they were already too late to stop him from destroying Yuri Kriskov. When they left the apartment, Grachev was already setting himself up to fire his first shot.

They had arrived in a motor-pool Lada with bad brakes. Elena, who was by far the better driver of the two, had picked up the vehicle and now was driving it to the house of Yuri Kriskov. They were no more than half a mile from their destination when the first shot was fired.

Elena stepped on the gas as more shots were fired. Sasha opened his window and saw a glint in the window of a house two streets away from the Kriskovs. It could have been a . . . another shot. The object in the window caught the early-morning sun again and jerked upward.

"Let me out here, now," said Sasha. "You go to the house."

Elena hit the faulty brakes and the car skidded to the side of the street, almost turning back in the direction from which they had come. Sasha was out of the car before it had quite stopped. He kicked the door closed behind him and took his gun from the holster inside his unzipped jacket as he moved.

He crouched low as Elena stepped on the gas behind him and headed for the Kriskov house. There were more shots now, and he was sure they were coming from that window.

Sasha got behind the house and made his way through a waist-high growth of wild bushes. His left hand was scratched by something sharp and he thought he might be bleeding but he didn't look. His eyes were fixed on the back of the house and the motor scooter parked next to the rear door.

As he stepped into the clearing, gun in two hands, knees slightly bent, the back door of the house suddenly opened. They saw each other at the same moment and hesitated. Sasha fired first. Valery Grachev fired next. Grachev's weapon was far more powerful and had great range and accuracy, but Sasha was a policeman who had been shot at before and who had shot at others.

Sasha's bullet went into Valery Grachev's left shoulder. Grachev's entered the ground in front of Sasha, who dropped to his stomach and rolled to his left. When he had rolled back to his right and leveled his weapon, he saw Grachev on the motor scooter, rifle in his hand. Sasha fired again. The bullet hit the front fender of the scooter just in front of Valery. The bullet made a strange *ziiiinging* sound as Valery started the bike with a kick of his foot and a twist of his hand.

Sasha got to his feet and ran toward the now-moving scooter.

He stopped, aimed, and fired again as Grachev started to speed away. This shot hit nothing and Grachev was gone. Sasha was certain he had hit Grachev with his first shot. He ran to the door and examined the ground quickly. Blood, yes, blood.

Sasha put his weapon back in the holster, moved quickly around the house, and headed for Kriskov's. As he crossed the small street and ran around another house, he saw two men in front of him, two men in uniforms, both with weapons, both aiming at the panting Sasha.

"Police," Sasha tried to shout, holding his hands in the air.

"What do we do?" one of the men asked the other.

"Shoot him," said the second.

"But if he is the police?"

"Shit," said the second. "He shot at us first. He's our man. He was rushing to finish the job. Shoot."

The first security guard was leveling his Kalishnikov rifle at Sasha, who knew what he would have to do. He would leap to one side, try to pull out his gun, and attempt to fire at the two men as he hit the ground. He knew he would fail. They were only thirty feet ahead of him. They didn't even have to be good shots.

"Stop. Now. Or you both die," came a calm voice.

Sasha looked beyond the two men at Elena, who held her weapon level, pointed at the backs of the two security guards.

The two guards stood, still aiming at Sasha.

"Drop your weapons or die," said Elena. "I am the police. He is the police. Drop them."

The two men didn't move. They exchanged glances that told Sasha they didn't intend to drop their weapons. The question was which one would kill Sasha and which would turn and fire blindly in the direction of Elena's voice.

Before they could make their move, Elena fired. Her bullet struck the wooden wall of the nearby house no more than a foot from one of the two guards.

Both men dropped their weapons.

"A man we were guarding has been shot," said one of the men. "We thought you were the shooter."

Sasha advanced on the two men, weapon now in his hand. Elena moved forward from behind.

"He got away," said Sasha. "That is all you need to know."

"Kriskov's dead," Elena said as Sasha picked up the automatic weapons and awkwardly cradled them in his arms while still holding his own pistol.

One of the security guards shook his head.

When they were in front of the Kriskov house, Sasha dropped the guns. The two security guards turned around to pick them up. Another security guard came running out of the house, weapon ready. He recognized Elena, who had been there only minutes before, and lowered his gun.

"I hit him, Elena," Sasha said. "He is hurt, bleeding. He's on a motor scooter, carrying a rifle. I'll call it in. He should be very easy to spot."

"Are you all right, Sasha Tkach?" Elena asked as they moved through the front door.

Sasha had to think about it for a moment. He had almost been killed, twice or more in the last few minutes, and yet he felt calm. He looked at his hands. They were shaking.

"No, I am not all right."

Sasha went to the phone, and Elena spoke briefly to one of the security guards. Then she moved to Vera Kriskov, who was seated on the white sofa, hugging herself and rocking forward and back. She was covered with blood, her face, hands, dress, hair. The white sofa was dabbed with red. Her head was down and she was sobbing.

"He's dead," she said, looking up at Elena.

Elena could not tell if the woman was acting or was sincere. She seemed sincere. The tears and terror seemed real.

"Where is he?" Elena asked gently.

"Where? Upstairs. In the bedroom," Vera said.

"No, not your husband. The man who shot him, Valery Grachev."

Vera Kriskov stopped rocking and looked up at Elena. "Where is he?"

Vera Kriskov's eyes showed panic. She was thinking, thinking quickly. No matter what she said, Elena was now certain of the woman's guilt.

"I don't know any Valery Grostov," she said. "What are you talking about?"

She was good, but Elena was now certain that she was watching a combination of shock, grief, and performance.

"Grachev. My partner shot him," Elena said. "He will be caught soon. But he might hurt more people. He might destroy the negatives."

"I don't care about negatives," shouted Vera. "My husband is dead. Find the man who killed him. Shoot him down like a rabid rat in the street."

The two security guards in the room and Sasha at the phone looked over at the shouting woman.

Vera looked at the head security guard, the one who had rushed into the bedroom. "You hear me," Vera shouted, standing, her hair tumbling across her face. "I'll pay ten thousand new rubles to the person who kills the man who murdered my husband. Twenty thousand."

Elena folded her arms and waited as Vera looked at Sasha and the two security officers. Then the two women faced each other.

"If we find the negatives," Elena said softly. "If Grachev kills no one else, I will ask my superior to do what he can for you. But first you must tell me where Grachev is."

"I don't know any Grachev," Vera said.

Sasha was standing next to Elena now. He heard the widow's words and paused till he was sure there was an impasse.

"The roads are being watched," he said. "A helicopter is circling the Outer Ring and another is following the road from here back to the center of the city. A wounded man on a motor scooter carrying a rifle will be easy to spot."

"My husband is dead," Vera moaned, her eyes now meeting Sasha's, searching for sympathy. "How do I tell the children? My two precious children."

"My wife has left me," he answered. "With my two children."

Elena looked at him. It was definitely not the thing to say in the situation. Sasha's eyes were moist. His hair had fallen over his forehead.

"I'm sorry," said Vera, reaching out to touch Sasha's arm. "There is so much I'm sorry for."

"And," said Elena, "if we don't find Grachev soon, there may be much more for you to be sorry for."

As soon as he had been sure that there was no one directly behind, following him, Valery had pulled off the Outer Ring onto Tverska, down Tverska a mile, and into a stand of trees to his right. He had hidden the motor scooter, buried the rifle with leaves and dirt, and headed toward the complex of tall gray apartment buildings a few hundred yards on the other side of the trees.

The wound was bleeding and his shoulder throbbing. He took off his thin jacket and pressed it against his left shoulder. Was the bullet still in there? Was he bleeding to death? Valery did not know. He moved on, searching for something, someone. The game should have been over. He had killed the king but he had then been shot by a pawn. The queen was back in that house. She was waiting for him to claim her. Valery was sweating, feverish. From the wound? From whatever illness had entered him the day before? From both? He had been feverish before he had broken into that house when the people who lived there had driven away just after dawn. He had been feverish looking out the window, waiting for Kriskov to step out or appear at the window.

The security guards didn't bother him. He would be gone before they had time to react. He had planned this well. Move by move. But somehow that young one, probably about Valery's age, had been there almost immediately, outside the rear door, shooting at him. It made no sense. The policeman's appearance had been a move he had not anticipated by whatever fate was playing against him, a fate that told him the game was not over even though the king was dead.

There were children playing outside the nearest tall building. These were not the homes of the wealthy but of those who worked and those who did not or could not. Laundry hung on lines from many of the windows, hung from one window to the next. He moved toward the children and saw a group of women, one with a baby carriage in front of her, sitting on a bench and talking. On another bench an old man sat, eyes closed, a workman's cap on his head, an unlit pipe in his mouth. He appeared to be dozing.

The woman didn't pay much attention to Valery, who had slung his jacket over his shoulder to hide the wound and forced his legs to move normally. He approached the old man on the bench and sat next to him, biting back the pain and fever.

For the women across the concrete square where small boys had moved to kick a sickly-looking soccer ball, Valery smiled as he spoke to the old man, trying to give the impression that they knew each other.

The old man, startled, opened his eyes and looked at Valery.

"I need something from you," Valery said, still smiling, putting his arm around the old man. "I'll pay."

"I have nothing," the old man said, looking at Valery as if he were mad, which, Valery admitted to himself, he might at this point be. "I have only a corner in my son's apartment and this bench when the weather permits and no one comes to sit next to me."

"One hundred and fifty new rubles," Valery said. "You bring

me a shirt, two shirts, and tell me how I get back to the city, and I give you one hundred and fifty new rubles."

"You killed someone," the old man said.

"What?"

"If you didn't kill someone, why are you offering me all that money for two shirts?"

"I killed no one," Valery said with a laugh. "I'm playing a game. Like a game of chess with some friends of mine. They are trying to find me."

"I worked on the railroad," said the old man, spitting on a crack in the concrete in front of him and looking up to watch the soccer game before him. "You are lying. But I need two hundred rubles."

"I said . . . yes, two hundred rubles, when you get back with the shirts and tell me where I can catch a bus or find a metro station or a train."

The old man nodded and said, "Wait."

"*Skahryehyeh,* 'be quick,' " said Valery.

The old man rose and walked toward the nearest apartment building.

Valery did his best to look like a man who had nothing to do but smile, spread his arms along the back of the bench, and watch the children play. He wiped his brow. It was drenched and hot. He would use one shirt to cover the wound as best he could and the other to wear over . . . The man who had shot him.

He knew the man who had shot him. It was the one Yuri Kriskov had brought to the editing room, the French producer. It made no sense. Why had a French producer been behind that building with a gun? Because he was not a French producer. He was the police. If he was the police, he knew that Valery had shot Yuri Kriskov and he would then know that Valery had the negative.

Valery could not go home.

Valery could not go anywhere.

But there had to be a move. Bargain with the negative? Vera, could she help? No, she would be surrounded by the police. He would have to protect her. He was her protector, Kon. They were attacking. He was, yes, now he was the king.

A helicopter spun overhead against the sun. Valery and the women and some of the children looked up, shading their eyes, and watched it follow the road beyond the trees.

Were they looking for him? Probably.

Valery closed his eyes. When he opened them, the old man had returned with two shirts. The women beyond the soccer game looked at the two men and wondered about the shirts. Was this a relative? It really didn't matter.

The old man handed him the shirts and sat exactly where he had before.

The shirts were old, frayed, both a faded blue. They looked as if they might fit, but Valery wouldn't know until he tried them on. No matter. They would have to do. Hiding the pain as best he could, Valery took out his wallet and found two hundred rubles. That left him with very little.

The old man reached for the bills. Valery held them tight and pulled them back. The women looked at the odd exchange taking place and wondered again.

"Transport," said Valery as the soccer ball sailed over their heads and small boys ran to retrieve it.

"On the other side of the buildings," the old man said, pointing at the buildings. "A bus stop. One will be there in . . ."

The old man took out a pocket watch.

". . . in sixteen minutes, if it is on time. You know I used to work on the railroad."

He reached for the money again and Valery let him take it.

"Do you play chess?" asked Valery.

"Everyone plays chess," the old man replied, pocketing the money and digging his pipe out of his pocket.

"What do you do if you are trapped? You have no place to

go. All you can do is buy a little time but you are bound to lose." Valery rose and looked down at the old man, who cupped a hand over the brim of his cap to block the sun as he looked up at Valery.

"What do I do? I attack. Suicidal, my son and grandson call it. Grandfather is suicidal again. Grandfather doesn't know when to quit. I attack, do something bold, take out an attacker even if it means ending the game five moves earlier than is essential. I do not concede. I do not tip over my king. You know why? Because I used to work on the railroad."

Valery nodded.

"Tell no one of me," said Valery. "They might take the money from you."

"I'll tell no one. My son could have worked on the railroad. Instead, he sells fish at the market. At least he has work."

Valery made a show of shaking the old man's hand and patting him on the shoulder.

The old man was a bit mad perhaps, but, Valery decided as he walked, so am I. And his advice had been good. There would be no concession. If he were to lose the game, it would be with panache. It would be with a flurry of ribbons and a shout over Moscow.

Tsimion Vladovka did not protest, did not grow angry, did not laugh and say that the block of a policeman who stood before him was insane or mistaken. Instead he wiped his hands on his pants and said, "What now?"

"We talk."

"Here?" asked Tsimion, looking around.

"Yes, I like it here," said Rostnikov.

"So do I, and we can see anyone approaching for more than two hundred yards in any direction. We are alone."

"What happened to your brother?"

"Konstantin had been sick for more than a year," the man said, looking toward the farmhouse. "Liver cancer. I sent money so he could go to St. Petersburg for treatment. He went a few times. My father called, told me Konstantin was dying. I knew sooner or later they would decide to kill me, so I came here, I came home. I didn't plan to stay, take my brother's life. It was my father's idea."

"A good one," said Rostnikov, "but it had problems. You and your brother look similar. The beard helps, but the photograph of you that was given to me shows a white mark on the back of your hand. A scar?"

Tsimion looked at his hand. "Yes."

"I must tell you that the man who calls himself Primazon may have noticed, as I did," said Rostnikov.

"Then I will have to run," said Tsimion, with a small sigh and a grunt.

"Not necessarily," said Rostnikov. "Tell me the secret of that space flight. I will tell my director. He will talk to the proper people, protect you, let you stay here."

"Why would he do that?" asked Tsimion.

"Because if he knows what happened, my director will be able to use it. Of course he will want you alive to confirm it. He will confront those who mean to kill you and keep them away. He will do it because my director is ambitious."

"And ambition is a grievous fault," said Vladovka in English.

"And grievously will he pay for it," Rostnikov replied in English. And then in Russian said, "but not for a long time, I hope. What happened? Who wants to kill you? Why?"

"It is really very simple," said Vladovka. "We had a biologist on the flight. Baklunov. He did not react well to life on the space station. He began to talk to himself, behave strangely. We, Kinotskin and I, reported his behavior on the computer safe line. We had no response. Then, one day, Kinotskin came to me while I was in the control pod. Baklunov had gone mad. He was breaking things. He had attacked Kinotskin with a metal bar. Do you know what it is like to have a nightmare come true?"

"Yes."

"I mean almost literally true."

"Yes," said Rostnikov.

"I followed Kinotskin through the tunnel into the living area. The chamber was alive with floating debris and hundreds of white worms, fat white worms from Baklunov's experiments. My nightmare, my precise nightmare, had come true. If I hadn't had the nightmares, I would have been able to better handle what happened next. We heard the noise in the pod where the air is supplied. The noise of metal against metal and the shouting of Baklunov. We made our way through food, metal, debris, fecal matter, the worms. I have nightmares of that more than what happened next."

"And that was?" Rostnikov prompted, looking toward the road beyond the farmhouse where a vehicle was moving quickly, sending up dust.

Vladovka's eyes followed Rostnikov's. He paused, and then continued his story. "When we entered the chamber, Baklunov attacked with the metal bar. He hit my hand. Blood splattered. Droplets floated. That is the reason for the scar."

Tsimion Vladovka paused again and continued, "We killed him. Kinotskin took the bar. I grabbed Baklunov from behind. He was ranting, spitting. I was angry. I had him around the neck. I choked him. He struggled. Kinotskin had the bar now. He began hitting Baklunov in the ribs, in the face. I kept choking, thinking that I would have to go back through those fat floating worms because of this madman. The blood didn't bother me. I know blood. It is life. It is not something to fear. It is something to regret losing. You understand?"

"I understand," said Rostnikov.

The vehicle, whatever and whoever it was, was now driving up to the Vladovka farmhouse.

"I'm not sure which of us killed him," Tsimion continued. "It doesn't matter. We both murdered him. The first murder in outer space, followed by the first burial in space. We sent him into eternity to cover our crime. For you see, we did not have to kill him. But we did. I have considered it many times. We could have subdued him, but we were in a chamber of madness, in a state of instant delirium. We didn't check with ground control. We simply put the body in a chamber and released it into space. We didn't watch. We spent hours cleaning up after we disposed of the body. Horrible hours. Nightmare hours. No one has experienced what we have. May no one have to again."

A man was now running through the field toward them.

"We were told to say nothing," Tsimion continued. "We were told that we would be brought back to earth immediately, that those who were coming for us would know what had happened. We were told that we were to act as if there had been a minor problem on the station and that all three of us were coming down. We had solved the problem. We were space heroes. The three of us were coming down. We were told that our space program did not have enough money. Our national pride was at stake during difficult political times, but when are there not difficult political times? We came down. We were silent. Kinotskin took it harder than I did. His career, his ambition, were gone. He grew gaunt and became a hollow man. And they thought about it, thought, as I knew they someday would, that we might decide to tell what happened, tell of the cover-up. They decided to kill us all. Those who came to bring us back to earth, and both of us."

"Why did you want me to be told of what happened on that flight? Why did you call my name?"

Tsimion Vladovka shook his head. "I made a mistake."

"A mistake?" asked Porfiry Petrovich.

"I was in a panic. I had heard your name in relation to some political situation a few years ago, but I really wanted to call out the name of my friend Peotor Rosnishkov. In my panic . . ."

". . . you called out my name."

Tsimion Vladovka shrugged. Rostnikov smiled.

"You have a weapon?" Tsimion was looking at the man running toward them.

"No," said Rostnikov. "You?"

"No."

A moment later it was clear to Vladovka as it had been minutes ago to Rostnikov that a weapon would not be necessary, at least not at that moment. The man running toward them was Iosef. When he was a dozen paces in front of them, he stopped, breathing hard.

"The man who called himself Primazon," Iosef said. "He came into the house. He asked where Konstantin was. Boris spoke to him. I couldn't hear, then Boris killed him. Before I could act, he had reached up and snapped his neck."

Tsimion Vladovka started toward the house. Rostnikov stopped him, gripping the bearded man with a solid grasp of his arm. Vladovka tried to pull away, grabbed Rostnikov's wrist and tried to free himself. He could not.

"We must think," said Rostnikov. "Pause and think. You understand?"

Tsimion stopped struggling and Rostnikov released his grip before saying, "The driver, Laminski, did he see? Where was he?"

"He was outside, at the car. When I came out of the house and started running to tell you, he asked me what was happening. I told him to get inside the car and wait. I ordered him to get inside the car. He did."

"Who else was there, in the house, when this happened?"

"We three were the only ones in the room," said Iosef.

The three men stood for a few seconds and then Rostnikov said, "We will walk back to the house very calmly. The three of us. And on the way, we will make a plan, a very good one. I don't know what it will be at the moment, but it will have to be a very good one."

"Wait," said Andrei Vanga, trying his best to think quickly. "My fingerprints are on that disk."

Both Karpo and the old man, Tikon Tayumvat, looked at the director of the Center for the Study of Technical Parapsychology. The director looked very, very nervous.

"I can explain," said Vanga.

"Then do so," said Karpo, holding the disk carefully by the edges.

"I will," said Vanga.

"Man can't think on his feet," Tayumvat said with derision. "No wonder it takes him so long to write a simple second-rate article."

"I promised Bolskanov that I would not allow anyone to see his private journals," said Vanga. "We had been working together for a long time, and from time to time he confided in me as I confided in him. You see?"

"I see nothing," said the old man. "Is this going to take long? I'll sit down if it's more than five minutes. Ah, I see. You have no idea how long you are going on. I'll sit at the desk and watch and listen."

"Yes, yes," Vanga went on, holding the fist of his left hand in the palm of his right. "His private diary is on the computer. It is very personal. He—he didn't want it to be made public if he were to die. I promised that it would never happen, and in return he promised me the same."

Karpo said nothing, simply stood at attention, disk in hand, watching and listening.

"I keep my promises," said Vanga.

"And what was in that diary that was so terrible?" said Tayumvat.

"I cannot tell you. You can take my job, put me in prison even, but I am sworn to secrecy."

"There may well have been something in his diary or in another file that would help us find his murderer. You have willfully destroyed potential evidence," said Karpo.

Vanga smiled ruefully. "I didn't think of it that way. I just thought of what I had promised my friend."

"You are under arrest, Dr. Andrei Vanga," said Karpo. "For possible concealment of knowledge regarding a murder, and for suspicion of murder."

"Why? Are you joking? Why would I kill my friend, my colleague?"

Karpo handed the disk to Tayumvat, who took it carefully by the edges, and then Karpo stepped toward Vanga, who backed away.

"Wait, wait," said Vanga. "What if I were to tell you what secrets he had in his diary, why he didn't want it seen? What if I did that?"

Karpo paused, and Tayumvat looked up with a smile that showed he anticipated another lie.

"Bolskanov was a homosexual," said Vanga.

"That's it?" said Tayumvat. "You can do no better than 'Bolskanov was a homosexual'?"

"And . . ." Vanga said, his voice breaking, "and he had committed crimes when he was young, terrible crimes, crimes of which he was very much ashamed. He stole other people's work, passed it on as his own."

"A terrible crime," Tayumvat said with a shake of his head. "Come, Vanga, this has turned into the most interesting human contact I have had in half a century. Don't disappoint me. Don't disappoint Inspector Karpo. Tell us more terrible crimes."

"What and . . . oh . . . yes, let me . . . he murdered someone, many years ago, in . . . in Lithuania, Kaunas. And in another country."

"Much better," said Tayumvat.

"Why?" asked Karpo.

"Why what?" said Vanga.

"Why did he kill these other people?"

"I don't know. He didn't tell me."

"In any case, you are guilty of concealing a murder, possibly several murders," said Karpo.

"But that was in another country," said Vanga. "Lithuania is no longer part of greater Russia, which may be good or bad, depending on your politics. But that is another country now and I do not know who he murdered. I think it was a cab driver. No, a—yes, it was a cab driver."

Vanga looked at Karpo, whose face revealed nothing, and then at Tayumvat, whose face revealed everything in its myriad lines and shadows.

"You don't believe me," Vanga said. "You think I am lying."

"You are under arrest," said Karpo.

"I stand by what I have told you," said Vanga indignantly. "I stand by the memory of my best friend and his wishes."

"But you told us his secrets," said Tayumvat. "In a bizarre attempt to save yourself, you told us what you had supposedly sworn to destroy. I wash my hands of you. Consistency is essential if one is to propose a scientific theory, especially one who works with the paranormal. You can't even create a decent lie. I will but guess why you killed Bolskanov. It was you who stole something from him, an article, speech. He caught you. You killed him."

"I don't need to steal someone else's ideas and work," Vanga said.

"Yes, you do," said Tayumvat. "You can't come up with an original thought of your own."

"I will get a good attorney," said Vanga. "I will see to it that

you, Inspector Karpo, are dismissed from service. I will demand
an apology from the highest levels."

"Karpo," said Tikon Tayumvat, "at my age I don't wish to hear
rehashed speeches from old television shows. Please, the scene is
over. Take me home and take him away."

And that is just what Emil Karpo did.

Chapter Thirteen

★ ★ ★ ★ ★ ★ ★ ★ ★ ★ ★ ★ ★

We will walk back rather slowly," said Rostnikov to his son
and Tsimion Vladovka. "For two reasons. First, I am
incapable of moving quickly, and, second, I do not want our
driver, Laminski, to think that anything is wrong. I am sure he
would prefer that nothing be wrong. Iosef, engage him. Tell Ivan
Laminski of your exploits in the theater or in Afghanistan or
with women. Smile, listen to him, and reassure him that everything is fine and that we will soon be going to St. Petersburg."

Iosef nodded as they moved forward through the field. Rostnikov turned his head to Tsimion and said, "And you will come
with me. We will talk calmly of farming. I will ask a question.
You will answer. And we will improvise if your father comes out
of the house."

"I have grown accustomed to improvising," said Tsimion.

"I like the smell of freshly harvested potatoes," said Rostnikov as they cleared the field and neared the farmhouse. Laminski stood waiting. He adjusted his blue uniform as they
approached. He said nothing, but there was certainly a look of
curiosity in his less-than-brilliant eyes. Iosef moved toward the
somewhat bewildered driver.

"What? . . ." Laminski began.

"I'll explain," said Iosef. "I made a mistake. There was no rea-

son for me to go running after Inspector Rostnikov. He had forgotten to take some medication and I wanted to be sure he got
it quickly."

"Are there parts of Russia where potatoes grow better?" asked
Porfiry Petrovich, loud enough for the driver to hear them.

"Different, not better necessarily," said Tsimion. "There are
different kinds of potato. In this region . . ."

And they were inside the door. Tsimion closed it behind them.
They found Boris in the kitchen, alone with the corpse. Boris
was sitting at the table, looking down at the body of the man
who had called himself Primazon. The dead man was sprawled
awkwardly, one leg straight, the other bent backwards in an L.
He was on his back. His head was turned toward the nearest wall
and he was looking upward at a spot where there was nothing
to see. His umbrella lay a foot or so away.

Boris looked up at his son and the detective.

"He said he wanted to talk to Konstantin," Boris said, looking at Rostnikov. "I could see in his eyes that he knew, just as I
saw in your eyes that you knew. It was the way he said it. I was
certain."

Rostnikov sat in a chair and motioned to Tsimion to do the
same.

"Where are the women, the child?" asked Rostnikov.

"Where? I don't know. I think they are in my bedroom."

"Did they see? . . ." asked Rostnikov.

"I don't know. I don't think so," said Boris.

"My son says they did not."

"Good," said Boris.

"I think it would be a good idea for your son to go to them,
comfort them, explain that our friend on the floor was here for
bad reasons, but that everything will now be fine."

Tsimion rose, nodded in understanding, and put his hand on
his father's shoulder. Boris put his hand on top of his son's. And
then Tsimion moved toward the bedrooms.

"Money is tight for our government security services," said Rostnikov. "That umbrella has an ejection button. By pressing it . . . it is on the handle . . . by pressing the button, a very thin needle with a very lethal dose of poison pops out. Death is swift and looks like a stroke or a heart attack to all but the best pathologists. It is an effective but rather old means of murder. The Bulgarians used it a great deal. Too much. There are far better ways, but they cost more. And I think our dead Primazon preferred this method. Are you following me, Boris Vladovka?"

"Yes," he answered, staring at the dead man. "I've never killed before."

"I, on six occasions, have killed," said Rostnikov. "It was, I believe, necessary in all six of those instances. At least it is what I have told myself. Four of those killed were Nazis during the war."

"You are too young to have been a soldier," Boris said.

"I was a boy soldier. There were many of us, some barely ten, some even younger. My leg was injured during the war."

"You said four Nazis. The other two, the ones you killed?"

"I am a policeman. It happens. I am not proud of what I did, but it was necessary, and like you, Vladovka, I killed one of them with my hands. I believed I had to kill to protect myself and a very small child."

Boris nodded and said, "And I must kill again. Yes, I must kill you and your son and Laminski and continue to kill every time someone comes to take my son or kill him."

"I too have but one son, Boris," said Rostnikov with a sigh. "I am afraid I would have to stop you. Besides, I think there is a better way. Killing us would certainly bring many more policemen here."

"I see no other way," said Boris.

"All right, let's begin with your killing me. If you fail, we will talk about other, more sensible, ways of handling this situation."

Boris rose from his chair, as did Porfiry Petrovich.

"You want me to kill you?"

"You have to start with someone. Come."

Boris looked a bit dazed as he moved toward the policeman. Yes, he thought, if I am to protect Tsimion, I must start somewhere.

Vladovka was larger across and certainly taller than Rostnikov, and he had the power of a farmer who had labored all of his life. He reached out for the thick neck of the policeman. Rostnikov grabbed the farmer's wrists. Boris Vladovka struggled to free himself as his son had only minutes before in the potato field. Boris pushed forward. Both men tripped over the corpse and fell to the floor. Still, Rostnikov held fast. They rolled away from the dead man over the umbrella and into the wall.

Their faces were inches apart. Rostnikov could smell coffee and the bile of fear on the other man's breath.

"Now we try my way," Rostnikov said gently as he held the larger man by his shoulders.

"We try your way," Boris agreed.

"When we get up, rise carefully," said Rostnikov. "Our dead friend pressed his umbrella button before he died. I think he meant to use it on you when he realized that you were going to kill him."

Rostnikov let the bigger man free, and Boris moved to his knees.

"Then I would have been the one to die," the farmer said with resignation.

"If he had used his weapon," said Rostnikov, trying to sit up, "you would have been dead almost instantly. I would appreciate it if you would help me up. It is difficult . . ."

"You, oh, of course, I'm sorry."

Boris stood and held out a hand. Rostnikov took it and with the farmer's help got to his feet.

"You are very strong," said Boris, stepping over the dead man and returning to his chair. "Would you like coffee?"

"Coffee," said Rostnikov, moving back to his chair.

Boris nodded and moved to the stove. He touched the coffeepot.

"It is still very warm, but not hot . . . Shall I? . . ."

"No, warm will be fine."

"Sugar? Milk?"

"Sugar, not too much. If your coffee is strong or bitter, a little milk would be nice."

Boris nodded, filled a brown mug, dropped in a sugar cube,
and went to the refrigerator for the milk.

While he finished preparing the mug of coffee, Rostnikov
leaned over, picked up the umbrella, found the button, pressed
it, and watched the very thin needle slide noiselessly back into
its slot.

Boris brought two mugs to the table, handed one to Rostnikov and took the other.

"What," asked Rostnikov, after taking a drink of the very strong
and not very good coffee, "if our friend here were to be found
tonight on a very dark street of a very bad neighborhood in St.
Petersburg, beaten to death, neck broken, arm broken, many
bruises, perhaps a broken rib, his money taken, his shoes taken,
his watch taken, his umbrella taken, his clothes and dignity taken?
What if his car were never found? The police would assume the
car had been sold to what the Americans call a 'chop shop.' Unless the pathologist who examines the body realizes that he was
dead before he was beaten, it will be assumed to be a routine
mugging and murder. It is unlikely the pathologist, if one is even
called in, will have that realization. Do you think our dead man
might meet that fate?"

"Yes," said Boris. "In my sixtieth year, I have become a murderer and will now commit further crimes by concealing that
murder like . . . like a criminal in some French movie."

"You have seen many French movies?" asked Rostnikov.

"Actually, no, and it has been many years since the last, but I
have a good memory."

"Remember then that Primazon came here to see me. I talked to him and left. Then our very-much-alive man left. In fact, he and I left at the same time. It would be best if many people saw him leaving the district."

"Many people will swear that they saw him drive away," said Boris, looking far more alive than when Rostnikov had entered the room.

"Good. Then I will finish my coffee, meet privately with your son, and go home."

"More will come, won't they?"

"I will act so that no one will follow," said Rostnikov. "I cannot guarantee it, but I believe you and your family will be left in peace."

"And why do you do this?"

"Why? I believe it is what should be done."

"But you are a policeman and I am a murderer."

"And I must wake up every morning and say to myself, Porfiry Petrovich, can you live with what you have done with your life so far? Can you live with what you did yesterday? And I wish to be able to answer yes. Now I must talk to your son. As soon as we leave, I suggest you put your dead visitor in the trunk of his car and keep him there till it is dark. I think it best if the women and the child do not see him."

"They are strong," said Boris.

"I have seen many dead people," said Rostnikov. "I would be quite content to see no more and to have never seen the first."

They stood up yet again. They shook hands, and Rostnikov went in search of Tsimion Vladovka.

Tayumvat rode with Karpo and Vanga to Petrovka. The three sat in the back of the car, Vanga in the middle. The driver whistled a nonsong, and Vanga struggled to find another, better lie. He could think of none.

"This is a mistake," he said.

"It is not," said Tayumvat.

The pale policeman looked straight ahead and said, "Before we went to Bolskanov's apartment, I asked Dr. Tayumvat to look at the files in your computer."

"You had no right . . ." Vanga said with indignation.

"I had the right and the obligation, but you may dispute that with the courts and my superiors if you wish," Karpo replied calmly. "He asked me to look at your paper on dream research. It meant nothing to me. He said he did not believe you had written it, though he could not prove it."

"That's—"

"Ah, there was one curiosity I have not yet mentioned," said the old man. "At my age, my memory. The cover page, dedication, and cover letter to a journal meant a great deal. The article itself has two spaces after each period. That is standard. The cover page, dedication, and letter are different. In each of those, and in all of your correspondence and memos, the period is followed by a single space. I would say that the text was written by one person and the cover page with your name on it was written by another, by you. I quickly examined the files of Bolskanov. They all contain documents with two spaces following the period."

"Dr. Tayumvat also says that the style of the article in question bears little resemblance to your style in other documents in your computer," said Karpo. "I believe his professional opinion will carry great weight, and I believe others who know of such things will agree with him."

"I know important people," said Vanga.

"I knew Einstein," said Tayumvat. "Met him twice. The first time he smelled of pipe tobacco and asked where he could get good food. That was in Vienna. Why he asked me, I don't know. What do I know of Vienna?"

Vanga went silent. A lawyer. Yes, he would get a lawyer. A very good lawyer. He would make calls. He would ask for favors. He

was a respected scientist, the director of a major research institute.

"It doesn't matter," said the old man, looking out the window.

"What doesn't matter?"

"That you are the director of a respected research institute,"
said the old man.

Vanga stared at the old man.

"You read my mind. I thought you didn't believe in such things."

"I didn't read your mind," said Tikon Tayumvat. "It was the
logical thing to think under the circumstances."

And the logical thing to think now, thought Andrei Vanga, is
that I wish you were dead.

"I soon will be," said the old man, still looking out the window. "But there is a very real chance that you will go first."

"Try again," Nadia Spectorski said, sitting across from Zelach
in her laboratory, a stack of photographs, facedown, in front of
her. "Or, rather, don't try, just close your eyes and tell me what
you see."

"I would prefer to keep my eyes open," he said.

"Then open. Do you see anything?"

"You. This room. No more."

She picked up a photograph and looked at it. It was a white
telephone on a black table.

"What am I looking at?"

"A photograph."

"Of what?"

"I don't know."

She adjusted her glasses and Zelach did the same. He would
not survive a battle of wits with this woman. I am, he told himself, going to become a test mouse or a monkey doing tricks.
No, Porfiry Petrovich will save me from this. He must save me.

"You are supposed to cooperate," she said evenly.

"I am," said Zelach, slouching in the chair as best he could.

"Then what is . . ."

She stopped. It was she who saw two quick, very quick, almost subliminal images. The first was of Andrei Vanga sitting next to Emil Karpo. Vanga was definitely frightened. The second was of her sitting in the office of the director, behind the desk, talking to . . . someone.

"Are you all right?" asked Zelach.

"Yes," she said.

"You saw something?"

"Yes. Did you see it?"

"No. Dr. Spectorski, I do not want to do this."

She sat back, took off her glasses, rubbed her forehead with one finger, and closed her eyes.

"Then," she said, "it will end."

When she opened her eyes, Zelach was looking at her in a way few men had done in the past.

"End?" asked Zelach.

"My—if you don't want to proceed, you should not have to do so. I think you are a good man who doesn't want to or have to be turned into a research phenomenon."

"Why have you changed your mind?"

"I don't know," she said, removing her glasses and placing them on the table. "May I ask you a question?"

"What?"

"Would you . . . I've never done anything like this before . . . would you go out for some coffee and cake with me? I will pay. If you say no, I will understand."

"I say yes," said Akardy Zelach. "And can we not talk about . . . this?" he asked, looking around the room and at the photographs.

"We will talk of other things," she said with a smile.

Zelach thought she had a most wonderful smile.

Valery Grachev existed no longer. There was only Kon. He had changed his mind after talking to the old man from whom he bought the shirts. He would only truly become a king if he were to survive to claim victory. An attack doomed to defeat had its compensations, but it did not create a king.

The bus, green and slow, made many stops. Each stop was painful. A sudden jerk and *stoy*, "stop." And it also hurt when the bus moved again. The bullet, he was sure, was still inside him. He was sure he could feel it. He could certainly imagine it, a small distortion of metal making its way through his blood, finding and jabbing into a pulsing organ.

The bus was not crowded, but it was far from empty. He had moved to the rear, covered his bleeding wound as well as he could, and gripped the top of the empty seat in front of him.

When he finally got off the bus, arms folded in front of him as if he had a chill, he staggered. Soon, he feared, fevered hallucinations would come. They would have to wait. The bus door closed and he knew the driver and the passengers on this side were looking at this young drunk as he moved down the street.

Will yourself to keep moving, he told himself. Your will can carry you through. Your will power. It can be done. You cannot quit before the game is ended.

He couldn't go home. He couldn't go to work. He did not have enough money left to buy bandages or a fresh jacket or shirt to cover his wound. And he certainly could not go to a hospital. He went the only place he could.

"You want to buy a bicycle?" the shopkeeper said.

"Yes," said Valery Grachev.

"I think you're sick," said the man, one hand on the wheel of the upside-down bicycle in front of him. "I think you have a fever and should go to the hospital."

"You want to sell a bicycle?"

"Yes, but I don't think you can drive one."

"That is the concern of Kon, not yours."

"Kon?"

"Yes, will you sell me a bicycle, now?"

The shopkeeper had a weak heart and no stomach for trouble. "How much can you afford?"

Kon shook his head and smiled.

"Price is no concern," he said. "Something simple, no gears."

The man moved down the aisle and selected a bicycle from the many lined up on both sides.

"This?" he asked, pointing to a bicycle.

"Fine, perfect. I'll take it."

"It will cost you . . ."

"I don't care. I told you, Kon doesn't care."

The shopkeeper shrugged. "You need to know so you can pay me," he said.

"I have no money with me. When I return, I'll pay you double whatever you ask."

"I don't think . . ."

"You do not have to think. Kon is thinking. I've been renting that closet from you for months. You have overcharged me. Have I ever missed a payment? Ever?"

"No, but . . ."

"I'm taking the bicycle. I have no time to argue."

"Take it. You'll pay today?"

"And for the rest of my life," said Valery Grachev.

The shopkeeper returned to his work. The man was drunk, in a fever, or crazy, or all of these, but he was surely trouble. He heard the man go to the closet, open it, make some noise. Then the man moved slowly to the bicycle, pulled it out of the line, and wheeled it past the shopkeeper. There was now a very large and clearly very heavy backpack strapped over the shoulders of the man who was now calling himself Kon.

The shopkeeper watched as the man struggled to get on the bicycle, the pack on his back heavy and awkward. Finally, he succeeded and managed to drive away down the street.

Fortunately, the bike he had given his customer was one he had been trying to get rid of for two years. It was fortunate because the shopkeeper had a feeling that he would not be seeing this young man again.

A man fitting the description of the one who had shot at Sasha and killed Yuri Kriskov had been reported to a policeman on the embankment of the Moscow River, across from the Kremlin. The policeman had been directing traffic when a man and woman approached him and said that a bleeding man was weaving back and forth on his bicycle and talking to himself. The policeman had nodded professionally, checked the traffic, and moved to the police phone station across the street to call in the report and then go back to directing traffic. The policeman thought little of the report, but he had learned that he should cover his back if he were to survive and possibly some day escape dodging maniacs in red cars. He had reported. He was done.

The report had been taken by a desk clerk who had just received a copy of the description of a Valery Grachev. Grachev, the report said, was dangerous, armed, and probably wounded. The clerk, like the policeman directing traffic, did not wish to lose his job should anything come of this coincidence, should it be but a coincidence, which was likely. The clerk had a wife, a grown daughter, and a gambling habit that required his small but steady salary. He picked up the phone and called the sighting of the wounded bicyclist in to Petrovka, suggesting that it be passed on immediately to the officers investigating the man named Grachev.

It was this that sent the helicopter allocated to the Kriskov murder down the embankment of the river where the pilot saw a man sitting on the narrow line of rocks along the water. The pilot dropped lower and reported over his radio that there was a child on one side of the man and a large cloth bag that looked like a backpack on the other. It was then that the man raised his arm and fired a shot at the helicopter.

The pilot heard the bullet hit not far from his window. He

took the helicopter up two hundred feet quickly and noisily and reported in again, trying to keep his voice calm as he told of the shot fired. The pilot was a veteran of the Afghan war. He had been shot at before, but it had been a long time ago, and now that it had happened again the knowledge of how close he had come to dying in that distant rocky wasteland rushed into his consciousness. He was afraid, but he would not show it.

"Man and boy on the embankment of the Moscow River almost directly across from the Kremlin," he said. "Man fits the description of Valery Grachev. There is a bag at his side. When I approached, he fired one shot from a handgun, hitting but, I believe, not causing serious injury to the craft. I could not determine if he might be wounded or the extent of any wounds."

"Very good," came the voice of the pilot's supervisor. "Remain in place until you see police vehicles at the scene and then return to base for a damage assessment."

The supervisor ended the transmission and the pilot allowed himself to take some serious deep breaths.

Grachev was still sitting in the same position that the pilot had reported, when Sasha Tkach and Elena Timofeyeva arrived at the embankment in the police car they had been in for the past hour and a half. By this time, other marked cars with flashing lights had converged and a pair of uniformed policemen were directing traffic away from the site, creating a lengthy traffic jam and drawing camera-armed tourists.

Sasha had said little during the ride. Elena had only repeated that she was certain that Vera Kriskov was involved in her husband's death. Sasha's mind was elsewhere. Once again he had almost died. He had imagined Maya and the children crying at his grave site. He imagined his mother shouting at Porfiry Petrovich, telling him how many times she had pleaded with him to give her only son a safe job behind a desk. The helicopter pilot and

Sasha had a great deal in common this morning: both had almost been shot by the same man.

When Elena and Sasha stepped out of the car, a uniformed policeman pointed to the concrete balustrade that ran along the river, keeping drunken motorists from plunging into the water. Elena reached the concrete barrier first and carefully looked over. Sasha moved to her side and looked down at Valery Grachev to their left. Grachev was holding a gun in his lap. The weapon was pointed at a boy of about eleven, no more than a foot or two from Grachev.

"A special-division marksman is here," the policeman said. "He says he can safely put a bullet into the man's head. It is an easy shot, the marksman says."

"If one puts a bullet into a man's head, the word *safe* cannot appropriately be applied," said Elena.

"I'm just reporting what my duty officer told me to report," the policeman said.

"And if Grachev, in the throes of death, pulls the trigger and puts a bullet into the head of that boy?" asked Elena.

"I'm just reporting what my duty officer told me to report," the policeman said.

"Tell the marksman to be ready but to do nothing unless I hold up my right arm," Elena said. "Then he is to safely put a bullet into Grachev's brain."

The policeman nodded and moved down the balustrade toward a young man, also in uniform, cradling a rifle in his arms.

"Now?" asked Elena.

"Now," said Sasha, leaning over the rough concrete to get a better look at Grachev.

Valery Grachev was talking to the boy, apparently ignoring the noise above and behind him.

"Grachev," Sasha shouted.

The gun came out of the man's lap and pressed into the stomach of the boy. Sasha looked at the boy, who seemed remarkably unafraid, perhaps even curious and excited. He was obviously not feeling the same sense of mortality as Sasha Tkach and the helicopter pilot.

"Stay away," shouted Grachev. "It will all be over soon. Stay away. I want you to watch what I am about to do, but I want you to stay away. This is the end. Kon will not simply surrender. Kon will go with defiance like Boribyonovich in the regionals. I do not wish to harm this boy, but what does it really matter if he dies today, in twenty years, in fifty years. It's all the same. All we have is the game."

"I'm coming down," said Sasha, starting to climb over to the rocks below. "I have no weapon. I won't get close."

Elena grabbed his sleeve. "What are you doing?"

"Climbing down to talk to him," he said calmly.

"That is insane," Elena said as he continued to climb. "I'm going to signal the marksman."

"No," said Sasha, one leg now over the side. "I remind you that I am the senior inspector here."

"You are the single insane inspector here," she said.

"A good match," said Sasha, now about to drop to the rocks. "A mad suspect and a mad inspector. We should have much to talk about."

With that, Sasha dropped, fell to his knees, and almost tumbled into the dark water.

"Go back. Go back. Go back," shouted Grachev.

"Very difficult," said Sasha, still on his knees, hands holding a jutting edge of rock. "I just want to talk."

"I have work to do," said Grachev. The young man was bleeding. The front of his shirt was soaked through.

"Perhaps I can help," Sasha said, moving up the rocks and sitting about a dozen feet from the other man.

"Help? You don't know what I have to do."

"I think I do," said Sasha.

"I . . ." Grachev began. "It's you. You shot me."

Sasha nodded.

"And you tried to shoot me," said Sasha. "And I think you would have had no trouble succeeding in killing me, had you a little practice with your weapon."

The boy, who had his dusty-brown hair cut short, was remarkably skinny. His face was clean and he was wearing a pair of jeans and what seemed to be a new black pullover T-shirt.

"I can kill you now," said Grachev.

Sasha shook his head. "Possibly, we are much closer now. But consider this, if you shoot me, a man with a rifle whom you cannot see will put a bullet through your brain. You stand a far better chance of missing me than he of missing you. Then you would be dead and unable to do whatever it is you plan to do."

Grachev, his face pale, seemed to smile. "And you are not afraid?"

"Oh, very much afraid," said Sasha. "Very much, but I said to myself up there that if I did not do this I would be afraid for whatever remains of my life."

"Yes," said Grachev. "Yes."

"May I ask a question?" asked Sasha.

"Yes, then I have one. I think we should be quick."

"Who is Boribyonovich?"

Grachev looked at the detective. "Don't you play chess?"

"A little, badly," Sasha said, looking across the water at the wall of the Kremlin. "My wife is the chess player."

"She is a true Russian."

"She's Ukrainian," said Sasha. "Her name is Maya. I have two children."

"You are trying to make me feel sympathy," said Grachev.

"Am I? I don't know. Maybe. I was ... I don't know," said Sasha.

Sasha continued to look across the river at the wall, at the flowing traffic, which paused as drivers looked across and saw the crowd of police vehicles and the two men and a boy on the rocks.

"I've always wanted to climb that tower," Sasha said, pointing across the river.

"The Moskvoretsky Tower," said Grachev.

"Yes. An interesting sight from this perspective. Have you ever been down on the rocks before?"

"No. I have a question. Do you love your wife?" asked Grachev.

"Is that the question you want to ask?"

"No, it just came to me. I'll ask the other soon, very soon. Now I have a third question. What's your name?"

"Sasha. And yours is Valery."

"Mine is Kon," he corrected.

"Yes, I love my wife. I love my children. My wife has taken them to Kiev, Kon."

"Why?"

"Because I have behaved like an animal, a brooding animal in the zoo. You've seen the tigers in those small cages. Pacing, pacing. They are depressed. I was told that by my chief inspector. When he told me about the tigers, I stopped taking my older daughter, Pulcharia, to see them."

"Sasha, I think I am dying. I have work to do and I don't understand what you are saying, but I do understand love. I am sitting here like this because of a woman I love. No, that is not fair, I am sitting here because of what I wanted and because I seem to be growing more and more mad as I lose blood. Also, I think I have the flu."

"I would say you are not having a good day," said Sasha.

Grachev laughed and then coughed. The boy at his side made it clear by his look that he had no idea what this madman who had kidnapped him was laughing at.

"A very bad day, but I mean to salvage something."

"That is understandable," Sasha said. "Who is the woman, the one you love?"

"No," Grachev said, shaking his head. "I am dying. I am going mad, but I am still playing and I will go down protecting my queen."

"All right, then what is the boy's name?"

"I don't know. What is your name?"

He turned his eyes to the boy, the gun touching the black T-shirt.

"B.B.," said the boy.

"Your real name," said Grachev.

"Artiom. Are you going to shoot me?"

The boy seemed more curious and excited than afraid.

"No."

"Are you going to shoot yourself?"

"You watch too many movies on television," said Grachev. "You should be playing chess."

"I don't like chess."

"Maybe I *will* shoot you."

The boy who called himself B.B. suddenly changed. He was afraid.

"I'm not going to shoot you," Grachev said. "And I'm not going to shoot Sasha here or anyone else. But that is our secret. I have killed enough for one morning. They are making a great deal of noise up there."

"A great deal," Sasha agreed, looking back over his shoulder. "I have no control over that."

"I don't mind," said Valery Grachev. "Now, my third question. You said you know what I am going to do, or you think you do. What am I going to do?"

"Take the negative out of that bag and throw it in the river," said Sasha. "The only reason you have not already done so is that you are waiting for a larger audience and the television cameras."

"You really should play chess," said Grachev.

Sasha shrugged.

"I don't think I can wait longer," said Grachev. "I think I see a television truck on the Kremlyovskaya Embankment over there across the river, and I am sure there are others and tourists with cameras. I would like your people to let the people with cameras come where they can see."

"I do not have that power, Kon," said Sasha.

"Then I will have to begin."

"Would you like some help?" asked Sasha, who was now certain that Grachev was dying. "It will be awkward for you, keeping the gun on B.B. with one hand, staying alert, reaching in for the film. It will be painful."

"I think I would prefer you to remain where you are," said Grachev. "You can watch."

With that, the young man reached into the bag and pulled out a tightly wound roll of film about one and a half feet across. Sasha could see the pain in the man's face.

"You are going to destroy Tolstoy," said Sasha.

"I am going to destroy a movie about the life of Tolstoy. I will tell you a secret, Sasha," said Grachev. "From what I have seen of it, it is a very bad, bloated, lying movie about Tolstoy. It turns him into a tragic romantic figure with a big-budget background. The world is better off without this Tolstoy."

"And without Kriskov?" asked Sasha.

"And without me," answered Grachev, unwinding the film.

"I can help," said B.B.

Grachev handed him the reel, and the boy began to unwind the film. There was a rattle and more than a murmur in the crowd behind the two men and the boy. Above the sound of voices and vehicles, Sasha could hear the crinkling of unwinding film. Soon the rocks in front of the boy and the man who now called himself Kon were covered with curls of black film. When there was still about half the film remaining in a tight circle, the circle collapsed and dropped into the boy's lap.

"Throw it in," said Grachev. "Stand up. Throw it in."

B.B. wiped his hands on his jeans and stood. "Really?" he asked.

"Throw," said Grachev.

And the boy threw.

Some people who had managed to make it to the concrete ledge began to applaud and some took pictures. The film now floated in a serpentine mass upon the water. The black bundle began to move away from the shore. Grachev reached for the second reel and handed it to the waiting boy, who eagerly took it and began to unwind.

"Sasha, would you like to cast black bread upon the water?" asked Grachev.

"No, thank you," said Sasha. "I'm content to watch."

And watch he did till there was no more film, just four dark clouds floating away on the water. The first cloud of film had begun to sink.

"Now," said Grachev, his eyes blinking away perspiration.

"Now?" asked Sasha.

"Now you come close and I tell you a secret," he said.

Sasha moved toward him carefully along the rocks, knowing that he was ruining a good pair of pants already stained by his earlier shoot-out with the man toward whom he crawled. Someone in the crowd gasped. When Sasha was a yard from the dying man, Grachev turned his weapon on the detective and said, "B.B., you may go now, clamber up the rocks, climb the wall, talk to the television people and the police. B.B., I have become the highlight of your life. You will remember me and what we have done till you die. You will tell the story many times. It will change. I don't know how. I know. I once made it to the Moscow chess semifinals when I was your age. I remember every move and the watching crowd and I have convinced myself that the game I lost was much closer than it probably really was. Go."

B.B. scampered up the rocks, slipped once, and continued.

Grachev was not watching, but Sasha was.

"Is he gone?"

"Yes," said Sasha. "You talked of a woman. Was it Vera Kriskov?"

"That is Kriskov's wife?"

"You know that it is. You love her," said Sasha.

"I have never seen her, don't know her, but I will perhaps do her a great favor when I tell you my secret. Lean close."

Sasha leaned toward the man, not worrying about being shot, though it would have been a reasonable cause of concern at that moment. Sasha could smell blood, fever, and death now.

"There is a bicycle shop off of Gorky Street. It is called Wheels. There is a closet in that shop, in the rear. Go to it. You will find my final surprise, my last move. I will be laughing. I will have protected my queen."

"What will I find in that closet?" asked Sasha.

"The original negative and the duplicate negative for the abomination of the life of Tolstoy. B.B. just threw away the negative of a movie I worked on two years ago, *The Gambler's Wife*. That was even worse than the film you will find in that closet. That is my gift to the widow."

"And from this you got? . . ."

"Look around you, Sasha. I got an audience for my final move. I got . . ."

He drew in a breath, broke off in the middle of it, stretched himself out, and died.

Chapter Fourteen

★ ★ ★ ★ ★ ★ ★ ★ ★ ★ ★ ★

Director Igor Yaklovev was sitting at the end of the conference table in his office when Rostnikov arrived with his writing pad, a neatly typed stack of reports, some notes, and a small box in his hands. The Yak motioned the chief inspector to his usual spot, and Rostnikov nodded as he moved to take his seat and place his bundle in front of him.

The Yak said nothing, sat with hands folded before him on the wooden table. There was nothing in front of him. In a few moments there was a knock at the door.

"Come in," called Yaklovev, and the diminutive Pankov entered, juggling a small tray with two cups.

Pankov moved slowly, afraid of dropping the coffee, and placed a cup before the director and another before the chief inspector. The Yak's was black. The chief inspector's was white with two sugars. Pankov took the small tray and departed.

"He is learning to make better coffee," said the Yak after taking a sip.

"Much better," Rostnikov agreed.

"Progress?" asked Yaklovev.

"Closure on all three current investigations," said Porfiry Petrovich, handing the director three reports in clean manila folders.

His leg was definitely bothering him. He would have to see

Leon, his wife's cousin, for an adjustment to his prosthesis. The park competition was coming soon. With any pain it would be difficult to lift.

"Andrei Vanga, director of the Center for the Study of Technical Parapsychology, has been arrested for the murder of Sergei Bolskanov," said Rostnikov, taking a sip of coffee and opening his pad.

"The motive?"

"The theft of Bolskanov's research. Vanga had produced nothing of note in almost two decades. He was afraid of losing his job and his reputation."

"And now he has lost both," said Yaklovev. "He has friends and enemies."

"Bolskanov's research paper is contained on a computer disk in the report before you," said Rostnikov, beginning to draw.

If the research was worth theft and murder, thought Yaklovev, it might well be of value to certain prominent people behind the center. They would definitely be grateful for the swift conclusion of the investigation and for the disk, of which Igor Yaklovev would make a copy.

"And Kriskov is dead?"

"Yes," said Rostnikov. "We did not succeed in protecting him."

"But the stolen negative has been recovered."

"Sasha Tkach and Elena Timofeyeva recovered it," said Rostnikov, letting his fingers mindlessly create the image on the pad.

"They are to be commended," said the Yak.

"Some time off with pay for Sasha Tkach would be . . ."

"He is a hero," said the Yak. "His picture was on television, in the newspaper. He generated very positive promotion for our office. He risked his life to save a boy. He can have a week."

"Three would be better," said Rostnikov.

"Three," Yaklovev agreed.

"Elena Timofeyeva believes Kriskov's wife was a party to the crime," said Rostnikov.

"Is there any evidence of this?"

"None. Valery Grachev died insisting he acted alone."

"Then tell Elena Timofeyeva that she will be commended and the issue dropped."

Rostnikov nodded.

"And the cosmonaut?"

"Vladovka is dead," said Rostnikov.

"And so is a State Security operative who was assigned to protect him," said the Yak. "Died in a St. Petersburg alley, apparently the victim of a random mugging."

"I have heard something of that," said Rostnikov. "Others will be sent to investigate, I presume."

"It is a reasonable presumption, Chief Inspector."

"It would be better if they did not," said Rostnikov.

The Yak finished his coffee, patted the reports before him, and took the small package being handed to him by Rostnikov.

"You might prefer that Konstantin Vladovka, the brother of TsimionVladovka the cosmonaut, not be bothered," said Rostnikov.

Rostnikov looked over at the package that lay before the director.

Yaklovev opened the package and found a cassette.

"That will explain," said Rostnikov.

"I am sure you did your best to save Vladovka," said the Yak.

"While I would far prefer that he remain buried, if it becomes essential for him to be resurrected, it might be a good idea that the resurrection take place when the dead man is somewhere safe, perhaps France or the United States. I would like to think that what is on that tape will protect a dead man."

The Yak nodded and played with the cassette.

"If what is on the tape is of value, I believe I have the power to keep State Security and Mikhail Stoltz from the village of Kiro-Stovitsk. One more question and you may leave. I'll give you new assignments tomorrow."

Rostnikov looked up.

"What have you just drawn?"

Rostnikov turned the pad and slid it across the table to Yaklovev, who looked down at it.

"It looks like two fat worms," he said.

"The tape will explain," said Rostnikov, getting up, deciding that he would see Leon that very day.

When the chief inspector had left the room, Yaklovev rose, tapping the cassette against the palm of his open hand, and moved to his desk where he kept his tape recorder.

He pulled the tape recorder from his desk drawer, placed it on his desk, inserted the tape, and pressed the *play* button.

"Fat worms," he said, shaking his head and wondering if his eccentric chief inspector might be going mad.

"My name is Tsimion Vladovka," came a voice with an echo behind it. "I was a cosmonaut and I have kept a terrible secret about my last flight."

Before the tape was over, Igor Yaklovev had decided that his chief inspector was not mad and that what he was listening to might well be the most valuable possession in his collection of well-protected secrets.

He would make his usual three copies, as he did of all documents and tapes for his private file, and while he was doing so would decide how best to make use of what he had. He was fairly certain that he would soon be having a talk with Mikhail Stoltz.

And that afternoon—

"You have a body for me?" asked Paulinin as Emil Karpo made his way through the tables and specimens.

"I have lunch for you," said Karpo.

"Lunch is fine. A corpse would make it better. They've taken my scientist and cosmonaut. I have no one to talk to now except the living. I prefer to talk to you and the dead."

"I accept the compliment," said Karpo.

"It is simply the truth," said Paulinin.

Paulinin had what appeared to be a rusty automobile part in front of him. He was working at it with a fine-haired brush. Karpo opened the bag in his hand and stood across the table, lit by the bright overhead light casting black shadows.

"Do you think I am mad because I talk to the dead, Emil Karpo? Do you ever talk to the dead?"

"Yes," Karpo said. "I talk to the dead."

"Do they answer you as they answer me when I probe and explore them?"

"No," said Karpo. "I talk to only one dead person. She does not answer. For me it must simply suffice that I talk to her."

"I understand," said Paulinin. "In many ways we are alike, you and I. In many ways. That is why we are friends."

"Yes," said Karpo. "I must acknowledge that. If it were not so, I would not be talking to you as I am, telling you things that I do not even tell Porfiry Petrovich and do not even tell myself."

"What did you bring?"

"Cheese, bread, water. And two apples."

Paulinin looked up from the rusty metal, still holding the brush, wiped his chin with his sleeve, and adjusted his glasses.

"Let us eat."

A knock at her door brought Anna Timofeyeva out of her near slumber. She had been sitting at her window with her cat, Baku, in her ample lap, looking out on the concrete courtyard where children played, mothers and grandmothers sat on benches and talked, and a regular group of jobless men gathered in a far corner to smoke, complain, and make weak jokes about those who were better or worse off than they were.

The door was locked, as were all apartment doors in Moscow, so she had to rouse herself, place Baku on the floor, and make her way across the room. The first step made her dizzy and ir-

ritable. Not long ago, before two heart attacks sent her into re-
tirement, Anna had been a procurator, a rising and respected figure in the Soviet Union. Porfiry Petrovich Rostnikov had worked
under her. They had all worked under her, and she had worked
tirelessly to enforce the law, to bring those who offended the
State to judgment.

And now, at the age of fifty-seven, she watched women and
children from her window and grew dizzy when she rose. Illness
did not become her. There was a rage within her which she quelled
with dreams, medication, and reading, because the rage did her
no good and could, according to the doctors, actually kill her.

"We must talk," shouted Lydia Tkach as soon as Anna opened
the door.

The wiry, nearly deaf woman carried a plastic shopping bag
from which a very pleasant odor reached out and struck the now-
awake Anna. Lydia moved into the room, and Anna considered
leaving the door open so that she could shoo the loud gnat from
her presence, but experience told her that such would not be the
case. Anna closed the door and turned.

"Did you see him?" Lydia shouted, moving to the kitchen area
and the small table to her right.

"See? . . ."

"Sasha, on the television. My son, the hero."

There was a bite to the word *hero* that required no special acu-
men to discern.

"No, I have not watched television today."

The smaller woman was taking things from the plastic bag she
had set on the table. There was a small cake, some croissants,
and a large white cylinder carton with the unmistakable smell of
coffee.

"I wish I had not," said Lydia, going to the cupboard behind
her to bring out two plates, two forks, a large knife, and two
cups. "Sit."

Anna, who had spent a lifetime giving orders, knew it was useless to argue with the woman. Besides, the confections and coffee drew her to the table. Listening to Lydia Tkach was the price she would have to pay for the guilty pleasure.

"He was there, on the riverbank, right across from the Kremlin," said Lydia, sitting and reaching over immediately to cut the cake. "Right in front, or almost, of the Hotel Baltschug Kempinski Moskau. You know?"

"I know where the—" Anna Timofeyeva began but was cut short by her guest, who served her a slice of wondrously aromatic lemon cake.

"Sitting there next to a madman with a gun. Hundreds of people watching, and thousands and thousands on television. He saved the life of a child. A madman—he had this child throwing moving-picture film into the river, as if the river is not dirty enough."

"Sasha had a child throw moving-picture film into the Moscow River?"

The cake was delicious. The coffee was hot.

"No, the madman had the child throw the film in the river."

"Why?"

"Why? Why? Why? Because he was a madman. He's dead now. Sasha is a hero. The madman had already killed someone in a dacha outside of the city. You like the cake? I have a new baker. The old one left his family and ran away to Lithuania or someplace with one of my clerks. Why would anyone run away to Lithuania? But it was a blessing. The new baker is better, a Greek, and the new clerk is his daughter."

"Sasha," Anna said, considering the wisdom of having yet another slice of cake after she finished the one before her.

"And your Elena," said Lydia, who had consumed a croissant and now sliced herself a generous portion of cake. "She was on television, too. Looking down from the embankment. You wouldn't see her if you weren't looking, but she was there."

Lydia Tkach consumed enormous quantities of food without

apparent joy in the process. She remained pole-thin. Anything
Anna ate turned to instant fat, which was a danger to her. Normally she dieted according to the order of her doctor, but at the
moment she told herself that she needed to fortify herself against
the intruder. Anna had gotten Lydia into an apartment on the
other side of the one-story building.

"He could have been killed," Lydia said. "I have one son and
he could have been killed. More cake?"

"A very thin slice, and then I want you to take the cake and
croissants away," said Anna.

"We'll leave the rest for Elena," said Lydia, putting an even
larger slice of cake than the first on Anna's plate.

Infinite are the ways this woman can be my death, thought
Anna, unable to resist the call of lemon and the white sugar
frosting. The new baker was very good indeed.

"So? . . ." Anna began.

"It is enough," shouted Lydia, whose outburst was certainly
being listened to by the pensioner and his wife who lived on the
other side of the thin wall of Anna Timofeyeva's apartment. "I
want him safe. I want him out. Sometimes I think he is suicidal.
That's what I think sometimes."

It was something which Anna also thought but not nearly as
often as his mother. When she had been a procurator, Sasha had
been a brooding young man, a protégé of Porfiry Petrovich. He
had a promising career ahead of him, but Sasha could be difficult and on more than one occasion he had been drawn from
his course not by bribery but by women who found the boyish
brooding young man irresistible.

"I want you to talk to Porfiry Petrovich," Lydia said, her eyes
meeting Anna's.

"To . . ."

"To insist that he get my son off the streets. Sasha is a hero
now. Heroes deserve to be protected whether they wish to be or
not. You agree?"

"Well, I think . . ."

"You can't talk to Sasha. I've thought of that. Sasha is on his
way to Kiev, on an airplane. I don't trust airplanes. I've never
been on one. I think they crash all the time and no one tells us.
They keep it secret. Sasha has been strange lately. Happy . . . he
even took me to a movie about men who for no apparent reason take off their clothes. And then he is back to feeling sorry
for himself. I want my grandchildren back. I made him take airplane money to bring them back. I told him the only way to get
Maya to come back with him would be to get off the streets,
have normal hours and a normal job where he wouldn't get into
trouble."

Anna sipped her coffee, which she should not be drinking. It
was excellent coffee. She would resist a second cup.

"I think you are right," said Anna.

"You think I am right? You never think I am right."

"This time," said Anna, "I think you are right."

"And what will you do about it?" Lydia asked insistently.

Anna felt like saying, "I'll consult the neighbors and get their
opinion," but instead she said, "I will give Baku the rest of what
I have on my plate and then I will call Porfiry Petrovich and ask
him to stop by for a talk. I have never asked him to come visit
me. He will come."

Lydia said nothing and then opened her mouth to speak. Nothing came out. She began to weep. As loud as her voice had been,
her weeping was nearly silent. Her thin shoulders shook and she
leaned her head forward. Anna had no experience comforting people. People, even her niece, had never really looked to her for
comfort. Anna was large, serious, stern in appearance. When she
was procurator, she always wore her dark uniform. One did not
go to such a woman for solace.

"I will do what I can, Lydia," she said. "I will do what I can."

*   *   *

"You are going out?" asked Rostnikov, sitting across the table from his wife.

Galina and the two little girls were watching television. The woman sat between the children, who were completely absorbed in the young men and women on very tall unicycles speeding around on a television-studio floor. The television was black and white. They could only imagine the spectrum of colorful glitter.

"Yes," said Sarah, finishing her coffee.

"I know where you go each Friday," he said softly as circus music vibrated excitedly from the television set.

"You are a detective, Porfiry Petrovich," Sarah said with a smile, reaching over to touch his hand. "I thought you would have figured it out long ago."

"I did," he said, picking up crumbs from the remains of the pastry on the plate between them and popping them into his mouth.

"And you want to know why?" she asked.

"It seems a logical question," he said.

"And an emotional one."

"And an emotional one," he agreed. "Is there any more cake?"

"No more cake," she said. "I don't believe in God, Porfiry Petrovich. Maybe sometime. Maybe never. I feel the need to make a connection to my history. It's . . . more a meditation than a worship. I can lose myself in the ritual, the prayers, the chants. I feel as if I'm making a connection and on good days I can walk away feeling a little better."

"Avrum Belinsky is good?"

"Very good," she said.

"He is very young."

"But he has studied much and been through much," she said. "Are you bothered by my going?"

"No," he said. "If you want to read the Bible or something at home, I don't mind."

"No," she said, still touching his hand. "I don't want to read the Bible at home. Porfiry, maybe someday I'll believe in a god, some kind of god. We have talked about this very little. What do you believe in?"

The crowd on the television set roared. Nina giggled. Laura clapped.

"You," he said. "Nature. Benches and spaceships and people who can move objects very slightly with their minds and dreams that sometimes become reality. Mystery. People who are not all good or all evil. Common sense."

"You are not really answering the question," Sarah said.

Rostnikov nodded and said, "You are going to be late. Would you like me to come with you?"

"No," she said, getting up. "I won't be late."

"All right," he said. "When the circus is over and the applause has died, I have a sink to fix."

"She did it," Elena said.

Iosef and Elena were sitting in his apartment. With the afternoon off, they were supposed to be making the final plans for their wedding. Iosef had hoped that she would be filled with ideas and that they might end the afternoon with something to eat and, perhaps, an hour or so in bed, just being together without their clothes. Iosef loved her smooth, full body. But it was clear that Elena was in no mood for food or love. She pushed her hair back, a sign, Iosef had learned, that she was agitated. This time he needed no sign.

"I would like to go back, confront her," Elena said, her arms folded.

"You've been ordered to forget about her," said Iosef. "Yaklovev will handle it."

"You know how he will handle it," she said. "He'll find some way to get something from the widow Vera Kriskov. He'll probably have the movie dedicated to him."

"That is not the kind of thing the Yak wants," said Iosef. "I know. Remember when . . ."

"Yes, and he doesn't want sex," Elena went on. "Vera Kriskov is very beautiful, you know?"

"As are you."

"I am not beautiful," she said. "I have a higher opinion of my looks than I once had, but I am not beautiful."

"I am entitled to my opinion," he said with a smile she did not return.

"She will get away with the murder of her husband."

"She will join the legions, the thousands, who have gotten away with murder and continue to do so," he said. "Why does this woman obsess you?"

"She doesn't. She . . ."

Elena stopped. A realization struck her, one she could not quite put into words. "She has wealth, two children, beauty, and . . ."

"You would like the same," Iosef said, watching her face.

"Perhaps, yes," she said with a sigh. "He loved her."

"Her husband?"

Elena smiled. "Grachev. He loved her. He died protecting her."

"Let us leave it as a tragic romance," said Iosef.

"You think like a playwright," Elena said.

"It is an ending out of Tolstoy. If she has guilt, she will have to live with it."

"Then she will live," said Elena.

"Feel better?"

"Yes, I think so."

"Good."

He leaned over to kiss her. She returned the kiss with a passion and hunger he had not expected.

Winter was still months away in Winnipeg.

It had taken Misha and Ivan only an hour to find a room they could share in the house of an old couple who spoke Ukrainian-accented Russian and who welcomed them as recent immigrants. They had stopped at a small restaurant and asked if there were places they might find a room. The incredibly thin man behind the counter had served them cherry pie and directed them to the old couple.

"We need new blood here," the old woman had said when they carried their luggage in. "New blood that won't freeze in the winter."

"People come from the United States. They say they love it here. They take deep breaths. The winter comes. They go home, usually at night. If they can get their car started or a ride to the airport."

"But," said the old woman, "you are Russians. Are you married?"

"No," said Misha.

"Then maybe . . . what is your work?" the man asked.

"We are mechanics," Ivan said.

"Mechanics? Like cars?" said the old man.

"Yes," said Misha. "Like cars."

The old woman motioned for them to pick up their luggage. They did and followed her to a wooden stairway.

The old man came after them and said, "My nephew, Frank. He has a garage. He is looking for help. You have papers?"

They were at the top of the stairs now. There was something familiar about the house. Ivan thought he might be comfortable. At the moment, he simply wanted to lie down on his stomach and hope that the pain in his back and behind would lose some of its anger.

"No," said Misha.

"I understand," said the old man. "I understand. Political?"

"Yes," said Misha. "We are merchant marines. We jumped from our ship in Nova Scotia."

"The water was cold," said the man. "Even in the summer. The water was cold."

"It was cold," Ivan agreed, following the old woman into the room.

There were two beds. Ivan felt both relief and guilt. Knowing now about Misha's sexual preference, he was relieved that they would not have to share a bed. Knowing that Misha had saved his life, Ivan felt guilt.

The room was large, furnished in old-country style, very simple. Ivan thought he could like it here.

"There are snowshoes downstairs for the winter," said the old man. "The snow comes right up to the window over there sometimes. Well . . . should I talk to Frank?"

"Yes, please," said Misha.

"He has friends, knows people. He can get you papers, but let me talk to him first."

"Leave them alone to settle," said the old woman, touching her husband's sleeve and guiding him toward the door.

"Yes, yes. Of course. Come down when you are ready. My wife will give you something to eat."

When they were gone and the door closed, Ivan moved in agony to the nearest bed, kicked off his shoes, and lay carefully on his stomach.

"I'll go to a drugstore, get you something for your bruises," said Misha.

"I—" Ivan began.

"I won't try to seduce you," Misha said. "Are we friends?"

"Yes," said Ivan. "I owe you my life."

"Then we shall be just friends," said Misha. "I have a feeling I will not lack companionship here when I feel the need."

"I'm too much in pain to think about sex," said Ivan.

Misha looked around the room and moved to the window. "I think we may like it here," he said.

"Misha?"

"I think I shall now be Casmir," said Misha. "Who would you like to be?"

"Ivan. There are probably thousands of Ivans here. Do you think we will ever get back to Russia?"

"Do you want to go back?" asked Misha, sitting on the second bed.

"I don't know. I can't think beyond my pain. Tomorrow I'll think. Maybe the day after. Maybe the week after. We are rather overtrained to be automobile mechanics."

"Which means," said Misha with a grin, "we will be the best automobile mechanics in Winnipeg. Think of it, Ivan. Perhaps in a few years we will have our own garage. Land of opportunity."

"And no rubles," said Ivan.

"And no rubles," Misha agreed. "I'll go get something for your wounds."

Misha rose and started for the door.

"Will they come for us, here?" asked Ivan.

"I don't know."

"The one bent over like a *V*. With the notches on both ends. The seat wrench," Rostnikov said.

Nina searched through the gray-metal toolbox and held up the wrench.

"This one?" she asked.

Rostnikov looked down from the faucet on which he was working. Bending down to the toolbox was more than difficult, though he could have done it had it been necessary. The child, however, made the maneuver unnecessary.

Nina handed the tool to Rostnikov, who smiled and looked at it as if she had handed him a wonderful treasure.

She was eight years old, a pleasant-looking child though no beauty. Yet her face, like that of her older sister, showed an intelligence and curiosity that made Rostnikov think they were capable of great things. No, neither he nor Sarah wanted Galina

Panishkoya and her granddaughters to move to their own apartment. Sarah had suggested that with his recent promotion, somewhat higher salary, and his connections, they might all move to an apartment with two bedrooms.

Porfiry Petrovich had been giving this idea serious thought. At the moment, however, he was trying to ignore the irritating minor pain in his leg at the very point where it was inserted neatly into the prosthesis with which he had been trying to form a friendship.

They were in the apartment two floors down from that of the Rostnikovs. The apartment was being rented by an American journalist who was writing about Russia for several magazines. The journalist had been in the apartment for six months. He planned to remain for a year.

The journalist, whose name was Schwartz, had been pleased to find a neighbor who could both speak English and fix his badly leaking sink. Schwartz had heard of Porfiry Petrovich from another neighbor, a Rumanian, who lived next door, and it was the Rumanian who had come to see Rostnikov about the American's problem.

This was the first time Rostnikov had been in the American's apartment. He had taken it all in without letting his curiosity show, and now, as he worked on the sink, the American sat at his desk in the other room, working at his computer.

"Why do you fix toilets and sinks and drains?" Nina asked.

Rostnikov inserted the wrench in the pitted seat of the faucet. He had already used his seat cutter on the problem and now began working with the wrench.

"Because," he told the eight year old, "plumbing presents a problem that always has a solution. During the day I must deal with people and problems that almost never have a clear solution. Plumbing, on the other hand, can always, with the right tools, be taken care of. There is a satisfaction to this. Do you understand?"

"I think so," said Nina, who was now seated on the closed toilet next to the sink. "Yes, I think so. Laura and I like to watch you fix plumbing and lift weights."

"Ah, the lifting is another story," Rostnikov said, removing the wrench and looking down at his work. "Lifting is a meditation. Plumbing presents problems. The weights are a friendly challenge. When I lift the weights I am absorbed by the challenge, and the world disappears so that there is only the action and the music. Do you understand?"

"No, but I am young. I will understand when I am older, older than Laura. Now, I just like watching."

"Good," he said, reaching over to touch the girl's cheek.

He left a smudge of grease. He unrolled some toilet paper, moistened it with the water from the faucet on which he was not working, and removed the smudge from the little girl's face. She giggled. When the girl and her sister had come to the Rostnikovs, their grandmother was in jail, their mother had left them, and they did not smile or talk. That had changed; gradually, that had changed.

Rostnikov had now repacked the faucet and replaced the washer. He put the handle back in place, tightened the screw, and tapped in the escutcheon.

"Finished," he said, turning the handle.

Water rushed into the sink. The faucet was fixed.

The child helped Rostnikov put the tools back and clean the sink.

On the way out, Rostnikov would ask the American writer if he knew Ed McBain or had read his books. Perhaps he would ask the American if he played chess. He was an American. He probably played badly, which was what Rostnikov needed. Porfiry Petrovich was not a great player of chess, but he liked to play.

He picked up the closed toolbox as the girl stood up.

"Enough," he said. "We have done enough this day."

The 4th Marine Division had been unable to embark adequate transportation for the Roi-Namur operation, as noted in Chapter II, and the trucks of the 15th Defense Battalion were now constantly in use. Nor was the lack of wheeled vehicles entirely the cause of the acute transportation problem.

It may be interesting to note that the real shortage was not in vehicles but rather in tire-patches. The preparatory bombardment. . . . resulted in a well-distributed coating of shell and bomb fragments and assorted junk all over both islands [Roi and Namur]. Hardly a square foot of airstrip or roadway existed but what it had its share of puncture-producing debris. The 15th Defense Battalion's transportation was operating simply because the battalion's Motor Transport officer . . . had somehow, before leaving Pearl Harbor, accumulated a great deal more tire-patching material than the TBA provided.[5]

On D-plus 3, the day after Namur was declared secure, the 2d Battalion, 23d Marines and the 2d Battalion, 24th Marines were embarked to relieve congestion on Roi-Namur. The following day the Division Scout Company was assigned to the Eniwetok force now forming, and the 4th Amphibian Tractor Battalion and the 1st Armored Amphibian Battalion were loaded for the South Pacific. Four days later the 14th Marines (less 1st Battalion), the 23d Marines and 2/24, all under General Underhill's command, departed the Kwajalein area for Maui. The remainder of the division (less Combat Team 25 [reinforced] and Company A, 10th Amphibian Tractor Battalion) followed in various echelons on 12, 14 and 15 February 1944.[6]

The 15th Defense Battalion had begun landing survey teams on Roi as soon as sufficient room permitted, and while fighting was still in progress. By the time Roi-Namur was secured "all antiaircraft units of the battalion were in position and ready in all respects to engage air and surface targets.[7]

During the early morning hours of 12 February, the Japanese retaliated to the Marshalls invasion with a bombing attack on Roi by some 12 to 14 seaplanes.[8] The raiders effected sur-

COLONEL L. R. JONES, commanding the 23d Marines, raises the flag on battered Roi.

prise by dropping large amounts of "window"[9] on the way to the target and thus fouled the defense battalion's radar scopes.[10] Droning in between 14,000 and 21,000 feet at 0249 hours, the planes made a sighting run over Roi and then followed with a bomb run.[11] Some of the explosives struck an ammunition dump, while others landed elsewhere on Roi's bare surface. "This explosion was seen as far away as Kwajalein Island, some 40 or more miles distant."[12]

Tracer ammunition lit up the sky as far as we could see, and for a full half hour red-hot fragments rained from the sky like so many hailstones, burning and piercing the flesh when they hit. . . . A jeep ex-

[5] Ltr Col Peter J. Negri to CMC, 5Feb53.

[6] 4th MarDiv War Diary, 25Mar44, 2–4.

[7] *Negri.*

[8] "My recollection is that at the time we believed

[the planes] had come from Saipan and probably been staged through Truk and perhaps Ponape or Kusaie." Ltr Adm Raymond A. Spruance to CMC 18Feb53.

[9] Strips of metal foil dispersed by aircraft to create a great many false targets for radar sets by causing them to register spurious readings.

[10] *Wendt;* Ltr LtCol Arthur E. Buck, Jr., to CMC 23Jan53, hereinafter cited as *Buck II.*

[11] Ltr Col Otto Lessing to CMC, 25Feb53.

[12] *Negri.*

ploded in our faces a few yards away. Yet half an hour after the first bomb hit, several hospitals and first-aid stations were functioning with all the efficiency of urban medical centers.[13]

For almost an hour colorful bursts of small-arms ammunition were punctuated by large explosions as unprotected ammunition and gasoline dumps blew up. Several badly dazed and wounded men made their way across the sandspit and the causeway to our location [on Namur] and on to medical aid at the pier. From our vantage point it appeared that Roi was completely

afire. Daylight showed the destruction to be almost complete. Little of anything appeared still serviceable.[14]

The devastating raid produced the greatest number of casualties that any United States land target had suffered since December 1941.[15] Thirty men were killed, some 300 more were wounded and evacuated to ships in the lagoon, and an additional 100 received treatment for wounds ashore and returned to duty. Damages

[13] Combat Correspondent Bernard Redmond, as quoted in Carl W. Proehl (ed), *The Fourth Marine Division in World War II*, Washington, 1946. Redmond was with the 20th Marines.

[14] *Buck II.*

[15] Robert Sherrod, *History of Marine Corps Aviation in World War II*, Combat Forces Press, Washington, 231, hereinafter cited as *Sherrod.*

ROOTING INDIVIDUAL JAPANESE out of hiding places was the major task in mopping up.

amounted to an estimated 85 percent of supplies (including all provisions except for a seven-day supply of K-rations) and 33 percent of construction equipment. In addition, 75 percent of all tentage and miscellaneous buildings on Roi were flattened and rendered unfit for further use. Two LCT's beached for unloading were burned out, as was the 20th Marines' command post, with the loss of regimental records and journals.[16] The Japanese had struck a heavy blow, but they made no attempt to follow it up, which was probably fortunate for them. On Admiral Conolly's recommendation, three Marine night fighters landed at Roi the next night prepared for any subsequent nocturnal raids.

While the bulk of the 4th Marine Division was reorganizing, clearing Roi-Namur and preparing to depart for Hawaii, Colonel Cumming's Combat Team 25 (reinforced) and Company A, 10th Amphibian Tractor Battalion searched the remaining islands in the northern portion of Kwajalein Atoll. This movement had begun on the morning of D-plus 2 when General Schmidt ordered Colonel Cumming to proceed with the seizure of those islands scheduled for the later phases of the over-all operation. Landing Team 2 under Lieutenant Colonel Hudson was picked to make the initial movement, its landings to be preceded by 14th Marines' artillery preparations. But after the first two landings were effected without meeting opposition, the 75mm pack howitzers remained silent. By utilizing LVT's, Hudson's unit secured eight islands during the day.

I remember distinctly the unusual sensation of navigating LVT's between the islands by means of a small pocket compass held as far as possible above the metal of the LVT. At times, due to the low freeboard[17] of the LVT, we were out of sight of all land.[18]

The Marines encountered no resistance and picked up 47 natives and three Japanese, the natives being established in a camp on Ennubirr (ALLEN) Island.[19]

[16] *CTF 53 Rpt FLINTLOCK*, 8, 22–23; *20thMar SAR*, 3; Report of Island Commander to Commander in Chief, United States Fleet, 4Apr44, 4.

[17] Freeboard is the height of a vessel's side from the water line to the main deck or gunwale.

[18] Ltr Col Lewis C. Hudson, Jr., to CMC, 12Feb53.

[19] "[The natives] were looked after by a detachment

COMMUNICATORS raised their wires from the ground to makeshift telephone poles when the shooting quieted down.

Lieutenant Colonel O'Donnell's Landing Team 1 was assigned the task of securing three islands: Boggerlapp (HUBERT), Boggerik (HOMER), and HOLLIS. This was accomplished in two days, no Japanese being met. On the afternoon of D-plus 4 Lieutenant Colonel Chambers' Landing Team 3/25 took over the mission, augmented by Battery C, 14th

of Regimental Weapons Company under the command of Maj James T. Kisgen. During the 30 days together, the natives and the men of R/W 25 became fast friends. . . . Upon leaving, the native chief made a most touching speech and presented the Marines with presents." Ltr Maj Thomas H. Rogers, Jr., to CMC, 13Feb53.

Marines, 34 LVT's and a miniature fleet of two LST's, two LCI's, six LSM's, and the destroyer, *Hopewell*. By the afternoon of D-plus 7 this force had secured 39 islands, met some 250 natives and found no Japanese.[20]

In addition to completing the Northern Landing Force's mission, Combat Team 25 was ticketed as a garrison force for Kwajalein Atoll. On D-plus 8 the unit, together with Company A, 10th Amphibian Tractor Battalion, was temporarily detached from the 4th Marine Division, and Colonel Cumming reported to Rear Admiral Alva D. Bernhard, atoll commander. Landing Team 1 constituted the defense force for Roi-Namur, Landing Team 2 for Kwajalein Island, and Landing Team 3 a mobile defense group stationed on the western islands.

The combat team retained these dispositions until February 29 when it was relieved by the 22d Marines.[21] It then departed the area and rejoined its parent division in the Hawaiians.

---

[20] Rpt on the 25th Marines (reinforced) in the FLINTLOCK Operation, 3–4.

[21] Earlier activities of the 22d Marines will be taken up in Chapter VIII.

ALL ISLANDS SECURED

On D-plus 2, the same date that Combat Team 25 began the seizure of minor islands in the northern zone, the Army's 7th Reconnaissance Troop initiated similar operations in the southern sector.

Between 0800 and 0900 this unit returned to Gehh (CHAUNCEY), the island it had hit by mistake in the dark early hours of D-Day. Light resistance was encountered, and with the assistance of *Overton's* guns, the Reconnaissance Troop overran the Japanese positions. The infantrymen counted 135 enemy dead that day at a cost of 14 wounded soldiers.[22]

North of Kwajalein lay Ebeye (BURTON) Island, 2,000 yards long and containing machine shops and warehouses before the preliminary bombardment. This became the target of Colonel Zimmerman's 17th Regimental Combat Team, an unopposed landing being effected the morning of D-plus 3 by BLT 17–1.

As the infantrymen pushed northward on the island, enemy resistance was encountered and

---

[22] *Gritta*.

NAMUR immediately after the 24th Marines secured the island.   In the background is Ennugarret (ABRAHAM).

JAMES V. FORRESTAL (center), Under Secretary of the Navy, visited Roi-Namur a few days after the battle ended. Here he is accompanied by (left to right) Admirals Spruance and Conolly, Generals Schmidt and Smith.

it steadily increased. Many of the island's defense installations had been destroyed during the preliminary bombardment, but the Japanese took full advantage of the remaining pillboxes, dugouts, and air-raid shelters to put up a disorganized fanatical fight. By nightfall BLT 17–1 had cleared two-thirds of Ebeye.

The morning of the second day, a Japanese prisoner pointed out the location of an ammunition dump and a requested air strike scored a direct hit on this choice target. The dump's elimination apparently took the heart out of the remaining defenders, for not a resisting shot was fired after it exploded. The Nipponese then surrendered or committed suicide, a majority of them choosing the latter course.

The 3d Battalion, 17th Infantry, relieved BLT 17–1 at 1130, and 40 minutes later Ebeye was declared secured.

While his main effort was being made on Ebeye, Colonel Zimmerman used the remaining troops available to him to secure four other nearby islands, resistance being encountered on one of them and that only light.

By D-plus 5 the 17th Regimental Combat Team and the 7th Reconnaissance Troop had secured all islands but one in the Southern Landing Force's zone. In addition to those already noted, 12 islands or islets were secured, only two of these offering any degree of resistance. The 7th Reconnaissance Troop neutralized an enemy force of about 100 men on Bigej (BENNETT) and Landing Team 17–2 subdued 102 Japanese on Eller (CLIFTON).[23]

On the morning of D-plus 6 Landing Team 17–2 took without opposition Ennugenliggelap

---

[23] *7th Div Rpt*, 9, 11–12.

DYESS FIELD on Roi after the Seabees completed their work there.

(COHEN), thus completing the mission of the Southern Landing Force.

The 7th Infantry Division was directed to embark for the Hawaiian Islands as soon as its mission was completed. At 0800 on 6 February, Regimental Combat Teams 184 and 32 began loading ship, followed two hours later by RCT 17. But transportation was not immediately available for the entire Southern Landing Force. The morning of 8 February (D-plus 8), General Corlett and the bulk of his command departed the Kwajalein area, followed a few days later by the Division Artillery Group, one company of RCT 17 and detachments of the tank LVT battalion which had been left behind, except for those earmarked for the next operation. Company A, 708th Amphibian Tank Battalion, the 708th Provisional Amphibian Tractor Battalion, and 30 DUKW's were all assigned to Tactical Group-1 to assist in the seizure of Eniwetok.

SUMMATION

The Kwajalein operation clearly showed that heavy casualties are not a requisite for seizure of an enemy-held atoll. As noted earlier, the Tarawa operation loomed large in the minds of the men planning the Kwajalein landings, and it was their intent to avoid a repetition of the costly assault on Betio. This was accomplished. Marines at Tarawa incurred 3,301 casualties in combating a Japanese force of 4,690.[24] At Kwajalein, the Northern Landing Force overran 3,563 Japanese and the Southern Landing Force defeated 4,823 of the enemy.[25] The 4th Marine Division's total casualties for the operation amounted to 313 killed in action or died of wounds, and 502 wounded in action.[26] The 7th Infantry Division lost 173 killed in action or died of wounds and 793 wounded in action.[27]

[24] Capt James R. Stockman, *The Battle for Tarawa*, historical monograph prepared by Historical Section, HQMC, 1947, Appendices B and C.

[25] VAC G-2 Rpt, 19Feb44, 12.

[26] Marine casualty figures furnished by Personnel Accounting Section, Records Branch, Personnel Department, HQMC. Figures certified and released 26Aug52.

[27] 7th InfDiv G-1 Rpt, 18-19 (7th InfDiv FLINTLOCK Rpt, Vol III).

This is no reflection on the 2d Marine Division's action at Betio. There it was conclusively demonstrated that much more artillery, air and naval assistance was required to seize an atoll without prohibitive losses. Such support was overwhelmingly provided at Kwajalein. Actually, only one more atoll operation remained in the war in the Pacific, and that was Eniwetok.

All elements of the Armed Forces participated as a team in the Kwajalein assault. Marines, Navy ships and aviation, Army air and ground units, Coast Guard, all worked together in the seizure of the first prewar enemy-held territory.

An important aspect from the Marine point of view was that the Roi-Namur operation was the initial one for the 4th Marine Division. One more Marine combat force was blooded and therefore better able to participate in subsequent amphibious assaults, as it conclusively demonstrated at Saipan,[28] Tinian,[29] and Iwo Jima.[30] As a direct result of the difficult lessons learned at Roi-Namur, the LVT units were

able to effect a smooth landing in their next operation, Saipan.[31]

Kwajalein was another steppingstone on the road across the Central Pacific, with Japan as the final goal. Kwajalein's seizure, together with that of Eniwetok a few weeks later, cleared the path for attacks on Truk, the capture of the Marianas,[32] and the other Central Pacific operations that followed.

In addition to providing aerial and naval bases for subsequent offensive operations, the

[28] Maj Carl W. Hoffman, *Saipan: The Beginning of the End*, historical monograph prepared by Historical Division, HQMC, 1950.
[29] Maj Carl W. Hoffman, *The Seizure of Tinian*, historical monograph prepared by Historical Division, HQMC, 1951.
[30] LtCol W. S. Bartley, *Iwo Jima, Amphibious Epic*, historical monograph prepared by Historical Branch, G-3, HQMC, 1954.
[31] *Croizat.*
[32] See monographs cited in preceding footnotes; also Maj O. R. Lodge, *The Recapture of Guam*, historical monograph prepared by Historical Branch, G-3, HQMC, 1954.

MEMBERS OF THE 4TH MARINE AIR WING on Roi devised a system of windmills to wash their laundry.

captured Marshall Islands also served as a springboard for neutralization of the by-passed atolls. From Kwajalein and Majuro the 4th Marine Air Wing pounded the Japanese fortresses of Mille, Maloelap, Wotje, and Jaluit, making it unnecessary for ground forces to assault and occupy those heavily held atolls.

What was involved in the Central Pacific was later explained by Vice Admiral Harry W. Hill:

If you will examine an air map of the Central Pacific, you will note that the successive objectives of attack, namely Kwajalein and Eniwetok, Saipan and Iwo Jima are all approximately 500 miles away from the last objective seized. At that time, none of our fighters was capable of operating 500 miles from base. Therefore, the job of fighter protection and ground supported troops devolved completely upon our carrier task forces. . . . The question naturally arises, therefore, why did we not utilize shorter sea hops in order to have better land based air support. . . . The only islands we wanted were ones which had sufficient land mass to provide a runway into the direction of the prevailing wind, which was northeast, and also to provide a harbor. Such islands and atolls were few and far between. Practically all that there were had been already occupied by the Japanese. For the same reason, therefore, we could not do in the Central Pacific as General MacArthur had done in the Southwest Pacific—make unopposed landings. Instead, we were forced to go to the atolls or islands already held by the Japanese and which, of course, were heavily defended.[33]

Although the Marines had to go to defended islands and atolls, there were varying degrees of defense at various objectives. Thus, Admiral Nimitz' decision to make a bold stroke into the heart of the Marshalls, by-passing the more heavily defended "anchored aircraft carriers," both increased the tempo of the war in the Central Pacific and obviously kept the casualty rate low. So quickly and successfully was the Kwajalein mission accomplished that the Eniwetok landings, tentatively planned for May, were shoved forward three months, and the first troops stormed ashore on 17 February.

[33] *Hill.*

CHAPTER VIII

Eniwetok[1]

THE OBJECTIVE

In the northwest corner of the Marshall Islands, 326 nautical miles from Roi-Namur, lies Eniwetok Atoll[2] (coded DOWNSIDE), some 30 islands arranged in an irregular circumference of 70 miles. Many of the coral bits of land are covered with underbrush, while the larger ones grow stunted coconut trees. At the outbreak of the war less than 100 natives were to be found there, and the agricultural output consisted of a few figs and coconuts.

---

[1] Unless otherwise indicated, this chapter is derived from the following sources: JICPOA Bulletin 3–44, 20Jan44; JICPOA Bulletin 88–44, 3Jun44; JICPOA Bulletin 89–44, 12Jun44; Task Group 51.11 Report of Eniwetok Operations, 7Mar44; Tactical Group-1, War Diary, 5Nov43–29Feb44; Tactical Group-1, Operation Order 2–44, 10Feb44; Tactical Group-1 Special Report Concerning FLINTLOCK and CATCHPOLE Operations, 1Mar44, hereinafter cited as TG–1 Spl Rpt; Tactical Group-1 Report of Attack on Eniwetok Atoll, 27Feb44; Tactical Group-1 Journal, 17Feb–22Mar44; 22d Marines, reinf, War Diary, 1Jan–29Feb44; 22d Marines, reinf, Report on DOWNSIDE Operation, 9Mar44, hereinafter cited as 22dMar SAR; Battalion Landing Team 1, 22d Marines, Report on FLINTLOCK II Operation, undated, hereinafter cited as *BLT 1 Rpt.*

[2] When he discovered the atoll in 1794, Capt Thomas Butler named it Brown's Range, and the Japanese Navy continued calling it Brown throughout World War II. *Morison,* 282.

The lagoon measures some 21 miles in length, northwest-southeast, and about 17 miles across, northeast-southwest. Wide Passage and Deep Entrance on the south and southeast sides respectively are the only navigable breaks in the rim of coral surrounding the atoll. Ships of all types may anchor in the sheltered waters, as did major units of the Japanese Fleet shortly before the invasion.

The principal islands include:

Engebi (FRAGILE) roughly shaped in the form of an equilateral triangle, each side measuring slightly over a mile in length. The northern end of this northernmost island was cleared, while mangrove and coconut palms covered the remaining portions. Here was found the atoll's only airstrip, concrete-surfaced and extending 4,025 feet.

Japtan (LADYSLIPPER) bounds the right of Deep Entrance. Measuring 800 yards (east-west) by 750 yards (north-south), this coral-sand island's northwestern area was covered by coconut palms in even rows, while dense underbrush grew elsewhere.

Parry (HEARTSTRINGS) lies immediately south of Japtan and bounds Deep Entrance's left. Shaped like an inverted tear drop, the island is two miles long, tapering from a 600-yard width in the north to a point in the south. In early 1944 it was covered with coconut palms.

Eniwetok (PRIVILEGE), the atoll's southernmost island, is formed like a blackjack and flanks the right of Wide Passage. Its length extends 4,700 yards and its width varies between 750 yards in the south to 170 yards in the north. Except for a few clearings and some fringes of mangrove, Eniwetok was covered with evenly spaced coconut palms.

THE JAPANESE

Prior to the arrival of the Japanese 1st Amphibious Brigade on 4 January 1944, the defense of Eniwetok Atoll was entrusted to the Eniwetok Detachment of the 61st Keibitai (Guard Unit), based at Kwajalein. The detachment never totaled more than 61 men, 45 of whom were stationed on Engebi where the atoll defenses were concentrated. These consisted of a battery of two 120mm guns, two twin-mount M93 13mm AA machine guns, two M96 light machine guns and a number of rifles, pistols and hand grenades. This token defense force reflected the tardy Japanese military interest in the northwestern Marshalls. In November and December 1942, some 800 construction workers of the 4th Shisetsubu (4th Fleet Construction Section) landed at Engebi and began work on an airstrip, which was completed the following July. The 61st Keibitai detachment then moved into the island in October 1943.

Engebi's airstrip began operating in November, but since it was used only for staging planes between Truk and points east, no flying personnel were stationed there. The maintenance force consisted of 38 petty officers and men under a warrant officer. As American air operations increased in the eastern Marshalls, however, and the threat of amphibious assault in that area became greater, Japanese air was evacuated from the forward areas to Eniwetok Atoll's air base. On 11 January 1944 an additional 110 aviation officers and men were billeted on Engebi "owing to present operations in the Roi, Wotje, Mille, and Taroa areas." [3] With the fall of Kwajalein Atoll, steps were taken to evacuate all air personnel to Truk by flying boat, but for most of them this began too late.

An estimated 150 grounded pilots and crewmen were still on Engebi and Parry when American assault forces sailed into the lagoon 17 February 1944.

The 1st Amphibious Brigade was formed from the 3d Independent Garrison Unit in Manchuria in November 1943 under Major General Yoshima Nishida. Japanese Army planners originally intended it as a mobile striking force within the Marshalls, initially designating it the 1st Mobile Shipborne Brigade and ticketing it for centrally located Kwajalein. When it arrived at Truk on 26 December, however, the increasing threat of American attack on the Marshalls made necessary the reinforcement of certain points. The brigade was therefore ordered to garrison duty on various atolls, as noted in Chapter II.

General Nishida's command arrived at Engebi on 4 January and four days later those elements earmarked for Wotje, Maloelap, and Kwajalein departed. Of the 3,940 men within the brigade, 2,586 were left to defend Eniwetok Atoll, and these were now distributed among Engebi, Parry, and Eniwetok. Although they did not know it, the defenders had about six weeks in which to transform a virtually undefended atoll into a stronghold.

Command of the Engebi garrison devolved upon Colonel Toshio Yano of the 3d Battalion. His total military force numbered 736 men, including 44 of the 61st Keibitai detachment, and was augmented by aviation personnel, civilian employees, and laborers. [4] In addition to his organic small arms, Yano had available two flame throwers, two 75mm mountain guns, three 20mm guns, two 120mm naval guns, two twin-mount 13mm AA machine guns, three light tanks and a variety of machine guns, mortars, and grenade dischargers. Organization and construction of defensive positions were begun immediately, and on 10 February the island commander issued an outline of his defensive plans in which he correctly estimated the events of a week later:

The enemy will bomb this island either with carrier or land-based planes and will bombard us from all sides with battleships and heavy cruisers. Directly

[3] JICPOA Bulletin 89–44, 3.

[4] Enemy strength on Engebi, estimated from the number buried, was set at 1,200.

following these bombardments, an amphibious force landing will be carried out.

It will be extremely difficult for the enemy to land here from the open sea because of the high waves and rugged reefs.

Whether or not they are able to carry out their plan to land on the islands to the east and west, it is expected that they will force their way through the north and south passages, or make a forced passage of either the east or west pass in order to enter the atoll and carry out landing operations from the lagoon. While making assaults on outlying islands, they will approach this island from all directions.

If any of the above happens, and if sea and air control are in the hands of the enemy, this defense garrison must put up a defense on its own.

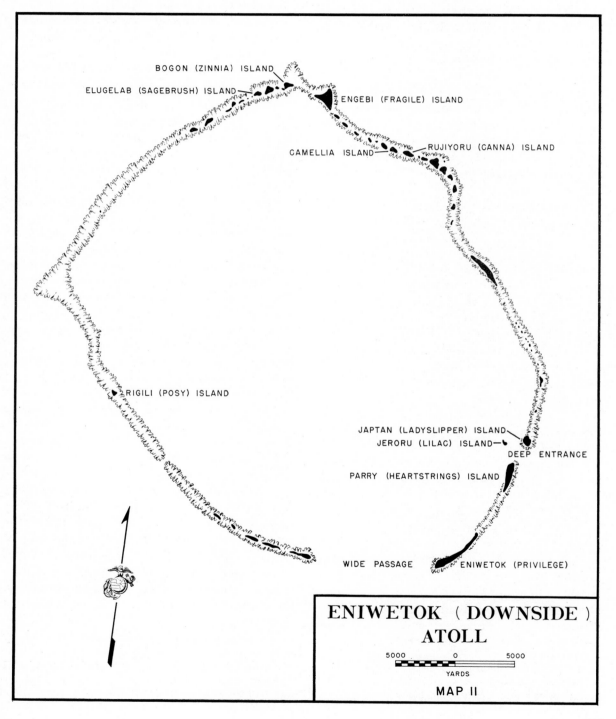

BOGON (ZINNIA) ISLAND

ELUGELAB (SAGEBRUSH) ISLAND

ENGEBI (FRAGILE) ISLAND

RUJIYORU (CANNA) ISLAND

CAMELLIA ISLAND

RIGILI (POSY) ISLAND

JAPTAN (LADYSLIPPER) ISLAND
JERORU (LILAC) ISLAND

DEEP ENTRANCE

PARRY (HEARTSTRINGS) ISLAND

WIDE PASSAGE   ENIWETOK (PRIVILEGE)

ENIWETOK (DOWNSIDE)
ATOLL

5000   0   5000

YARDS

MAP II

119

In view of these things, it is essential that this force make complete use of every available man and all fortified positions, carrying out each duty to the utmost. Plans must be followed to lure the enemy to the water's edge and then annihilate him with withering fire power and continuous attacks.[5]

In an operational order issued 13 February, Colonel Yano instructed his forces to give "particular attention" to the construction of positions facing the lagoon. He directed that Company 8 (reinforced) occupy the eastern corner of the island; the Battalion Artillery Company (reinforced) station itself in the western corner; the Battalion Mortar Company occupy the central area with main fire directed toward the lagoon; the Machine Cannon Platoon occupy positions on the shore southeast of the main positions, and all other units take positions in the "main strength area," just inland of the lagoon beaches.

The island defenses were principally trenches and dugouts, protected by coconut log barricades, usually covered with light wood or sheet metal. In addition, a series of "spider traps" were installed. These consisted of oil-drum tunnels and each hole was covered with an innocuous piece of metal, a palm frond or coral rubble. No blockhouses such as those found at Tarawa and Kwajalein Atoll were constructed. In the limited time available to him, Yano had concrete pillboxes set up, but these were not reinforced and in comparison with those on other atolls, definitely weak. Despite these limitations, Admiral Hill described Engebi as the most heavily defended of the three islands attacked in Eniwetok Atoll.

Lieutenant Colonel Masahiro Hashida, commanding the 1st Battalion, took charge of the Eniwetok Island Garrison Force. Its strength was set originally at 779 men, subsequently reinforced by an additional 129 from brigade reserve.[6] Armament was essentially the same as that allocated Engebi. In his defense plan, Hashida concentrated his force on the lagoon beaches and exhorted them to destroy the enemy at the water's edge. Beginning about midway of the island and extending southward, the following forces were established:

Right flank rear guard force: Infantry platoon, mortars, observation forces.

Right water's edge force: One mountain gun, one infantry platoon (less two squads).

Middle water's edge force: One mountain gun, one rapid fire gun, one infantry platoon (less one squad).

Left water's edge force: Two infantry squads, one mountain gun, one rapid fire gun.

Support force: One infantry platoon and one squad, three engineer platoons, tanks.

Defense works resembled those on Engebi, so effectively camouflaged with natural foliage they were unidentifiable from the air. In addition, new concrete pillboxes were rushed to completion on the island's southwestern tip and some land mines laid.

General Nishida established brigade headquarters and reserve on Parry, and this, together with a garrison force of 305 men, gave the island a total of 1,115 defending troops.[7] Aviation personnel and civilian surveyors added slightly more than 100 men to this force. The armament available consisted of the same types as Engebi's and Eniwetok's, but in greater quantities, with the exception of tanks and mountain guns.

The defense plan for Parry was embodied in an order issued 5 February 1944. As a general policy Nishida directed that "each unit will split up the enemy's infantry attack landing craft at the water's edge, and annihilate the enemy forces piecemeal. . . . If the enemy does land, we shall annihilate him by original creative night attacks." The battle for Parry was visualized in three stages, the "outcome of the battle and the fate of the Brigade" being decided in the second. In the third stage "the Brigade investigates and analyzes the over-all situation and decides to die gloriously."[8] Approximately one-half of the total troops were assigned to three strong points on the lagoon beaches, the remainder making up the island reserve force.

Parry's defensive positions were essentially

---

[5] JICPOA Bulletin 89–44, 12Jun44.

[6] TG 51.11 Rpt estimated enemy strength on Eniwetok Island as 900, based on the number buried.

[7] Enemy strength on Parry estimated at 1,300, based on the number buried.

[8] JICPOA Bulletin 89–44, 31, 32.

the same as those on Eniwetok, though not as well constructed. They were so well camouflaged, however, that not only were they virtually invisible from the air, but later attacking ground troops had difficulty spotting them. On the whole, they consisted of roofed over foxholes and trenches which protected the occupants from all gunfire and bombing, short of direct hits. An extensive mine field was laid on the northern tip of the island, and smaller ones set up in other areas. Some were buried just under the ground's surface, while others were concealed by lantanna and palm fronds.

PLANNING FOR ENIWETOK

The decision to seize Eniwetok was made during the planning phase for Kwajalein, Admiral Nimitz regarding it as a preliminary to a landing on Truk or other islands in the Carolines. Originally the CATCHPOLE plan called for the 2d Marine Division to seize Eniwetok Atoll on 19 March 1944, and the 27th Infantry Division to assault Kusaie ten days later.[9] As far along as January this concept was in force, the only change being that of revising the target date to 1 May in order that the naval units might participate in the proposed assault on Kavieng in April.[10] During January both the 2d Marine Division and the 27th Infantry Division (less 106th RCT) were undergoing intensive training for the operation.[11]

But there appeared to be some general reflection along the lines of seizing Eniwetok immediately after the Kwajalein operation. On 14 January 1944 Admiral Spruance expressed such a desire to Admiral Nimitz. The Fifth Fleet Commander said he would like to proceed against Eniwetok then rather than waiting until the fleet returned from the Kavieng assault.[12] And during the FLINTLOCK planning at Pearl Harbor, Admiral Turner's staff considered capture of Eniwetok as a part of that operation, staff studies being prepared "should success at Kwajalein prove rapid enough to justify the extension of the operation westward."[13]

Nor were these thoughts limited to the Navy. En route to Kwajalein Major General Holland Smith's staff drew up a tentative study dealing with the rapid seizure of Eniwetok. Dated 26 January 1944 and embodied in a memorandum to the corps chief of staff, the paper first reviewed the existent concept of two divisions striking on or about 1 May 1944. It then pointed out what could be gained by a quick attack:

> The advantage of seizing DOWNSIDE as a part of the FLINTLOCK operation are numerous and obvious. The task would be greatly facilitated if the operation could be executed before the Japanese have had an opportunity to strengthen his defenses. It would result in the savings of lives, equipment, money and effort. Furthermore, it would advance the progress of the war, and would serve to keep the enemy under continuing pressure.[14]

On 2 February conditions appeared propitious for pushing on to Eniwetok. It was apparent that Kwajalein Atoll could be secured without the assistance of the Expeditionary Reserve, Tactical Group-1. Moreover, carrier plane photos of Eniwetok, made on 30 January, coupled with the fortunate capture by the 7th Reconnaissance Troop of secret navigational charts of the atoll, provided enough information to make definite plans for landing attacks.[15] Rear Admiral Turner thereupon recommended to Vice Admiral Spruance that the assault on Eniwetok be undertaken in the immediate future. Two days later Admiral Nimitz radioed Spruance asking his recommendations concerning the capture of Eniwetok, as well as a carrier strike on Truk. The Fifth Fleet commander promptly recommended approval.

Admiral Nimitz arrived at Kwajalein on 5 February, and during his 42-hour visit on the atoll approved final plans for the Eniwetok and Truk operations.

---

[9] CATCHPOLE Plan, CinCPac and CinCPOA, 29Nov-43, serial 00272.

[10] Canceled by JCS on 12Mar44.

[11] VAC War Diary, Jan44, 11, and Capt Edmund G. Love, *The 27th Infantry Division in World War II*, Washington, Infantry Journal Press, 59.

[12] Jeter A. Isely & Philip A. Crowl, *The U. S. Marines and Amphibious War*, Princeton University Press, 1951, 291–292, hereinafter cited as *Isely & Crowl*.

[13] Ltr Adm R. K. Turner to CMC, 13Apr53, hereinafter cited as *Turner II*.

[14] Memo for Chief of Staff from J. C. Anderson, Acting ACofS G–5, 26Jan44, serial 007–2.

[15] *Turner II*.

ADMIRAL HILL AND GENERAL WATSON directed the seizure of Eniwetok Atoll.

As soon as it was evident that Eniwetok would follow Kwajalein, Rear Admiral Harry W. Hill, who had directed the successful occupation of Majuro Atoll, was instructed to report to Admiral Turner.[16] He did so on 3 February, and the next day the two admirals conferred with Major General Holland Smith and Brigadier General Thomas E. Watson on plans for the project (coded CATCHPOLE). Initially the target date for D-Day was set at 12 February, but was later changed to 17 February in order to permit Task Force 58 to replenish fuel and ammunition for the Truk strike.

Admiral Hill was given over-all amphibious command, his force being designated Task Group 51.11.[17] Watson's recently created Tac-

tical Group-1 would provide the assault troops. But the problem of garrison troops was another matter, as Admiral Turner later recalled:

. . . No garrison elements for Eniwetok were carried along from Hawaii when the Expeditionary Force began departing . . . none were available, nor was there enough shipping to lift any. When the decision was made to capture Eniwetok without waiting for additional forces, we had to rob both Kwajalein Island and Roi-Namur of considerable proportions of their garrisons and carry them forward in order to start the more urgent development and defense of the new base.[18]

Organized under V Amphibious Corps General Order No. 55–43 on 16 November 1943, Tactical Group-1 was originally composed of Tactical Group Headquarters and the 22d Marines (Colonel John T. Walker), reinforced by 2d Separate Pack Howitzer Battalion, 2d Separate Tank Company, 2d Separate Engineer Company, 2d Separate Motor Transport Company, 2d Separate Medical Company, and Shore Party and JASCO elements.

The tactical group was not an administrative unit except where tactical matters were concerned,[19] and it contained a streamlined type of staff, partly as an experiment and partly due to the lack of suitable staff personnel.[20]

The 22d RCT had been formed in early 1942 at Linda Vista, near San Diego, California, and had spent some 18 months on garrison duty in Samoa before receiving orders to proceed to the Hawaiian Islands. It was preceded by General Watson, who had commanded the 3d Marine Brigade in Samoa until its deactivation in early November 1943. Between its arrival in the Hawaiian Islands and its departure for Kwajalein in late January, the 22d Marines reinforced, camped at Maui and engaged in amphibious exercises, these being marred by a training accident on 6 December in which 21 men were killed and 27 wounded. On 23 December, the 106th Infantry Regiment (less 2d

---

[16] "I had no forewarning of the possibilities of my being put in command of the Eniwetok operations. The first intimation was a dispatch directing me to proceed from Majuro by air to Kwajalein and report to Admiral Turner." Ltr VAdm Harry W. Hill to CMC, 24Feb53, hereinafter cited as *Hill II*.

[17] "Owing to the fact that Task Forces 52 and 53 were not dissolved until 11 Feb, and because some departing groups still retained designations in those forces, no *force* numbers were available for assigning to Hill's command. Consequently, he was assigned a *group* number as a part of TF 51, which remained in existence and under my command until sunset 24 Feb. . . ." *Turner II.*

[18] *Ibid.*

[19] Ltr LtGen Thomas E. Watson to CMC, 1Mar53, hereinafter cited as *Watson.*

[20] "Events proved that this type of staff was inadequate to handle anything but a quick 'Flash' type of operation of a few days duration. . . . The streamlined staff idea died a rapid and just death. . . ." Ltr Col W. M. Greene, Jr., to CMC, 4Mar53, hereinafter cited as *Greene II.*

Battalion), reinforced, was detached from the Army's 27th Infantry Division and placed under General Watson's group. The 106th RCT had been earmarked for Nauru during the Gilberts Operation, but upon the cancellation of that island objective the regiment had sat out the campaign.

During the amphibious training phase for Kwajalein, attention was centered on the assault units rather than on the elements of Tactical Group-1, since the latter was scheduled for corps reserve. Watson's command trained with what it had, but it had precious little, as the general caustically pointed out in a later report:

In the actual operation (Eniwetok), most of the troops were landed in amtracs for their first time. The artillery battalion landed for its first time in DUKW's. We were sent to attack a coral atoll. We rehearsed on the large island of Maui on terrain and approaches totally unlike those of the target. Troops did not land in rehearsal supported by naval gunfire, air and artillery fires to accustom them to actual attack conditions. The artillery had no practice in landing in DUKW's and firing under situations experienced at Eniwetok. The rehearsal at Maui permitted no appreciable advance inland, no combat firing, no infantry-tank team movement. . . . In the attack on Eniwetok, the infantry, amtracs, amtanks, tanks, aircraft, supporting naval ships and most of the staffs concerned had never worked together before.[21]

But if amphibious training was lacking, small unit ground training was not, as Colonel Wallace M. Greene, Jr., Tactical Group-1's operations officer, later pointed out:

Although it is only too true that both regiments [22d Marines and 106th Infantry] had received very little amphibious training prior to participation in the Eniwetok operation, it is also a fact that the 22d Marines was at its peak in small unit training—training which was anchored firmly around a basic fire team organization. This was accomplished by tough, vigorous jungle training given the unit . . . during its stay in Western Samoa. Colonel Floyd Moore [then R–3] was largely responsible for the planning and supervision of this training. And it was this excellence in the fire teams which really paid off at Eniwetok. . . . This regiment was one of the best trained and spirited units I observed. . . . It was this period of isolation in Samoa and opportunity to train which made the 22d Marines far superior to the 106th Infantry in the close tough fighting on the beaches and in the bush of Eniwetok Atoll.[22]

[21] *TG–1 Spl Rpt*, 7.
[22] *Greene II*.

COLONEL JOHN T. WALKER, commanding the 22d Marines, reinforced.

Tactical Group-1, constituting the reserve group for the Kwajalein operation, sailed from the Hawaiian Islands on 22 January with the other elements of the Joint Expeditionary Force. Between 31 January and 3 February, while the 4th Marine Division and the 7th Infantry Division were seizing their objectives, Tactical Group-1 cruised eastward of Kwajalein Atoll anchoring in the lagoon at the latter date.

To augment Watson's striking force for Eniwetok, he was allotted V Amphibious Corps Reconnaissance Company, Company D (Scout) of the 4th Tank Battalion, 708th Provisional Amphibian Tractor Battalion less one LVT group (102 LVT's), Company A of the 708th Amphibian Tank Battalion (17 LVTA's), and a Provisional DUKW Battery (30 DUKW's and 4 LVT's). The assault elements counted some 5,820 Marines and 4,556 soldiers, giving a total troop strength of 10,376. In addition, initial occupation forces included the Marine 10th Defense Battalion, 3d Army Defense Battalion, and 47th Army Engineer Battalion.

Admiral Hill, accompanied by General Watson, carried his flag on board an attack transport, *Cambria*, which had been specially fitted out as an amphibious troop command flagship.[23] To lift the troops to their objective there were five other attack transports (APA), one transport (AP), two attack cargo ships (AKA), one cargo ship (AK), two destroyer transports (APD), two submarine chasers (SC), nine landing ships, tank (LST), and six landing craft, infantry (LCI). Ten destroyers made up the transport screen. Rear Admiral Jesse B. Oldendorf commanded the Fire Support Group, consisting of the battleships *Colorado*, *Tennessee*, and *Pennsylvania*, three heavy cruisers, and seven destroyers. Three escort carriers and four destroyers composed the Escort Carrier Group, under Rear Admiral V. H. Ragsdale, while Carrier Task Group Four, under Rear Admiral Ginder, consisted of one heavy carrier, two light carriers, two heavy cruisers, one light antiaircraft cruiser, and eight destroyers. In addition, there was a Minesweeping Group with two high-speed mine sweepers, three mine sweepers, and two motor mine sweepers; a Service Group with two tugs and two oilers, and an Ocean Tug Group containing one destroyer and two tugs.

It has been previously noted that Japanese defense forces in Eniwetok Atoll at this time amounted to nearly 3,500 troops. But intelligence derived from prisoners and documents taken at Kwajalein, as well as aerial photographs of Eniwetok, led American staff planners to estimate that Eniwetok Atoll was defended by some 800 Japanese: 500 from the 61st Naval Guard Force and a detachment of 300 of the 4th Civil Engineers. It was conceded, however, that "some portion of the 1st Mobile Shipborne Force, of 2,000 to 3,000 Army troops, may be in this area." It was assumed that the majority of the defenders were stationed on Engebi, about 100 to 150 on Parry, and a small detachment on Eniwetok. There was no evidence of any enemy on any other islands within the atoll.

In considering the Japanese dispositions, General Watson decided to strike first at Engebi. His plan for the seizure of the atoll included four phases, the first involving occupation of nearby islands or islets by artillery as was done at Kwajalein Atoll.

> Phase I: On D-Day, Company D (Scout) of the 4th Tank Battalion secure ZINNIA Island to the west of Engebi; simultaneously, V Amphibious Corps Reconnaissance Company secure five islands to the southeast of Engebi and cover the landings of the 2d Separate Pack Howitzer Battalion and the 104th Field Artillery Battalion on CAMELLIA and CANNA respectively.
>
> Phase II: On D-plus 1, 22d Marines, reinforced by the 2d Separate Tank Company (medium) and one platoon of the 106th Infantry's Cannon Company (two 105mm self-propelled guns), seize Engebi. Support fires provided by the two artillery battalions from CAMELLIA and CANNA.
>
> Phase III: On D-plus X, 106th Infantry, reinforced by 2d Separate Tank Company (medium), seize Eniwetok and two hours later be prepared to seize Parry. One battalion, 22d Marines, would be assigned the 106th Infantry for the latter landing, inasmuch as BLT 106–2 was not present.
>
> Phase IV: Complete seizure of all islands within the atoll.

An important aspect of the plan for Eniwetok, from the Marine viewpoint, was a new development in the troop command picture. Admiral Hill's plan provided that the Expeditionary Troops Commander (General Watson) be specifically placed in command of landings and garrison forces when ashore. At Roi-Namur, General Schmidt had received this command only after he stated he was ready to assume it. "In other words, [this command] formerly required positive action on the Ground Force Commander's part. Now it is established before the operation begins."[24]

---

[23] "Although it did not have the extensive facilities of the AGC, it served the purpose adequately, not only in the Majuro and Eniwetok operations, but also in the Saipan and Tinian operations which followed." *Hill II.*

[24] Memo from BrigGen O. T. Pfieffer to BrigGen G. C. Thomas, 23Feb44.

TRUK HARBOR as it appeared to planes from the *Intrepid* on the first carrier strike at that Japanese stronghold. (Navy photo.)

Planning also included a massive carrier strike on Truk concurrently with the invasion of Eniwetok. Truk lies 670 nautical miles from the latter atoll and was still regarded by many Americans as "Japan's Pearl Harbor" and the "Gibraltar of the Pacific." The Japanese Combined Fleet under Admiral Mineichi Koga, IJN, had been based there since mid-1942, as was headquarters, Sixth Fleet (submarines), and Admiral Spruance hoped that by striking a blow at the base, a major naval battle could be joined. Also, a strike on Truk was the necessary preliminary to a continuing advance westward through the Central Pacific. Thus, this planned attack (coded HAILSTONE) by Rear Admiral Marc Mitscher's Task Force 58 was closely connected with Hill and Watson's Eniwetok assault.[25]

[25] *Morison*, 315–317.

PRELIMINARY OPERATIONS

Reconnaissance flights over Eniwetok had been underway irregularly since the preceding December, but the first concentrated preliminary strikes were performed by Rear Admiral Ginder's Task Group 58.4 while the amphibious assault force still lay off Kwajalein.

Planes from *Saratoga, Langley, Princeton, Sangamon, Suwanee, and Chenango* plastered every structure above ground that they could spot. Fourteen enemy planes were destroyed on the ground at Engebi, and aerial photographs of targets were rushed back to *Cambria*. Admiral Hill later reported that these strikes destroyed all buildings of consequence, rendered the airfield at Engebi temporarily useless, and demolished at least one of the two coastal defense guns on the northeast corner of that island.

On 3 February 1944 a Marine scouting plane from Bougainville flew over Truk, spotting an imposing array of vessels at anchor. This aggregation was duly reported, but Admiral Koga knew the plane had flown over and realized that an air attack would probably follow. He thereupon ordered the *Yamato* and *Nagato* plus elements of the 2d Fleet to Palau on 4 February. A week later the Combined Fleet, with Admiral Koga in *Musashi*, sailed for Japan, leaving two cruisers, some destroyers, and a great many cargo and transport vessels in Truk lagoon.[26]

Admiral Spruance in *New Jersey* and Admiral Mitscher in *Yorktown* sortied from

Majuro with Task Force 58 (less TG 58.4) during the early morning hours of 12 February, bound for Truk.[27] Included in the armada were Carrier Group 1 (Rear Admiral John W. Reeves), Carrier Group 2 (Rear Admiral A. E. Montgomery), Carrier Group 3 (Rear Admiral F. C. Sherman), and Task Force 17, Patrol Submarines (Vice Admiral C. A. Lockwood). The list of ships counted five heavy carriers, four light carriers, six battleships (including *New Jersey*), five heavy cruisers, five

---

[26] *Nakajima.*

[27] Although TF 58 began operations against Truk the same day that the assault was made on Eniwetok Atoll, the Truk strike is narrated as a preliminary operation here because, among other things, it covered the Eniwetok operation.

JAPANESE NAVY YARD at Dublon Island, Truk Atoll, attacked by Admiral Mitscher's carrier-based planes. (Navy photo.)

light cruisers, 28 destroyers, and ten submarines.[28] At dawn on 17 February a total of 70 planes took off from five of Admiral Mitscher's carriers. As they appeared over Truk they were engaged by 80 Japanese planes which rose to contest the intrusion. Some 60 of these Nipponese craft were shot down with a loss of four American planes, while another 40 enemy planes were destroyed on the ground by strafing. A fragmentation and incendiary bomb run followed. Of 365 planes on Truk when the attacking force arrived, less than 100 remained unscathed, and not one rose into the skies the next day.

At 0443, 18 February, fighters, dive bombers, and torpedo bombers began their attacks on Japanese shipping in Truk lagoon. By the end of the day two cruisers (one *Naka* class and the *Kashima*), four destroyers, nine auxiliary craft, and 24 cargo and transport vessels had been sunk.[29] But the Japanese got in one blow. During the night of 17 February a group of "Kate" torpedo bombers sought out Mitscher's force and sent a torpedo into *Intrepid*, putting that carrier out of operation for several months. While the carriers were engaged in aerial assaults on Truk, Admiral Spruance conducted an around-the-atoll search for any fleeing enemy shipping. A cruiser and two destroyers were encountered and only one destroyer escaped. Spruance and Mitscher rendezvoused on 18 February and retired toward Kwajalein.[30] The strike had not produced the hoped-for fleet action, but it had materially damaged Japanese naval forces and, most important, had torn the mask of dark mystery from Truk, revealing it as virtually an empty shell.

LOADING OUT

On 3 February General Watson issued verbal instructions to his subordinates concerning the Eniwetok operation, and his written operation

order was issued one week later. V Amphibious Corps formally released Tactical Group-1 as Landing Force Reserve for the Kwajalein operation on 6 February, and assigned it duty under Admiral Hill's Task Group 51.11.

Only two weeks separated the decision to take Eniwetok and the departure for that objective, and Tactical Group-1 utilized the time to prepare feverishly for its new assignment. Perhaps no major amphibious operation in the Pacific was handled in such an impromptu manner. When General Watson's command had departed Pearl Harbor as floating reserve for the Kwajalein operation, it had no inkling that it would be assigned the Eniwetok mission. Furthermore, both regiments within the Tactical Group were as yet untried in combat.

Preparations for departure included reloading the 2d Separate Pack Howitzer Battalion on LST 246, and the 2d Separate Tank Company on LSD 1. By 15 February Admiral Hill's task group was ready to sail for Eniwetok, and at 0700 that day the Southern Group, composed of LST's, LCI's, and other slow-moving craft, departed Kwajalein lagoon. Seven hours later the Northern Group, consisting of transports, battleships, and carriers, was under way.

CANNA, CAMELLIA, AND ZINNIA

In the early morning hours of 17 February, Warrant Officer Shionoya, IJA, was interrupted in his labors on Parry Island's defenses by an air alarm and naval bombardment. He later recorded in his diary:

I was amazed at the severity of the bombardment.
The bombardment was most severe from 0500 to 0600.
. . . Everyone was looking on fully prepared for battle.
We all passed the night [sic] with the idea that they were finally going to land that very night [sic]. Planes circled the sky all day, and the bombardment also lasted all day. There was one man killed and four wounded. . . . There were some who were buried by the shells from the ships. . . . How many times shall we bury ourselves in the sand . . .[31]

While Warrant Officer Shionoya and his comrades buried themselves in the sand, *Colorado* and *Louisville* shelled Engebi, *Portland*

[28] *Morison*, 352–353.

[29] *Nakajima*.

[30] "I returned to Kwajalein in the New Jersey. . . . Adm Mitscher took Task Force 58 for a carrier strike on the Marianas. This strike included our first photographs of Saipan and Tinian, which islands were later taken in June and July, respectively." Ltr Adm Raymond A. Spruance to CMC, 11Mar53.

[31] Diary of Warrant Officer Shionoya, JICPOA Item 7005, hereinafter cited as *Shionoya*.

and *Trathen* poured fire onto Parry and Japtan, and *Indianapolis* and *Hoel* bombarded Eniwetok. Not a return shot was fired. Between 0700 and 0900 naval gunfire was lifted only to permit the planes from Task Group 58.4 to make their bomb and strafing runs on the islands under attack. During this period mine sweepers moved into Wide Passage, where 28 moored mines were found, swept, and destroyed. This was the first Japanese mine field encountered by United States naval forces in the war.[32] As soon as the mine sweepers had completed their work the shallow draft vessels of the Southern Group entered Eniwetok lagoon. At 0915 the Northern Group started into the lagoon via Deep Entrance. Moving in column, the fast mine sweepers led the way followed by destroyers, battleships, and transports.[33] Flanking 40mm fire raked Japtan and Parry, but still the enemy did not reply.

A naval officer who was present subsequently described the maneuver:

In my study of naval history I do not recall any other instance where a naval force of this size and composition has steamed up to an enemy-held harbor, formed column and entered in much the same manner as it would enter its home port. . . . To see the force enter this lagoon in column through a narrow entrance and between the shores of islands on either flank, and steam something over 20 miles through the enemy lagoon was one of the most thrilling episodes which I witnessed during the entire war.[34]

On Parry Island Major General Nishida reacted to the invasion by radioing a futile plea to his superiors in Tokyo: "Enemy fleet entering the lagoon in large numbers. Request reinforcements."[35]

By 1034 Admiral Hill's task group completed entrance into Eniwetok lagoon, and 45 minutes later 14-inch shells from *Tennessee* and *Pennsylvania* exploded with destructive fury on Engebi. While the larger ships were thus engaged, the heavy cruiser *Portland* and the destroyers *Heermann* and *McCord* worked over CAMELLIA and Rujiyoru (CANNA) Islands[36] in preparation for landings by the V Amphibious Corps Reconnaissance Company. At 1150 in the lagoon the Marines transferred from APD *Kane* to LST 272, clambered into six LVT–2's of the Army's 708th Provisional Amphibian Tractor Battalion and roared toward the two islands. Two LCI gunboats provided support, their rockets and 40mm guns producing geysers of sand and water. But there were no Japanese on either island. Captain James L. Jones, the company commander, reported CAMELLIA secured and uninhabited at 1355. Five minutes later Rujiyoru was reported in Marine hands. Five natives found on the latter island estimated Japanese strength at 1,000 on Engebi, Eniwetok, and Parry, respectively, with an additional 1,000 laborers on Engebi. Later on D-Day, Jones' command occupied five other islands in the chain southeast of Engebi, finding all of them devoid of enemy.

At 1344 General Watson directed his artillery to land in DUKW's according to schedule, the 2d Separate Pack Howitzer Battalion proceeding to CAMELLIA and the 104th Field Artillery Battalion (105mm) going to Rujiyoru. But progress of the former unit did not please Brigadier General Watson[37] who thereupon relieved the Marine artillery commander,[38] Major Alfred M. Mahoney assuming command of the howitzers.

Both artillery battalions, with five units of fire, were ashore at 1602 and ready for registration 30 minutes later. This was begun promptly, aerial artillery spotters having been on station for 45 minutes. By 1902 registration on Engebi was complete and 50 minutes

---

[32] *Hill II.*

[33] ". . . Deep Entrance had been chosen for use by the larger ships because due to the high currents through this passage it was not expected that it would be practicable to plant mines there, which assumption proved to be correct." *Ibid.*

[34] Ltr Capt Claude V. Ricketts, USN, to CMC, 9Mar53.

[35] *Ibid.*

[36] As has been done previously, the native name for an island is followed by the code name in parentheses. Where a code name is used alone, no record can be found of a native name.

[37] *Watson.*

[38] Col Walker quickly installed the relieved officer as artillery officer on the regimental staff, although no such billet was authorized. He was subsequently wounded in action on Engebi, awarded the Silver Star for his actions there, and resumed command of his battalion as soon as that unit reverted to control of the 22d Marines at the end of the operation.

ENGEBI AS IT APPEARED three weeks before the 22d Marines stormed ashore. In the left center of the photograph is the small pier separating Beaches White 1 and Blue 3. In the background is the western end of the airstrip. (Navy photo.)

later night-long harassing fires against the next day's objective were begun by the artillerymen. During registration and under the protection of naval gunfire, underwater demolition teams moved to within 100 yards of Engebi's shore in amphibian tractors and then swam 50 yards closer, reconnoitering the beaches and their approaches. No obstacles or mines were located.

One task remained before the day's work was ended. At 1848 Company D (Scout), 4th Tank Battalion, embarked in rubber boats from APD *Schley* with orders to land on Bogon (ZINNIA), the island lying directly west of Engebi, and prevent any attempted Japanese exodus in that direction. The darkness, heavy sea, and wind combined to split the company, one portion returning to the *Schley* and the remainder

landing three islands away on Elugelab (SAGEBRUSH). Working their way across the reefs, the latter group eventually secured its original objective at 0327 without meeting opposition.

Thus Phase I was accomplished on schedule without meeting any enemy or incurring any casualties. All hands could now turn their attention to the seizure of Engebi on D-plus 1, Phase II in the over-all plan.

FRAGILE IS SHATTERED

The 22d Marines' plan for Engebi (FRAGILE) designated Battalion Landing Team 1 (Lieutenant Colonel Walfried H. Fromhold) and Battalion Landing Team 2 (Lieutenant Colonel Donn C. Hart) assault elements, Battalion Landing Team 3 (Major Clair W. Shisler) constituting regimental reserve. Landing beaches were located on the approximate center of the lagoon side of the island, with a short finger pier separating them and demarking the initial BLT boundaries. (See Map 12, Map Section.) Once ashore, the line between the 1st and 2d Landing Teams extended along WHOOPIE Trail to ENERVATE Trail, thence along the latter to its terminal point and from there to the island's northern tip. Fromhold's command would land on Beach White 1 and handle the regiment's right zone, while the left, Hart's unit, would land on Beach Blue 3. Reinforcing elements to be landed under 22d RCT control were the 2d Separate Tank Company and one platoon (two 105mm self-propelled guns) from the 106th Infantry's Cannon Company. During the afternoon of D-Day the troops transferred from their transports to the LST's where LVT's awaited them, and readied themselves for W-Hour, set for 0845.

LANDING TEAMS 1 AND 2 churn their way toward Engebi's shore. (Navy photo.)

ENGEBI as it appeared after the aerial and naval bombardment. (Coast Guard photo.)

At 0655 on D-plus 1 (18 February) the guns of *Colorado* and *Louisville* heralded the opening attack on Colonel Yano's Engebi defenses. Minutes later *Pennsylvania* and *Tennessee*—1,000 yards offshore—joined in with a full-throated roar, and four destroyers, *McCord*, *Heermann*, *Phelps*, and *Hall*, got into the act.[39] From nearby Rujiyoru and CAMELLIA the 75mm and 105mm howitzers stepped up their fire, which had been harassing the defending Nipponese all night. Shortly before 0800 planes from *Sangamon* and *Suwanee* appeared on the scene, and the bombardment was halted abruptly to permit the aviators to get in their wallop. The naval guns and artillery resumed their discordant chant at 0811 and continued without cessation until one minute before the first wave of LVT's stormed ashore.

Reveille at 0400 had roused the assault troops on board the LST's, and by 0805 the loaded amtracs were in the rendezvous area. Ten minutes later the first wave crossed the line of departure and churned its way toward the beaches.[40] Preceding the LVT's were six LCI(G)'s, three on each flank, and these poured forth a torrent of rocket and 40mm fire. The gunfire hit the beach as planned, but because of an error in estimating the range, the rockets landed in the water, thereby providing no assistance whatsoever to the assault troops. The LVT(A)'s were the next in formation, five echeloned on each flank immediately behind the LCI's and seven in a V-shape between the leading elements of the assault landing teams. Thus, the amphibian tanks [41] did not go before the troop-carrying tractors, but were a part of the same wave. Smoke and dust from the bombardment drifted out over the water, obscuring

[39] Action Report of Bombardment of Eniwetok Atoll by Task Unit 51.17.2, 4, hereinafter cited as *TU 51.17.2 AR.*

[40] Gen Watson ordered his aide and a radio team into an LCVP which was dispatched to the flank of one assault battalion. This group's mission was to locate enemy guns by drawing fire. Later it was directed to report the progress of fighting ashore. In the attacks on Eniwetok and Parry Islands, Watson sent ashore OP teams under the command of various staff officers. The OP team leaders were instructed to report directly to the general on the progress of the respective operations. *Greene II.*

[41] The term, "amphibian tank," is used here because that is the Army designation and the LVT's were a part of an Army unit.

LANDING TEAM 1 encountered this emplaced Japanese tank on Engebi. (Navy photo.)

vision, and the amphibian vehicles tended to separate.[42] On the left, amtracs bearing elements of Company F (assault) and Company G (support) went 200–250 yards to the left of their assigned beach (Blue 3) and landed the troops at the western end of the airstrip. In the zone of Landing Team 1, the LVT's hit the correct beach, but the amtracs bearing the right platoon of Company A (assault) broke down, thus delaying this unit's arrival.[43]

Two minutes before W-Hour the first wave ground ashore on the sandy beach, but here the LVT's themselves contributed to a certain amount of congestion.

After the troops were landed, the first wave of LVT's remained in the vicinity of the beach, and thus added to the congestion there. According to plans and orders issued, they were to proceed inland to WHISKEY Road, and support the advance of the infantry. Their failure to proceed inland, as directed, was attributed to fallen coconut trees and debris blocking their passage. However, it is felt that with more determination the prescribed position could have been reached and the mission could have been accomplished. They

would then have been in a position to render excellent support with their machine guns and facilitated the seizure of SKUNK Point [44] [a strong point on the southern tip of Engebi].

Once the troops were ashore, the Japanese reacted by firing rifles, machine guns, and mortars at the Marines. But the stunned defenders did not put up an organized defense, their fire being anything but intense.

In Landing Team 1's area, Companies A and B moved forward on the right and left, respectively. Moments later Company C landed in support, wheeling to the right in order to overrun SKUNK Point. Company A's 3d Platoon landed somewhat later than its parent unit because of the LVT breakdown (noted earlier). Its mission was to echelon itself to the right rear of Company A and close the gap between that organization and Company C on the right.

Over on the regiment's left, Landing Team 2 was advancing with Companies E and F on the right and left respectively, the latter company covering a front slightly larger than that planned because of the shift to the left during landing. Company G, landing in support, wheeled left to assault WEASEL Point, a strong point on the island's northwestern tip.

Shortly after 0900 the medium tanks of the 2d Separate Tank Company began landing and moved in support of BLT 2/22 on the airstrip. But this was not accomplished without incident. One LCM operator inadvertently lowered his ramp prematurely, and the craft flooded and capsized. The tank on board had buttoned up before this occurred and only one of its crew escaped.[45]

Lieutenant Colonel Fromhold's battalion continued to advance on the right, but as it did so the flanks of Companies A and C were stretched to the breaking point in an effort to maintain physical contact. Sometime after 0900 this tenuous contact was broken and a gap created with an utterly unforeseen result. As noted earlier, Company A's 3d Platoon was to retain

[42] "This situation was investigated and the fault was determined to exist in the fact that the wave guides (Navy) had not led their waves close enough to their beaches before turning them loose on their own." Comments LtCol John P. Lanigan on prelim script, hereinafter cited as *Lanigan*.

[43] Notes of LtCol W. F. Frombold, undated, hereinafter cited as *Fromhold*.

[44] Ltr MajGen John T. Walker to LtCol Harry W. Edwards, 9Apr53. The LVT unit, on the other hand, reported that it "initially supported the advance of the infantry inland." Special Action Report, Eniwetok Operation, 708th Amphibian Tank Bn, 19Mar44.

[45] USS *Ashland*, Action Report for Eniwetok Atoll, 3May44, 6. hereinafter cited as *Ashland Rpt*.

contact between Companies A and C. When the break finally came this platoon remained with Company C, rather than with its parent unit.[46] Thus Company A was now working its way forward with only two platoons and its right flank exposed.

As Company C began exerting its inexorable pressure on SKUNK Point, many of the defending Japanese sought to escape by running up the southeastern beach. Because of the gap existing between Companies A and C, the fleeing enemy were thus in a position to fire on the former unit's right flank and rear—and this they did. At 0955 Company A had to turn and fight off a heavy attack on the southeastern beach. At the same time Company C threw in one platoon to plug the gap between its left flank

and that beach, thus bottling the remaining Nipponese in their strong point.

Faced by a maze of trenches and interconnected spider holes, the men of the 22d RCT quickly improvised an effective means of rooting out the Nipponese:

> Due to the many exits from the defenses and spider-type trenches, it was found expedient to toss smoke grenades into these prior to exploding main demolition charges. Thus, the exits were exposed by escaping smoke. These exits were then covered by fire or flame thrower when the main charge was exploded.[47]

As soon as the Regimental Weapons Company's half-tracks were ashore, two were assigned each assault landing team. But the shell holes and debris made movement difficult for the vehicles, particularly in the forward areas. Although they executed a few fire missions, half-tracks were used principally to haul

---

[46] Memo LtCol Glen E. Martin to LtCol Harry W. Edwards, 12Mar53, hereinafter cited as *Martin*.

[47] *Fromhold*.

MARINES work their way forward by fire and movement.

water and ammunition to the front and remove wounded to the rear. Experience typical of the difficulties encountered by these troops is related in a report of the 2d Heavy Platoon (half-track) which was attached to Landing Team 2 (Beach Blue 3):

> The platoon landed in the 8th wave on Beach White 1, which was not the beach planned on. . . . We turned left down the beach in an effort to reach BLT 2 on Beach Blue 3. We were held up at the pier by debris. . . . Finally we decided to force our way across the debris; in doing this the radiator of No. 1 half-track was punctured, thereby partially disabling the vehicle. While still on the beach the radios in No. 1 and No. 2 TCS jeeps went out also. . . . Eventually we reached a position on the right boundary of BLT 2, when we received orders to move out behind BLT 1. . . .[48]

At about 1100 Company A was reinforced by two 105mm self-propelled guns,[49] but 15 minutes later these were diverted to Company C, still busily hammering away at SKUNK Point. By this time Companies A and B had entered the wooded area which stretched about halfway between the landing beaches and the final objective, NEWT Point. Dense vegetation and trees knocked down by the naval bombardment impeded progress. In addition, a great many Japanese had taken refuge in the area and were now putting up a fanatical last-ditch fight.

Landing Team 3, which was now ashore, was directed to send Company I to BLT 1/22, and that company moved in behind Company A.

Contrasted with the difficulties Landing Team 1 was meeting, Lieutenant Colonel Hart's organization on the left was pushing forward rapidly over the airstrip and open terrain. Companies E and F, working with Marine medium tanks, had encountered four Japanese tanks, dug in, which were being utilized as pillboxes. These "fortifications" were knocked

out[50] and the advance continued. Enemy defenses which could not be easily overrun were by-passed on the premise that mopping up details could handle them.[51]

Colonel Walker was ashore by 1030. An hour later he was informed that Company G was still at work on WEASEL Point, Company F was attacking NEWT Point and Company E was well forward on line with F/22. Despite the differences in distance of advance, contact between the two battalions was still intact.

Meanwhile, Company I had taken over from Company A in the assault, the latter unit reverting to landing team reserve. While Companies B and I worked their way through the woods toward the airstrip, Company A busied itself with Japanese defensive positions on the southeastern beach.

At 1310 Colonel Walker notified General Watson that WEASEL Point and that portion of NEWT Point in Landing Team 2's zone were secure; that the island was in possession of the 22d Marines except for a pocket of enemy stretching across Landing Team 1's line of advance and lying between that unit and the airstrip. At 1400 the Tactical Group commander came ashore and 50 minutes later Engebi was officially listed as secure.

At 1456 Company C announced that SKUNK Point was overrun and at 1600 Companies B and I debouched from the wooded area onto the airstrip. At this point, I/22 reverted to control of Landing Team 3 and once again Company A moved in as the right flank assault unit. At 1830 Companies A and B reported secure that portion of NEWT Point falling within their zone.

An hour earlier Landing Team 3 and the 2d Separate Tank Company had been reembarked for action with the 106th Infantry Regiment in its D-plus 2 assault on Eniwetok.

The 22d RCT's first night on Engebi was "uncomfortable," one participant recalls.[52] Many Japanese had been by-passed during the rapid movement across the island, and complete mopping up was not conducted simultane-

---

[48] Combat Report of 2d Heavy Platoon for Engebi and Parry Islands, 15Mar44.

[49] "From personal experience, the 105mm self-propelled guns proved to be more of a hazard than a help. They made a very inviting target for Japanese mortar and small-arms fire, and consequently were not a very comforting thing to have around. After experiencing one of these barrages directed at the 105's, most of the Marines in my particular sector didn't like to see a 105 approach." Comments Maj Thomas D. Scott on prelim script, hereinafter cited as *Scott*.

[50] Ltr Maj Robert S. Reinhardt, Jr., to CMC 18Mar53, hereinafter cited as *Reinhardt*.

[51] *Lanigan.*

[52] *Ibid.*

MARINE TANKS work their way across Engebi's airstrip and onto NEWT Point. (Navy photo.)

ously with the initial attack. Moreover, little attention had been paid to collecting both United States and Japanese weapons which were left lying about the battlefield. Thus individual Nipponese were able to supply themselves with sufficient arms and ammunition to make isolated attacks on the Marines throughout the night.[53] Nor should it be forgotten that this was the first night in combat for these particular troops, and a certain amount of firing on their part was to be expected.

At 0800 on 19 February 1944 (D-plus 2), Colonel Walker raised the American flag on Engebi, as "To the Colors" was blown on a captured bugle. Mopping up continued throughout the day with demolition teams and flame throwers of the 2d Separate Engineer Company in the forefront.

[53] *Fromhold.*

While attention was focused on Engebi during D-plus 1, the V Amphibious Corps Reconnaissance Company and Company D (Scout) were not idle. The Reconnaissance Company surveyed two islets southeast of Engebi and found no signs of enemy or natives. But as it landed on Muzinbaarikku (ARBUTUS) Island, next to Engebi, it was met by grazing machine-gun fire. The Marines returned this fire and threw 60mm mortar shells toward the northern point of the island. Later it developed that the island contained enemy positions but no enemy, the fire coming from the vicinity of SKUNK Point on Engebi, where C/22 was heavily engaged.

As noted earlier, the Scout Company secured several islands southwest of Engebi in the early morning hours of D-plus 1. During the remainder of the day these Marines occupied five other islands in the chain, using rubber boats

and finding only one Japanese soldier, whom they took prisoner.

General Watson noted that on Engebi the enemy had conducted only a passive defense and that operations were proceeding according to plan. From captured documents it was determined that elements of the 1st Mobile Seaborne Infantry Brigade were on the atoll, and estimated enemy strength for Parry and Eniwetok was revised upwards to 400–550 and 700–800 respectively. The stage was now set for Phase III, the seizure of Eniwetok, to begin on schedule on the morning of D-plus 2.[54]

PRIVILEGE IS TAKEN

During the afternoon of D-plus 1 the 106th Regimental Combat Team (less BLT 106–2 [55]) was released from its status of floating reserve for Engebi, and at 1500 Colonel Ayers issued Field Order #4 for the seizure of Eniwetok Island (PRIVILEGE). Plans still optimistically called for Ayers' command to seize Parry (HEARTSTRINGS) as soon as Eniwetok was secured, and landing team assignments were made accordingly.

As previously described, Eniwetok is shaped like a blackjack. The selected landing beaches were situated on the lagoon side of the island on the northern portion of the blackjack's head, and designated Yellow 1 and Yellow 2, from left to right. The two assault units would land abreast, BLT 106–1 [56] on Beach Yellow 2 and BLT 106–3 on Beach Yellow 1. (See Map 13, Map Section.) This latter unit was instructed to send a rifle company across the island, form a defensive line facing northeast and prevent the Japanese from moving southwest. The remainder of the landing team would serve in regimental reserve. BLT 106–1 would secure the southwestern end of the island, utilizing not more than one rifle company, then pass through BLT 106–3's rifle company and

secure the northeastern portion of Eniwetok. The 104th Field Artillery Battalion would move into the southern end of the objective as soon as it was secured. Upon occupation of the target, RCT 106 would be prepared to move into LVT's for the planned assault on Parry Island. During the attack on Eniwetok, LT 3/22 would constitute a floating reserve.[57] One platoon of the 2d Separate Tank Company (medium) was attached to BLT 106–3, while the remainder of the Marine tanks were attached to BLT 106–1.[58]

The problem of getting the 2d Separate Tank Company refueled, rearmed, and transferred from the northern portion of Eniwetok Atoll to the southern area was one faced by the vessel which transported the tanks and LCM's from Kwajalein. Moving *Ashland* during darkness was considered hazardous, so at 0247 on D-plus 2 (19 February) 12 LCM's loaded with tanks and their crews, and accompanied by *SC 1066* departed on a dark 25-mile voyage across the choppy waters of the lagoon. "The results were satisfactory, all boats arrived as planned, but considerable risk of breakdown was present. The commanding officer recommended this course of action, but would hesitate to do so again." [59]

Eniwetok was subjected to harassing naval gunfire from D-Day until the morning of the landing, D-plus 2. Because there were few above-ground defenses and naval gunfire's flat trajectory is not especially damaging to underground fortifications, the total bombardment, in both quantity and quality, did not equal that for Engebi and Parry. Some 204.6 tons of projectiles, none larger than 8-inch, were poured

---

[54] TG-1 Unit Report 2, 18Feb44, 1–3.

[55] It is well to recall that BLT 106–2 was involved in the Majuro occupation and did not participate in the Eniwetok operation in any way. The basic infantry organization of RCT 106 was the 1st and 3d Battalion Landing Teams.

[56] As noted previously in this monograph, when taken from Army reports, Army terms and designations will be used in referring to Army actions.

[57] "Effective combat units are achieved by effective unit training, and can never be replaced by assorted combinations of component units, however highly trained. The make-up of the landing force on Eniwetok Island illustrates my point. A two battalion regiment is difficult to fight, and when the reserve normal to a regiment is made up of a totally strange battalion from a different service . . . unit integrity is being sorely violated." Ltr Col Joseph C. Anderson, USA, to CMC, 27Feb53, hereinafter cited as *Anderson II*.

[58] RCT 106, reinf, (less BLT 106–2) Unit Operations Report (DOWNSIDE), 15Apr44, hereinafter cited as *RCT 106 Rpt*.

[59] *Ashland Rpt*, 3, 6.

on Eniwetok by *Tennessee, Portland, Indianapolis, Trathen, Phelps, Hailey, Hoel,* and *Haggard.* In contrast Engebi received 1,179.7 tons and 944.4 tons were scheduled for Parry. Further, there was no preliminary artillery bombardment as had been placed on Engebi and would be laid on Parry because there were no nearby islands on which the guns could be positioned. The concept of a light naval bombardment (in comparison with the other islands) was based on the belief that Eniwetok was lightly held and that the 106th RCT would have little trouble taking it.

With Y-Hour set for 0900, *Portland, Indianapolis,* and two destroyers stepped up their harassing fire to preliminary bombardment strength at 0710. An hour later this was checked to permit an air strike and then resumed at 0826. Fearing that the tank-loaded LCM's would not arrive on schedule, Admiral Hill reset Y-Hour to 0915 and later moved it to 0922. The armor arrived on time, however, and the soldiers were ordered into the beach, the first wave crossing the line of departure shortly after 0900.

The assault troops had been awakened at 0430 and departed their LST's for the rendezvous area three hours later. Now as their LVT's lurched toward the shore, they were preceded by the usual groupings of LVT(A)'s and rocket-carrying LCI's. At 0918 the first soldiers touched ground and began moving inland against light opposition, preceded by the amphibian tanks.

BLT 106–3 (Lieutenant Colonel Harold I. Mizony) landed on Beach Yellow 1 with Companies L and K abreast Company I in reserve. Company L, in the left, was to pivot on its left flank, face north and extend toward the ocean beaches. Company K was to drive straight across the island to the ocean shore and then mop up in L/106's rear. On Beach Yellow 2, BLT 106–1 (Lieutenant Colonel Winslow Cornett) scheduled a similar maneuver. Company

ASSAULT FORCES of RCT 106 on their way into Yellow Beaches 1 and 2 on Eniwetok Island. (Navy photo.)

137

LANDING TEAM 3/22 prepares to assault a coconut log emplacement on Eniwetok Island.

B, on the left, was to cross the island, while Company A pivoted on its right flank and moved southward between the lagoon beach and a north-south trail.

But these plans went awry. Before the LVT(A)'s could go the prescribed 100 yards inland, they encountered a steep bluff some nine feet high which blocked their progress. As they ground to a halt, the troop-carrying amphibians followed suit, and the end result was congestion on the beaches that kept succeeding waves afloat beyond their scheduled landing time. A network of insidious spider traps, backed up by machine-gun and mortar fire, helped keep the advance at a standstill.

General Watson reacted to this stalemate by sending a message to Colonel Ayers at 1004, "Push your attack." Six minutes later the

beachmaster notified Admiral Hill that he was holding up all waves because of the congested beaches "due to slowness of movement of troops inland." At 1023 General Watson prodded the attacking troops once more. He ordered Colonel Ayers to "move troops forward and inland, clear beaches. Advance."

By 1100 the 3d Battalion had pushed inland about 100 yards, Companies L and K abreast, the former's left flank on the lagoon beach and K/106's right flank in the air about two-thirds of the way across the island. An hour later the landing team had pushed northward a short distance, the right flank resting about 70 yards from the ocean beach.[60]

In the 1st Battalion area the cross-island attack was somewhat more successful, but the

---

[60] *RCT 106 Rpt.*

138

southward advance was slow, the soldiers fighting dense undergrowth and undulating ground as well as the ever-present spider trap defenses. Elements of Company B managed to reach the ocean shore by 1145, but this was an isolated group which had lost contact with the remainder of the unit. Company A was moving slowly, attempting to execute its pivot maneuver to the right. Scheduled to land behind Company B, Company C approached Beach Yellow 2, which was badly congested, in the fifth and sixth waves. Four LCVP's were somehow diverted some distance south of the prescribed beach and landed against stiff opposition. But Company A came to the rescue by advancing along the beach.[61]

By 1200 contact was established between Lieutenant Colonel Cornett's units, and his command faced south, in the shape of a huge "S". The farthest advance was made by Company A, its right flank extending to the lagoon beach. Company C was in the center, forming the bend in the line. Company B extended to the left with its left flank on the ocean beach. Although a line had been established, opposition in the rear from by-passed Japanese was far from eliminated as the 3d Battalion, 22d Marines would soon discover.

By landing on Beach Yellow 2 and advancing to the south, BLT 106–1 was in a position to take the bulk of the Japanese defenses from the rear. Enemy reaction took the form of a strong counterblow in an attempt to ward off the inevitable. No sooner had contact been effected within the battalion and the "S"-line formed, than some 400 Nipponese hit it furiously. Company B's line was broken momentarily, but quickly reformed and by 1245 the soldiers had thrown back the Japanese. Despite this blow to the enemy, however, progress did not improve, and Cornett's command inched its way forward, assisted by Marine medium tanks and 105mm self-propelled guns of the Cannon Company.

At 1230 Colonel Ayers visited the 3d Battalion's command post and directed that unit to push forward and secure the northern end of Eniwetok. Reinforcing elements included one platoon from the 2d Separate Tank Company (medium) and one platoon of self-propelled 105mm guns. Company I replaced Company K on line, the latter organization taking over the mop-up mission in the rear. Shortly thereafter the battalion stretched across the island from beach to beach and began advancing slowly.

Eniwetok was proving a much tougher nut to crack than had been originally expected, and Colonel Ayers ordered the reserve (3d Battalion, 22d Marines) to land, but refused Major Shisler's request to take his half-tracks ashore. At 1330 the Marines began debarking from LCVP's on Beach Yellow 1 and moved to an assembly area north of the pier, fighting Japanese on the way.[62] Shisler was directed to take over BLT 106–1's left flank, relieving Companies B and C. Company B would revert to landing team reserve and Company C would move into Company A's area, beefing up the force there. A general attack to the south was scheduled for 1515.

The boundary between 3/22 and 106–1 lay just southeast of the trail that ran the length of Eniwetok Island. Thus the Marines assumed responsibility for approximately two-thirds of the entire southern zone. And as they began moving forward to relieve BLT 106–1's left flank, once again they were forced to fight by-passed Japanese.

The attack to the south began promptly at 1515. BLT 106–1 moved forward with Companies A and C on the right and left respectively, Company B in reserve. Landing Team 3/22 advanced with Company L on the right, Company K on the left and Company I in reserve. Some 300 yards were covered before stiff opposition was encountered in the form of mutually supporting coconut log emplacements.

Most of these positions could not be discerned until the troops were within 25 or 30 yards of them. Because of the close proximity of the troops to the positions, the dense jungle with consequent lack of proper observation, it was determined that naval gunfire was

---

[61] *Crowl and Love*, XIX–42.

[62] Historical Branch interview with Col. Clair W. Shisler, 24Apr53, hereinafter cited as *Shisler*.

not practicable. Mortar fire had very little effect on the positions. . . .[63]

Once again Major Shisler requested permission to bring his half-tracks ashore and once again Colonel Ayers refused. The Marine commander then requested tank support, but this was not forthcoming. Nor were all the assault weapons available, only one bazooka being on hand.[64] Infantrymen and a platoon from the 2d Separate Engineer Company attacked the positions with flame throwers and satchel charges, and the Marines continued to advance slowly through the dense undergrowth.

As the afternoon wore on BLT 106–3 pushed slowly northward through the same sort of undergrowth which proved a serious obstacle as well as providing concealment to the enemy. Shortly after 1800 Lieutenant Colonel Mizony reported his lines about 500 yards north of the pier at Beach Yellow 1. He informed his superior that he doubted if he could reach the end of the island by dark, but was in a position to set up a defensive line for the night.

Meanwhile, at 1635 General Watson had radioed Colonel Ayers: "Absolutely necessary that you land your artillery prior to darkness today so that it may register on HEART-STRINGS early tomorrow morning. . . ." Sixty-five minutes later Tactical Group-1 was notified that one battery of the 104th Field Artillery Battalion was on Beach Yellow 1.

At 1850 Colonel Ayers dispatched a message to the units under his command: "You will continue to advance until you reach the end of the island. Call for illumination when necessary." BLT 106–3, operating in the northern portion of Eniwetok, attempted to do this, picking up about 200 yards during the entire night. Although searchlight and star shell illumination were utilized, the battalion took a dim view of such nocturnal operations:

Movement at night proved to be both difficult and costly. It was impossible to see the camouflaged holes, contact was poor, and the troops as a whole did not seem to have the confidence in themselves that was so apparent throughout the day. . . .[65]

When the RCT commander's message reached the battalions in the south, they were some 600 yards short of their objective. And in contrast to BLT 106–3 in the north, they were attacking a heavily fortified area. At dusk a few tanks finally arrived at Major Shisler's command post, but when he informed the tank commander of the plan to push on during darkness, the armor's leader pronounced it "impossible" and withdrew.[66] Moreover, the expected illumination did not materialize.[67]

Since no tank support was received and no illumination given prior to the time when the night attack was scheduled, the commanding officer of LT 3/22 informed his unit commanders no attack would be made. Orders were issued for the units of LT 3/22 to hold their present positions for the night.[68]

Groups of Japanese, usually numbering six to ten individuals, attacked the Marine lines during the night, but no large coordinated attack was forthcoming. Many of the enemy who did attack were armed with crude spears, knives and rifles. All their attempts to break through were frustrated.[69]

Dawn brought a surprise to Major Shisler's command. On the landing team's right flank, where BLT 106–1 was supposed to be, there was only one soldier from that unit.[70] During the night the Army organization, with the exception of the lone infantryman, had withdrawn some 300 yards to the rear without notifying the adjoining Marines.[71] Thus a sizeable gap in the lines existed through most of the night. Major Shisler quickly ordered elements of Company I forward to plug the hole, while a

[63] Document dated 10Apr44, submitted by Capt Buenos A. W. Young, believed to be Eniwetok Action Rpt of 3d Bn, 22d Marines, hereinafter cited as *BLT 3/22 SAR*.

[64] Some Army troops from Kwajalein had come on board 3/22's troop ship while it lay off that island and passed the word that bazookas were ineffective. The men of the 3d Bn had not experienced combat and they accepted this statement from men whom they regarded as combat veterans. Thus when 3/22 was engaged in Eniwetok Island it suddenly found itself lacking these important weapons. *Shisler*.

[65] *RCT 106 Rpt*. BLT 106–3 S–3 Summary.

[66] *Shisler*.

[67] Illumination was provided BLT 106–3 in the north, but available information indicates that this was not the case in the south.

[68] Maj William E. Sperling, III, an undated paper titled "BLT 3/22 on Eniwetok Island," hereinafter cited as *Sperling*.

[69] Ltr LtCol Earl J. Cook to CMC, 23Feb53.

[70] *Shisler*.

[71] Ltr LtCol Robert A. McCabe to CMC, 12Mar53, hereinafter cited as *McCabe*.

coordinated attack which had been planned for dawn had to await BLT 106–1's return to its original positions.

At about 0830 on the morning of D-plus 3 (20 February) between 40 and 50 Japanese suddenly attacked the Marines' battalion command post. Surprise was on the side of the enemy and an estimated eight Marines were killed (including the battalion operations officer) and an equal number wounded [72] before Master Sergeant John J. Nagazyna organized a force which eliminated the attackers.[73]

Meanwhile, both LT 3/22 and BLT 106–1 had begun attacking to the south, and enemy opposition was much the same as that encountered on the preceding day. At 1000 it appeared that Major Shisler's repeated requests for tank

support had borne fruit. Four light tanks belonging to the 106th RCT rumbled up into the Marine area at that time, but these rumbled away before actually engaging in combat.[74]

Shortly after the four tanks disappeared, however, the Marines managed to persuade two Army self-propelled 105mm gun crews to assist them with their weapons. These guns "did render excellent assistance and worked in fine

---

[72] Accounts vary as to the exact number of casualties suffered by 3/22 in this action. The number given here is an estimate based on available information.

[73] Ltr Capt Buenos A. W. Young to CMC, 9Mar53.

[74] *BLT 3/22's SAR* cites numerous instances where tank support was promised by RCT 106 but was not delivered. Moreover, *Shisler* relates that it was particularly "disheartening" to him that he was not allowed his half-tracks, nor was he given tank support. *22dMar SAR*, 3, states: "During the attack on PRIVILEGE, BLT #3 was unassisted by tanks though two full tank companies were ashore and being used by the regiment. This left a feeling of desire on the part of the higher echelon of command to save their other troops at the expense of BLT #3." Inasmuch as one of the tank companies was a Marine unit, disappointment was intensified.

MARINES advance toward the southwestern tip of Eniwetok.

cooperation with the infantry units of LT 3/22 in the reduction of numerous enemy strong points."[75]

At 1445 Marine and Army elements reached the tip of Eniwetok, and 15 minutes later General Watson was notified that the southern end of the island was secure. As is always the case, mopping-up operations continued.

During the morning, the remainder of the 104th Field Artillery Battalion landed with the mission of supporting the attack on Parry Island, tentatively scheduled for 21 February but later firmed for the 22d. Permission was granted for the artillerymen to support the advance of BLT 106–3 up the northeastern neck of Eniwetok, and this was initiated at 1155.

Lieutenant Colonel Mizony's command began its D-plus 3 daylight advance to the north shortly after 0800. Company L continued as the left flank unit, while Company K replaced Company I on the battalion right. Marine medium tanks continued to give close support, and engineers carrying pole charges, flame throwers and shaped charges materially assisted

in the reduction of enemy strong points. By nightfall the landing team was 1,000 yards from the northern tip of Eniwetok. The attack was resumed the next morning and continued in the usual manner. At 1430 on D-plus 4 (21 February) Mizony informed Ayers that the northern end of the island was secure. With Admiral Hill and General Watson on hand, the Stars and Stripes were raised on Eniwetok Island at 1721.

Altogether, it took three days to overrun Eniwetok, and the 3d Battalion, 22d Marines bore the brunt of the operation during a sustained 24-hour advance. Its area included the most heavily defended portion of the island. But it was clear that the commanding general was not pleased with the performance of the 106th RCT:

> . . . In the assault against PRIVILEGE Island by the 106th Infantry . . . the assault troops did not move forward rapidly from the beaches (thereby causing a serious congestion), did not operate in close cooperation with tanks and failed to realize the capabilities of and to use to the fullest extent naval gunfire and close support aviation.[76]

---

[75] *Sperling.*

[76] *TG–1 Spt Rpt 7;* "It would be wrong and even un-

UNOPPOSED LANDINGS were made on a number of small islands in Eniwetok Atoll. Here a group of Marines goes ashore on one of them. (Navy photo.)

Although Eniwetok Island was secured, the battle for Eniwetok Atoll was not yet complete and movements were under way to bring this to an expeditious end.

SIDESHOW

While primary attention was focused on the assault of Eniwetok Island, other units were actively engaged in other portions of the atoll.

The chain of islands making up the eastern rim of Eniwetok Atoll had been assigned to Captain Jones' V Amphibious Corps Reconnaissance Company. On the morning of D-plus 2 this unit continued with its mission.

Operating from the APD *Kane*, the Marines secured ten islands and islets during the day without meeting any natives or enemy. At 1600 General Watson ordered the company to occupy Japtan (LADYSLIPPER) before dark, and two hours later the unit was ashore. A Japanese flag flying from a mast in the center of the island indicated the presence of the enemy, but it turned out that the invaders were the only human beings there.

Inasmuch as Japtan bounds Deep Entrance and lies immediately north of Parry, Watson selected it as a position for the 2d Separate Pack Howitzer Battalion to support the Parry operation.[77] The Reconnaissance Company selected landing beaches for the DUKW-borne artillery, and at 1000 the next day (20 February) guided the howitzer battalion ashore.

In the midst of these multiple activities, a survey of Jeroru Island (LILAC) was overlooked. This minute bit of coral lies just inside the lagoon between Japtan and Parry. On 21 February a reconnaissance patrol reported it unoccupied. The Corps Reconnaissance Company thereupon reembarked in *Kane*, awaiting the attack on Parry the following day.

The western chain of islands in the atoll was the responsibility of Company D (Scout), 4th Tank Battalion under Captain Edward L.

Katzenbach, Jr. As noted earlier, the northern portion of these small islands was secured by the evening of D-plus 1. The next morning the Marines began their landings on the southern group, starting with Rigili (POSY). Here enemy fire was received, and a brisk five-minute fire fight followed. When it was over nine Japanese lay dead. The remaining seven islands in the chain were secured during the day without meeting any natives or Nipponese. At the close of the day the scouts reembarked on *Schley* and stood by for the Parry attack.

Thus, when both Eniwetok Island and the islet of Jeroru were reported secured on the afternoon of 21 February (D-plus 4), there remained only one island to be taken in the entire atoll—Parry.

BREAKING HEARTSTRINGS

The first few hours on Eniwetok Island clearly indicated the original invasion schedule could not be maintained, but for a time General Watson still hoped that the island would be secured at the end of the day. By 2100, however, he was convinced that "the capture of PRIVILEGE Island would not be completed before the evening of 20 February at the earliest." Therefore, he decided to take the victors of Engebi (Colonel Walker's 22d Marines) off their island and turn the Parry (HEARTSTRINGS) mission over to them, with a target date of 21 February.[78] Walker was ordered to begin reembarkation immediately and arrive in the transport area by 1600 the following day.

At 0800 D-plus 3 (20 February) LT 1/22 was afloat in the transport area. Four hours later responsibility for Engebi was assumed by the 3d Army Defense Battalion, reinforced by Companies A and D, 111th Infantry Regiment.[79] And later that afternoon Landing

---

fair to ignore the brave and competent performance of many fine and highly trained individuals and small units who collectively made up the 106th Infantry . . . ." *Anderson II.*

[77] As has already been noted, the 104th Field Artillery Battalion would support the Parry assault from the island of Eniwetok.

[78] "When it became apparent that this operation [Eniwetok Island] would require two or three days, it became necessary to revise the entire operations for the assault on Parry Island . . . . The change in plans was effected very expeditiously and efficiently by Gen Watson and Col Walker, together with members of my staff." *Hill II.*

[79] These were forward elements of the 111th Infantry Regiment. That organization later relieved RCT 106 in its duties as garrison for Eniwetok Atoll.

PARRY ISLAND (looking south) under bombardment the day before the 22d Marines landed there.   (Navy photo.)

Team 2, 22d Marines, arrived in the transport area.

Following a conference of unit commanders at 1400 on 20 February, General Watson issued Tactical Group-1 Operation Order 3–44. This postponed the attack on Parry until 0845 (later changed to 0900), 22 February. It also provided for the relief and reembarkation of the 3d Battalion, 22d Marines, and the 2d Separate Tank Company the morning of 21 February in order that these organizations might participate in the Parry assault. Further, additional forces were assigned the regimental combat team to bolster its striking power.

In the midst of this planning a shift was made in landing beach designations, which was to play an important part in the operation. As originally established, a small 20-yard-long pier on the northern lagoon shore of Parry separated Beach Green 2 and Beach Green 3, the latter being south of the marker. On Beach Green 3's southern flank was a larger 30-yard-long pier,

designated VALENTINE Pier. During the planning it was decided that too much territory was involved in this scheme, and the beach designations were shifted northward about 300 yards, Beach Green 3's southern flank then resting just south of the smaller of the two piers. "This information apparently was not known in time by all naval forces," [80] and the effect of this will be subsequently seen. (See Map 14, Map Section.)

On 21 February Colonel Walker issued his Operation Order 10–44. The landings would be executed from the lagoon on the northern portion of Parry on Beach Green 2 (north) and Beach Green 3 (south). The northern one-third of the island constituted the first objective. Separating this area from the southern two-thirds was an 0–1 line running east-west. The attack south of the 0–1 line would be made on order by two battalions abreast, the battalion

[80] *Fromhold;* Historical Branch interview with Col Floyd R. Moore, 1Mar53, hereinafter cited as *Moore.*

144

boundary running north-south in the center of the island.

LT 1/22 would land on Beach Green 3 at Z-Hour, drive straight across the island and secure that area falling within its zone. It would then be prepared to attack south, being responsible for the eastern sector.

LT 2/22 would land on Beach Green 2 at Z-Hour, secure the portion of island in its zone, thoroughly mop up the northern one-third of Parry and then revert to regimental reserve.

LT 3/22 would land on Beach Green 3 on order and take over the western area in the drive to the south.

The 2d Separate Tank Company (medium) would land in the 4th wave, attack enemy defenses in the northern portion of Parry and prepare to support the attack to the south.

Major James L. Rogers' 708th Provisional Amphibian Tractor Battalion would once again take the troops ashore and support the landing in the same formation as was used at both Engebi and Eniwetok Islands.

Other organizations which would be prepared to land on order included Company C, 766th Light Tank Battalion (RCT 106), V Amphibious Corps Reconnaissance Company, Company D (Scout) of the 4th Tank Battalion, and a Provisional Landing Force consisting of five provisional companies organized within the 10th Defense Battalion (Marine).[81] Ticketed for Group reserve was BLT 106–3, which would be reembarked from Eniwetok the morning of 22 February.

One aspect of preparing for the Parry assault was the diligent search among the ships for hand grenades, demolition charges, and small arms.[82] These were now in short supply, as were artillery shells. Some grenades and demolitions were found, but it was necessary to fly in an additional 775 grenades and 1,500 demolition caps from Kwajalein. A number of BAR's and rifles were acquired from RCT 106 to make up deficiencies in RCT 22, and artillerymen were directed to reduce planned harassing fires.

At 2100 on D-plus 4 Colonel Walker reported to General Watson that his men were transferred to the LVT-bearing LST's and "all preparations for the attack on HEART-STRINGS Island on 22 February [are] complete."

While the Marines prepared for their landings on Parry, Warrant Officer Shionoya and his comrades on that island were impatiently awaiting the assault.[83] On the morning that the 22d Marines went into Engebi, the Japanese warrant officer wrote:

We thought they would land this morning, but there was only a continuation of their bombardment and no landing. As this was contrary to our expectations, we were rather disappointed.

The next morning preparations were underway for the landing on Eniwetok. To the defenders of Parry it seemed that they would be the target that day, and once more Shionoya recorded his reactions:

When I looked out to sea there were four transports and three destroyers lined up. That surely made me angry. At 0540 the enemy was in the midst of preparations for landing. Each unit got orders to prepare for battle and fell to its respective position. . . .[84]

On the basis of resistance encountered on Eniwetok Island, Admiral Hill decided to intensify the naval bombardment of Parry. On D-plus 3 (20 February), *Tennessee* and *Pennsylvania* lay a mere 850 yards off the island and "conducted a close, destructive enfilade bombardment."[85] The next day *Pennsylvania* delivered plunging main battery fire from 0740 to 1630, and both battleships repeated this from 1730 to 1900. That night the 2d Separate Pack Howitzer Battalion on Japtan Island and the 104th Field Artillery Battalion on Eniwetok

---

[81] 10th Defense Battalion (Marine) Operation Order 4–44, 21Feb44. This provisional group was not landed. The battalion operations officer later recalled, "enthusiasm ran high among the troops and there was much grumbling when, on the morning of the scheduled landing, the men were ordered to secure." Ltr Col Paul A. Fitzgerald to CMC, 12Mar53.

[82] "One of the basic reasons for shortage of grenades, equipment and workable weapons was because of the fact that casualties [on Engebi and Eniwetok] were not stripped of their equipment, weapons and ammunition prior to evacuation. A great proportion of this equipment, etc., was later found to be in the hands of ships' companies and was recovered. . . ." *Lanigan.*

[83] Whether Shionoya survived until the day Parry was assaulted is a moot question. The final entry in his diary is dated 19Feb44.

[84] *Shionoya.*

[85] *TU 51.17.2 AR,* 4.

placed harassing fire on Parry, as did four destroyers.

At 0600 on D-plus 5 (22 February) the two artillery battalions stepped up their harassing fire to preparatory strength, the Marine cannoneers augmenting their howitzer fire with bullets from sixteen .50 caliber machine guns.[86] At 0700 the Navy joined in with a full scale bombardment from *Tennessee, Pennsylvania, Louisville, Indianapolis,* and *Hailey.* At 0845 the first wave of Marines left the line of departure and headed for Beaches Green 2 and 3, accompanied by LVT(A)'s and preceded by LCI's. A string of buoys had been set up from the line of departure to within 500 yards of the beach to indicate the division between landing teams during the approach.[87] But the smoke and dust generated by the bombardment of Parry rolled out over the choppy water, curtailing vision and making the buoys little help. Moreover, as the LVT's butted their way toward shore, they were guided toward the original landing beaches rather than toward the ones newly established 300 yards northward.[88]

The LCI(G)'s supporting the right flank approached shore and began firing their 40mm batteries, when suddenly all three craft were struck by 5-inch fire from *Hailey,* apparently because they were further south than had been expected. The acting-gunboats lost 13 men killed and 46 wounded, as well as receiving extensive damage, but nevertheless they fired their rockets before retiring from the scene.[89]

On the 22d RCT's right flank, the first wave of LT 1/22 hit the beach at 0900 just south of VALENTINE Pier, some 300 yards south of its scheduled landing position; the second wave followed at 0908, landing 200 yards north of

the pier, and the third wave came in three minutes later, debarking in the gap between the first and second waves.[90] Units were intermingled on the beach, and as at Namur junior officers and noncommissioned officers used their initiative.

During hand-to-hand encounters in the shell holes which pockmarked the beach, officers and non-coms rose splendidly to the task of reorganizing confused men who were separated from their units and leaders.[91]

The Marines under Lieutenant Colonel Fromhold were meeting stiff resistance from intense Japanese machine-gun and mortar fire, and casualties on the beach were described as "fairly heavy."

It is well to note here that when landing on an enemy-held island, it is often difficult, if not virtually impossible, to determine whether the landing has been made on the correct beaches. Unless something is obviously wrong, it is generally assumed that the landing has been correctly performed. This was the case of both assault landing teams at Parry. Initially they were under the impression that they had landed some 300 yards north of where they actually were.[92]

In the combat teams' northern zone, Landing Team 2/22 hit the beach on schedule and in contact with the unit on its right. Thus, it too was some 300 yards south of its landing beach and accordingly had a greater area of responsibility than originally planned. Initially, resistance was light, but some men on the left flank were killed by an enemy mine field.[93] Lieutenant Colonel Hart's battalion began pushing across the island with Companies G, F, and E from left to right. The landing team moved roughly as a line, the left flank attempting to move along the northwestern and northern shore line, while the right flank remained in contact with Landing Team 1/22 to the south. As had been the case on Engebi, there was no organized Japanese resistance, only fanatical

---

[86] The artillerymen had 20 units of fire for these weapons. Ltr LtCol Alfred M. Mahoney to CMC, 25Mar53, hereinafter cited as *Mahoney.*

[87] Whether these buoys marked the old or new beach designations is not known.

[88] A possible factor in the confusion regarding the landing beaches was that the smaller, or northern pier, was destroyed by naval gunfire. Thus the only pier visible was VALENTINE Pier. *Martin.*

[89] At about the same time a spotter plane carrying the Marine artillery aerial observer flew too low and into the artillery barrage. It burst into flames and crashed.

[90] The components of each wave are unknown to the author. Inasmuch as the landing units were intermingled and based on available records, it is assumed for the purpose of this narrative that LT 1/22's line included Companies A, C, and B, from right to left.

[91] *Fromhold.*

[92] *Ibid.*

[93] *Reinhardt.*

defenders in isolated groups who had to be rooted from their spider traps and individual strong points.

The intensive fires placed on Landing Team 1/22 were not limited to the Marines ashore. Thirty minutes after the first wave of Marines touched the beach, Japanese mortar and machine gun fire grew so severe that both the *Pennsylvania* and the control vessel (*SC 1066*) had to shift position, the latter not regaining her original station until 1500.[94]

Meanwhile, assault elements of Companies B and C had knifed their way across to the ocean (eastern) beach of Parry within an hour after the landing,[95] but not in sufficient force adequately to clear the intervening ground. The bulk of Landing Team 1/22 was continuing to fight its way across, ably assisted by tanks of the 2d Separate Tank Company which had landed in the fourth wave. A short distance off the beach, three Japanese tanks had been emplaced to resist invasion, and these vehicles had remained in position until the Marine medium tanks came ashore. For reasons best known to the enemy, his light armor thereupon emerged from the emplacements and attempted to give battle to the Marine tanks, with disastrous results to the Japanese and no damage to the Marine armor.[96]

As enemy resistance increased, particularly from what were believed to be several 75mm guns on the right flank, Lieutenant Colonel Fromhold requested naval gunfire. As noted earlier, the landing team commander was under the impression he was considerably north of his actual position, and what occurred was subsequently recalled by him:

[Naval gunfire] was requested on the basis that troops had landed where planned, as the much bombarded pier and building foundations indicated. This request was denied by higher channels who, through air spot, had knowledge that the troops had been outside the planned area and would be endangered by this fire. However, a direct request from a naval liaison team spotter did get through. Five salvos were furnished as requested. . . . The Naval gunfire struck some

TANKS AND INFANTRY worked together to secure Parry in one day.

of our medium tanks . . . [and] also partially landed among our own troops. . . . Less than 10 of our troops were lost by this fire, whereas the Japs suffered heavily both in men and field pieces. . . .[97]

Captain Harry Calcutt, the tank commander, made his own caustic comments regarding the naval salvos:

Five-inch guns will penetrate the two-inch armor of medium tanks and generally raise hell with them. We would appreciate it if they would call their gunfire somewhere else, especially when we are forced to hold the tanks static in the gunfire in order to cover the infantry in the same area in an attempt to silence what we thought to be enemy opposition.[98]

The naval gunfire apparently broke the back of enemy resistance, for after it had ended the landing team, assisted by the tanks, moved forward with relative ease and rapidity. As the Marines reached the opposite shore shortly after 1100, between 150 and 200 heavily armed Japanese were seen moving along in column. Evidently they were caught by surprise and were able to put up only token resistance before being eliminated.

In the northern portion of Parry, Lieutenant Colonel Hart's Landing Team 2 had pushed to

[94] Transport Division 30, Action Report—Amphibious Phase of Eniwetok and Parry Islands, Eniwetok Atoll, 6Mar44, 5.
[95] Ltr LtCol Charles F. Widdecke to CMC, 10Mar53.
[96] *Scott.*

[97] *Fromhold.*
[98] 2d Separate Tank Company, Report on DOWNSIDE Operation, 26Feb44.

HEARTS CIRCLE, a cleared mound in the center of the unit's zone. Here Company H [99] placed all of its machine guns on line to provide overhead fire for the advancing troops. While this was in progress a hidden ammunition dump exploded under the machine gunners, wounding six men and eliminating a section of guns.[100] But this did not hamper the landing team's progress.

Landing Team 3/22, regimental reserve, was originally scheduled to land on Beach Green 3, but as it was dispatched from the line of departure at 0945, its destination was changed to Beach Green 2. Because Landing Team 2 had gone ashore south of its prescribed beach, the reserve battalion now landed north of all assault units at 1000, receiving "heavy machine-gun, rifle and mortar fire."[101] Moreover, a portion of the unit landed in a mine field and incurred several casualties.

Company I, reinforced by a platoon from Company K, neutralized the enemy positions on the beach, and Major Shisler directed his command south to ADONIS Road, where Company I relieved Company A at 1100. The latter unit thereupon reverted to reserve for Landing Team 1/22.

The 22d Marines' command post was estab-

[99] *Lanigan.*
[100] *Ibid.*
[101] *BLT 3/22 SAR,* 4.

lished just off Green Beach 2 at 1145, Colonel Walker having gone ashore an hour earlier. At noon General Watson ordered V Amphibious Corps Reconnaissance Company ashore to reinforce LT 2/22, and 45 minutes later directed Company D (Scout) to land and assist LT 1/22.

Landing Team 2/22 continued to press its attack northward and eastward, assisted by RCT 106's light tanks which had landed at 1100. Captain Jones' Reconnaissance Company was evenly divided between Companies E and F, providing about 55 additional men to each rifle company, and with this added strength the 2d Battalion pushed on across the island.[102] The northern portion of Parry was reported secure at 1400, but mopping up continued to engage the unit's attention until reembarkation.

Shortly after 1300, Landing Teams 1/22 and 3/22 were poised on the 0–1 line, ready to advance southward. This boundary was the line secured across the island by Lieutenant Colonel Fromhold's organization. Originally, of course, it had been drawn on the maps considerably north of its present position, but now it lay just south of VALENTINE Pier.

Landing Team 1 occupied the eastern half (left sector) of the jumpoff line, Companies B and C on the left and right, respectively. Both

[102] "We needed some extra zip to complete the job." *Lanigan.*

MARINES FOUGHT THEIR WAY through shattered coconut groves which the Japanese had filled with spider traps and log emplacements.

front-line units were reinforced by one platoon each from Company A, the remainder of that organization acting as battalion reserve. Responsibility for the western half (right sector) of the island lay with Landing Team 3/22, which would move forward in column of companies, Company I leading the attack, Company L mopping up, and Company K in reserve.[103]

Following a 15-minute artillery preparation, the two landing teams began their southward movement at 1330, the 2d Separate Tank Company moving in support shortly thereafter. It was the same story as before, the enemy putting up a static defense from spider traps and other subsurface positions. Landing Team 1/22 was reinforced by Company D (Scout) of the 4th Tank Battalion at 1422, the scouts joining with Company A (less two platoons) in the mission of mopping up and landing team reserve.

> We were closely supported by medium tanks which, while moving very slowly, fired their machine guns at random and occasionally let go with their 75's. When the tanks had exhausted their ammunition the advance would halt, the tanks would leave to resupply, a 60mm mortar barrage would be brought down close to the front, a 75mm pack howitzer barrage would be laid down beyond the mortar barrage, half-tracks [104] and DUKW's would bring forward more supplies for the infantry.[105]

The advancing Marines had covered some 350 yards when Company I encountered an enemy strong point consisting of underground barracks and extensive tunnels.[106] All tanks in both landing team areas were quickly dispatched to Company I's assistance, and after a short, fierce fight the enemy positions were overrun.

Artillery was active all during the afternoon, combining with naval gunfire in shelling the southern portion of the island and softening

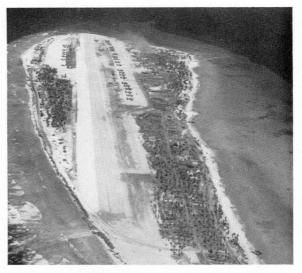

A 7,000-FOOT BOMBER STRIP was created on Eniwetok Island. (Air Force photo.)

the way for the advancing troops.[107] Additional support was provided by RCT 106's light tanks which moved southward after they were no longer needed by Landing Team 2 in the north.

After Company I's successful reduction of the Japanese strong point, the attack progressed with increasing velocity. Principal resistance came from Japanese in the heavy brush on Landing Team 1's left flank. By nightfall the two landing teams were some 450 yards from the southernmost tip of Parry (SLUMBER Point). Here the intervening ground narrowed to such an extent that there was danger of troops firing into each other if the advance were pushed, so the landing teams were directed to dig in for the night.

With a small area remaining to be covered, Colonel Walker considered Parry in his hands. Its possession meant the successful completion of the Eniwetok operation, and a general feeling of pleasure and satisfaction was reflected in the various radio messages that followed.

Colonel Walker started the ball rolling. He radioed General Watson: "I present you with Parry at 1930. Request this unit be relieved

---

[103] *Shisler.*

[104] "The battalion commanders' lack of mobile logistic support prompted them to use the attached half-track platoons to haul supplies and wounded. Also, as I recall, the tank company commander made repeated recommendations against the use of half-tracks in any zone which he was to work." Ltr LtCol Cecil D. Ferguson to CMC, 9Mar53.

[105] *Scott.*

[106] *Moore; McCabe.*

---

[107] ". . . [Army] artillery was firing directly at the troops who were advancing southward on Parry. This firing was handled most capably by a young Army captain who was liaison officer with the 22d Marines. . . ." Ltr BrigGen M. F. Schneider to CMC, 9Mar53.

ENGEBI'S AIRSTRIP was improved by the Seabees and taken over by the 4th Marine Air Wing.

for reembarkation in the morning." To which General Watson replied, "Well done, Johnny. My sincere congratulations to the 22d Marines and their supporting units. You have done a magnificent job."

The last congratulatory message of the night was sent to all units from General Watson at 2000: "With the capture of Parry at 1930 today, Eniwetok Atoll is now in our possession. My sincere congratulations to the officers and men of this group whose aggressive spirit and combat efficiency made the capture of this atoll possible. Well done."

CATCHPOLE CONCLUDED

The night of 22–23 February on Parry Island could hardly be described as "quiet" in the accepted sense of the word. Under the circumstances, however, it was a quiet night. There were no organized attacks against the Americans, but Japanese as individuals and in small groups emerged from camouflaged holes bypassed during the day and used rifles and grenades against the invaders. This was futile business at best. Naval vessels in the lagoon fired 5-inch star shells over the island all night, marking the first time in the Pacific that continuous illumination was provided.[108]

Enemy activity . . . during the night was light, and our casualties were few. The relatively peaceful night can be attributed to several things. Great care had been taken during the day to thoroughly mop up and remove ordnance and munitions from the areas covered by the assault units. Thus, any surviving enemy troops did not have loose weapons readily available to them. The star shells fired by the naval guns were invaluable. . . . The battalion night S. O. P. proved sound, and the troops followed it well—demonstrating the fact that they were seasoned troops.[109]

On the morning of D-plus 6 (23 February) elements of Landing Teams 1 and 3, Company D (Scout), and tanks of the 2d Separate Tank Company jumped off from the defense line of the night before. Enemy opposition was light between the jumpoff and SLUMBER Point, the Marines declaring the area secure shortly after 0900. But mopping-up operations continued.

---

[108] "Based on our experience at Tarawa and the known tactics of the Japs in regard to night infiltration and counterattack, we decided . . . that we would utilize 5-inch star shells from our Force to keep the island . . . under continuous illumination. . . . This was the first time that such a procedure had been developed, and as I watched the demand for them grow during succeeding operations . . . I always looked back on this with a great deal of satisfaction. . . ." *Hill II.*

[109] *BLT 1 Rpt.*

At 1045 the American flag was raised over Parry, indicating that the atoll, as well as the island, was in American hands.

The next few days were filled with the arrival, departure, and shifting of troops, debarkation and reembarkation, unloading and loading. The 10th Defense Battalion (Marine) had been released from its reserve status 22 February, and the next day began unloading at Eniwetok, assuming responsibility for that island on 25 February.

BLT 106–3, which had remained in floating reserve for Parry, was landed on the island 23 February and began policing and mopping up. Colonel Walker reembarked his Landing Team 2 and the 2d Separate Tank Company that day, followed by the remainder of the exhausted RCT 22 on 24 February. The next day the 22d Marines, reinforced, departed Eniwetok for Kwajalein, where it relieved the 25th Marines.[110] Various attached units were ordered to Hawaii at the same time. Of the assault force that had arrived at Eniwetok on 17 February, only RCT 106 (less BLT 106–2) remained. On 2 March it left the operational control of Tactical Group-1 and became a part of the Eniwetok Atoll garrison force.

General Watson departed Eniwetok by air on 3 March, arriving at Pearl Harbor the following day. And on 22 March Tactical Group-1 was disbanded.[111]

The combat elements assigned to Tactical Group-1 had been floating reserve for the Kwajalein operation, and on extremely short notice had gone in to take Eniwetok Atoll. They had entered Eniwetok's lagoon as men untried in combat,[112] but they performed like veterans in seizing their objectives. As added evidence for this view, the 22d Marines and virtually all the attached units were awarded the Navy Unit Commendation.

Marine and Army troops went into Eniwetok outnumbering the defenders roughly three-to-one. At the end of five days of intensive combat some 3,400 Japanese were buried and the Americans held the atoll. Statistically, the Marines lost 254 dead and 555 wounded. RCT 106 (less BLT 106–2) casualties numbered 94 dead and 311 wounded.[113] The figures by themselves are not representative. RCT 22 took both Engebi and Parry. RCT 106 (less BLT 106–2) assaulted only Eniwetok, and then it was reinforced by a tank company and a landing team from RCT 22. Thus, any comparison between Marine and Army casualty figures for the over-all operation must take into account the amount of combat experienced by the respective units as well as the number of troops involved.

After training in the Samoan area for some 18 months, the 22d Marines, reinforced, had at last experienced combat and was now a blooded regiment, as it capably demonstrated later at Guam and Okinawa.

In deciding to proceed ahead of schedule with the Eniwetok operation, Navy and Marine commanders had greatly advanced the war effort. Now the 2d Marine Division and the remainder of the 27th Infantry Division were free for other operations and would not be held down by the Marshalls. Eniwetok was secure in February instead of May. Admiral Nimitz was able to move up the target date for the Marianas by at least 20 weeks.[114] And Truk was revealed as being incapable of operations against U. S. forces.

---

[110] As noted in Chapter VII. Activities of RCT 22 after effecting this relief will be treated in Chapter IX.

[111] V Amphibious Corps General Order 51–44, 22Mar44.

[112] With the exception of the 708th Provisional Amphibian Tractor Company, VAC Reconnaissance Company, and Company D (Scout), 4th Tank Battalion.

[113] Marine casualty figures from Personnel Accounting Section, Records Branch, Personnel Department, HQMC, 1Aug52. RCT 106 casualty figures from *RCT 106 Rpt*, 15Apr44.

[114] *Isely and Crowl*, 303.

CHAPTER IX # Mopping Up the Marshalls[1]

FLINTLOCK, JR. BEGINS

The 22d Marines arrived at Kwajalein Atoll on 26 February 1944 and began the relief of Colonel Cumming's 25th Marines, that 4th Marine Division unit having remained as a temporary garrison force. By 5 March Colonel Walker's command was disposed as follows: 1st Battalion, Bigej Island; 2d Battalion, Roi-Namur; 3d Battalion on Edgigen, and the remainder of the regiment on Ennubirr and Obella Islands, with the regimental command post on Ennubirr. The 2d Separate Pack Howitzer Battalion relieved 1st Battalion, 14th Marines, on Edgigen,[2] but Company A, 10th Amphibian

---

[1] Unless otherwise indicated, this chapter is a synthesis of the following sources: 22d Marines Report of Operations into Lesser Marshalls, 6Apr44; Maj Paul H. Bird, "Atoll Hopping—The Lesser Marshalls," an undated report dealing with the 22d Marines in the Lesser Marshalls hereinafter cited as *Atoll Hopping;* Atoll Commander, Report of Occupation of Wotho, Ujae and Lae Atolls, 28Mar44; Atoll Commander, Report of Occupation of Ailinglapalap and Namu, 2Apr44; Atoll Commander, Report of Occupation of Ebon and Namorik Atolls and Kili Island, undated; Atoll Commander, Report of Occupation of Ailuk Atoll, Mejit Island, Jemo Island and Likiep Atoll, 12Apr44; Atoll Commander, Report of Occupation of Bikini, Ailinginae, Rongelap, Rongerik, Utirik, Bikar and Taka Atolls, 14Apr44; *Campaign; Sherrod.*

[2] "This consisted of a relief in place to continue the defense. . . . During this relief the pack howitzers of [1/14] were left in place and exchanged for those of

Tractor Battalion, was directed to remain at Kwajalein and work with the 22d Marines.

But if the tired victors of Eniwetok thought that they would merely occupy Kwajalein Atoll, this illusion was quickly dispelled. On 1 March Rear Admiral Alva D. Bernhard, Atoll Commander, received orders to neutralize and control the Lesser Marshalls, consisting of those atolls and islands thought to be undefended or lightly held. Specifically, the admiral was directed to:

1. Destroy Japanese installations or materials which might be of benefit to their submarines, aircraft or surface forces.
2. Make prisoner Japanese or suspicious natives.
3. Instruct the natives in the war situation and their changed sovereignty.
4. Assist them in any way practicable economically, and establish relations of friendliness and good will.

Admiral Bernhard and Colonel Walker set up a joint staff to direct the Lesser Marshalls campaign, which was dubbed FLINTLOCK, JR. Five areas of operations were established:

1. West Group (Wotho, Ujae, and Lae Atolls).
2. South Group (Namu, Ailinglapalap,

---

the 2d SepPkHowBn. Such procedure is often recommended but seldom accomplished." *Mahoney.*

Namorik, Ebon Atolls, and Kili Island.)
3. North Group (Bikini, Rongelap, Ailinginae, and Rongerik Atolls).
4. Northeast Group (Bikar, Utirik, Taka, Ailuk, Likiep Atolls, Jemo and Mejit Islands).
5. Separate (Lib Island).

Each atoll and island was reconnoitered by low-level PBY flights prior to moving troops to the objective, and aerial photographs were delivered to the various naval and troop commanders. The naval force for each operation usually consisted of one LST transporting six to nine LVT's, two LCI's, one destroyer or destroyer escort, and one mine sweeper. Three

SBD's from VMSB–151 [3] were called on to furnish air support.

Inasmuch as native reaction was considered important in the scheduled operations, a flag-raising ceremony was evolved to be carried out whenever this formality took place. One civil affairs report best describes it:

After the proclamation explanation and posting formality, the American flag was raised . . . one platoon at present arms, staff officers at hand salute, natives in a group in the center. A Marine photographer made a picture record of each raising. The ceremony appealed to the natives, and was an aid in inculcating

[3] The squadron at this time was divided into two echelons, one based at Roi, the other at Engebi. The air support mentioned was to be provided from Roi.

THE AMERICAN FLAG was raised on a great many islands of the Lesser Marshalls in the six weeks following the Eniwetok operation.

the idea that they now were under American protection and no longer subject to Japanese rule.[4]

It was further planned that each force of Marines would be augmented by civil affairs officers, medical personnel to examine the natives, interpreters and native scouts from Kwajalein.

On 7 March the first reconnaissance group departed Kwajalein Atoll with the West Group as its objective. The Marines included two reinforced companies from 1st Battalion, under Major Crawford B. Lawton, battalion executive officer.[5] The next morning this force lay off Wotho Atoll where it was learned that the only Japanese at hand numbered 12, the stranded crew of a crashed bomber. On the morning of 9 March 180 Marines landed on Wotho Island without opposition. During the night the 12 Nipponese had fled to a nearby island where they committed suicide when later they were pursued by 1st Platoon, Company C. On Wotho the proclamations were read, the flag raised and the expeditionary group departed, but not before one Marine had been killed by the accidental explosion of a hand grenade.

At Ujae Atoll the following day, Major Lawton learned that only six Japanese were there, the crew of a weather station. Once again 180 Marines landed, and once again the enemy reacted by committing suicide—with one exception. One of the six, not so fervent as his comrades, made a halfhearted attempt at suicide and then permitted himself to be taken prisoner.

Lae Atoll was secured next. No Japanese were found, but the naval officer in charge of the task force noted that "the natives were not as friendly as at the other atolls." This unfriendly attitude was apparently due to an unfortunate event which occurred a few days prior to the Marines' arrival. A hand grenade box containing one grenade floated ashore. The bomb had exploded, killing a child. When the armed troops landed on Lae the natives connected them with the hand grenade and decided that the Marines were in some measure respon-

sible for the child's death.[6] The reconnaissance force returned to Kwajalein, arriving there the evening of 14 March, mission successfully completed.

During the absence of the 1st Battalion group there had been a change in regimental command. On 10 March Colonel Walker was detached to V Amphibious Corps and was succeeded in command by Colonel Merlin F. Schneider, regimental executive officer.

One other reconnaissance took place during the 22d Marines' first two weeks at Kwajalein Atoll. On 11 March a reinforced platoon from the 1st Battalion landed on Lib Island, listed as a separate operation on the schedule. No trace of Japanese was found, natives were assembled and questioned, proclamations read, and at 1130 that day the American flag was raised. The platoon returned to its home base the same day.[7]

SECURE IN THE SOUTH

On 19 March, after a false start the preceding day,[8] two landing forces, each containing about 325 Marines, departed Kwajalein Atoll to clear the South Group. Both forces were taken from the 3d Battalion with Major Shisler and his executive officer, Major William E. Sperling III, the respective commanders. It was planned that the two forces would part company after securing Ailinglapalap Atoll, which objective was reached the morning of 20 March. Native scouts reported some 40 armed Japanese on Ailinglapalap Island, and that afternoon Major Sperling's force landed, followed the next morning by Major Shisler's group.

Company I, reinforced by both a heavy machine-gun platoon and an 81mm mortar platoon, made contact with the enemy the morning of 21 March. The Japanese defense line was entrenched across a narrow portion of the island, and the 81mm mortars began pounding it, the Marines overrunning it in the early afternoon.

[6] LtCol Crawford B. Lawton, comments on preliminary script.

[7] Report of Reconnaissance Unit, Landing on Lib Island, 11Mar44, 1–2.

[8] The force originally included an LCT loaded with medium tanks. Upon departing the lagoon on 18Mar44, however, the craft began shipping water and all vessels returned to the lagoon. There it was decided to dispense with the LCT and the tanks.

[4] Report of Reconnaissance of Wotho, Ujae and Lae Atolls, Chief of Civil Affairs Section, 15Mar44, 1–2.

[5] Atoll Commander, Report of Occupation of Wotho, Ujae and Lae Atolls, 28Mar44.

SEVENTH AIR FORCE B–24 banks toward Wotje during the bombing of the by-passed atolls. (Air Force photo.)

Two Marines were wounded and 39 Nipponese killed,[9] two surviving enemy escaping to other islands in the atoll where they were eventually picked up.

Having overcome this resistance, Major Shisler's force reembarked the afternoon of 21 March and steamed toward Ebon Atoll, the southernmost of the Marshalls. Major Sperling's unit remained to bury the enemy dead, scout the other islands in the atoll [10] and proceed with proclamations and flag-raising formalities.

Ailinglapalap Atoll is the residence of the clan which controls the Ralik (western) chain of islands in the Marshalls, and the civil affairs officers took pains to make clear the new order of things. Chief Jemata, the head of the clan, assured the Marines that his people would adhere to the proclamation notices, and that he looked upon all Americans as friends—as no doubt he had previously looked upon all Japanese.

Major Sperling's group next proceeded to Namu Atoll where native scouts were dispatched to reconnoiter the islands. The scouts duly reported that the Japanese on the atoll consisted of one policeman and one schoolteacher together with his wife and three children. The next day (24 March) the Marine commander sent a surrender note to the Nipponese who quickly gathered on the beach waving white flags. Major Sperling noted that the number of Japanese present was correct "with addition of one child." The seven interned civilians were taken on board ship, and the troops departed, arriving at Kwajalein the next afternoon.

Meanwhile, Major Shisler's command arrived at Ebon Atoll on the morning of 23 March. Native scouts landed, followed shortly by Marines. Only friendly natives were found during the day, but the next morning contact was made with the enemy on Ebon Island. A 20-minute fire fight ensued in which two Marines were killed and 17 armed Japanese wiped out.[11]

---

[9] Included in the enemy armament were several 1903 Springfield rifles, a Browning light machine gun, and two cases of United States hand grenades. *McCabe.*

[10] Seven Japanese civilians were found and taken back to Kwajalein.

[11] The Japanese force consisted of one woman, 11 male civilians, and five soldiers.

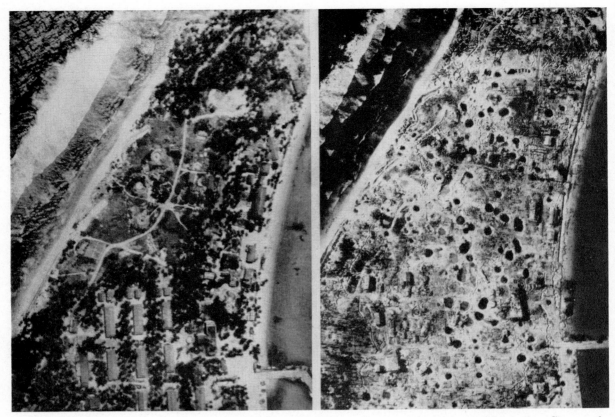

GRAPHIC EVIDENCE of the aerial pounding given the by-passed Japanese strongholds in the Marshalls. Six months intervened between these photographs of Emidj Island, Jaluit Atoll. (Air Force photo.)

Six civilians were picked up at Ebon for internment, and the troops thereupon proceeded to Namorik Atoll and Kili Island. No Japanese were found at either objective. Consequently, the usual formalities were expeditiously accomplished, and the Marines returned to Kwajalein Atoll, arriving there 28 March.

MEJIT, AILUK AND LIKIEP

Two days after Major Shisler's return to Kwajalein, a reinforced company from his 3d Battalion, under Major Earl J. Cook, moved toward the Northeast Group. The entire group was not assigned this force, however. Its objectives were Ailuk, Likiep and Taka Atolls, Jemo and Mejit Islands. Aerial reconnaissance indicated that Jemo and Taka were uninhabited, and inasmuch as native scouts confirmed this, it was decided to by-pass them.

Ailuk was reconnoitered by the Marines on 31 March and 1 April and the usual formalities followed. No Japanese were found, but an important question was settled as far as the natives were concerned.

On Ailuk the question was raised [by Typhoon, the native chief] as to whether the people could now pray again, and considerable pleasure was expressed when they were assured that they could.[12]

The reconnaissance force stood off Mejit Island on the morning of 2 April, and six LVT's carried the troops ashore. Six Japanese assigned to a naval weather station there were killed resisting the landing.

During reembarkation, however, trouble developed. The LST ramp chains parted, leaving three LVT's still in the water with no way to be loaded on board. Rather than risk the vehicles falling into enemy hands, the naval commander ordered them stripped of equipment and then sunk by gunfire.

On Likiep Atoll, which was reconnoitered on 3 April, no Japanese were located, but the

[12] Reconnaissance of Ailuk and Likiep Atolls and Mejit Island, Report of Civil Affairs Section, 7Apr44.

Marines met a plantation owner, Carl F. Hahn, who said he had been an American citizen since 1900. Hahn, a native German, told the Marines he was shipwrecked in the Marshalls in 1891, had married a native woman and had lived there ever since.[13]

With its mission completed, Major Cook's reconnaissance force returned to Roi-Namur, arriving there at 0800 on 5 April.

FINALE IN THE NORTH

While elements of the 3d Battalion were reconnoitering to the south and north, a reinforced company of the 2d Battalion was equally active. On 27 March this unit, under Major Robert P. Felker, 2d Battalion executive officer, stood out to sea with the mission of raising the flag in the North Group and a portion of the Northeast Group. Aerial reconnaissance and native reports indicated that Ailinginae, Rongerik, and Bikar Atolls were uninhabited.

These were ignored, therefore, Major Felker concerning himself with only Bikini, Rongelap, and Utirik Atolls.[14]

From the morning of 28 March until the evening of 30 March the Marines scouted Bikini Atoll. Only five Japanese were found, but they committed suicide instead of resisting or surrendering. The proclamations were read, the flag was raised, and the miniature task force steamed toward Rongelap Atoll. Here the reconnaissance elements paused until 3 April, fruitlessly searching for a reported group of six Japanese soldiers.

Utirik Atoll was reached the morning of 5 April, but the naval commander decided the pass was dangerous and the lagoon "exceptionally full" of coral heads. He thereupon ruled that his vessels could not enter the lagoon. This made it necessary for the Marines to make a seven-mile run in amphibian tractors in order

[13] How Hahn could have established American citizenship in 1900 is not disclosed.

[14] Likiep Atoll was originally included in this list, but Adm Bernhard canceled it for Felker's group and turned it over to Maj Cook's force.

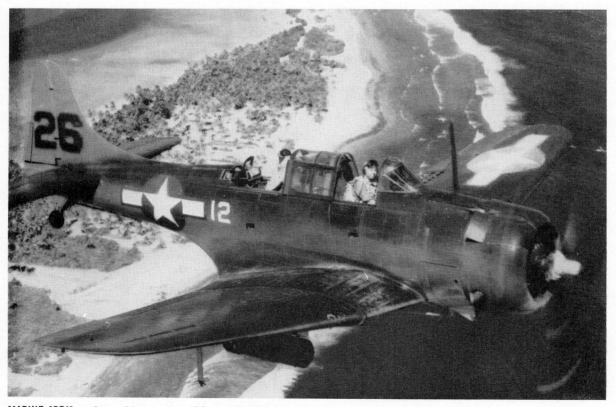

MARINE SBD'S such as this one over Majuro helped keep the Japanese "anchored aircraft carriers" ineffective until the war ended.

TWO COMMANDERS of the 4th Marine Air Wing during the tour of duty in the Marshalls were Generals Cushman (left) and Woods.

to land on Utirik Island. Fourteen armed Japanese resisted the invasion, but they were quickly overrun. A motor generator set was blown up, the flag raised, and the troops departed, reaching Kwajalein the next afternoon.

Major Felker's group arrived not a moment too soon, for the 22d Marines were loading transports. "The force [Felker's] . . . tied up alongside APA's and transferred troops just in time to sail with the regiment . . . to another staging area for preparations for further operations against the enemy." [15]

Between 7 March and 6 April 1944, elements of the 22d Marines, reinforced, had established American sovereignty over 12 atolls and three islands of the Lesser Marshalls, a water area of some 60,000 square miles. Thus the American forces fixed grip on what had been Japanese territory only three months earlier. And definitely on the profit side was the experience gained by junior officers in exercising command during actual landing operations.

---

[15] *Atoll Hopping*, 10.

As noted in Chapter VIII, Tactical Group-1 was disbanded on 22 March. On that same date the 1st Provisional Marine Brigade was organized and the 22d Marines assigned to it. A week later Colonel Schneider was alerted for a move to Guadalcanal, and on 6 April the 22d Marines, together with attached units,[16] departed for the new base.

LAST STAGE

During the month of April, Marine and Army forces reconnoitered three other atolls, the last to be secured in the Marshalls before the end of the war.

On 17 April a force of 199 Marines from the 1st Defense Battalion, VAC, embarked from Majuro on two LCI(L)'s with the mission of reconnoitering Erikub and Aur Atolls. Erikub lies a mere five miles from Wotje, and Aur only ten miles from Maloelap. Despite the proximity of the small atolls to the two formidable Japanese bases, no enemy was found on either. The Marines thereupon returned to Majuro only four days after departing it.[17]

The seizure of Ujelang Atoll, westernmost of the Marshalls, was virtually a repetition of the 22d Marines' landings in the smaller eastern atolls. A reinforced company from 3d Battalion, 111th Infantry, proceeded from Kwajalein 20 April and stood off the tiny atoll the next afternoon. For two days the infantrymen reconnoitered the various islands at Ujelang, killing 18 Japanese in the process. The American flag was raised and the soldiers reembarked, arriving at their home base on 24 April.[18]

---

[16] Included here is the amphibian tractor company. During the period just covered, the 10th Amphibian Tractor Battalion was at Maui and another LVT company there was designated Company A, 10th Amphibian Tractor Battalion. The LVT company then working with the 22d Marines was thereupon redesignated as a unit within the 11th Amphibian Tractor Battalion, then forming, and it sailed to Guadalcanal with the 22d Marines.

[17] War Diary for April 1944, 1st Defense Bn, VAC. Troops from this organization also conducted reconnaissance of Arno Atoll which had been reconnoitered shortly after the occupation of Majuro. No enemy was found on Arno.

[18] Company I, 111th Infantry, Report of Operations, Occupation of Ujelang Atoll, 27Apr44.

Remaining in enemy hands were Kusaie Island in the western Marshalls, and Wotje, Maloelap, Mille, and Jaluit Atolls in the east, and the Japanese garrisons of these were left to winter on the vine.[19] (See Map 15, Map Section.) To apply the heat necessary to keep them withered, the 4th Marine Base Defense Air Wing[20] (4th MBDAW) staged into the Marshalls. In mid-February 17 planes of MAG–31 arrived at Dyess Field[21] on Roi,

joining the ground echelon which had arrived a few days earlier. At the newly acquired fleet base of Majuro the Seabees completed an airstrip on 19 February, and the planes of MAG–13 flew in during the next seven days. Aviation elements also followed on the heels of Marine landing forces at Eniwetok Atoll. On 19 February a ground echelon of MAG–22 arrived at Engebi, planes setting down there 10 days later.

The 4th Marine Base Defense Air Wing's campaign against Mille, Maloelap, Jaluit, and Wotje, a campaign that was to continue until Japan's surrender, began on 4 March 1944 when VMSB–331 of MAG–13 conducted a bombing mission against Jaluit. Five days later Brigadier General Lewie G. Merritt, commander of

[19] The remainder of this narrative is taken principally from *Campaign; Sherrod.*

[20] The "Base Defense" portion of the Wing's designation was dropped 10Nov44.

[21] Named in honor of LtCol Aquilla J. Dyess, who was posthumously awarded the Medal of Honor for his actions on Namur, as previously noted in Chapter V.

JAPANESE SURRENDER OF MILLE ATOLL, 22 August 1945. Captain Masanori Shiga, IJN (left) and Captain H. B. Grow, USN (right). (Navy photo.)

the 4th MBDAW,[22] established his headquarters at Kwajalein.

Navy carrier planes had flown 1,671 sorties against Wotje, Jaluit, Mille, and Maloelap before the Marine pilots got in on the act. Since the preceding November, Navy and Army planes, principally the bombers of the Seventh Air Force, had struck at the four atolls. The Army planes continued attacking the by-passed targets until the Seventh Air Force moved to Saipan in June 1944, and Navy land-based planes struck at the atolls throughout the remainder of the year.

But the bulk of the dull job of pounding the enemy bases in the Marshalls until the end of the war fell to the Marine pilots.[23] For awhile the Japanese attempted to repair airstrips, just as they continued constructing realistic dummy gun positions. But a shortage of food and supplies, plus the progressive deterioration of morale, eventually put a stop to their efforts. As long as their antiaircraft guns were operational, the Nipponese continued to handle them against attacking planes, sometimes with telling effect.

But strength and time were on the side of the American forces. The Japanese on the by-passed atolls could only sit out the war, concentrating on a struggle for survival. Wotje, Maloelap, Mille, and Jaluit had been considered by the enemy as "unsinkable aircraft carriers," key links in the chain of defenses protecting Japan's eastern perimeter. Strong reinforcements had been rushed to them in order to contain or delay the inexorable American advance across the Pacific. But with war's end, the tattered, starving garrisons could only surrender.

---

[22] Succeeding commanders of the 4thMBDAW while in the Marshalls were BrigGen Thomas J. Cushman, MajGen Louis E. Woods, and BrigGen Lawson H. M. Sanderson.

[23] One pilot subsequently recalled that as he was returning from a mission he spotted two LCI(L)'s which had reconnoitered Aur Atoll and were on the way back to Majuro. Somehow the two vessels made an incorrect turn and were inadvertently heading for Mille. The pilot flew low over the craft, sending them a message in Morse by means of a flashing light. He thus notified them of their error and in all probability saved the lives of the men on board. Capt Ernesto H. Giusti, comments on preliminary script.

APPENDIX I

Bibliography

This bibliography cites only those sources which were particularly important and helpful in compiling the monograph. Literally hundreds of records were consulted. Some duplicated others, and some merely confirmed information already available. Preliminary drafts of the monograph were sent to participants in the operations in order to solicit their comments, corrections, and elaborations. A great many individuals contributed invaluable material, which has been cited in the course of the narrative. Lack of space prevents a separate listing of them here. Letters and interviews are on file in the offices of Historical Branch, G–3 Division, Headquarters Marine Corps, and are available to bona fide students within the limitations of security and restrictions imposed by originators.

DOCUMENTS

CCS 239/1 "Operations in the Pacific and Far East in 1943–44," a JCS paper approved by CCS 21May43. Pertains to plans for operations in the Pacific and Far East during late 1943 and early 1944.

CinCPac–CinCPOA. Dispatch to CominCh, 1Jul43, serial 096. A tentative proposal for operations in the Marshalls, depending on the outcome of photocoverage.

CinCPac-CinCPOA. Operation Plan 16–43, 12Oct43. Serial 00218. Early FLINTLOCK Plan.

CinCPac-CinCPOA. Dispatch to CominCh, 25Oct43, serial 00247, revising Marshalls target date.

CinCPac-CinCPOA. Dispatch to CG, Army Forces, CenPac, 30Oct43, serial 022120. Directs that 106th RCT be made available for the Marshalls operations.

CinCPac–CinCPOA. CATCHPOLE Detail Plan, 29Nov 43. Early plan for seizure of Eniwetok. Serial 00272.

CinCPac–CinCPOA. Base Development Plan, Kwajalein Island, 29Nov43. Serial 001612.

CinCPac-CinCPOA. Dispatch to JCS, 13Dec43, serial 001685, regarding decision to drop Wotje-Maloelap and concentrate on Kwajalein.

CinCPac–CinCPOA. Memorandum Report of Conference held in the Office of CinCPOA, 18Dec43. Pertains to LVT and DUKW program. Discussion of LVT performance in the Tarawa operation and future possibilities.

CinCPac–CinCPOA. FLINTLOCK II, Joint Staff Study, 20Dec43. A staff study based on the assumption of seizing Kwajalein Atoll and neutralizing the more heavily defended atolls.

CinCPac–CinCPOA. FLINTLOCK II, Alternate Joint Staff Study, 23Dec43. A staff study based on the assumption of seizing Wotje and and Maloelap Atolls and neutralizing other atolls.

CinCPac–CinCPOA. Base Development Plan, Majuro Atoll, 2Jan44. Serial 000201.

CinCPac–CinCPOA. Operations in the Pacific Ocean Areas, December 1943. Serial 001035, 31Mar44. Naval operations in the Pacific during this period.

CinCPac–CinCPOA. Bulletin 126–44. A Guide to the Western Pacific. An island-by-island study of the Pacific.

JICPOA Bulletin 53–43, "Kwajalein," 1Dec43.

JICPOA Bulletin 3–44, 20Jan44. A study of Eniwetok Atoll.

JICPOA Bulletin 46–44, 15Apr44. An analysis of base installations found on Roi, Namur, and Ennubirr Islands. Accompanied by maps and photographs.

JICPOA Bulletin 48–44, Japanese Defenses, Kwajalein Atoll, 10Apr44.

JICPOA Bulletin 88–44, 1st Amphibious Brigade, Japanese Army. A study of the brigade from its organization through its defense of Eniwetok Atoll.

JICPOA Bulletin 89–44, 12Jun44. Information compiled from captured documents and prisoners-of-war interrogations pertaining to the Japanese defense plans for Eniwetok Atoll.

JICPOA Item 7005, Translation of Diary of Warrant Officer Shionoya, a member of the 3d Battalion, 1st Amphibious Brigade.

CenPacForce. Capture of the Marshalls, Outline Plan, 1Oct43, Serial 0053. Includes dispatch from CinCPac–CinCPOA to CominCh, 20Aug43, and from CinCPac–CinCPOA to ComCenPacForce, 22Sept43.

CenPacForce. Operation Plan Cen 1–44, 6Jan44. Adm Spruance's plan for seizure of Kwajalein and Majuro Atolls.

CenPacForce. War Diary, December 1943. Serial 0082, 27Feb44. A day-by-day account of activities of the Central Pacific Force during the period covered.

CenPacForce. War Diary, January 1944. Serial 0095, 1Mar44. A day-by-day account of activities of the Central Pacific Force during the period covered.

Task Force 51. Operation Plan A6–43, 17Jan44. Admiral Turner's operation plan for Kwajalein Atoll. Includes appropriate annexes.

Task Force 51. Operation Plan A9–44, 7Feb44. A detailed operation plan for the Eniwetok Expeditionary Group (Task Group 51.11) was signed by RAdm R. K. Turner.

Task Force 51. Report of Amphibious Operations for the capture of the Marshall Islands (FLINTLOCK and CATCHPOLE Operations), 25Feb44. A detailed report containing 11 enclosures, including a narrative of operations, intelligence, troop landings, beach and shore parties, naval and air bombardment, support aircraft, communications, LVT's and DUKW's, medical, ship loading and recommendations.

Task Force 52. Attack Order A1–44, 14Jan44. Contains appropriate annexes and maps for the attack on southern Kwajalein.

Task Force 53. Operation Order A157–44, 16Jan44. Includes Movement Order A156–44, 11Jan44, together with appropriate annexes, maps and charts for operations against northern Kwajalein.

Task Force 53. Report of Amphibious Operations for the capture of Roi and Namur Islands (FLINTLOCK), 23Feb44. Report of Commander, Group 3, Fifth Amphibious Force. Includes nine enclosures containing operations narrative, and comments on naval gunfire, air support, communications, intelligence, material, logistics, loading and unloading, casualties.

Task Group 50.15. Action Report, Marshall Islands Campaign, 15Feb44. Comments and summary of events for the period 29Jan–3Feb44.

Task Group 51.11. Report of Eniwetok Operation, 7Mar44. A comprehensive report of the Eniwetok Operation signed by RAdm Hill. It is divided into seven separate parts and deals with planning, conduct of the operation and unloading after combat was concluded.

Task Group 51.2. Majuro Action Report, 15Feb44. Detailed report of the Majuro operation. Includes composition of forces, narrative, training and rehearsal, air and fire support narratives.

Task Group 58.2. Action Report of Marshall Islands Operation, 25Feb44. Narrative and chronological account of the organization's participation in the Kwajalein operation. Includes three enclosures.

Task Unit 52.5.1. Operation Report, FLINTLOCK, undated. Transport Division 4's summary and comments pertaining to training for the Kwajalein operation and conduct of operations.

Task Unit 53.5.5. Action Report on the Attack, Capture and Occupation of Kwajalein Atoll, 9Feb44. Chronological account of the bombardment of the islands of northern Kwajalein, 30Jan–1Feb44.

Task Unit 58.2.2. Action Report of Bombardment of of Roi-Namur Islands, 3Feb44. Account of battleship and destroyer bombardment of Roi-Namur, 30Jan44.

Battleship Division Two. Action Report of Bombardment of Eniwetok Atoll, 28Feb44. A 19-page report containing a narrative of events, bombardment plan for Eniwetok, and two track charts of the flagship during the Eniwetok operation.

V Amphibious Corps. G–5 Estimate of the Situation, FLINTLOCK Operation, 21Oct43. Discussion of various proposed courses of action in the Marshalls.

V Amphibious Corps. G–2 Study of the Theater of Operations: Marshall Islands, 26Nov43. A detailed terrain study of Mille, Maloelap, Wotje, Jaluit, Kwajalein, and Majuro Atolls. Includes maps and annexes.

V Amphibious Corps. Memorandum to Chief of Staff, 29Dec43. Report of conference with Cdr Dodge, USS *Seal*. Attached is report by USS *Seal* of photographic reconnaissance of Kwajalein Atoll.

V Amphibious Corps. Estimate of Japanese Troops and Defense Organizations, CARILLON Atoll, 17Jan44. A study of enemy potentialities on the islands to be invaded in Kwajalein Atoll. Includes maps and overlays. Signed by LtCol St. Julien R. Marshall.

V Amphibious Corps. G–1 Journal. Résumé of messages received and sent during the period 17Jan–7Feb44.

V Amphibious Corps. G–2 Journal. Covers period 17Jan–7Feb44.

V Amphibious Corps. G–3 Journal. Résumé of dispatches and messages received and sent from 22Jan44 through 7Feb44.

V Amphibious Corps. Study of Japanese Defensive Works, Kwajalein Atoll, 15Feb44. A 61-page detailed report containing maps and photographs of Japanese defenses at Kwajalein. Signed by LtCol A. Vincent Wilson, CE, USA.

V Amphibious Corps. Operations Report of the FLINTLOCK Operation, 6Mar44. A comprehensive report

of the Kwajalein operation. Contains narrative report of operations and nine annexes. These are: Corps Operation Plan 1–44; G–5 Report; G–3 Report; G–2 Report; G–1 Report; G–4 Report; Liaison Team Report; Special Staff Officers' Report; Reconnaissance Company Report.

V Amphibious Corps. Report of Logistical Aspects of FLINTLOCK Operation, 23Mar44. A 15-page report signed by MajGen H. M. Smith. It discusses all VAC logistical matters pertaining to the Kwajalein operation.

V Amphibious Corps. Special Action Report CATCH-POLE Operation, 1Apr44. Includes comments of MajGen H. M. Smith, Commanding General, VAC, pertaining to Tactical Group-1's Special Report; Naval Gunfire Report on CATCHPOLE; 708th Amphibian Tank Bn, Special Action Report on Eniwetok Operation; Final Report of Civil Affairs, Eniwetok Atoll.

V Amphibious Corps. Miscellaneous Orders and Plans. Folder containing miscellaneous orders, plans, memoranda, maps, and charts. Majority of the material pertains to Eniwetok.

V Amphibious Corps. Units and Ships Upon Which Embarked, FLINTLOCK, undated. Breakdown of ships with units embarked including unit strength and preferred and alternate loading plans.

V Amphibious Corps. War Diary, Jan44, 4Feb44. Contains list of VAC components as well as all orders issued during the month. Narrative of VAC activities during the period covered is included.

V Amphibious Corps. War Diary, Feb44, 5Mar44. A narrative of VAC activities during February 1944. Includes a list of all VAC orders issued during the month. Signed by MajGen H. M. Smith.

V Amphibious Corps. War Diary, Mar44, 8Apr44. Contains list of VAC components as well as copies of all orders issued during the period. A narrative of events is included.

4th Marine Division. Operation Plan 3–43 (revised), 31Dec43. Sets forth the mission of the Northern Landing Force in the Kwajalein operation, and how it is to be effected. Contains appropriate annexes and maps.

4th Marine Division. Journal. Contains a résumé of all messages sent and received by the division from 31Jan44 through 2Feb44 and an operational narrative covering the period 13Jan44 through 2Feb44.

4th Marine Division. Final Report on FLINTLOCK Operation, 17Mar44. A comprehensive report of the division's participation in the Kwajalein operation. Includes division organization and training, preliminary planning and conduct of operations. Ten enclosures include narrative of operations; extracts from the division journal; Report of Commanding General, IVAN Landing Group; CT 23 Report; CT 24 Report; CT 25 Report; 14th Marines Report; 20th Marines Report; Medical report; comments.

4th Marine Division. Communications—Operations Report, 29Mar44. Enclosures include report of Landing Team 1, 24th CT; letter from Commanding Officer, CT 24; letter from Commanding Officer, CT 23; Reports of the 1st, 2d and 3d Bns, 25th Marines.

4th Marine Division. War Diary, Mar44–23Apr44. A day-by-day account of the division's activities during March. Contains a station list and combat readiness report.

4th Marine Division. Record of Events, 5May44. Day-by-day account of division activities from 13Jan44 through 8Feb44.

4th Marine Division. Intelligence Report on FLINTLOCK, undated. A collection of nine intelligence summaries, 31Jan–12Feb44, as well as POW interrogations, Japanese defense plan for Roi-Namur, and a D–2 analysis of the conduct of the Japanese defense.

20th Marines. Bomb Disposal Unit 1 Report of Activities in the FLINTLOCK Operation, 27Apr44. Report accompanied by 12 photographs.

23d Marines. Journal. Résumé of messages sent and received during the period 31Jan–4Feb44.

Landing Team 1, 23d Marines. Report on the FLINTLOCK Operation, 10Feb44. Bn commander's report of his organization's assault on Roi. Attached are reports by the Bn executive officer and each staff section.

2d Battalion, 23d Marines. Comments on Landing Operations on Roi-Namur, 14Feb44. Contains a narrative of operations, record of events, comments and recommendations. Attached are reports from the Bn commander and executive officer, each staff section, each company commander and each attached unit commander. Also sketches of Japanese defenses.

3d Battalion, 23d Marines. Record of Events, 12Feb44. Comments and recommendations of the Bn commander and executive officer and each staff section during the period 31Jan–5Feb44. Includes overlays and sketches.

1st Battalion, 24th Marines. Preliminary Report of Operations on Namur, 8Feb44.

2d Battalion, 24th Marines. Narrative, Battle of Roi-Namur, undated. Brief account of the Bn's participation in the assault on Namur.

2d Battalion, 24th Marines. Preliminary report of operations on Namur, 7Feb44.

3d Battalion, 24th Marines. Undated and incomplete report of operations on Namur.

Landing Team 1, 25th Marines. Report of Activities on D-Day and D-plus 1, 16Feb44. Narrative, followed by questions and answers pertaining to the Kwajalein operation.

Landing Team 2, 25th Marines. Report of Activities, 20Feb44. Chronological account of the Bn's activities on 31Jan–1Feb44.

Landing Team 3, 25th Marines. Report on D-Day and D-plus 1, 9Feb44. Brief account of the Bn's activities during the Kwajalein operation.

Landing Team 3, 25th Marines. History. A mimeographed paper, source not indicated, covering the period 11Jan–8Mar44.

4th Tank Battalion. Report of Activities in the FLINTLOCK Operation, 31Mar44. Contains summary of activities, comments and recommendations as well as combat reports by each platoon.

10th Amphibian Tractor Battalion. Report on Operations, FLINTLOCK Operation, 17Mar44. An analysis of the unit's activities during its organization, training and combat operations. Contains individual reports from each company, as well as an earlier Bn action report dated 17Feb44.

1st Joint Assault Signal Company. Report of Commanding Officer on the FLINTLOCK Operation, 6Mar44. Attached are individual reports from each liaison team. Carries endorsements by MajGen Schmidt and MajGen Smith.

7th Infantry Division. Report of Participation in the FLINTLOCK Operation, 8Feb44. Includes a narrative of operations, recommendations for future operations, proposed operating procedures for LVT's, and commendatory messages.

7th Infantry Division. Report on FLINTLOCK Operation, 6Mar44. A detailed list of questions and answers pertaining to the Kwajalein operation.

7th Infantry Division. Report of the Southern Force Artillery, FLINTLOCK Operation, 22Feb44. An account of planning and conduct of operations, followed by recommendations.

7th Infantry Division. G–3 Reports. G–3 daily reports of division's activities during the period 31Jan–5Feb44. Overlays.

7th Infantry Division. FLINTLOCK Report. Volumes III, IV, VII, IX, XI. The division's formal report of participation in the Kwajalein operation.

Tactical Group-1. Report of Attack on Eniwetok Atoll, 27Feb44. A 14-page narrative report concerning operations against Eniwetok Atoll. Carries endorsement of RAdm H. W. Hill.

Tactical Group-1. Special Report concerning FLINTLOCK and CATCHPOLE Operations, 1Mar44. A comprehensive report dealing with the attack on Eniwetok Atoll. Includes daily unit reports with overlays from 17Feb44 through 23Feb44; radio log for the operation; action report by Company D (Scout), 4th Tank Bn; action report, VAC Reconnaissance Co; Japanese map of Parry Island; Group Operation Order 2–44, DOWNSIDE, 10Feb44.

Tactical Group-1. Journal. Contains memoranda, dispatches, training orders, reports and maps. Covers period 7Dec43 through 22Mar44.

Tactical Group-1. War Diary, 5Nov43–29Feb44. A day-by-day account of TG–1 activities during the period covered.

Tactical Group-1. War Diary, March 1944. Signed by BrigGen T. E. Watson, with endorsement by BrigGen G. B. Erskine, CofS, VAC. Covers period 1Mar-22Mar44.

22d Marines, reinforced, Operation Orders. A folder containing combat instructions, field messages, regimental operations plans for FLINTLOCK, and regimental operations orders for CATCHPOLE. Inclusive dates are 26Sept43–21Feb44.

22d Marines. Record of Events. A folder containing various orders, reports, copies of war diaries, dispatches and records of events from 6Aug42 through 2Mar44.

22d Marines. Journal. A record of all messages sent and received by 22d Marines Headquarters, 17Feb–24Feb44. Included is a penciled report dated 15Mar44 dealing with activities of the Regimental Weapons Co during the Eniwetok operations.

22d Marines, reinforced. Report on DOWNSIDE Operation, 9Mar44. A detailed 25-page report dealing principally with an analysis of all aspects of the Eniwetok operation and containing pertinent recommendations for future activities.

22d Marines. Reports, undated. A folder containing reports relating to the Eniwetok operation from the following organizations: 2d Separate Transport Co; 2d Separate Pack Howitzer Bn; BLT 2; Service & Supply Plt, H&S Co.; 2d Separate Engineer Co; 2d Separate Tank Co; 2d Separate Medical Co; Regimental Weapons Co.

22d Marines. Action Reports on Lesser Marshalls. Detailed reports from each group participating in the occupation of the Lesser Marshalls. Also a regimental report covering the over-all Lesser Marshalls operations. Dates are 11Mar44 through 24Apr44. Each report carries the endorsement of the atoll commander and the Marine Administrative Command, VAC.

22d Marines, reinforced. War Diary, 3Mar44. Signed by Col. J. T. Walker, with endorsement by MajGen H. M. Smith, Commanding General, VAC. Covers period 1Jan44 through 29Feb44.

1st Battalion, 22d Marines. Report on FLINTLOCK II Operation, undated. A report on Landing Team 1's activities at Eniwetok Atoll and signed by W. H. Fromhold. Includes a history of operations, operation overlay, unit journal and message abstract and comments and recommendations.

2d Battalion, 22d Marines. Record of Events. A day-by-day report from 19Jul42 through 6Feb45.

106th Infantry Regiment. Unit Operation Report (DOWNSIDE), 15Apr44. A detailed report of the organization's participation in the Eniwetok operation. Includes operation plans and orders, maps, unit journal, casualty report and a report by BLT 106–3. Carries endorsements by VAC and the 27th Infantry Division.

1st Defense Battalion, VAC. War Diary for April 1944. A day-by-day account of activities during the month of April. Signed by LtCol J. H. Buckner, and carrying an endorsement from VAC.

708th Amphibian Tank Battalion. Report of 708th Provisional Amphibian Tractor Bn on FLINTLOCK Operation, 14Feb44. Includes a narrative of oper-

ations and recommendations for future operations. Signed by Maj J. L. Rogers.

708th Amphibian Tank Battalion. Special Action Report, Kwajalein operation, 12Mar44. A day-by-day account of the organization's participation in the FLINTLOCK Operation, 31Jan44–6Feb44.

708th Amphibian Tank Bn. Unit History, 22Jan45. A brief and generalized history of the organization covering its activation and participation in the Marshall Islands and Guam operations. Signed by K. C. Heise, Adjutant.

Company I, 111th Infantry. Report of Operations, Occupation of Ujelang Atoll, 27Apr44.

USS *Alabama*. Bombardment of Roi-Namur, 6Feb44. Report of bombardment on 30Jan44.

USS *New Orleans*. Report of Action, 8Feb44. Chronological account of activities during the bombardment of Roi, 30Jan44.

USS *Overton*. Action Report, 8Feb44. Chronological account of *Overton's* participation in the Kwajalein operation from 30Jan44 through 5Feb44.

USS *Arthur Middleton*. Report of Landing Phase of Operations at Eniwetok Atoll, 7Mar44. Contains narrative reports as well as operations plans and order for Eniwetok.

USS *Ashland*. Action Report, Eniwetok Atoll, 3May44. Chronological account and comments on the Eniwetok operation during the period 11–23Feb44.

Island Commander, Roi. Report of Action, 4Apr44. Chronological account of Japanese air attack on 12Feb44, with pertinent comments.

Fleet Orders. Folder containing orders issued by RAdm Alva D. Bernhard, Kwajalein Atoll Commander, pertaining to operations in the Lesser Marshalls. Orders issued between 27Feb44 and 24Mar44, inclusive.

Marine Corps Headquarters. Advanced Base Operations in Micronesia, 712. Approved by the Commandant on 23Jul21; this document was the plan for Marine participation in the event of war with Japan. It is a detailed estimate of the situation on each of the numerous possible targets in the Pacific.

Document submitted by Capt Buenos A. W. Young, dated 10Apr44 and believed to be the Action Report, 3d Bn, 22d Marines, on the Eniwetok Operation.

BOOKS, PAMPHLETS, PERIODICALS

Amphibious Operations in the Marshall Islands, January–February 1944. Issued by CominCh, United States Fleet, 20May44.

Bartley, Whitman S. *Iwo Jima: Amphibious Epic.* Washington: Government Printing Office, 1954.

Craven, W. F. and Cate, J. L. *The Army Air Forces in World War II,* Vol IV, *The Pacific—Guadalcanal to Saipan.* University of Chicago Press, 1950.

Crowl, Philip A., and Love, Edmund G. *United States Army in World War II, The Seizure of the Gilberts and Marshalls.* A forthcoming volume to be published by the Office of the Chief of Military History, Department of the Army.

Heinl, Robert D., Jr. *The Defense of Wake.* Washington: Government Printing Office, 1947.

Heinl, Robert D., Jr. *Marines at Midway.* Washington: Government Printing Office, 1948.

Hoffman, Carl W. *Saipan: The Beginning of the End.* Washington: Government Printing Office, 1950.

Hoffman, Carl W. *The Seizure of Tinian.* Washington: Government Printing Office, 1951.

Hough, Frank O. *The Island War.* New York: J. B. Lippincott Co., 1947.

Isely, Jeter A., and Crowl, Philip A. *The U. S. Marines and Amphibious War.* Princeton University Press, 1951.

Lodge, O. R. *The Recapture of Guam.* Washington: Government Printing Office, 1954.

Love, Edmund G. *The 27th Infantry Division in World War II.* Washington: Infantry Journal Press, 1949.

Marine Corps Gazette. "Personalities—Men Who Differed," by Maj Frank O. Hough, USMCR, November 1950.

Marshall, S. L. A. *Island Victory.* Infantry Journal Press, 1945.

Military Review. "The Marshall Islands Operation," by VAdm Harry W. Hill, USN.

Morison, Samuel E. *History of United States Naval Operations in World War II,* Vol VII, *Aleutians, Gilberts and Marshalls.* Little Brown and Co., 1951.

Proehl, Carl W. (ed) *The Fourth Marine Division in World War II.* Washington: Infantry Journal Press, 1946.

Rentz, John N. *Marines in the Central Solomons.* Washington: Government Printing Office, 1952.

Robson, R. M. *The Pacific Islands Handbook, 1944.* New York: The MacMillan Company, 1945.

Sailing Directions for the Pacific Islands. Washington: Hydrographic Office, U. S. Navy Department, 1938.

Saturday Evening Post. "The Marines' First Spy," by Maj John L. Zimmerman, USMCR, 23 November 1946.

Sherrod, Robert. *History of Marine Corps Aviation in World War II.* Washington: Combat Forces Press, 1952.

Smith, Holland M. *Coral and Brass.* New York: Charles Scribner's Sons, 1949.

Stockman, James R. *The Battle for Tarawa.* Washington: Government Printing Office, 1947.

The War Reports of General Marshall, General Arnold and Admiral King. New York: J. B. Lippincott, 1947.

United States Strategic Bombing Survey. *The American Campaign Against Wotje, Maloelap, Mille and Jaluit.* Washington: Government Printing Office, 1947.

United States Strategic Bombing Survey. *The Campaigns of the Pacific War.* Washington: Government Printing Office, 1946.

United States Strategic Bombing Survey. *The Reduction of Truk.* Washington: Government Printing Office, 1947.

Wendell, William G. *The Marshall Islands Operations.* Unpublished manuscript, 1945.

Zimmerman, John L. *The Guadalcanal Campaign.* Washington: Government Printing Office, 1949.

MISCELLANEOUS

Maj Paul H. Bird, "Atoll Hopping—The Lesser Marshalls," an undated report dealing with the 22d Marines in the Lesser Marshalls.

LtCol Austin R. Brunelli, Historical Tactical Study, The Capture of Namur Island, 1–2 February 1944, written for Amphibious Warfare School, Quantico, Senior Course 1946–1947.

Notes of LtCol W. F. Fromhold, undated. Prepared by Capt W. G. Wendell.

S. L. A. Marshall. Kwajalein Notes. Col Marshall was with the 7th Infantry Division during the Kwajalein operation and conducted a series of interviews with participants as soon as organized resistance ceased. Maps and sketches accompany his notes.

Ltr Col O. T. Pfeiffer to Col. G. B. Erskine, 23Oct43.

Memo BrigGen O. T. Pfeiffer to BrigGen G. C. Thomas, 23Feb44.

LtCol Richard Rothwell, A Study of An Amphibious Operation, The Battle of Namur, 31Jan44–2Feb44, written for Amphibious Warfare School, Quantico, Senior Course 1946–1947.

Maj William E. Sperling III, an undated paper titled "BLT 3/22 on Eniwetok Island," filed in Archives, HQMC.

Memo Adm H. R. Stark to SecNav, 12Nov40.

APPENDIX II

Chronology

1943

11 May	TRIDENT Conference in Washington; CCS decides to seize the Marshalls and to move against Japanese outer defenses.
Mid-June	JCS directs Adm Nimitz to submit plan for occupation of the Marshalls.
1 July	Adm Nimitz submits concept for operations.
20 July	JCS directs Adm Nimitz to organize and train forces for operations in the Marshalls on 1 January 1944.
15 August	4th Marine Division organized.
20 August	Adm Nimitz submits outline plan for occupation of Kwajalein, Wotje and Maloelap.
17–24 August	At the QUADRANT Conference at Quebec, routes of advance on Japan laid out and operations in the Marshalls agreed to.
24 August	Fifth Amph Force set up, RAdm Turner commanding.
1 September	JCS dispatches directive to Adm Nimitz, allocating troops and naval forces for the Marshalls.
16 September	7th Inf Div arrives at Oahu, T. H. to begin preparations for the Marshalls.
20 September	4th MarDiv assigned to VAC.
12 October	Adm Nimitz issues OP Plan 16–43, first formal operation plan for the Marshalls.
15 November	MajGen Smith issues OP Plan 2–43, first over-all troop directive for the Marshalls.
16 November	TG–1 organized under VAC GenOrd No. 55–43.
20 November	2d MarDiv assaults Tarawa.
4 December	First aerial photo coverage of Kwajalein Atoll effected.
5 December	VAdm Yamada assumes command of Japanese aviation in the Marshalls.
14 December	Adm Nimitz revises OP Plan 16–43; target date postponed.
20 December	Adm Nimitz issues final JCS Study, FLINTLOCK II in which all changes have been ratified.

1944

3 January	RAdm Turner issues OP Plan A6–43, listing components and setting forth mission of Joint Expeditionary Force.
4 January	1st Amphibious Brigade (Japanese) arrives at Eniwetok Atoll.
5 January	VAC OP Plan 1–44 released, superseding OP Plan 3–43.
13 January	Main body of TF 53 departs San Diego.
22 January	Joint Expeditionary Force sails from Hawaii.
31 January	D-Day in the Marshalls: Landings effected on small islands in both northern and southern Kwajalein Atoll. VAC Reconn Co lands on Majuro Atoll.
1 February	Combat Teams 23 and 24 land on Roi-Namur. RCT's 32 and 184 land on Kwajalein Island.
4 February	RAdm Harry W. Hill given command of Task Group 51.11, with the mission of seizing Eniwetok Atoll. Kwajalein Island overrun. 109th NavConsBn begins repair on Roi airfield.
7 February	Ground elements of 4th MBDAW arrive at Roi.
8 February	Kwajalein Atoll secured.
12 February	Japanese retaliate with air attack on Roi.
17 February	Landings effected on small islands of Eniwetok Atoll.
17–18 February	TF 58 attacks Truk.
18 February	22d Marines land on Engebi and secure it.
19 February	Landing by 106th RCT and 3d Bn, 22d Marines, on Eniwetok Island.
21 February	Eniwetok Island secured.
22 February	22d Marines land on Parry and secure it.
26 February	22d Marines relieve 25th Marines on Kwajalein.
1 March	RAdm Bernhard receives orders to neutralize and control the Lesser Marshalls.
4 March	4th MBDAW begins bombing campaign against Wotje, Jaluit, Mille and Maloelap.
10 March	Wotho Island taken.
11 March	Ujae Atoll occupied. American flag raised on Lib Island.
21 March	Ailinglapalap Atoll taken.
22 March	TG–1 disbanded; 1st Prov-MarBrig organized.
24 March	Ebon Atoll secured.
30 March	Flag raised on Bikini Atoll.
1 April	Ailuk Atoll taken.
2 April	Marines land on Mejit Island.
3 April	Likiep and Rongelap Atolls secured.
5 April	Utirik Atoll secured.
6 April	22d Marines depart for Guadalcanal.
17 April	Marines from 1st Defense Bn, VAC, land on Erikub and Aur Atolls.
22 April	Soldiers of 111th Inf raise flag on Ujelang Atoll.

1945

22 August	Mille Atoll surrendered to American naval forces; the first of the by-passed atolls to surrender.
2 September	Japan formally surrenders.

APPENDIX III

Casualties

MARINE ORGANIZATIONS [1]	Killed or Died of Wounds [2]		Wounded		Total	
	Officers	Enlisted	Officers	Enlisted	Officers	Enlisted
4th Marine Division:						
Hq Co, Hq Bn...............			2	2	2	2
4th Sig Co...................				2		2
MP Co.......................			1		1	
4th Spec Wpns Bn...........			1	8	1	8
4th Tank Bn.................	1	6	1	7	2	13
4th Serv Bn.................				2		2
4th MT Bn..................			2	2	2	2
4th Amph Trac Bn...........				1		1
10th Amph Trac Bn..........		9		8		17
11th Amph Trac Bn..........		6				6
1st Armd Amph Bn...........		9		8		17
14th Marines:						
1st Bn......................				2		2
2d Bn.......................		1		6		7
3d Bn.......................		5	1	2	1	7
20th Marines:						
H&S Co....................		7	3	17	3	24
1st Bn......................	1	22	2	21	3	43
2d Bn.......................	2	3	1	10	3	13
23d Marines:						
H&S and Wpns Cos............			1	3	1	3
1st Bn......................		2	2	13	2	15
2d Bn.......................		13	1	36	1	49
3d Bn.......................		3	2	10	2	13

[1] Marine casualty figures furnished by Personnel Accounting Section, Records Branch, Personnel Department, HQMC. These figures were certified and released on 26 August 1952, and includes those casualties incurred in the Marshalls within the period 31 January through 6 April 1944.

[2] Includes MIA and Missing, Presumed Dead figures.

MARINE ORGANIZATIONS	Killed or Died of Wounds		Wounded		Total	
	Officers	Enlisted	Officers	Enlisted	Officers	Enlisted
24th Marines:						
H&S and Wpns Cos.............	1	6	2	9	3	15
1st Bn.......................	3	44	3	64	6	108
2d Bn........................	3	91	5	123	8	214
3d Bn........................	6	72	5	94	11	166
25th Marines:						
H&S and Wpns Cos.............			1	3	1	3
1st Bn.......................		9	1	7	1	16
2d Bn........................		13		8		21
3d Bn........................		1		14		15
1st JASCO.......................	2	4		4	2	8
Reconn Co, VAC..................		7	1	11	1	18
10th Defense Bn.....................				1		1
15th Defense Bn....................		5	1	39	1	44
22d Marines:						
H&S and Wpns Cos.............		8		19		27
1st Bn.......................	1	97	12	193	13	290
2d Bn........................	1	60	1	128	2	188
3d Bn........................	2	72	9	145	11	217
2d Sep Pk How Bn.............		2	2	8	2	10
2d Sep Tank Co.................		6	1	13	1	19
2d Sep Engr Co.................		5	1	23	1	28
4th Marine Base Defense Air Wing:						
MAG–13:						
VMSB–231.....................	1	2	1	1	2	3
VMSB–331....................			2	2	2	2
MAG–22:						
Hq Sq–22.....................			1	2		3
AWS–1.......................			1	2		3
SMS–22.......................				4		4
VMF–113......................				3		3
VMF–422......................			1	4		5
MAG–31:						
Hq Sq–31.....................			9	16		25
SMS–31.......................			6	23		29
VMF–111......................	1		4	9	5	9
VMF–224.....................		2	3	17	3	19
VMF–311......................			2		2	
VMF–441......................	1		4	2	5	2
Total [3]......................	26	610	81	1, 151	107	1, 761

[3] The following organizations suffered no casualties during the operation: 1st Defense Bn, 2d Sep Transport Co, 2d Sep Med Co and 3d Bn, 20th Marines.

NAVY MEDICAL [4]	Killed or Died of Wounds		Wounded		Total	
	Officers	Enlisted	Officers	Enlisted	Officers	Enlisted
4th Marine Division		1	2	15	2	16
22d Marines		6		13		19
MAG–31		2				2
Photo Sq No. 3		1				1
Total		10	2	28	2	38

ARMY ORGANIZATIONS [5]						
7th Infantry Division:						
17th Inf		16	2	77	2	93
32d Inf	2	55	19	303	21	358
184th Inf	1	64	17	252	18	316
13th Engr Bn		10		31		41
57th FA Bn		2	1	9	1	11
48th FA Bn	1				1	
49th FA Bn				5		5
145th FA Bn		9		22		31
7th Div Arty	1				1	
7th Med Bn		1	1	1	1	2
7th Reconn Trp		2	2	18	2	20
7th Div Hqs	1				1	
91st Chem Co		1		13		14
75th Sig Co				4		4
47th Engr Co		3		1		4
767th Tank Bn		1	2	5	2	6
111th Inf		2	1	5	1	7
867th AAA				1		1
4th Army Def Bn		1		1		2
Total	6	167	45	748	51	915
708th Amph Tank Bn [6]		1	3	33	3	34

[4] Navy Hospital Corpsmen, Medical and Dental Officer casualty figures furnished by U. S. Navy Bureau of Medicine and Surgery, Statistics Division, World War II Casualties, 1Aug52.

[5] These figures taken from 7th Infantry Division FLINTLOCK Operation, ACofS, G–1 Report of Operation.

[6] This unit participated in both the Kwajalein and Eniwetok operations. Casualty figures are taken from the 708th Amph Tank Bn History, 27Oct43–31Dec44, which lumps together all casualty figures for the Marshalls.

ARMY ORGANIZATIONS [7]	Killed or Died of Wounds	Wounded	Total
RCT 106 (Reinf) (less BLT 106–2):			
106th Inf................................	82	281	363
104th FA Bn.............................	2	8	10
104th Engr Bn...........................	6	10	16
Co B, 102d Engr Bn......................	1	4	5
Co C, 102d Med Bn.......................	2		2
Det, 295th Sig Co.......................		1	1
Co C, 766th Tk Bn.......................	1	5	6
Det, 727th Ord Co.......................	1		1
Hq Btry, 27th Div Arty..................		1	1
Hq, 27th Inf Div........................		1	1
Yank Magazine...........................	1		1
Total..............................	96	311	407

[7] These figures taken from 106th RCT Operation Report, Eniwetok. No breakdown into officers and enlisted was shown.

THE MARSHALLS: INCREASING THE TEMPO

APPENDIX IV

Task Organization

NORTHERN LANDING FORCE—MajGen Harry Schmidt

PHASE I

IVAN Landing Group—BrigGen James L. Underhill
Det Hq Co, Hq Bn, 4thMarDiv
Det Sig Co, Hq Bn, 4thMarDiv
25th Marines (plus Band Sec)
14th Marines
1st Composite Engr Bn (plus Cam Det, H&S Co, 20th Mar)
Co A, 4th Tk Bn (less 1st Plat)
Btry B, 4th Spl Wpns Bn
10th Amph Trac Bn
1st Plat, Btry A, 4th Spl Wpns Bn
Co A, 11th Amph Trac Bn (plus Prov LVT(2) Plat, 1st Armd Amph Bn)
Cos B and D, 1st Armd Amph Bn
Co A, 4th Med Bn
Co A, 4th MT Bn
1st Plat, Ord Co, 4th Serv Bn
1st Plat, Serv & Sup Co, 4th Serv Bn
1st Plat, 4th MP Co
Det 1st JASCO
Co D, 4th Tk Bn (Scout)   (All less Rear Echelon)

PHASE II

Combat Team 23—Col Louis R Jones
23d Marines (plus Band Sec)
3d Composite Engr Bn (plus Cam Det, Com Plat, H&S Co, 20th Mar)
Co C, 4th Tk Bn (Medium)
1st Plat, Co A, 4th Tk Bn
Btry C, 4th Spl Wpns Bn
3d Plat, Btry A, 4th Spl Wpns Bn
4th Amph Trac Bn
Cos A and C, 1st Armd Amph Bn

Co C, 4th Med Bn
Co C, 4th MT Bn
3d Plat, Ord Co, 4th Serv Bn
3d Plat, 4th MP Co
Dets 1st JASCO   (All less Rear Echelon)
Combat Team 24—Col Franklin A. Hart
24th Marines (plus Band Sec)
2d Composite Engr Bn (plus Cam Det, H&S Co, 20th Mar)
Co B, 4th Tk Bn
Btry D, 4th Spl Wpns Bn
2d Plat, Btry A, 4th Spl Wpns Bn
10th Amph Trac Bn
Cos B and D, 1st Armd Amph Bn
Co B, 4th Med Bn
Co B, 4th MT Bn
2d Plat, 4th MP Co
Dets 1st JASCO   (All less Rear Echelon)
Division Reserve—Col Samuel C. Cumming
25th Marines (plus Band Sec)
1st Composite Engr Bn (plus Cam Det, H&S Co, 20th Mar)
Co A, 4th Tk Bn (less 1st Plat)
Co D, 4th Tk Bn (Scout)
Btry B, 4th Spl Wpns Bn
1st Plat, Btry A, 4th Spl Wpns Bn
Co A, 11th Amph Trac Bn (plus Prov Plat, 1st Armd Amph Bn)
Co A, 4th Med Bn
Co A, 4th MT Bn
1st Plat, Ord Co, 4th Serv Bn
1st Plat, Serv & Sup Co, 4th Serv Bn
1st Plat, 4th MP Co
Det 1st JASCO   (All less Rear Echelon)
14th Marines (less Rear Echelon)—Col Louis G. DeHaven
Support Group—Col Emmett W. Skinner
Hq Bn 4th MarDiv (less dets)

20th Mar (less 1st, 2d and 3d Bns, and less Com Plat and Cam Sec, H&S Co, 20th Mar)
4th Tk Bn (less dets)
1st Armd Amph Bn (less dets)
4th Med Bn (less Cos A, B and C)
4th Serv Bn (less dets)
4th MT Bn (less dets)
1st JASCO (less dets)
4th Spl Wpns Bn (less dets)
15th Defense Bn (Marine)

SOUTHERN LANDING FORCE—MajGen Charles H. Corlett, USA

7th Infantry Division—MajGen Charles H. Corlett, USA
RCT's 17, 32 and 184
7th Reconnaissance Troop
13th Engr Bn
Co D, 34th Engr Bn
1st Bn, 47th Engr Bn
50th Engr Bn
7th Sig Co
75th Sig Co
GAU 7, 163d Sig Photo Co
767th Tk Bn
Det, 8th Chem Co
91st Chem Co
7th QM Co
MP Platoon
707th Ord Co
93d Bomb Disposal Squad
Cannon Co, 111th Inf
1st Bn, 111th Inf (less Co C)
708th Prov Amph Trac Bn
Co A, 708th Amph Tk Bn
7th Med Bn
31st Field Hospital
Btry A, 55th CA
Btrys E and F, 57th CA
Btrys A, B, C and D, 96th AAA Bn
Btrys A and C, 98th AAA Bn
Det, 296th AAA Bn
Co B, 376th Port Bn
Btrys A and B, 753d AAA Bn
Btrys A and D, 867th AAA Bn
Dets, 87th ASSRON

3d Army Defense Bn
4th Army Defense Bn

Division Artillery Group—BrigGen Archibald V. Arnold, USA

31st, 48th, 49th, 57th and 145th FA Bns

SUNDANCE LANDING FORCE—LtCol Frederick B. Sheldon, USA

2d Bn, 106th Inf (reinforced)
V Amphibious Corps Reconnaissance Co
1st Defense Bn (Marine)

RESERVE LANDING FORCE (Tactical Group-1)— BrigGen Thomas E. Watson

22d Marines (reinforced)
106th Inf (reinforced) (less 2d Bn reinforced)

ENIWETOK LANDING FORCES (Tactical Group-1)—BrigGen Thomas E. Watson

22d Marines
2d Sep Pack How Bn
2d Sep Engr Co
2d Sep Med Co
2d Sep Tank Co
2d Sep Transport Co
Co D (Scout), 4th Tank Bn
V Amphibious Corps Reconnaissance Co
10th Defense Bn (Marine)
Nav Const Co (Acorn 22)
106th Inf (less 2d Bn)
104th FA Bn
104th Engr Bn (less 1 Co)
Co B, 102d Engr Bn (less 1 Plat)
Cos C and D, 102d Med Bn (less 2 Plats)
Portable Surgical Hospital #1 (Prov)
Co C, 766 Tk Bn
Det, 727th Ord Co
Det, 97th Ord Co
Det, 295th Sig Co
Co A, 708th Amph Tk Bn
708th Prov Amph Trac Bn (less 1 LVT Grp)
Prov DUKW Btry
47th Engr Bn
3d Army Defense Bn

Command and Staff

APPENDIX V

KWAJALEIN ATOLL [1]

(31 January 1944–8 February 1944)

V Amphibious Corps [2]

Commanding General....	MajGen Holland M. Smith
Chief of Staff...........	BrigGen Graves B. Erskine
G–1....................	LtCol Albert F. Metze
G–2....................	LtCol St. Julien R. Marshall
G–3....................	Col John C. McQueen
G–4....................	Col Raymond E. Knapp
G–5....................	Col Joseph T. Smith

4th Marine Division

Commanding General.....	MajGen Harry Schmidt
Asst. Div. Commander....	BrigGen James L. Underhill
Chief of Staff...........	Col William W. Rogers
D–1....................	Col Merton J. Batchelder
D–2....................	Maj Gooderham L. McCormick
D–3....................	Col Walter W. Wensinger
D–4....................	Col William F. Brown

1st Armored Amphibian Battalion

Commander Officer.......	Maj Louis Metzger
Executive Officer........	Capt Richard G. Warga
Bn–3..................	1stLt Thomas M. Crosby

[1] Tactical Group-1 was in reserve for the FLINTLOCK Operation. Inasmuch as this unit participated in CATCHPOLE its command and staff organization is listed only under the latter operation.

[2] In the case of VAC staff, the officers shown herein occupied their respective billets during the important planning phase of FLINTLOCK, although not all of them accompanied MajGen Holland M. Smith on the *Rocky Mount* to Kwajalein.

4th Amphibian Tractor Battalion [3]

Commanding Officer......	LtCol Clovis C. Coffman

10th Amphibian Tractor Battalion [4]

Commanding Officer......	Maj Victor J. Croizat
Executive Officer........	Maj Warren H. Edwards

4th Tank Battalion

Commanding Officer.....	Maj Richard K. Schmidt
Executive Officer........	Capt Francis L. Orgain
Bn–3..................	Capt Leo B. Case

23d Marines

Commanding Officer......	Col Louis R. Jones
Executive Officer........	LtCol John R. Lanigan
R–1....................	Capt Frank E. Phillips, Jr.
R–2....................	Capt Richard W. Mirick
R–3....................	Maj Edward W. Wells
R–4....................	Capt Henry S. Campbell

Regimental Weapons Company

Commanding Officer......	Capt George W. E. Daughtry
Executive Officer........	Capt Raymond C. Kraus

1st Battalion, 23d Marines

Commanding Officer......	LtCol Hewin O. Hammond
Executive Officer........	Maj Hollis U. Mustain
Bn–3..................	Capt James R. Miller

[3] Executive Officer and Bn–3 not shown in available records.

[4] Bn–3 not shown in available records.

2d Battalion, 23d Marines

Commanding Officer...... LtCol Edward J. Dillon
Executive Officer........ Maj Lawrence V. Patterson
Bn–3.................... Capt James W. Sperry

3d Battalion, 23d Marines

Commanding Officer..... LtCol John J. Cosgrove, Jr.
Executive Officer........ LtCol Ralph Haas
Bn–3.................... Maj Robert J. J. Picardi

24th Marines

Commanding Officer..... Col Franklin A. Hart
Executive Officer........ LtCol Homer L. Litzenberg, Jr.
R–1.................... Capt Kenneth N. Hilton
R–2.................... Capt Arthur B. Hanson
R–3.................... LtCol Charles D. Roberts
R–4.................... Maj Clyde T. Smith

Regimental Weapons Company

Commanding Officer..... Maj Richard McCarthy, Jr.
Executive Officer........ Capt Edward J. Schofield

1st Battalion, 24th Marines

Commanding Officer..... LtCol Aquilla J. Dyess
(KIA 2 February)
Maj Maynard C. Schultz
Executive Officer........ Maj Maynard C. Schultz
(to 2 February)
Bn–3.................... Capt Gene G. Mundy

2d Battalion, 24th Marines

Commanding Officer..... LtCol Francis H. Brink
Executive Officer........ LtCol Richard Rothwell
Bn–3.................... Maj Claude M. Cappelmann

3d Battalion, 24th Marines

Commanding Officer..... LtCol Austin R. Brunelli
Executive Officer........ Maj John V. V. Veeder
Bn–3.................... Capt Webb D. Sawyer

25th Marines

Commanding Officer..... Col Samuel C. Cumming
Executive Officer........ LtCol Walter I. Jordan
R–1.................... WO Daniel H. Nelson [5]
R–2.................... Capt Charles D. Gray
R–3.................... LtCol William F. Thyson, Jr.
R–4.................... Capt Edward Sherman

Regimental Weapons Company

Commanding Officer..... Capt James T. Kisgen
Executive Officer........ Capt Thomas H. Rogers
Capt Delbert A. Graham
(from 1 February)

---

[5] WO Nelson was actually assistant R–1 of the 25th Marines. He accompanied the regiment to Kwajalein, however, while Capt Francis A. Norton, R–1, remained with the rear echelon.

1st Battalion, 25th Marines

Commanding Officer..... LtCol Clarence J. O'Donnell
Executive Officer........ Maj Michael Davidowitch, Jr.
Bn–3.................... Capt Fenton J. Mee

2d Battalion, 25th Marines

Commanding Officer..... LtCol Lewis C. Hudson, Jr.
Executive Officer........ Maj William P. Kaempfer
Bn–3.................... Capt Victor J. Barringer

3d Battalion, 25th Marines

Commanding Officer..... LtCol Justice M. Chambers
Executive Officer........ Maj James Taul
Bn–3.................... Maj John H. Jones

14th Marines

Commanding Officer..... Col Louis G. DeHaven
Executive Officer........ LtCol Randall M. Victory
R–1.................... 1stLt Cecil D. Snyder
R–2.................... Capt Harrison L. Rogers
R–3.................... Maj Frederick J. Karch
R–4.................... Maj Richard J. Winsborough

1st Battalion, 14th Marines

Commanding Officer..... LtCol Harry J. Zimmer
Executive Officer........ Maj Clifford B. Drake
Bn–3.................... Maj Thomas M. Fry

2d Battalion, 14th Marines

Commanding Officer..... LtCol George B. Wilson, Jr.
Executive Officer........ Maj William McReynolds
Bn–3.................... Capt Ralph W. Boyer, Jr.

3d Battalion, 14th Marines

Commanding Officer..... LtCol Robert E. MacFarlane
Executive Officer........ Maj Harvey A. Feehan
Bn–3.................... Maj Donald M. Love, Jr.

4th Battalion, 14th Marines

Commanding Officer..... Maj Carl A. Youngdale
Executive Officer........ Maj John B. Edgar, Jr.
Bn–3.................... Maj Roland J. Spritzen

20th Marines

Commanding Officer..... Col Lucian W. Burnham
Executive Officer........ LtCol Nelson K. Brown
R–1.................... Capt Martin M. Calcaterra
R–2.................... Capt Carl A. Sachs
R–3.................... Maj. Melvin D. Henderson
R–4.................... Capt Samuel G. Thompson

1st Battalion, 20th Marines

Commanding Officer..... Maj Richard G. Ruby
Executive Officer........ Capt George F. Williamson
Bn–3.................... Capt Martin H. Glover

2d Battalion, 20th Marines

Commanding Officer..... LtCol Otto Lessing
Executive Officer........ Maj John H. Partridge
Bn–3.................. Capt George L. Smith

3d Battalion, 20th Marines [4]

Commanding Officer..... LtCdr William G. Byrne
Executive Officer........ LtCdr Thomas H. Flinn

15th Defense Battalion

Commanding Officer..... LtCol Francis B. Loomis, Jr.
Executive Officer........ LtCol Peter J. Negri
Bn–3.................. Capt Guy L. Wharton

7th Infantry Division

Commanding General..... MajGen Charles H. Corlett
Asst. Commanding General BrigGen Joseph L. Ready
Chief of Staff............. Col LeRoy J. Stewart
G–1.................... LtCol Charles V. Wilson
G–2.................... LtCol Robert G. Fergusson
G–3.................... LtCol George B. Sloan
G–4.................... LtCol David X. Angluin
Adjutant General........ LtCol Arthur J. Salisbury

7th Medical Battalion

Commanding Officer..... LtCol Robert J. Kamish
Executive Officer......... Maj Alan B. Eaker
S–3..................... Capt Sidney Cohen

7th Reconnaissance Troop

Commanding Officer..... Capt Paul B. Gritta

13th Engineer Battalion

Commanding Officer..... LtCol Harold K. Howell
Executive Officer......... Capt George G. McCormick
S–3..................... Capt Myrl A. Reaugh

17th Infantry Regiment

Commanding Officer..... Col Wayne C. Zimmerman
Executive Officer......... LtCol William B. Moore
S–1..................... Capt Henry R. Sievers
S–2..................... Maj Harry L. Beatty
S–3..................... Capt James E. Simmons
S–4..................... Capt Paul S. Foster, Jr.

1st Battalion, 17th Infantry

Commanding Officer..... LtCol Albert V. Hartl
Executive Officer......... Maj Maynard B. Weaver
S–3..................... Capt Robert H. Johnson

2d Battalion, 17th Infantry

Commanding Officer..... LtCol Edward P. Smith
Executive Officer......... Maj Delbert L. Bjork
S–3..................... Capt Robert J. Edwards

3d Battalion, 17th Infantry

Commanding Officer..... LtCol Lee Wallace
Executive Officer......... Maj Earl W. Nelson
S–3..................... Capt Mervin A. Elliot

32d Infantry Regiment

Commanding Officer..... Col Marc J. Logie
Executive Officer......... LtCol John M. Finn
S–1..................... Capt Jack L. Oliver
S–2..................... Maj Charles F. Manov
S–3..................... Maj Leigh H. Mathias
S–4..................... 1stLt Wayne K. Yenni

1st Battalion, 32d Infantry

Commanding Officer..... LtCol Ernest H. Bearss
Executive Officer......... Maj Leonard E. Wellendorf
S–3..................... Capt James R. Hurt

2d Battalion, 32d Infantry

Commanding Officer..... LtCol Glen A. Nelson
Executive Officer......... Maj Charles A. Whitcomb
S–3..................... Capt Robert E. Goodfellow

3d Battalion, 32d Infantry

Commanding Officer..... LtCol Francis T. Pachler
Executive Officer......... Maj James H. Keller
S–3..................... Capt John P. Connor

184th Infantry Regiment

Commanding Officer..... Col Curtis D. O'Sullivan
Executive Officer......... LtCol Merl W. Bremer
S–1..................... Capt Charles J. Simon
S–2..................... Maj Jackson C. Gillis
S–3..................... Maj James K. Bullock
S–4..................... Maj Otto G. Niemann

1st Battalion, 184th Infantry

Commanding Officer..... LtCol Roy A. Green
Executive Officer......... Maj Cortez A. Kitchen
S–3..................... Capt Clark G. Campbell

2d Battalion, 148th Infantry

Commanding Officer..... LtCol Carl H. Aulick
Executive Officer......... Maj Richard W. Robison
S–3..................... Capt John R. Palmer

3d Battalion, 184th Infantry

Commanding Officer..... LtCol William P. Walker
Executive Officer......... Maj Daniel C. Maybury
S–3..................... Capt Paul L. Smith

Division Artillery Group

Commanding General.... BrigGen Archibald V. Arnold
Executive Officer......... Col William C. Lucas
S–1..................... Maj Waldo W. Montgomery

S-2 . . . . Maj John W. Pritchard
S-3 . . . . Maj Ara G. Lindley
R-4 . . . . Maj Waldo W. Montgomery

31st Field Artillery Battalion

Commanding Officer . . . . . LtCol Stanley Sawicki
Executive Officer . . . . Maj Clement B. Harts
S-3 . . . . Capt Edward L. Smith

48th Field Artillery Battalion

Commanding Officer . . . . . Maj Harold S. Dillingham
Executive Officer . . . . Capt Stanley C. Anderson
S-3 . . . . Maj Ray D. Free

49th Field Artillery Battalion

Commanding Officer . . . . . LtCol Francis B. Harrison
Executive Officer . . . . Maj Jack D. Beck
S-3 . . . . Maj Carroll Mitchell

57th Field Artillery Battalion

Commanding Officer . . . . . LtCol Donald F. Slaughter
Executive Officer . . . . Maj Stuart M. George
S-3 . . . . Maj John F. Hanson, Jr.

145th Field Artillery Battalion

Commanding Officer . . . . . LtCol George D. Preston
Executive Officer . . . . Maj Ralph W. Morgan
S-3 . . . . Maj George F. Seacat

767th Tank Battalion

Commanding Officer . . . . . LtCol William G. Bray
Executive Officer . . . . Maj Walter S. Hahn
S-3 . . . . Capt Joseph L. Lohner

708th Provisional Amphibian Tractor Battalion

Commanding Officer . . . . . Maj James L. Rogers
Executive Officer . . . . Maj William Rossing
S-3 . . . . Capt John D. Kooken

50th Engineer Battalion

Commanding Officer . . . . . LtCol Leonard L. Kingsbury
Executive Officer . . . . Capt George S. Baumgartner
S-3 . . . . Capt Charles J. Bainum

3d Army Defense Battalion [6]

Commanding Officer . . . . . LtCol Ralph W. Oakley

4th Army Defense Battalion [6]

Commanding Officer . . . . . Col Clifford R. Jones

---

[6] Executive Officer and S-3 not shown in available records.

MAJURO ATOLL
(31 January 1944–1 February 1944)

2d Battalion, 106th Infantry [7]

Commanding Officer . . . . . LtCol Frederick B. Sheldon
Executive Officer . . . . Maj Almerin C. O'Hara

1st Defense Battalion

Commanding Officer . . . . . LtCol Lewis A. Hohn
Executive Officer . . . . Maj Jean H. Buckner
Bn-3 . . . . Capt Charles S. Roberts

V Amphibious Corps Reconnaissance Company

Commanding Officer . . . . . Capt James L. Jones
Executive Officer . . . . 1stLt Merwin H. Silverthorn, Jr.

ENIWETOK ATOLL
(17 February 1944–24 February 1944)

Tactical Group-1

Commanding General . . . . BrigGen Thomas E. Watson
S-2 . . . . Maj Robert W. Shaw
S-3 . . . . LtCol Wallace M. Greene, Jr.
S-4 . . . . Col Robert J. Straub
Artillery Officer . . . . Maj Joseph L. Stewart
Naval Gunfire Officer . . . . Maj Ellsworth G. Van Orman

D Company (Scout), 4th Tank Battalion

Commanding Officer . . . . . . Capt Edward L. Katzenbach, Jr.
Executive Officer . . . . 1stLt James R. Barbour

V Amphibious Corps Reconnaissance Company [8]

22d Marines

Commanding Officer . . . . . Col John T. Walker
Executive Officer . . . . Col Merlin F. Schneider
R-1 . . . . Capt Curtis G. Callan
R-2 . . . . Maj Paul H. Bird
R-3 . . . . LtCol Floyd R. Moore
R-4 . . . . Capt Roland A. Wright

Regimental Weapons Company

Commanding Officer . . . . . Maj Theodore M. Sheffield
Executive Officer . . . . Maj Cecil D. Ferguson

1st Battalion, 22d Marines

Commanding Officer . . . . . . LtCol Walfried H. Fromhold
Executive Officer . . . . Maj Crawford B. Lawton
Bn-3 . . . . Capt Peter R. Dyer

---

[7] S-3 not shown in available records.
[8] Command and staff for this unit shown under Majuro Operation.

2d Battalion, 22d Marines

Commanding Officer..... LtCol Donn C. Hart
Executive Officer........ Maj Robert P. Felker
Bn-3.................. Capt William B. Koren

3d Battalion, 22d Marines

Commanding Officer..... Maj Clair W. Shisler
Executive Officer........ Maj William E. Sperling, III
Bn-3.................. Capt Leighton M. Clark, (KIA 20 February)
Capt Harry D. Hedrick

2d Separate Pack Howitzer Battalion

Commanding Officer..... LtCol Edwin C. Ferguson
Maj Alfred M. Mahoney (from 17 February)
Executive Officer........ Maj Alfred M. Mahoney
Maj Nathan C. Kingsbury (from 17 February)
Bn-3.................. Maj Nathan C. Kingsbury
Capt Robert T. Gillespie (from 17 February)

2d Separate Engineer Company

Commanding Officer..... Maj Paul F. Sackett
Executive Officer........ Capt Frederick G. Bloomfield

2d Separate Medical Company [9]

Commanding Officer..... Lt Llewellyn E. Wilson

2d Separate Tank Company

Commanding Officer..... Capt Harry Calcutt
Executive Officer........ 1stLt Robert Hall

2d Separate Transport Company [9]

Commanding Officer..... Maj Joseph A. Meyer

10th Defense Battalion

Commanding Officer..... LtCol Wallace O. Thompson
Executive Officer........ LtCol Robert E. Hommel
Bn-3.................. Maj Paul A. Fitzgerald

106th Infantry Regiment

Commanding Officer..... Col Russell G. Ayers
Executive Officer........ LtCol Joseph J. Farley
S-1.................... Capt George E. White
S-2.................... Capt William A. Foxen
S-3.................... Capt. George H. Temme, Jr.
S-4.................... Capt Jacob Ludwig

1st Battalion, 106th Infantry [7]

Commanding Officer..... LtCol Winslow Cornett
Executive Officer........ Maj John M. Nichols

3d Battalion, 106th Infantry [7]

Commanding Officer..... LtCol Harold J. Mizony
Executive Officer........ Maj Ernest C. Delear

104th Field Artillery Battalion [6]

Commanding Officer..... LtCol Van Nostrand

708th Provisional Amphibian Tractor Battalion [10]

3d Army Defense Battalion [10]

---

[9] Executive Officer not shown in available records.
[10] Command and staff for this unit shown under Kwajalein Operation.

179

Index

NORA Point, 89n, 97
NORA Road, 104, 105
NORBERT Circle, 72, 77
Northern Attack Force. *See* Task Force 53.
Northern Landing Force. *See* Task Group 56.2.
North Pacific Area, 6n
North Pacific Force, 9n
NUBBIN Lane, 91, 92
NUT Lane, 91, 92, 97

Oahu, 7, 26, 41
Obella Island, 49, 50, 152
Ocean Island, 5
O'Donnell, LtCol Clarence J., 42, 43, 46, 111
Okinawa, 151
Oldendorf, RAdm Jesse B., 124
ORANGE Plan, 3, 4, 4n
Ormsby, USS, 55n
O'Sullivan, Col Curtis D., USA, 100
Overton, USS, 53, 54, 112

Pacific Fleet, 6, 6n, 14, 15n, 37n
Pacific Ocean, 1–3, 3n, 5, 17, 28, 35, 36, 48, 115, 125, 150, 160
PAL Blockhouse, 65, 65n, 81
Palaus, 2, 126
Paramount Studios, 17n
Parry Island, 117, 118, 120, 120n, 124, 127, 128, 131n, 136, 137, 140, 142, 143, 143n, 144, 145, 145n, 146–149, 149n, 150, 151
PAULINE Point, 81, 92, 96
Pearl Harbor, 14, 18, 21, 26, 28, 37, 41, 60, 109, 121, 125, 127, 151
Pendleton, Camp Joseph H. 20, 23, 25
Pennsylvania, USS, 56, 56n, 57, 124, 128, 131, 145–147
Pensacola, USS, 39
Peter Road, 74n, 84
Pfeiffer, Col Omar T., 15n; BrigGen, 124n
Phelps, USS, 43, 43n, 44, 45, 48, 49, 49n, 50, 66, 68, 131, 137
Philippines 4, 31
Polynesians 3
Ponape Branch Bureau, 2
Ponape Island, 37, 109n
PORCELAIN. *See* Kwajalein Island.
Porterfield, USS, 42, 50
Portland, USS, 58, 60, 128, 137
POSY. *See* Rigili Island.
Power, 1stLt John V., 88
Pownall, RAdm Charles A., 38, 39
President Polk, USS, 55n
Princeton, USS, 39, 41, 125
PRIVILEGE. *See* Eniwetok Island.

QUADRANT Conference, 8
Quantico, 53n
Quebec, 8

Rabaul, 5, 30
Ragsdale, RAdm, V. H., 124
RAINBOW Plans, 4n

Ralik, 1, 3
Ralik Chain, 155
Ratak, 1, 3
Ready, BrigGen Joseph L., USA, 58
Reconnaissance Company. *See* Marine Units.
Reconnaissance Troop. *See* Army Units.
Redmond, Bernard, 110n
Reeves, RAdm John W., 39, 126
Regiment. *See* Army Units; Marine Units; Japanese Units.
Reinhardt, Maj Robert S., Jr., 134n, 146n
Relief, USS, 37
Rentz, Maj John N., 5n
Reserve Group, 36
Reserve Landing Force. *See* Task Group 56.3.
Rickets, Capt Claude V., USN, 128n
Rigili Island, 143
Ringgold, USS, 56, 57
RITA. *See* Darrit Island.
Roberts, LtCol Charles D., 20n
Rocky Mount, USS, 17, 30
Rogers, Maj James L., USA, 36, 145
Rogers, Maj Thomas H., Jr., 111n
Rogers, Col William W., 21, 21n, 22n, 51n, 53n, 82n, 99, 99n
Roi Island, 12, 13, 17, 18, 19n, 20, 21, 21n, 22, 22n, 23–26, 28, 29, 31–34, 37–40, 42–46, 46n, 48, 53, 64, 64n, 65, 65n, 66–74, 74n, 75–77, 79–81, 85, 85n, 87, 88, 91, 94, 96, 105, 108, 108n, 109–112, 115, 117, 118, 122, 124, 152, 153n, 157, 159
Rongerik Atoll, 153, 157
ROSALIE. *See* Uliga Island.
Ross, Capt John F., Jr., 84n, 85, 85n, 86n, 94, 94n
Rothwell, LtCol Richard 81n, 85n
Rujiyoru Island, 124, 127, 128, 131
Runway Able, 74n

Saavedra, Albaro de, 2
SAGEBRUSH. *See* Elugelab Island.
Saipan 28, 115, 115n, 116, 124n, 127n, 160
Salamaua 5
Salerno, 17
SALLY, 32
SALLY Point, 44, 49, 67, 81, 86
SALOME. *See* Dalap Island.
Salt Lake City, USS, 39
Samoa, 3, 8, 35, 122, 123
Samoan area, 151
San Clemente Island, 23–25
Sanders, LtCol Alvin S., 108n
Sanderson, BriGen Lawson H. M., 159n
San Diego, 17n, 20, 23n, 25, 67, 122
San Francisco, USS, 39, 56, 57
Sangamon, USS, 40, 73, 125, 131
Santa Fe, USS, 43, 45n, 65, 66, 75
Saratoga, USS, 39, 41, 108n, 125
Scales, Maj James S., 75n, 79n
Schley, USS, 42n, 129, 143
Schmidt, MajGen Harry, 13, 17, 17n, 19, 23, 35, 44, 64, 67, 71, 75, 79, 79n, 82, 82n, 83, 94, 94n, 96, 96n, 99, 111, 124

AL

Attu

Kis

Paramushiru To

USSR

CHISHIMA RETTO
(Kuril Islands)

Vladivostok   HOKKAIDO

JAPAN SEA

Chefoo
Shantung
Tsingtao   KOREA
YELLOW   HONSHU

SEA   TOKYO
Tsushima

Nagasaki   KYUSHU

Shanghai
Ningpo   EAST CHINA SEA

NANSEI SHOTO

Okinawa Shima

Kazan Retto • Iwo Jima   • Marcus
(Volcano Is)

TAIWAN
(FORMOSA)

LUZON STR.   • Wake

Lingayen G   • Pagan
SOUTH CHINA   LUZON   MARIANAS
SEA   Tinian• Saipan
Manila   • Rota
Mindoro   • Guam
Eniwetok• Bikini
Panay   Rongelap
Samar   Wotho• RONGELAP
Yap• Ulithi Is   Kwajalein Wotje
Maloelap
Namu   Majuro
MINDANAO Palau Is   Jaluit Mili
Peleliu   Babelthuap   Truk Is   • Ponape
CAROLINE   ISLANDS   Kusaie

CELEBES SEA   Makin

Morotai   Tarawa
BORNEO   HALMAHERA   Apamama

Str. of Makassar   Biak Schouten Is   Nauru•   •Ocean
CELEBES   Hollandia   Admiralty
Is   New Ireland   ELLICE Is   Nanom
BISMARCK   Bougainville
ARCHIPELAGO   Choiseul SOLOMON ISLANDS
NEW GUINEA   New   Vella Lavella• Sta. Isabel
Lae   Britain   New Georgia
TIMOR   D'Entrecasteaux   Russell Is• Malaita
P. Moresby   Is   Guadalcanal San
MILNE BAY   Cristobal

Darwin   CORAL SEA

Espiritu Santo   NEW   FIJI
HEBRIDES IS   •Efate

Townsville

AUSTRALIA   NEW   Noumea
CALEDONIA

PACIFIC   OCE

PHILIPPINE ISLANDS

MARSHALL ISLANDS

GILBERT ISLANDS

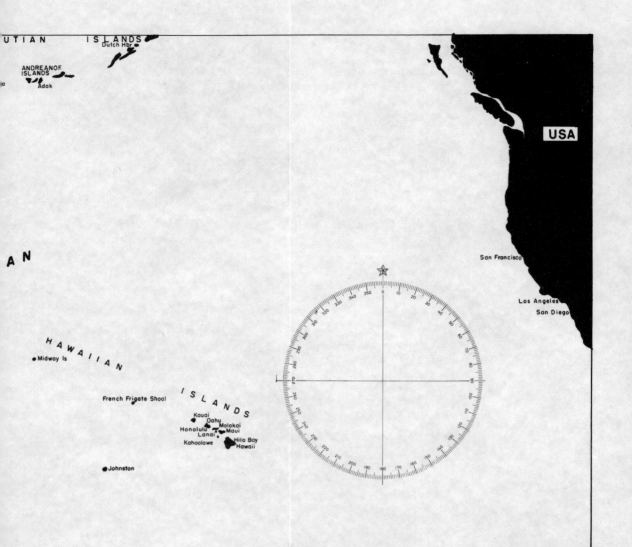

HAWAIIAN

ISLANDS

Midway Is

French Frigate Shoal

Kauai
Oahu
Honolulu Molokai
Lanai Maui
Kahoolawe Hilo Bay
Hawaii

Johnston

Palmyra

Christmas

Howland
Baker

PHOENIX Canton
ISLANDS

Nuku Fetau
Funafuti

UNION
GROUP

SAMOA ISLANDS
Savaii Upolu
Tutuila

ISLANDS

TONGA
ISLANDS
Tongatabu Gp

COOK ISLANDS

USA

San Francisco

Los Angeles

San Diego

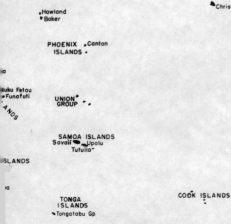

TABLE OF DISTANCES FROM KWAJALEIN ATOLL

In Nautical Miles

Eniwetok Atoll	356
Guam	1374
Jaluit Atoll	203
Kusaie	347
Majuro Atoll	220
Maloelap Atoll	209
Mille Atoll	285
Palau	1993
Pearl Harbor	2175
Rabaul	1205
Saipan	1355
San Diego	4368
Tarawa	540
Tokyo	2228
Truk	955
Wotje Atoll	156

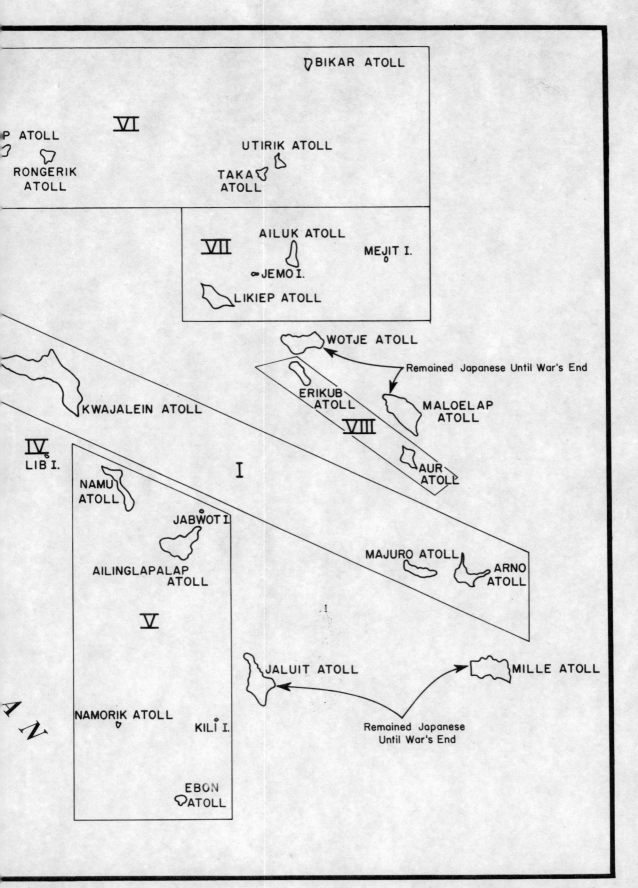

BIKAR ATOLL

VI

P ATOLL

RONGERIK
ATOLL

UTIRIK ATOLL

TAKA
ATOLL

VII

AILUK ATOLL

MEJIT I.

JEMO I.

LIKIEP ATOLL

WOTJE ATOLL

Remained Japanese Until War's End

KWAJALEIN ATOLL

ERIKUB
ATOLL

MALOELAP
ATOLL

VIII

IV
LIB I.

I

NAMU
ATOLL

JABWOT I.

AUR
ATOLL

AILINGLAPALAP
ATOLL

V

MAJURO ATOLL

ARNO
ATOLL

NAMORIK ATOLL

KILI I.

JALUIT ATOLL

MILLE ATOLL

Remained Japanese
Until War's End

EBON
ATOLL

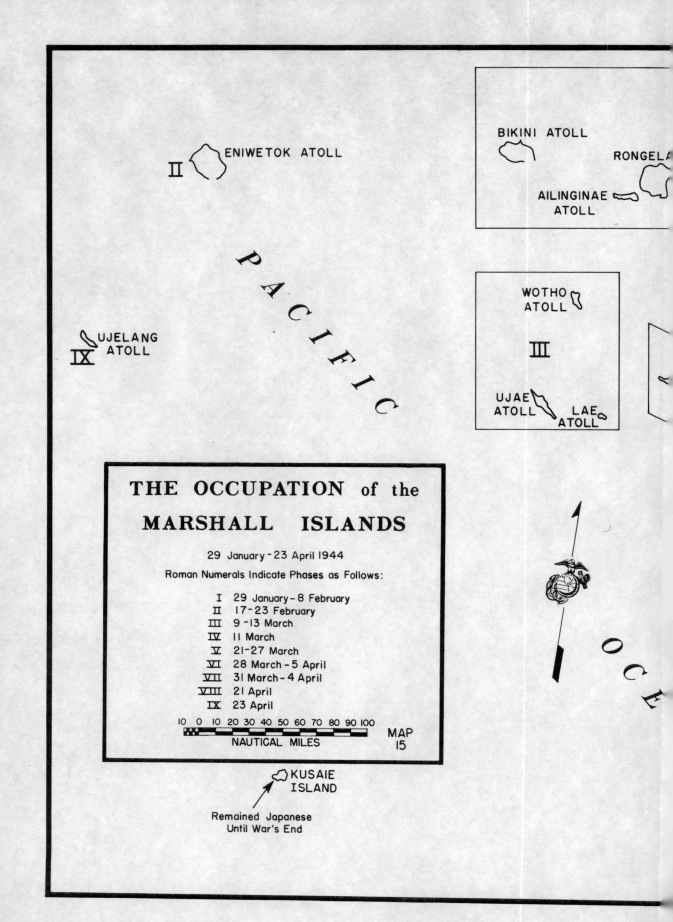

II   ENIWETOK ATOLL

BIKINI ATOLL   RONGELA

AILINGINAE ATOLL

P A C I F I C

IX   UJELANG ATOLL

WOTHO ATOLL

III

UJAE ATOLL   LAE ATOLL

THE OCCUPATION of the MARSHALL ISLANDS

29 January - 23 April 1944

Roman Numerals Indicate Phases as Follows:

I	29 January - 8 February
II	17 - 23 February
III	9 - 13 March
IV	11 March
V	21 - 27 March
VI	28 March - 5 April
VII	31 March - 4 April
VIII	21 April
IX	23 April

10   0   10 20 30 40 50 60 70 80 90 100

NAUTICAL MILES   MAP 15

KUSAIE ISLAND

Remained Japanese Until War's End

O C E

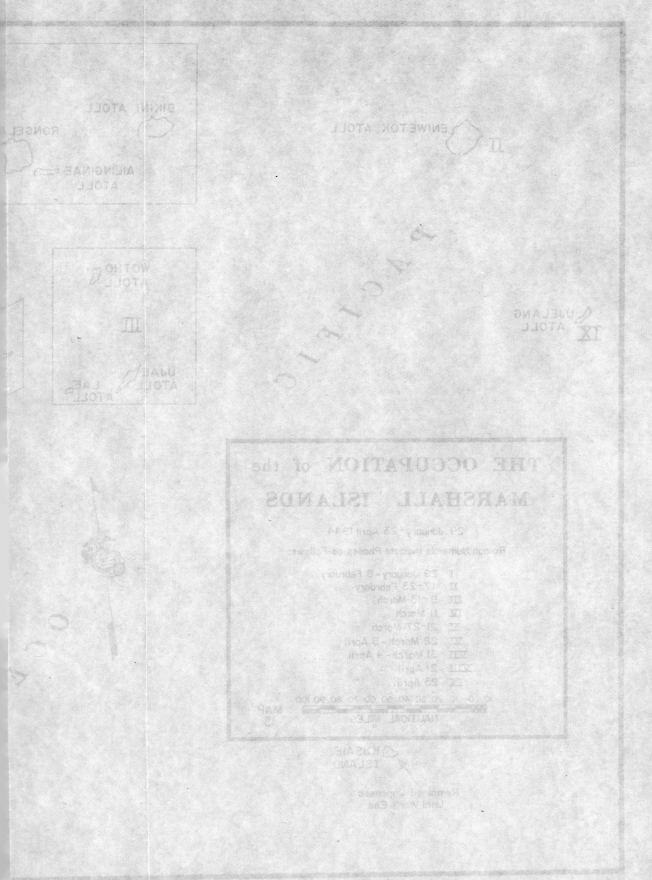

amounted to an estimated 85 percent of supplies (including all provisions except for a seven-day supply of K-rations) and 33 percent of construction equipment. In addition, 75 percent of all tentage and miscellaneous buildings on Roi were flattened and rendered unfit for further use. Two LCT's beached for unloading were burned out, as was the 20th Marines' command post, with the loss of regimental records and journals.[16] The Japanese had struck a heavy blow, but they made no attempt to follow it up, which was probably fortunate for them. On Admiral Conolly's recommendation, three Marine night fighters landed at Roi the next night prepared for any subsequent nocturnal raids.

While the bulk of the 4th Marine Division was reorganizing, clearing Roi-Namur and preparing to depart for Hawaii, Colonel Cumming's Combat Team 25 (reinforced) and Company A, 10th Amphibian Tractor Battalion searched the remaining islands in the northern portion of Kwajalein Atoll. This movement had begun on the morning of D-plus 2 when General Schmidt ordered Colonel Cumming to proceed with the seizure of those islands scheduled for the later phases of the over-all operation. Landing Team 2 under Lieutenant Colonel Hudson was picked to make the initial movement, its landings to be preceded by 14th Marines' artillery preparations. But after the first two landings were effected without meeting opposition, the 75mm pack howitzers remained silent. By utilizing LVT's, Hudson's unit secured eight islands during the day.

I remember distinctly the unusual sensation of navigating LVT's between the islands by means of a small pocket compass held as far as possible above the metal of the LVT. At times, due to the low freeboard [17] of the LVT, we were out of sight of all land.[18]

The Marines encountered no resistance and picked up 47 natives and three Japanese, the natives being established in a camp on Ennubirr (ALLEN) Island.[19]

COMMUNICATORS raised their wires from the ground to makeshift telephone poles when the shooting quieted down.

Lieutenant Colonel O'Donnell's Landing Team 1 was assigned the task of securing three islands: Boggerlapp (HUBERT), Boggerik (HOMER), and HOLLIS. This was accomplished in two days, no Japanese being met. On the afternoon of D-plus 4 Lieutenant Colonel Chambers' Landing Team 3/25 took over the mission, augmented by Battery C, 14th

---

[16] *CTF 53 Rpt FLINTLOCK*, 8, 22–23; *20th Mar SAR*, 3; Report of Island Commander to Commander in Chief, United States Fleet, 4Apr44, 4.

[17] Freeboard is the height of a vessel's side from the water line to the main deck or gunwale.

[18] Ltr Col Lewis C. Hudson, Jr., to CMC, 12Feb53.

[19] "[The natives] were looked after by a detachment

of Regimental Weapons Company under the command of Maj James T. Kisgen. During the 30 days together, the natives and the men of R/W 25 became fast friends. . . . Upon leaving, the native chief made a most touching speech and presented the Marines with presents." Ltr Maj Thomas H. Rogers, Jr., to CMC, 13Feb53.

Marines, 34 LVT's and a miniature fleet of two LST's, two LCI's, six LSM's, and the destroyer, *Hopewell*. By the afternoon of D-plus 7 this force had secured 39 islands, met some 250 natives and found no Japanese.[20]

In addition to completing the Northern Landing Force's mission, Combat Team 25 was ticketed as a garrison force for Kwajalein Atoll. On D-plus 8 the unit, together with Company A, 10th Amphibian Tractor Battalion, was temporarily detached from the 4th Marine Division, and Colonel Cumming reported to Rear Admiral Alva D. Bernhard, atoll commander. Landing Team 1 constituted the defense force for Roi-Namur, Landing Team 2 for Kwajalein Island, and Landing Team 3 a mobile defense group stationed on the western islands.

The combat team retained these dispositions until February 29 when it was relieved by the 22d Marines.[21] It then departed the area and rejoined its parent division in the Hawaiians.

---

[20] Rpt on the 25th Marines (reinforced) in the FLINTLOCK Operation, 3–4.

[21] Earlier activities of the 22d Marines will be taken up in Chapter VIII.

ALL ISLANDS SECURED

On D-plus 2, the same date that Combat Team 25 began the seizure of minor islands in the northern zone, the Army's 7th Reconnaissance Troop initiated similar operations in the southern sector.

Between 0800 and 0900 this unit returned to Gehh (CHAUNCEY), the island it had hit by mistake in the dark early hours of D-Day. Light resistance was encountered, and with the assistance of *Overton's* guns, the Reconnaissance Troop overran the Japanese positions. The infantrymen counted 135 enemy dead that day at a cost of 14 wounded soldiers.[22]

North of Kwajalein lay Ebeye (BURTON) Island, 2,000 yards long and containing machine shops and warehouses before the preliminary bombardment. This became the target of Colonel Zimmerman's 17th Regimental Combat Team, an unopposed landing being effected the morning of D-plus 3 by BLT 17–1.

As the infantrymen pushed northward on the island, enemy resistance was encountered and

---

[22] *Gritta.*

NAMUR immediately after the 24th Marines secured the island. In the background is Ennugarret (ABRAHAM).

JAMES V. FORRESTAL (center), Under Secretary of the Navy, visited Roi-Namur a few days after the battle ended. Here he is accompanied by (left to right) Admirals Spruance and Conolly, Generals Schmidt and Smith.

it steadily increased. Many of the island's defense installations had been destroyed during the preliminary bombardment, but the Japanese took full advantage of the remaining pillboxes, dugouts, and air-raid shelters to put up a disorganized fanatical fight. By nightfall BLT 17–1 had cleared two-thirds of Ebeye.

The morning of the second day, a Japanese prisoner pointed out the location of an ammunition dump and a requested air strike scored a direct hit on this choice target. The dump's elimination apparently took the heart out of the remaining defenders, for not a resisting shot was fired after it exploded. The Nipponese then surrendered or committed suicide, a majority of them choosing the latter course.

The 3d Battalion, 17th Infantry, relieved BLT 17–1 at 1130, and 40 minutes later Ebeye was declared secured.

While his main effort was being made on Ebeye, Colonel Zimmerman used the remaining troops available to him to secure four other nearby islands, resistance being encountered on one of them and that only light.

By D-plus 5 the 17th Regimental Combat Team and the 7th Reconnaissance Troop had secured all islands but one in the Southern Landing Force's zone. In addition to those already noted, 12 islands or islets were secured, only two of these offering any degree of resistance. The 7th Reconnaissance Troop neutralized an enemy force of about 100 men on Bigej (BENNETT) and Landing Team 17–2 subdued 102 Japanese on Eller (CLIFTON).[23]

On the morning of D-plus 6 Landing Team 17–2 took without opposition Ennugenliggelap

_____

[23] *7th Div Rpt*, 9, 11–12.

113

DYESS FIELD on Roi after the Seabees completed their work there.

(COHEN), thus completing the mission of the Southern Landing Force.

The 7th Infantry Division was directed to embark for the Hawaiian Islands as soon as its mission was completed. At 0800 on 6 February, Regimental Combat Teams 184 and 32 began loading ship, followed two hours later by RCT 17. But transportation was not immediately available for the entire Southern Landing Force. The morning of 8 February (D-plus 8), General Corlett and the bulk of his command departed the Kwajalein area, followed a few days later by the Division Artillery Group, one company of RCT 17 and detachments of the tank LVT battalion which had been left behind, except for those earmarked for the next operation. Company A, 708th Amphibian Tank Battalion, the 708th Provisional Amphibian Tractor Battalion, and 30 DUKW's were all assigned to Tactical Group-1 to assist in the seizure of Eniwetok.

SUMMATION

The Kwajalein operation clearly showed that heavy casualties are not a requisite for seizure of an enemy-held atoll. As noted earlier, the Tarawa operation loomed large in the minds of the men planning the Kwajalein landings, and it was their intent to avoid a repetition of the costly assault on Betio. This was accomplished. Marines at Tarawa incurred 3,301 casualties in combating a Japanese force of 4,690.[24] At Kwajalein, the Northern Landing Force overran 3,563 Japanese and the Southern Landing Force defeated 4,823 of the enemy.[25] The 4th Marine Division's total casualties for the operation amounted to 313 killed in action or died of wounds, and 502 wounded in action.[26] The 7th Infantry Division lost 173 killed in action or died of wounds and 793 wounded in action.[27]

---

[24] Capt James R. Stockman, *The Battle for Tarawa*, historical monograph prepared by Historical Section, HQMC, 1947, Appendices B and C.

[25] VAC G–2 Rpt, 19Feb44, 12.

[26] Marine casualty figures furnished by Personnel Accounting Section, Records Branch, Personnel Department, HQMC. Figures certified and released 26Aug52.

[27] 7th InfDiv G–1 Rpt, 18–19 (7th InfDiv FLINT-LOCK Rpt, Vol III).

This is no reflection on the 2d Marine Division's action at Betio. There it was conclusively demonstrated that much more artillery, air and naval assistance was required to seize an atoll without prohibitive losses. Such support was overwhelmingly provided at Kwajalein. Actually, only one more atoll operation remained in the war in the Pacific, and that was Eniwetok.

All elements of the Armed Forces participated as a team in the Kwajalein assault. Marines, Navy ships and aviation, Army air and ground units, Coast Guard, all worked together in the seizure of the first prewar enemy-held territory.

An important aspect from the Marine point of view was that the Roi-Namur operation was the initial one for the 4th Marine Division. One more Marine combat force was blooded and therefore better able to participate in subsequent amphibious assaults, as it conclusively demonstrated at Saipan,[28] Tinian,[29] and Iwo Jima.[30] As a direct result of the difficult lessons learned at Roi-Namur, the LVT units were

able to effect a smooth landing in their next operation, Saipan.[31]

Kwajalein was another steppingstone on the road across the Central Pacific, with Japan as the final goal. Kwajalein's seizure, together with that of Eniwetok a few weeks later, cleared the path for attacks on Truk, the capture of the Marianas,[32] and the other Central Pacific operations that followed.

In addition to providing aerial and naval bases for subsequent offensive operations, the

[28] Maj Carl W. Hoffman, *Saipan: The Beginning of the End*, historical monograph prepared by Historical Division, HQMC, 1950.

[29] Maj Carl W. Hoffman, *The Seizure of Tinian*, historical monograph prepared by Historical Division, HQMC, 1951.

[30] LtCol W. S. Bartley, *Iwo Jima, Amphibious Epic*, historical monograph prepared by Historical Branch, G–3, HQMC, 1954.

[31] *Croizat.*

[32] See monographs cited in preceding footnotes; also Maj O. R. Lodge, *The Recapture of Guam*, historical monograph prepared by Historical Branch, G–3, HQMC, 1954.

MEMBERS OF THE 4TH MARINE AIR WING on Roi devised a system of windmills to wash their laundry.

captured Marshall Islands also served as a springboard for neutralization of the by-passed atolls. From Kwajalein and Majuro the 4th Marine Air Wing pounded the Japanese fortresses of Mille, Maloelap, Wotje, and Jaluit, making it unnecessary for ground forces to assault and occupy those heavily held atolls.

What was involved in the Central Pacific was later explained by Vice Admiral Harry W. Hill:

> If you will examine an air map of the Central Pacific, you will note that the successive objectives of attack, namely Kwajalein and Eniwetok, Saipan and Iwo Jima are all approximately 500 miles away from the last objective seized. At that time, none of our fighters was capable of operating 500 miles from base. Therefore, the job of fighter protection and ground supported troops devolved completely upon our carrier task forces. . . . The question naturally arises, therefore, why did we not utilize shorter sea hops in order to have better land based air support. . . . The only islands we wanted were ones which had sufficient land mass to provide a runway into the direction of the prevailing wind, which was northeast, and also to provide a harbor. Such islands and atolls were few and far between. Practically all that there were had been already occupied by the Japanese. For the same reason, therefore, we could not do in the Central Pacific as General MacArthur had done in the Southwest Pacific—make unopposed landings. Instead, we were forced to go to the atolls or islands already held by the Japanese and which, of course, were heavily defended.[33]

Although the Marines had to go to defended islands and atolls, there were varying degrees of defense at various objectives. Thus, Admiral Nimitz' decision to make a bold stroke into the heart of the Marshalls, by-passing the more heavily defended "anchored aircraft carriers," both increased the tempo of the war in the Central Pacific and obviously kept the casualty rate low. So quickly and successfully was the Kwajalein mission accomplished that the Eniwetok landings, tentatively planned for May, were shoved forward three months, and the first troops stormed ashore on 17 February.

---

[33] *Hill.*

CHAPTER VIII

Eniwetok[1]

THE OBJECTIVE

In the northwest corner of the Marshall Islands, 326 nautical miles from Roi-Namur, lies Eniwetok Atoll[2] (coded DOWNSIDE), some 30 islands arranged in an irregular circumference of 70 miles. Many of the coral bits of land are covered with underbrush, while the larger ones grow stunted coconut trees. At the outbreak of the war less than 100 natives were to be found there, and the agricultural output consisted of a few figs and coconuts.

---

[1] Unless otherwise indicated, this chapter is derived from the following sources: JICPOA Bulletin 3–44, 20Jan44; JICPOA Bulletin 88–44, 3Jun44; JICPOA Bulletin 89–44, 12Jun44; Task Group 51.11 Report of Eniwetok Operations, 7Mar44; Tactical Group-1, War Diary, 5Nov43–29Feb44; Tactical Group-1, Operation Order 2–44, 10Feb44; Tactical Group-1 Special Report Concerning FLINTLOCK and CATCHPOLE Operations, 1Mar44, hereinafter cited as TG–1 Spl Rpt; Tactical Group-1 Report of Attack on Eniwetok Atoll, 27Feb44; Tactical Group-1 Journal, 17Feb–22Mar44; 22d Marines, reinf, War Diary, 1Jan–29Feb44; 22d Marines, reinf, Report on DOWNSIDE Operation, 9Mar44, hereinafter cited as 22dMar SAR; Battalion Landing Team 1, 22d Marines, Report on FLINTLOCK II Operation, undated, hereinafter cited as *BLT 1 Rpt.*

[2] When he discovered the atoll in 1794, Capt Thomas Butler named it Brown's Range, and the Japanese Navy continued calling it Brown throughout World War II. *Morison*, 282.

The lagoon measures some 21 miles in length, northwest-southeast, and about 17 miles across, northeast-southwest. Wide Passage and Deep Entrance on the south and southeast sides respectively are the only navigable breaks in the rim of coral surrounding the atoll. Ships of all types may anchor in the sheltered waters, as did major units of the Japanese Fleet shortly before the invasion.

The principal islands include:

Engebi (FRAGILE) roughly shaped in the form of an equilateral triangle, each side measuring slightly over a mile in length. The northern end of this northernmost island was cleared, while mangrove and coconut palms covered the remaining portions. Here was found the atoll's only airstrip, concrete-surfaced and extending 4,025 feet.

Japtan (LADYSLIPPER) bounds the right of Deep Entrance. Measuring 800 yards (east-west) by 750 yards (north-south), this coral-sand island's northwestern area was covered by coconut palms in even rows, while dense underbrush grew elsewhere.

Parry (HEARTSTRINGS) lies immediately south of Japtan and bounds Deep Entrance's left. Shaped like an inverted tear drop, the island is two miles long, tapering from a 600-yard width in the north to a point in the south. In early 1944 it was covered with coconut palms.

Eniwetok (PRIVILEGE), the atoll's southernmost island, is formed like a blackjack and flanks the right of Wide Passage. Its length extends 4,700 yards and its width varies between 750 yards in the south to 170 yards in the north. Except for a few clearings and some fringes of mangrove, Eniwetok was covered with evenly spaced coconut palms.

THE JAPANESE

Prior to the arrival of the Japanese 1st Amphibious Brigade on 4 January 1944, the defense of Eniwetok Atoll was entrusted to the Eniwetok Detachment of the 61st Keibitai (Guard Unit), based at Kwajalein. The detachment never totaled more than 61 men, 45 of whom were stationed on Engebi where the atoll defenses were concentrated. These consisted of a battery of two 120mm guns, two twin-mount M93 13mm AA machine guns, two M96 light machine guns and a number of rifles, pistols and hand grenades. This token defense force reflected the tardy Japanese military interest in the northwestern Marshalls. In November and December 1942, some 800 construction workers of the 4th Shisetsubu (4th Fleet Construction Section) landed at Engebi and began work on an airstrip, which was completed the following July. The 61st Keibitai detachment then moved into the island in October 1943.

Engebi's airstrip began operating in November, but since it was used only for staging planes between Truk and points east, no flying personnel were stationed there. The maintenance force consisted of 38 petty officers and men under a warrant officer. As American air operations increased in the eastern Marshalls, however, and the threat of amphibious assault in that area became greater, Japanese air was evacuated from the forward areas to Eniwetok Atoll's air base. On 11 January 1944 an additional 110 aviation officers and men were billeted on Engebi "owing to present operations in the Roi, Wotje, Mille, and Taroa areas."[3] With the fall of Kwajalein Atoll, steps were taken to evacuate all air personnel to Truk by flying boat, but for most of them this began too late.

An estimated 150 grounded pilots and crewmen were still on Engebi and Parry when American assault forces sailed into the lagoon 17 February 1944.

The 1st Amphibious Brigade was formed from the 3d Independent Garrison Unit in Manchuria in November 1943 under Major General Yoshima Nishida. Japanese Army planners originally intended it as a mobile striking force within the Marshalls, initially designating it the 1st Mobile Shipborne Brigade and ticketing it for centrally located Kwajalein. When it arrived at Truk on 26 December, however, the increasing threat of American attack on the Marshalls made necessary the reinforcement of certain points. The brigade was therefore ordered to garrison duty on various atolls, as noted in Chapter II.

General Nishida's command arrived at Engebi on 4 January and four days later those elements earmarked for Wotje, Maloelap, and Kwajalein departed. Of the 3,940 men within the brigade, 2,586 were left to defend Eniwetok Atoll, and these were now distributed among Engebi, Parry, and Eniwetok. Although they did not know it, the defenders had about six weeks in which to transform a virtually undefended atoll into a stronghold.

Command of the Engebi garrison devolved upon Colonel Toshio Yano of the 3d Battalion. His total military force numbered 736 men, including 44 of the 61st Keibitai detachment, and was augmented by aviation personnel, civilian employees, and laborers.[4] In addition to his organic small arms, Yano had available two flame throwers, two 75mm mountain guns, three 20mm guns, two 120mm naval guns, two twin-mount 13mm AA machine guns, three light tanks and a variety of machine guns, mortars, and grenade dischargers. Organization and construction of defensive positions were begun immediately, and on 10 February the island commander issued an outline of his defensive plans in which he correctly estimated the events of a week later:

The enemy will bomb this island either with carrier or land-based planes and will bombard us from all sides with battleships and heavy cruisers. Directly

---

[3] JICPOA Bulletin 89–44, 3.

[4] Enemy strength on Engebi, estimated from the number buried, was set at 1,200.

following these bombardments, an amphibious force landing will be carried out.

It will be extremely difficult for the enemy to land here from the open sea because of the high waves and rugged reefs.

Whether or not they are able to carry out their plan to land on the islands to the east and west, it is expected that they will force their way through the north and south passages, or make a forced passage of either the east or west pass in order to enter the atoll and carry out landing operations from the lagoon. While making assaults on outlying islands, they will approach this island from all directions.

If any of the above happens, and if sea and air control are in the hands of the enemy, this defense garrison must put up a defense on its own.

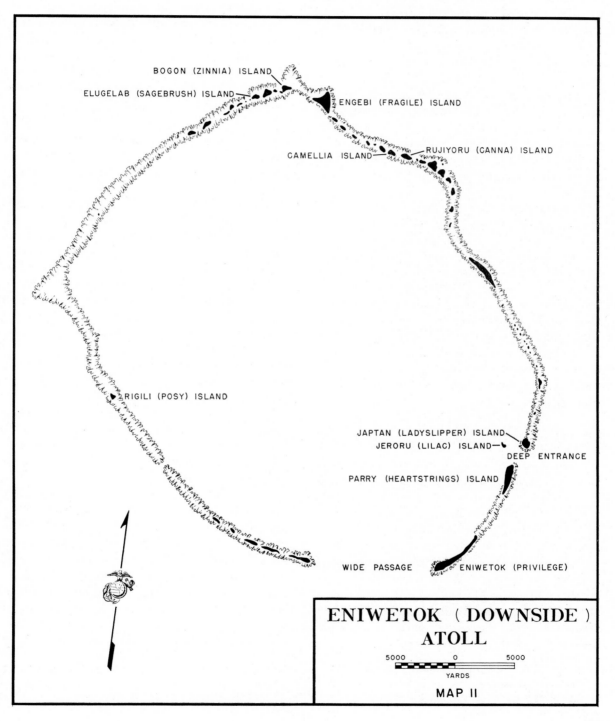

BOGON (ZINNIA) ISLAND
ELUGELAB (SAGEBRUSH) ISLAND
ENGEBI (FRAGILE) ISLAND
CAMELLIA ISLAND
RUJIYORU (CANNA) ISLAND
RIGILI (POSY) ISLAND
JAPTAN (LADYSLIPPER) ISLAND
JERORU (LILAC) ISLAND
DEEP ENTRANCE
PARRY (HEARTSTRINGS) ISLAND
WIDE PASSAGE
ENIWETOK (PRIVILEGE)

**ENIWETOK (DOWNSIDE)
ATOLL**

5000   0   5000
YARDS

MAP II

In view of these things, it is essential that this force make complete use of every available man and all fortified positions, carrying out each duty to the utmost. Plans must be followed to lure the enemy to the water's edge and then annihilate him with withering fire power and continuous attacks.[5]

In an operational order issued 13 February, Colonel Yano instructed his forces to give "particular attention" to the construction of positions facing the lagoon. He directed that Company 8 (reinforced) occupy the eastern corner of the island; the Battalion Artillery Company (reinforced) station itself in the western corner; the Battalion Mortar Company occupy the central area with main fire directed toward the lagoon; the Machine Cannon Platoon occupy positions on the shore southeast of the main positions, and all other units take positions in the "main strength area," just inland of the lagoon beaches.

The island defenses were principally trenches and dugouts, protected by coconut log barricades, usually covered with light wood or sheet metal. In addition, a series of "spider traps" were installed. These consisted of oil-drum tunnels and each hole was covered with an innocuous piece of metal, a palm frond or coral rubble. No blockhouses such as those found at Tarawa and Kwajalein Atoll were constructed. In the limited time available to him, Yano had concrete pillboxes set up, but these were not reinforced and in comparison with those on other atolls, definitely weak. Despite these limitations, Admiral Hill described Engebi as the most heavily defended of the three islands attacked in Eniwetok Atoll.

Lieutenant Colonel Masahiro Hashida, commanding the 1st Battalion, took charge of the Eniwetok Island Garrison Force. Its strength was set originally at 779 men, subsequently reinforced by an additional 129 from brigade reserve.[6] Armament was essentially the same as that allocated Engebi. In his defense plan, Hashida concentrated his force on the lagoon beaches and exhorted them to destroy the enemy at the water's edge. Beginning about midway of the island and extending southward, the following forces were established:

Right flank rear guard force: Infantry platoon, mortars, observation forces.

Right water's edge force: One mountain gun, one infantry platoon (less two squads).

Middle water's edge force: One mountain gun, one rapid fire gun, one infantry platoon (less one squad).

Left water's edge force: Two infantry squads, one mountain gun, one rapid fire gun.

Support force: One infantry platoon and one squad, three engineer platoons, tanks.

Defense works resembled those on Engebi, so effectively camouflaged with natural foliage they were unidentifiable from the air. In addition, new concrete pillboxes were rushed to completion on the island's southwestern tip and some land mines laid.

General Nishida established brigade headquarters and reserve on Parry, and this, together with a garrison force of 305 men, gave the island a total of 1,115 defending troops.[7] Aviation personnel and civilian surveyors added slightly more than 100 men to this force. The armament available consisted of the same types as Engebi's and Eniwetok's, but in greater quantities, with the exception of tanks and mountain guns.

The defense plan for Parry was embodied in an order issued 5 February 1944. As a general policy Nishida directed that "each unit will split up the enemy's infantry attack landing craft at the water's edge, and annihilate the enemy forces piecemeal. . . . If the enemy does land, we shall annihilate him by original creative night attacks." The battle for Parry was visualized in three stages, the "outcome of the battle and the fate of the Brigade" being decided in the second. In the third stage "the Brigade investigates and analyzes the over-all situation and decides to die gloriously."[8] Approximately one-half of the total troops were assigned to three strong points on the lagoon beaches, the remainder making up the island reserve force.

Parry's defensive positions were essentially

---

[5] JICPOA Bulletin 89–44, 12Jun44.

[6] TG 51.11 Rpt estimated enemy strength on Eniwetok Island as 900, based on the number buried.

[7] Enemy strength on Parry estimated at 1,300, based on the number buried.

[8] JICPOA Bulletin 89–44, 31, 32.

the same as those on Eniwetok, though not as well constructed. They were so well camouflaged, however, that not only were they virtually invisible from the air, but later attacking ground troops had difficulty spotting them. On the whole, they consisted of roofed over foxholes and trenches which protected the occupants from all gunfire and bombing, short of direct hits. An extensive mine field was laid on the northern tip of the island, and smaller ones set up in other areas. Some were buried just under the ground's surface, while others were concealed by lantanna and palm fronds.

PLANNING FOR ENIWETOK

The decision to seize Eniwetok was made during the planning phase for Kwajalein, Admiral Nimitz regarding it as a preliminary to a landing on Truk or other islands in the Carolines. Originally the CATCHPOLE plan called for the 2d Marine Division to seize Eniwetok Atoll on 19 March 1944, and the 27th Infantry Division to assault Kusaie ten days later.[9] As far along as January this concept was in force, the only change being that of revising the target date to 1 May in order that the naval units might participate in the proposed assault on Kavieng in April.[10] During January both the 2d Marine Division and the 27th Infantry Division (less 106th RCT) were undergoing intensive training for the operation.[11]

But there appeared to be some general reflection along the lines of seizing Eniwetok immediately after the Kwajalein operation. On 14 January 1944 Admiral Spruance expressed such a desire to Admiral Nimitz. The Fifth Fleet Commander said he would like to proceed against Eniwetok then rather than waiting until the fleet returned from the Kavieng assault.[12] And during the FLINTLOCK planning at Pearl Harbor, Admiral Turner's staff considered capture of Eniwetok as a part of that operation, staff studies being prepared "should success at Kwajalein prove rapid enough to justify the extension of the operation westward." [13]

Nor were these thoughts limited to the Navy. En route to Kwajalein Major General Holland Smith's staff drew up a tentative study dealing with the rapid seizure of Eniwetok. Dated 26 January 1944 and embodied in a memorandum to the corps chief of staff, the paper first reviewed the existent concept of two divisions striking on or about 1 May 1944. It then pointed out what could be gained by a quick attack:

The advantage of seizing DOWNSIDE as a part of the FLINTLOCK operation are numerous and obvious. The task would be greatly facilitated if the operation could be executed before the Japanese have had an opportunity to strengthen his defenses. It would result in the savings of lives, equipment, money and effort. Furthermore, it would advance the progress of the war, and would serve to keep the enemy under continuing pressure.[14]

On 2 February conditions appeared propitious for pushing on to Eniwetok. It was apparent that Kwajalein Atoll could be secured without the assistance of the Expeditionary Reserve, Tactical Group-1. Moreover, carrier plane photos of Eniwetok, made on 30 January, coupled with the fortunate capture by the 7th Reconnaissance Troop of secret navigational charts of the atoll, provided enough information to make definite plans for landing attacks.[15] Rear Admiral Turner thereupon recommended to Vice Admiral Spruance that the assault on Eniwetok be undertaken in the immediate future. Two days later Admiral Nimitz radioed Spruance asking his recommendations concerning the capture of Eniwetok, as well as a carrier strike on Truk. The Fifth Fleet commander promptly recommended approval.

Admiral Nimitz arrived at Kwajalein on 5 February, and during his 42-hour visit on the atoll approved final plans for the Eniwetok and Truk operations.

[9] CATCHPOLE Plan, CinCPac and CinCPOA, 29Nov-43, serial 00272.

[10] Canceled by JCS on 12Mar44.

[11] VAC War Diary, Jan44, 11, and Capt Edmund G. Love, *The 27th Infantry Division in World War II*, Washington, Infantry Journal Press, 59.

[12] Jeter A. Isely & Philip A. Crowl, *The U. S. Marines and Amphibious War*, Princeton University Press, 1951, 291–292, hereinafter cited as *Isley & Crowl.*

[13] Ltr Adm R. K. Turner to CMC, 13Apr53, hereinafter cited as *Turner II.*

[14] Memo for Chief of Staff from J. C. Anderson, Acting ACofS G-5, 26Jan44, serial 007-2.

[15] *Turner II.*

ADMIRAL HILL AND GENERAL WATSON directed the seizure of Eniwetok Atoll.

As soon as it was evident that Eniwetok would follow Kwajalein, Rear Admiral Harry W. Hill, who had directed the successful occupation of Majuro Atoll, was instructed to report to Admiral Turner.[16] He did so on 3 February, and the next day the two admirals conferred with Major General Holland Smith and Brigadier General Thomas E. Watson on plans for the project (coded CATCHPOLE). Initially the target date for D-Day was set at 12 February, but was later changed to 17 February in order to permit Task Force 58 to replenish fuel and ammunition for the Truk strike.

Admiral Hill was given over-all amphibious command, his force being designated Task Group 51.11.[17] Watson's recently created Tac-

tical Group-1 would provide the assault troops. But the problem of garrison troops was another matter, as Admiral Turner later recalled:

> . . . No garrison elements for Eniwetok were carried along from Hawaii when the Expeditionary Force began departing . . . none were available, nor was there enough shipping to lift any. When the decision was made to capture Eniwetok without waiting for additional forces, we had to rob both Kwajalein Island and Roi-Namur of considerable proportions of their garrisons and carry them forward in order to start the more urgent development and defense of the new base.[18]

Organized under V Amphibious Corps General Order No. 55–43 on 16 November 1943, Tactical Group-1 was originally composed of Tactical Group Headquarters and the 22d Marines (Colonel John T. Walker), reinforced by 2d Separate Pack Howitzer Battalion, 2d Separate Tank Company, 2d Separate Engineer Company, 2d Separate Motor Transport Company, 2d Separate Medical Company, and Shore Party and JASCO elements.

The tactical group was not an administrative unit except where tactical matters were concerned,[19] and it contained a streamlined type of staff, partly as an experiment and partly due to the lack of suitable staff personnel.[20]

The 22d RCT had been formed in early 1942 at Linda Vista, near San Diego, California, and had spent some 18 months on garrison duty in Samoa before receiving orders to proceed to the Hawaiian Islands. It was preceded by General Watson, who had commanded the 3d Marine Brigade in Samoa until its deactivation in early November 1943. Between its arrival in the Hawaiian Islands and its departure for Kwajalein in late January, the 22d Marines reinforced, camped at Maui and engaged in amphibious exercises, these being marred by a training accident on 6 December in which 21 men were killed and 27 wounded. On 23 December, the 106th Infantry Regiment (less 2d

---

[16] "I had no forewarning of the possibilities of my being put in command of the Eniwetok operations. The first intimation was a dispatch directing me to proceed from Majuro by air to Kwajalein and report to Admiral Turner." Ltr VAdm Harry W. Hill to CMC, 24Feb53, hereinafter cited as *Hill II*.

[17] "Owing to the fact that Task Forces 52 and 53 were not dissolved until 11 Feb, and because some departing groups still retained designations in those forces, no *force* numbers were available for assigning to Hill's command. Consequently, he was assigned a *group* number as a part of TF 51, which remained in existence and under my command until sunset 24 Feb. . . ." *Turner II.*

[18] *Ibid.*

[19] Ltr LtGen Thomas E. Watson to CMC, 1Mar53, hereinafter cited as *Watson.*

[20] "Events proved that this type of staff was inadequate to handle anything but a quick 'Flash' type of operation of a few days duration. . . . The streamlined staff idea died a rapid and just death. . . ." Ltr Col W. M. Greene, Jr., to CMC, 4Mar53, hereinafter cited as *Greene II.*

Battalion), reinforced, was detached from the Army's 27th Infantry Division and placed under General Watson's group. The 106th RCT had been earmarked for Nauru during the Gilberts Operation, but upon the cancellation of that island objective the regiment had sat out the campaign.

During the amphibious training phase for Kwajalein, attention was centered on the assault units rather than on the elements of Tactical Group-1, since the latter was scheduled for corps reserve. Watson's command trained with what it had, but it had precious little, as the general caustically pointed out in a later report:

In the actual operation (Eniwetok), most of the troops were landed in amtracs for their first time. The artillery battalion landed for its first time in DUKW's. We were sent to attack a coral atoll. We rehearsed on the large island of Maui on terrain and approaches totally unlike those of the target. Troops did not land in rehearsal supported by naval gunfire, air and artillery fires to accustom them to actual attack conditions. The artillery had no practice in landing in DUKW's and firing under situations experienced at Eniwetok. The rehearsal at Maui permitted no appreciable advance inland, no combat firing, no infantry-tank team movement. . . . In the attack on Eniwetok, the infantry, amtracs, amtanks, tanks, aircraft, supporting naval ships and most of the staffs concerned had never worked together before.[21]

But if amphibious training was lacking, small unit ground training was not, as Colonel Wallace M. Greene, Jr., Tactical Group-1's operations officer, later pointed out:

Although it is only too true that both regiments [22d Marines and 106th Infantry] had received very little amphibious training prior to participation in the Eniwetok operation, it is also a fact that the 22d Marines was at its peak in small unit training—training which was anchored firmly around a basic fire team organization. This was accomplished by tough, vigorous jungle training given the unit . . . during its stay in Western Samoa. Colonel Floyd Moore [then R–3] was largely responsible for the planning and supervision of this training. And it was this excellence in the fire teams which really paid off at Eniwetok. . . . This regiment was one of the best trained and spirited units I observed. . . . It was this period of isolation in Samoa and opportunity to train which made the 22d Marines far superior to the 106th Infantry in the close tough fighting on the beaches and in the bush of Eniwetok Atoll.[22]

<hr>

[21] *TG–1 Spl Rpt,* 7.
[22] *Greene II.*

COLONEL JOHN T. WALKER, commanding the 22d Marines, reinforced.

Tactical Group-1, constituting the reserve group for the Kwajalein operation, sailed from the Hawaiian Islands on 22 January with the other elements of the Joint Expeditionary Force. Between 31 January and 3 February, while the 4th Marine Division and the 7th Infantry Division were seizing their objectives, Tactical Group-1 cruised eastward of Kwajalein Atoll anchoring in the lagoon at the latter date.

To augment Watson's striking force for Eniwetok, he was allotted V Amphibious Corps Reconnaissance Company, Company D (Scout) of the 4th Tank Battalion, 708th Provisional Amphibian Tractor Battalion less one LVT group (102 LVT's), Company A of the 708th Amphibian Tank Battalion (17 LVTA's), and a Provisional DUKW Battery (30 DUKW's and 4 LVT's). The assault elements counted some 5,820 Marines and 4,556 soldiers, giving a total troop strength of 10,376. In addition, initial occupation forces included the Marine 10th Defense Battalion, 3d Army Defense Battalion, and 47th Army Engineer Battalion.

Admiral Hill, accompanied by General Watson, carried his flag on board an attack transport, *Cambria*, which had been specially fitted out as an amphibious troop command flagship.[23] To lift the troops to their objective there were five other attack transports (APA), one transport (AP), two attack cargo ships (AKA), one cargo ship (AK), two destroyer transports (APD), two submarine chasers (SC), nine landing ships, tank (LST), and six landing craft, infantry (LCI). Ten destroyers made up the transport screen. Rear Admiral Jesse B. Oldendorf commanded the Fire Support Group, consisting of the battleships *Colorado*, *Tennessee*, and *Pennsylvania*, three heavy cruisers, and seven destroyers. Three escort carriers and four destroyers composed the Escort Carrier Group, under Rear Admiral V. H. Ragsdale, while Carrier Task Group Four, under Rear Admiral Ginder, consisted of one heavy carrier, two light carriers, two heavy cruisers, one light antiaircraft cruiser, and eight destroyers. In addition, there was a Minesweeping Group with two high-speed mine sweepers, three mine sweepers, and two motor mine sweepers; a Service Group with two tugs and two oilers, and an Ocean Tug Group containing one destroyer and two tugs.

It has been previously noted that Japanese defense forces in Eniwetok Atoll at this time amounted to nearly 3,500 troops. But intelligence derived from prisoners and documents taken at Kwajalein, as well as aerial photographs of Eniwetok, led American staff planners to estimate that Eniwetok Atoll was defended by some 800 Japanese: 500 from the 61st Naval Guard Force and a detachment of 300 of the 4th Civil Engineers. It was conceded, however, that "some portion of the 1st Mobile Shipborne Force, of 2,000 to 3,000 Army troops, may be in this area." It was assumed that the majority of the defenders were stationed on Engebi, about 100 to 150 on Parry, and a small detachment on Eniwetok. There was no evidence of any enemy on any other islands within the atoll.

In considering the Japanese dispositions, General Watson decided to strike first at Engebi. His plan for the seizure of the atoll included four phases, the first involving occupation of nearby islands or islets by artillery as was done at Kwajalein Atoll.

> Phase I: On D-Day, Company D (Scout) of the 4th Tank Battalion secure ZINNIA Island to the west of Engebi; simultaneously, V Amphibious Corps Reconnaissance Company secure five islands to the southeast of Engebi and cover the landings of the 2d Separate Pack Howitzer Battalion and the 104th Field Artillery Battalion on CAMELLIA and CANNA respectively.
>
> Phase II: On D-plus 1, 22d Marines, reinforced by the 2d Separate Tank Company (medium) and one platoon of the 106th Infantry's Cannon Company (two 105mm self-propelled guns), seize Engebi. Support fires provided by the two artillery battalions from CAMELLIA and CANNA.
>
> Phase III: On D-plus X, 106th Infantry, reinforced by 2d Separate Tank Company (medium), seize Eniwetok and two hours later be prepared to seize Parry. One battalion, 22d Marines, would be assigned the 106th Infantry for the latter landing, inasmuch as BLT 106–2 was not present.
>
> Phase IV: Complete seizure of all islands within the atoll.

An important aspect of the plan for Eniwetok, from the Marine viewpoint, was a new development in the troop command picture. Admiral Hill's plan provided that the Expeditionary Troops Commander (General Watson) be specifically placed in command of landings and garrison forces when ashore. At Roi-Namur, General Schmidt had received this command only after he stated he was ready to assume it. "In other words, [this command] formerly required positive action on the Ground Force Commander's part. Now it is established before the operation begins."[24]

---

[23] "Although it did not have the extensive facilities of the AGC, it served the purpose adequately, not only in the Majuro and Eniwetok operations, but also in the Saipan and Tinian operations which followed." *Hill II.*

---

[24] Memo from BrigGen O. T. Pfieffer to BrigGen G. C. Thomas, 23Feb44.

TRUK HARBOR as it appeared to planes from the *Intrepid* on the first carrier strike at that Japanese stronghold. (Navy photo.)

Planning also included a massive carrier strike on Truk concurrently with the invasion of Eniwetok. Truk lies 670 nautical miles from the latter atoll and was still regarded by many Americans as "Japan's Pearl Harbor" and the "Gibraltar of the Pacific." The Japanese Combined Fleet under Admiral Mineichi Koga, IJN, had been based there since mid-1942, as was headquarters, Sixth Fleet (submarines), and Admiral Spruance hoped that by striking a blow at the base, a major naval battle could be joined. Also, a strike on Truk was the necessary preliminary to a continuing advance westward through the Central Pacific. Thus, this planned attack (coded HAILSTONE) by Rear Admiral Marc Mitscher's Task Force 58 was closely connected with Hill and Watson's Eniwetok assault.[25]

---

[25] *Morison*, 315–317.

PRELIMINARY OPERATIONS

Reconnaissance flights over Eniwetok had been underway irregularly since the preceding December, but the first concentrated preliminary strikes were performed by Rear Admiral Ginder's Task Group 58.4 while the amphibious assault force still lay off Kwajalein.

Planes from *Saratoga, Langley, Princeton, Sangamon, Suwanee, and Chenango* plastered every structure above ground that they could spot. Fourteen enemy planes were destroyed on the ground at Engebi, and aerial photographs of targets were rushed back to *Cambria*. Admiral Hill later reported that these strikes destroyed all buildings of consequence, rendered the airfield at Engebi temporarily useless, and demolished at least one of the two coastal defense guns on the northeast corner of that island.

On 3 February 1944 a Marine scouting plane from Bougainville flew over Truk, spotting an imposing array of vessels at anchor. This aggregation was duly reported, but Admiral Koga knew the plane had flown over and realized that an air attack would probably follow. He thereupon ordered the *Yamato* and *Nagato* plus elements of the 2d Fleet to Palau on 4 February. A week later the Combined Fleet, with Admiral Koga in *Musashi*, sailed for Japan, leaving two cruisers, some destroyers, and a great many cargo and transport vessels in Truk lagoon.[26]

Admiral Spruance in *New Jersey* and Admiral Mitscher in *Yorktown* sortied from

Majuro with Task Force 58 (less TG 58.4) during the early morning hours of 12 February, bound for Truk.[27] Included in the armada were Carrier Group 1 (Rear Admiral John W. Reeves), Carrier Group 2 (Rear Admiral A. E. Montgomery), Carrier Group 3 (Rear Admiral F. C. Sherman), and Task Force 17, Patrol Submarines (Vice Admiral C. A. Lockwood). The list of ships counted five heavy carriers, four light carriers, six battleships (including *New Jersey*), five heavy cruisers, five

[26] *Nakajima.*

[27] Although TF 58 began operations against Truk the same day that the assault was made on Eniwetok Atoll, the Truk strike is narrated as a preliminary operation here because, among other things, it covered the Eniwetok operation.

JAPANESE NAVY YARD at Dublon Island, Truk Atoll, attacked by Admiral Mitscher's carrier-based planes. (Navy photo.)

light cruisers, 28 destroyers, and ten submarines.[28] At dawn on 17 February a total of 70 planes took off from five of Admiral Mitscher's carriers. As they appeared over Truk they were engaged by 80 Japanese planes which rose to contest the intrusion. Some 60 of these Nipponese craft were shot down with a loss of four American planes, while another 40 enemy planes were destroyed on the ground by strafing. A fragmentation and incendiary bomb run followed. Of 365 planes on Truk when the attacking force arrived, less than 100 remained unscathed, and not one rose into the skies the next day.

At 0443, 18 February, fighters, dive bombers, and torpedo bombers began their attacks on Japanese shipping in Truk lagoon. By the end of the day two cruisers (one *Naka* class and the *Kashima*), four destroyers, nine auxiliary craft, and 24 cargo and transport vessels had been sunk.[29] But the Japanese got in one blow. During the night of 17 February a group of "Kate" torpedo bombers sought out Mitscher's force and sent a torpedo into *Intrepid*, putting that carrier out of operation for several months. While the carriers were engaged in aerial assaults on Truk, Admiral Spruance conducted an around-the-atoll search for any fleeing enemy shipping. A cruiser and two destroyers were encountered and only one destroyer escaped. Spruance and Mitscher rendezvoused on 18 February and retired toward Kwajalein.[30] The strike had not produced the hoped-for fleet action, but it had materially damaged Japanese naval forces and, most important, had torn the mask of dark mystery from Truk, revealing it as virtually an empty shell.

LOADING OUT

On 3 February General Watson issued verbal instructions to his subordinates concerning the Eniwetok operation, and his written operation order was issued one week later. V Amphibious Corps formally released Tactical Group-1 as Landing Force Reserve for the Kwajalein operation on 6 February, and assigned it duty under Admiral Hill's Task Group 51.11.

Only two weeks separated the decision to take Eniwetok and the departure for that objective, and Tactical Group-1 utilized the time to prepare feverishly for its new assignment. Perhaps no major amphibious operation in the Pacific was handled in such an impromptu manner. When General Watson's command had departed Pearl Harbor as floating reserve for the Kwajalein operation, it had no inkling that it would be assigned the Eniwetok mission. Furthermore, both regiments within the Tactical Group were as yet untried in combat.

Preparations for departure included reloading the 2d Separate Pack Howitzer Battalion on LST 246, and the 2d Separate Tank Company on LSD 1. By 15 February Admiral Hill's task group was ready to sail for Eniwetok, and at 0700 that day the Southern Group, composed of LST's, LCI's, and other slow-moving craft, departed Kwajalein lagoon. Seven hours later the Northern Group, consisting of transports, battleships, and carriers, was under way.

CANNA, CAMELLIA, AND ZINNIA

In the early morning hours of 17 February, Warrant Officer Shionoya, IJA, was interrupted in his labors on Parry Island's defenses by an air alarm and naval bombardment. He later recorded in his diary:

I was amazed at the severity of the bombardment. The bombardment was most severe from 0500 to 0600. . . . Everyone was looking on fully prepared for battle. We all passed the night [sic] with the idea that they were finally going to land that very night [sic]. Planes circled the sky all day, and the bombardment also lasted all day. There was one man killed and four wounded. . . . There were some who were buried by the shells from the ships. . . . How many times shall we bury ourselves in the sand . . .[31]

While Warrant Officer Shionoya and his comrades buried themselves in the sand, *Colorado* and *Louisville* shelled Engebi, *Portland*

[28] *Morison*, 352–353.

[29] *Nakajima*.

[30] "I returned to Kwajalein in the New Jersey. . . . Adm Mitscher took Task Force 58 for a carrier strike on the Marianas. This strike included our first photographs of Saipan and Tinian, which islands were later taken in June and July, respectively." Ltr Adm Raymond A. Spruance to CMC, 11Mar53.

[31] Diary of Warrant Officer Shionoya, JICPOA Item 7005, hereinafter cited as *Shionoya*.

and *Trathen* poured fire onto Parry and Japtan, and *Indianapolis* and *Hoel* bombarded Eniwetok. Not a return shot was fired. Between 0700 and 0900 naval gunfire was lifted only to permit the planes from Task Group 58.4 to make their bomb and strafing runs on the islands under attack. During this period mine sweepers moved into Wide Passage, where 28 moored mines were found, swept, and destroyed. This was the first Japanese mine field encountered by United States naval forces in the war.[32] As soon as the mine sweepers had completed their work the shallow draft vessels of the Southern Group entered Eniwetok lagoon. At 0915 the Northern Group started into the lagoon via Deep Entrance. Moving in column, the fast mine sweepers led the way followed by destroyers, battleships, and transports.[33] Flanking 40mm fire raked Japtan and Parry, but still the enemy did not reply.

A naval officer who was present subsequently described the maneuver:

> In my study of naval history I do not recall any other instance where a naval force of this size and composition has steamed up to an enemy-held harbor, formed column and entered in much the same manner as it would enter its home port. . . . To see the force enter this lagoon in column through a narrow entrance and between the shores of islands on either flank, and steam something over 20 miles through the enemy lagoon was one of the most thrilling episodes which I witnessed during the entire war.[34]

On Parry Island Major General Nishida reacted to the invasion by radioing a futile plea to his superiors in Tokyo: "Enemy fleet entering the lagoon in large numbers. Request reinforcements."[35]

By 1034 Admiral Hill's task group completed entrance into Eniwetok lagoon, and 45 minutes later 14-inch shells from *Tennessee* and *Pennsylvania* exploded with destructive fury on Engebi. While the larger ships were thus engaged, the heavy cruiser *Portland* and the destroyers *Heermann* and *McCord* worked over CAMELLIA and Rujiyoru (CANNA) Islands [36] in preparation for landings by the V Amphibious Corps Reconnaissance Company. At 1150 in the lagoon the Marines transferred from APD *Kane* to LST 272, clambered into six LVT–2's of the Army's 708th Provisional Amphibian Tractor Battalion and roared toward the two islands. Two LCI gunboats provided support, their rockets and 40mm guns producing geysers of sand and water. But there were no Japanese on either island. Captain James L. Jones, the company commander, reported CAMELLIA secured and uninhabited at 1355. Five minutes later Rujiyoru was reported in Marine hands. Five natives found on the latter island estimated Japanese strength at 1,000 on Engebi, Eniwetok, and Parry, respectively, with an additional 1,000 laborers on Engebi. Later on D-Day, Jones' command occupied five other islands in the chain southeast of Engebi, finding all of them devoid of enemy.

At 1344 General Watson directed his artillery to land in DUKW's according to schedule, the 2d Separate Pack Howitzer Battalion proceeding to CAMELLIA and the 104th Field Artillery Battalion (105mm) going to Rujiyoru. But progress of the former unit did not please Brigadier General Watson [37] who thereupon relieved the Marine artillery commander,[38] Major Alfred M. Mahoney assuming command of the howitzers.

Both artillery battalions, with five units of fire, were ashore at 1602 and ready for registration 30 minutes later. This was begun promptly, aerial artillery spotters having been on station for 45 minutes. By 1902 registration on Engebi was complete and 50 minutes

---

[32] *Hill II.*

[33] ". . . Deep Entrance had been chosen for use by the larger ships because due to the high currents through this passage it was not expected that it would be practicable to plant mines there, which assumption proved to be correct." *Ibid.*

[34] Ltr Capt Claude V. Ricketts, USN, to CMC, 9Mar53.

[35] *Ibid.*

[36] As has been done previously, the native name for an island is followed by the code name in parentheses. Where a code name is used alone, no record can be found of a native name.

[37] *Watson.*

[38] Col Walker quickly installed the relieved officer as artillery officer on the regimental staff, although no such billet was authorized. He was subsequently wounded in action on Engebi, awarded the Silver Star for his actions there, and resumed command of his battalion as soon as that unit reverted to control of the 22d Marines at the end of the operation.

ENGEBI AS IT APPEARED three weeks before the 22d Marines stormed ashore. In the left center of the photograph is the small pier separating Beaches White 1 and Blue 3. In the background is the western end of the airstrip. (Navy photo.)

later night-long harassing fires against the next day's objective were begun by the artillerymen. During registration and under the protection of naval gunfire, underwater demolition teams moved to within 100 yards of Engebi's shore in amphibian tractors and then swam 50 yards closer, reconnoitering the beaches and their approaches. No obstacles or mines were located.

One task remained before the day's work was ended. At 1848 Company D (Scout), 4th Tank Battalion, embarked in rubber boats from APD *Schley* with orders to land on Bogon (ZINNIA), the island lying directly west of Engebi, and prevent any attempted Japanese exodus in that direction. The darkness, heavy sea, and wind combined to split the company, one portion returning to the *Schley* and the remainder landing three islands away on Elugelab (SAGEBRUSH). Working their way across the reefs, the latter group eventually secured its original objective at 0327 without meeting opposition.

Thus Phase I was accomplished on schedule without meeting any enemy or incurring any casualties. All hands could now turn their attention to the seizure of Engebi on D-plus 1, Phase II in the over-all plan.

FRAGILE IS SHATTERED

The 22d Marines' plan for Engebi (FRAG-ILE) designated Battalion Landing Team 1 (Lieutenant Colonel Walfried H. Fromhold) and Battalion Landing Team 2 (Lieutenant Colonel Donn C. Hart) assault elements, Battalion Landing Team 3 (Major Clair W. Shisler) constituting regimental reserve. Landing beaches were located on the approximate center of the lagoon side of the island, with a short finger pier separating them and demarking the initial BLT boundaries. (See Map 12, Map Section.) Once ashore, the line between the 1st and 2d Landing Teams extended along WHOOPIE Trail to ENERVATE Trail, thence along the latter to its terminal point and from there to the island's northern tip. Fromhold's command would land on Beach White 1 and handle the regiment's right zone, while the left, Hart's unit, would land on Beach Blue 3. Reinforcing elements to be landed under 22d RCT control were the 2d Separate Tank Company and one platoon (two 105mm self-propelled guns) from the 106th Infantry's Cannon Company. During the afternoon of D-Day the troops transferred from their transports to the LST's where LVT's awaited them, and readied themselves for W-Hour, set for 0845.

LANDING TEAMS 1 AND 2 churn their way toward Engebi's shore. (Navy photo.)

ENGEBI as it appeared after the aerial and naval bombardment.   (Coast Guard photo.)

At 0655 on D-plus 1 (18 February) the guns of *Colorado* and *Louisville* heralded the opening attack on Colonel Yano's Engebi defenses. Minutes later *Pennsylvania* and *Tennessee*—1,000 yards offshore—joined in with a full-throated roar, and four destroyers, *McCord*, *Heermann*, *Phelps*, and *Hall*, got into the act.[39] From nearby Rujiyoru and CAMELLIA the 75mm and 105mm howitzers stepped up their fire, which had been harassing the defending Nipponese all night. Shortly before 0800 planes from *Sangamon* and *Suwanee* appeared on the scene, and the bombardment was halted abruptly to permit the aviators to get in their wallop. The naval guns and artillery resumed their discordant chant at 0811 and continued without cessation until one minute before the first wave of LVT's stormed ashore.

Reveille at 0400 had roused the assault troops on board the LST's, and by 0805 the loaded amtracs were in the rendezvous area. Ten minutes later the first wave crossed the line of departure and churned its way toward the beaches.[40] Preceding the LVT's were six LCI(G)'s, three on each flank, and these poured forth a torrent of rocket and 40mm fire. The gunfire hit the beach as planned, but because of an error in estimating the range, the rockets landed in the water, thereby providing no assistance whatsoever to the assault troops. The LVT(A)'s were the next in formation, five echeloned on each flank immediately behind the LCI's and seven in a V-shape between the leading elements of the assault landing teams. Thus, the amphibian tanks[41] did not go before the troop-carrying tractors, but were a part of the same wave. Smoke and dust from the bombardment drifted out over the water, obscuring

[39] Action Report of Bombardment of Eniwetok Atoll by Task Unit 51.17.2, 4, hereinafter cited as *TU 51.17.2 AR*.

[40] Gen Watson ordered his aide and a radio team into an LCVP which was dispatched to the flank of one assault battalion. This group's mission was to locate enemy guns by drawing fire. Later it was directed to report the progress of fighting ashore. In the attacks on Eniwetok and Parry Islands, Watson sent ashore OP teams under the command of various staff officers. The OP team leaders were instructed to report directly to the general on the progress of the respective operations. *Greene II.*

[41] The term, "amphibian tank," is used here because that is the Army designation and the LVT's were a part of an Army unit.

LANDING TEAM 1 encountered this emplaced Japanese tank on Engebi. (Navy photo.)

vision, and the amphibian vehicles tended to separate.[42] On the left, amtracs bearing elements of Company F (assault) and Company G (support) went 200–250 yards to the left of their assigned beach (Blue 3) and landed the troops at the western end of the airstrip. In the zone of Landing Team 1, the LVT's hit the correct beach, but the amtracs bearing the right platoon of Company A (assault) broke down, thus delaying this unit's arrival.[43]

Two minutes before W-Hour the first wave ground ashore on the sandy beach, but here the LVT's themselves contributed to a certain amount of congestion.

After the troops were landed, the first wave of LVT's remained in the vicinity of the beach, and thus added to the congestion there. According to plans and orders issued, they were to proceed inland to WHISKEY Road, and support the advance of the infantry. Their failure to proceed inland, as directed, was attributed to fallen coconut trees and debris blocking their passage. However, it is felt that with more determination the prescribed position could have been reached and the mission could have been accomplished. They

would then have been in a position to render excellent support with their machine guns and facilitated the seizure of SKUNK Point[44] [a strong point on the southern tip of Engebi].

Once the troops were ashore, the Japanese reacted by firing rifles, machine guns, and mortars at the Marines. But the stunned defenders did not put up an organized defense, their fire being anything but intense.

In Landing Team 1's area, Companies A and B moved forward on the right and left, respectively. Moments later Company C landed in support, wheeling to the right in order to overrun SKUNK Point. Company A's 3d Platoon landed somewhat later than its parent unit because of the LVT breakdown (noted earlier). Its mission was to echelon itself to the right rear of Company A and close the gap between that organization and Company C on the right.

Over on the regiment's left, Landing Team 2 was advancing with Companies E and F on the right and left respectively, the latter company covering a front slightly larger than that planned because of the shift to the left during landing. Company G, landing in support, wheeled left to assault WEASEL Point, a strong point on the island's northwestern tip.

Shortly after 0900 the medium tanks of the 2d Separate Tank Company began landing and moved in support of BLT 2/22 on the airstrip. But this was not accomplished without incident. One LCM operator inadvertently lowered his ramp prematurely, and the craft flooded and capsized. The tank on board had buttoned up before this occurred and only one of its crew escaped.[45]

Lieutenant Colonel Fromhold's battalion continued to advance on the right, but as it did so the flanks of Companies A and C were stretched to the breaking point in an effort to maintain physical contact. Sometime after 0900 this tenuous contact was broken and a gap created with an utterly unforeseen result. As noted earlier, Company A's 3d Platoon was to retain

---

[42] "This situation was investigated and the fault was determined to exist in the fact that the wave guides (Navy) had not led their waves close enough to their beaches before turning them loose on their own." Comments LtCol John P. Lanigan on prelim script, hereinafter cited as *Lanigan.*

[43] Notes of LtCol W. F. Fromhold, undated, hereinafter cited as *Fromhold.*

[44] Ltr MajGen John T. Walker to LtCol Harry W. Edwards, 9Apr53. The LVT unit, on the other hand, reported that it "initially supported the advance of the infantry inland." Special Action Report, Eniwetok Operation, 708th Amphibian Tank Bn, 19Mar44.

[45] USS *Ashland,* Action Report for Eniwetok Atoll, 3May44, 6, hereinafter cited as *Ashland Rpt.*

contact between Companies A and C. When the break finally came this platoon remained with Company C, rather than with its parent unit.[46] Thus Company A was now working its way forward with only two platoons and its right flank exposed.

As Company C began exerting its inexorable pressure on SKUNK Point, many of the defending Japanese sought to escape by running up the southeastern beach. Because of the gap existing between Companies A and C, the fleeing enemy were thus in a position to fire on the former unit's right flank and rear—and this they did. At 0955 Company A had to turn and fight off a heavy attack on the southeastern beach. At the same time Company C threw in one platoon to plug the gap between its left flank

and that beach, thus bottling the remaining Nipponese in their strong point.

Faced by a maze of trenches and interconnected spider holes, the men of the 22d RCT quickly improvised an effective means of rooting out the Nipponese:

Due to the many exits from the defenses and spider-type trenches, it was found expedient to toss smoke grenades into these prior to exploding main demolition charges. Thus, the exits were exposed by escaping smoke. These exits were then covered by fire or flame thrower when the main charge was exploded.[47]

As soon as the Regimental Weapons Company's half-tracks were ashore, two were assigned each assault landing team. But the shell holes and debris made movement difficult for the vehicles, particularly in the forward areas. Although they executed a few fire missions, half-tracks were used principally to haul

---

[46] Memo LtCol Glen E. Martin to LtCol Harry W. Edwards, 12Mar53, hereinafter cited as *Martin*.

[47] *Fromhold*.

MARINES work their way forward by fire and movement.

water and ammunition to the front and remove wounded to the rear. Experience typical of the difficulties encountered by these troops is related in a report of the 2d Heavy Platoon (half-track) which was attached to Landing Team 2 (Beach Blue 3):

> The platoon landed in the 8th wave on Beach White 1, which was not the beach planned on. . . . We turned left down the beach in an effort to reach BLT 2 on Beach Blue 3. We were held up at the pier by debris. . . . Finally we decided to force our way across the debris; in doing this the radiator of No. 1 half-track was punctured, thereby partially disabling the vehicle. While still on the beach the radios in No. 1 and No. 2 TCS jeeps went out also. . . . Eventually we reached a position on the right boundary of BLT 2, when we received orders to move out behind BLT 1. . . .[48]

At about 1100 Company A was reinforced by two 105mm self-propelled guns,[49] but 15 minutes later these were diverted to Company C, still busily hammering away at SKUNK Point. By this time Companies A and B had entered the wooded area which stretched about halfway between the landing beaches and the final objective, NEWT Point. Dense vegetation and trees knocked down by the naval bombardment impeded progress. In addition, a great many Japanese had taken refuge in the area and were now putting up a fanatical last-ditch fight.

Landing Team 3, which was now ashore, was directed to send Company I to BLT 1/22, and that company moved in behind Company A.

Contrasted with the difficulties Landing Team 1 was meeting, Lieutenant Colonel Hart's organization on the left was pushing forward rapidly over the airstrip and open terrain. Companies E and F, working with Marine medium tanks, had encountered four Japanese tanks, dug in, which were being utilized as pillboxes. These "fortifications" were knocked

out[50] and the advance continued. Enemy defenses which could not be easily overrun were by-passed on the premise that mopping up details could handle them.[51]

Colonel Walker was ashore by 1030. An hour later he was informed that Company G was still at work on WEASEL Point, Company F was attacking NEWT Point and Company E was well forward on line with F/22. Despite the differences in distance of advance, contact between the two battalions was still intact.

Meanwhile, Company I had taken over from Company A in the assault, the latter unit reverting to landing team reserve. While Companies B and I worked their way through the woods toward the airstrip, Company A busied itself with Japanese defensive positions on the southeastern beach.

At 1310 Colonel Walker notified General Watson that WEASEL Point and that portion of NEWT Point in Landing Team 2's zone were secure; that the island was in possession of the 22d Marines except for a pocket of enemy stretching across Landing Team 1's line of advance and lying between that unit and the airstrip. At 1400 the Tactical Group commander came ashore and 50 minutes later Engebi was officially listed as secure.

At 1456 Company C announced that SKUNK Point was overrun and at 1600 Companies B and I debouched from the wooded area onto the airstrip. At this point, I/22 reverted to control of Landing Team 3 and once again Company A moved in as the right flank assault unit. At 1830 Companies A and B reported secure that portion of NEWT Point falling within their zone.

An hour earlier Landing Team 3 and the 2d Separate Tank Company had been reembarked for action with the 106th Infantry Regiment in its D-plus 2 assault on Eniwetok.

The 22d RCT's first night on Engebi was "uncomfortable," one participant recalls.[52] Many Japanese had been by-passed during the rapid movement across the island, and complete mopping up was not conducted simultane-

---

[48] Combat Report of 2d Heavy Platoon for Engebi and Parry Islands, 15Mar44.

[49] "From personal experience, the 105mm self-propelled guns proved to be more of a hazard than a help. They made a very inviting target for Japanese mortar and small-arms fire, and consequently were not a very comforting thing to have around. After experiencing one of these barrages directed at the 105's, most of the Marines in my particular sector didn't like to see a 105 approach." Comments Maj Thomas D. Scott on prelim script, hereinafter cited as *Scott*.

[50] Ltr Maj Robert S. Reinhardt, Jr., to CMC 18Mar53, hereinafter cited as *Reinhardt*.

[51] *Lanigan.*

[52] *Ibid.*

MARINE TANKS work their way across Engebi's airstrip and onto NEWT Point.   (Navy photo.)

ously with the initial attack.   Moreover, little attention had been paid to collecting both United States and Japanese weapons which were left lying about the battlefield.   Thus individual Nipponese were able to supply themselves with sufficient arms and ammunition to make isolated attacks on the Marines throughout the night.[53]   Nor should it be forgotten that this was the first night in combat for these particular troops, and a certain amount of firing on their part was to be expected.

At 0800 on 19 February 1944 (D-plus 2), Colonel Walker raised the American flag on Engebi, as "To the Colors" was blown on a captured bugle.   Mopping up continued throughout the day with demolition teams and flame throwers of the 2d Separate Engineer Company in the forefront.

[53] *Fromhold.*

While attention was focused on Engebi during D-plus 1, the V Amphibious Corps Reconnaissance Company and Company D (Scout) were not idle.   The Reconnaissance Company surveyed two islets southeast of Engebi and found no signs of enemy or natives.   But as it landed on Muzinbaarikku (ARBUTUS) Island, next to Engebi, it was met by grazing machine-gun fire.   The Marines returned this fire and threw 60mm mortar shells toward the northern point of the island.   Later it developed that the island contained enemy positions but no enemy, the fire coming from the vicinity of SKUNK Point on Engebi, where C/22 was heavily engaged.

As noted earlier, the Scout Company secured several islands southwest of Engebi in the early morning hours of D-plus 1.   During the remainder of the day these Marines occupied five other islands in the chain, using rubber boats and finding only one Japanese soldier, whom they took prisoner.

General Watson noted that on Engebi the enemy had conducted only a passive defense and that operations were proceeding according to plan. From captured documents it was determined that elements of the 1st Mobile Seaborne Infantry Brigade were on the atoll, and estimated enemy strength for Parry and Eniwetok was revised upwards to 400–550 and 700–800 respectively. The stage was now set for Phase III, the seizure of Eniwetok, to begin on schedule on the morning of D-plus 2.[54]

PRIVILEGE IS TAKEN

During the afternoon of D-plus 1 the 106th Regimental Combat Team (less BLT 106–2 [55]) was released from its status of floating reserve for Engebi, and at 1500 Colonel Ayers issued Field Order #4 for the seizure of Eniwetok Island (PRIVILEGE). Plans still optimistically called for Ayers' command to seize Parry (HEARTSTRINGS) as soon as Eniwetok was secured, and landing team assignments were made accordingly.

As previously described, Eniwetok is shaped like a blackjack. The selected landing beaches were situated on the lagoon side of the island on the northern portion of the blackjack's head, and designated Yellow 1 and Yellow 2, from left to right. The two assault units would land abreast, BLT 106–1 [56] on Beach Yellow 2 and BLT 106–3 on Beach Yellow 1. (See Map 13, Map Section.) This latter unit was instructed to send a rifle company across the island, form a defensive line facing northeast and prevent the Japanese from moving southwest. The remainder of the landing team would serve in regimental reserve. BLT 106–1 would secure the southwestern end of the island, utilizing not more than one rifle company, then pass through BLT 106–3's rifle company and

secure the northeastern portion of Eniwetok. The 104th Field Artillery Battalion would move into the southern end of the objective as soon as it was secured. Upon occupation of the target, RCT 106 would be prepared to move into LVT's for the planned assault on Parry Island. During the attack on Eniwetok, LT 3/22 would constitute a floating reserve.[57] One platoon of the 2d Separate Tank Company (medium) was attached to BLT 106–3, while the remainder of the Marine tanks were attached to BLT 106–1.[58]

The problem of getting the 2d Separate Tank Company refueled, rearmed, and transferred from the northern portion of Eniwetok Atoll to the southern area was one faced by the vessel which transported the tanks and LCM's from Kwajalein. Moving *Ashland* during darkness was considered hazardous, so at 0247 on D-plus 2 (19 February) 12 LCM's loaded with tanks and their crews, and accompanied by *SC 1066* departed on a dark 25-mile voyage across the choppy waters of the lagoon. "The results were satisfactory, all boats arrived as planned, but considerable risk of breakdown was present. The commanding officer recommended this course of action, but would hesitate to do so again." [59]

Eniwetok was subjected to harassing naval gunfire from D-Day until the morning of the landing, D-plus 2. Because there were few above-ground defenses and naval gunfire's flat trajectory is not especially damaging to underground fortifications, the total bombardment, in both quantity and quality, did not equal that for Engebi and Parry. Some 204.6 tons of projectiles, none larger than 8-inch, were poured

---

[54] TG–1 Unit Report 2, 18Feb44, 1–3.

[55] It is well to recall that BLT 106–2 was involved in the Majuro occupation and did not participate in the Eniwetok operation in any way. The basic infantry organization of RCT 106 was the 1st and 3d Battalion Landing Teams.

[56] As noted previously in this monograph, when taken from Army reports, Army terms and designations will be used in referring to Army actions.

[57] "Effective combat units are achieved by effective unit training, and can never be replaced by assorted combinations of component units, however highly trained. The make-up of the landing force on Eniwetok Island illustrates my point. A two battalion regiment is difficult to fight, and when the reserve normal to a regiment is made up of a totally strange battalion from a different service . . . unit integrity is being sorely violated." Ltr Col Joseph C. Anderson, USA, to CMC, 27Feb53, hereinafter cited as *Anderson II*.

[58] RCT 106, reinf, (less BLT 106–2) Unit Operations Report (DOWNSIDE), 15Apr44, hereinafter cited as *RCT 106 Rpt.*

[59] *Ashland Rpt*, 3, 6.

on Eniwetok by *Tennessee, Portland, Indian-apolis, Trathen, Phelps, Hailey, Hoel,* and *Haggard.* In contrast Engebi received 1,179.7 tons and 944.4 tons were scheduled for Parry. Further, there was no preliminary artillery bombardment as had been placed on Engebi and would be laid on Parry because there were no nearby islands on which the guns could be positioned. The concept of a light naval bombardment (in comparison with the other islands) was based on the belief that Eniwetok was lightly held and that the 106th RCT would have little trouble taking it.

With Y-Hour set for 0900, *Portland, Indian-apolis,* and two destroyers stepped up their harassing fire to preliminary bombardment strength at 0710. An hour later this was checked to permit an air strike and then resumed at 0826. Fearing that the tank-loaded LCM's would not arrive on schedule, Admiral Hill reset Y-Hour to 0915 and later moved it to 0922. The armor arrived on time, however,

and the soldiers were ordered into the beach, the first wave crossing the line of departure shortly after 0900.

The assault troops had been awakened at 0430 and departed their LST's for the rendezvous area three hours later. Now as their LVT's lurched toward the shore, they were preceded by the usual groupings of LVT(A)'s and rocket-carrying LCI's. At 0918 the first soldiers touched ground and began moving inland against light opposition, preceded by the amphibian tanks.

BLT 106–3 (Lieutenant Colonel Harold I. Mizony) landed on Beach Yellow 1 with Companies L and K abreast Company I in reserve. Company L, in the left, was to pivot on its left flank, face north and extend toward the ocean beaches. Company K was to drive straight across the island to the ocean shore and then mop up in L/106's rear. On Beach Yellow 2, BLT 106–1 (Lieutenant Colonel Winslow Cornett) scheduled a similar maneuver. Company

ASSAULT FORCES of RCT 106 on their way into Yellow Beaches 1 and 2 on Eniwetok Island. (Navy photo.)

LANDING TEAM 3/22 prepares to assault a coconut log emplacement on Eniwetok Island.

B, on the left, was to cross the island, while Company A pivoted on its right flank and moved southward between the lagoon beach and a north-south trail.

But these plans went awry. Before the LVT(A)'s could go the prescribed 100 yards inland, they encountered a steep bluff some nine feet high which blocked their progress. As they ground to a halt, the troop-carrying amphibians followed suit, and the end result was congestion on the beaches that kept succeeding waves afloat beyond their scheduled landing time. A network of insidious spider traps, backed up by machine-gun and mortar fire, helped keep the advance at a standstill.

General Watson reacted to this stalemate by sending a message to Colonel Ayers at 1004, "Push your attack." Six minutes later the

beachmaster notified Admiral Hill that he was holding up all waves because of the congested beaches "due to slowness of movement of troops inland." At 1023 General Watson prodded the attacking troops once more. He ordered Colonel Ayers to "move troops forward and inland, clear beaches. Advance."

By 1100 the 3d Battalion had pushed inland about 100 yards, Companies L and K abreast, the former's left flank on the lagoon beach and K/106's right flank in the air about two-thirds of the way across the island. An hour later the landing team had pushed northward a short distance, the right flank resting about 70 yards from the ocean beach.[60]

In the 1st Battalion area the cross-island attack was somewhat more successful, but the

[60] *RCT 106 Rpt.*

138

southward advance was slow, the soldiers fighting dense undergrowth and undulating ground as well as the ever-present spider trap defenses. Elements of Company B managed to reach the ocean shore by 1145, but this was an isolated group which had lost contact with the remainder of the unit. Company A was moving slowly, attempting to execute its pivot maneuver to the right. Scheduled to land behind Company B, Company C approached Beach Yellow 2, which was badly congested, in the fifth and sixth waves. Four LCVP's were somehow diverted some distance south of the prescribed beach and landed against stiff opposition. But Company A came to the rescue by advancing along the beach.[61]

By 1200 contact was established between Lieutenant Colonel Cornett's units, and his command faced south, in the shape of a huge "S". The farthest advance was made by Company A, its right flank extending to the lagoon beach. Company C was in the center, forming the bend in the line. Company B extended to the left with its left flank on the ocean beach. Although a line had been established, opposition in the rear from by-passed Japanese was far from eliminated as the 3d Battalion, 22d Marines would soon discover.

By landing on Beach Yellow 2 and advancing to the south, BLT 106–1 was in a position to take the bulk of the Japanese defenses from the rear. Enemy reaction took the form of a strong counterblow in an attempt to ward off the inevitable. No sooner had contact been effected within the battalion and the "S"-line formed, than some 400 Nipponese hit it furiously. Company B's line was broken momentarily, but quickly reformed and by 1245 the soldiers had thrown back the Japanese. Despite this blow to the enemy, however, progress did not improve, and Cornett's command inched its way forward, assisted by Marine medium tanks and 105mm self-propelled guns of the Cannon Company.

At 1230 Colonel Ayers visited the 3d Battalion's command post and directed that unit to push forward and secure the northern end of Eniwetok. Reinforcing elements included one platoon from the 2d Separate Tank Company (medium) and one platoon of self-propelled 105mm guns. Company I replaced Company K on line, the latter organization taking over the mop-up mission in the rear. Shortly thereafter the battalion stretched across the island from beach to beach and began advancing slowly.

Eniwetok was proving a much tougher nut to crack than had been originally expected, and Colonel Ayers ordered the reserve (3d Battalion, 22d Marines) to land, but refused Major Shisler's request to take his half-tracks ashore. At 1330 the Marines began debarking from LCVP's on Beach Yellow 1 and moved to an assembly area north of the pier, fighting Japanese on the way.[62] Shisler was directed to take over BLT 106–1's left flank, relieving Companies B and C. Company B would revert to landing team reserve and Company C would move into Company A's area, beefing up the force there. A general attack to the south was scheduled for 1515.

The boundary between 3/22 and 106–1 lay just southeast of the trail that ran the length of Eniwetok Island. Thus the Marines assumed responsibility for approximately two-thirds of the entire southern zone. And as they began moving forward to relieve BLT 106–1's left flank, once again they were forced to fight by-passed Japanese.

The attack to the south began promptly at 1515. BLT 106–1 moved forward with Companies A and C on the right and left respectively, Company B in reserve. Landing Team 3/22 advanced with Company L on the right, Company K on the left and Company I in reserve. Some 300 yards were covered before stiff opposition was encountered in the form of mutually supporting coconut log emplacements.

Most of these positions could not be discerned until the troops were within 25 or 30 yards of them. Because of the close proximity of the troops to the positions, the dense jungle with consequent lack of proper observation, it was determined that naval gunfire was

[61] *Crowl and Love*, XIX–42.

[62] Historical Branch interview with Col. Clair W. Shisler, 24Apr53, hereinafter cited as *Shisler*.

not practicable. Mortar fire had very little effect on the positions. . . .[63]

Once again Major Shisler requested permission to bring his half-tracks ashore and once again Colonel Ayers refused. The Marine commander then requested tank support, but this was not forthcoming. Nor were all the assault weapons available, only one bazooka being on hand.[64] Infantrymen and a platoon from the 2d Separate Engineer Company attacked the positions with flame throwers and satchel charges, and the Marines continued to advance slowly through the dense undergrowth.

As the afternoon wore on BLT 106–3 pushed slowly northward through the same sort of undergrowth which proved a serious obstacle as well as providing concealment to the enemy. Shortly after 1800 Lieutenant Colonel Mizony reported his lines about 500 yards north of the pier at Beach Yellow 1. He informed his superior that he doubted if he could reach the end of the island by dark, but was in a position to set up a defensive line for the night.

Meanwhile, at 1635 General Watson had radioed Colonel Ayers: "Absolutely necessary that you land your artillery prior to darkness today so that it may register on HEART-STRINGS early tomorrow morning. . . ." Sixty-five minutes later Tactical Group-1 was notified that one battery of the 104th Field Artillery Battalion was on Beach Yellow 1.

At 1850 Colonel Ayers dispatched a message to the units under his command: "You will continue to advance until you reach the end of the island. Call for illumination when necessary." BLT 106–3, operating in the northern portion of Eniwetok, attempted to do this, picking up about 200 yards during the entire night. Although searchlight and star shell illumination were utilized, the battalion took a dim view of such nocturnal operations:

Movement at night proved to be both difficult and costly. It was impossible to see the camouflaged holes, contact was poor, and the troops as a whole did not seem to have the confidence in themselves that was so apparent throughout the day. . . .[65]

When the RCT commander's message reached the battalions in the south, they were some 600 yards short of their objective. And in contrast to BLT 106–3 in the north, they were attacking a heavily fortified area. At dusk a few tanks finally arrived at Major Shisler's command post, but when he informed the tank commander of the plan to push on during darkness, the armor's leader pronounced it "impossible" and withdrew.[66] Moreover, the expected illumination did not materialize.[67]

Since no tank support was received and no illumination given prior to the time when the night attack was scheduled, the commanding officer of LT 3/22 informed his unit commanders no attack would be made. Orders were issued for the units of LT 3/22 to hold their present positions for the night.[68]

Groups of Japanese, usually numbering six to ten individuals, attacked the Marine lines during the night, but no large coordinated attack was forthcoming. Many of the enemy who did attack were armed with crude spears, knives and rifles. All their attempts to break through were frustrated.[69]

Dawn brought a surprise to Major Shisler's command. On the landing team's right flank, where BLT 106–1 was supposed to be, there was only one soldier from that unit.[70] During the night the Army organization, with the exception of the lone infantryman, had withdrawn some 300 yards to the rear without notifying the adjoining Marines.[71] Thus a sizeable gap in the lines existed through most of the night. Major Shisler quickly ordered elements of Company I forward to plug the hole, while a

[63] Document dated 10Apr44, submitted by Capt Buenos A. W. Young, believed to be Eniwetok Action Rpt of 3d Bn, 22d Marines, hereinafter cited as *BLT 3/22 SAR*.

[64] Some Army troops from Kwajalein had come on board 3/22's troop ship while it lay off that island and passed the word that bazookas were ineffective. The men of the 3d Bn had not experienced combat and they accepted this statement from men whom they regarded as combat veterans. Thus when 3/22 was engaged in Eniwetok Island it suddenly found itself lacking these important weapons. *Shisler.*

[65] *RCT 106 Rpt.* BLT 106–3 S–3 Summary.

[66] *Shisler.*

[67] Illumination was provided BLT 106–3 in the north, but available information indicates that this was not the case in the south.

[68] Maj William E. Sperling, III, an undated paper titled "BLT 3/22 on Eniwetok Island," hereinafter cited as *Sperling.*

[69] Ltr LtCol Earl J. Cook to CMC, 23Feb53.

[70] *Shisler.*

[71] Ltr LtCol Robert A. McCabe to CMC, 12Mar53, hereinafter cited as *McCabe.*

coordinated attack which had been planned for dawn had to await BLT 106–1's return to its original positions.

At about 0830 on the morning of D-plus 3 (20 February) between 40 and 50 Japanese suddenly attacked the Marines' battalion command post. Surprise was on the side of the enemy and an estimated eight Marines were killed (including the battalion operations officer) and an equal number wounded [72] before Master Sergeant John J. Nagazyna organized a force which eliminated the attackers.[73]

Meanwhile, both LT 3/22 and BLT 106–1 had begun attacking to the south, and enemy opposition was much the same as that encountered on the preceding day. At 1000 it appeared that Major Shisler's repeated requests for tank support had borne fruit. Four light tanks belonging to the 106th RCT rumbled up into the Marine area at that time, but these rumbled away before actually engaging in combat.[74]

Shortly after the four tanks disappeared, however, the Marines managed to persuade two Army self-propelled 105mm gun crews to assist them with their weapons. These guns "did render excellent assistance and worked in fine

---

[72] Accounts vary as to the exact number of casualties suffered by 3/22 in this action. The number given here is an estimate based on available information.

[73] Ltr Capt Buenos A. W. Young to CMC, 9Mar53.

[74] *BLT 3/22's SAR* cites numerous instances where tank support was promised by RCT 106 but was not delivered. Moreover, *Shisler* relates that it was particularly "disheartening" to him that he was not allowed his half-tracks, nor was he given tank support. *22dMar SAR,* 3, states: "During the attack on PRIVILEGE, BLT #3 was unassisted by tanks though two full tank companies were ashore and being used by the regiment. This left a feeling of desire on the part of the higher echelon of command to save their other troops at the expense of BLT #3." Inasmuch as one of the tank companies was a Marine unit, disappointment was intensified.

MARINES advance toward the southwestern tip of Eniwetok.

cooperation with the infantry units of LT 3/22 in the reduction of numerous enemy strong points." [75]

At 1445 Marine and Army elements reached the tip of Eniwetok, and 15 minutes later General Watson was notified that the southern end of the island was secure. As is always the case, mopping-up operations continued.

During the morning, the remainder of the 104th Field Artillery Battalion landed with the mission of supporting the attack on Parry Island, tentatively scheduled for 21 February but later firmed for the 22d. Permission was granted for the artillerymen to support the advance of BLT 106–3 up the northeastern neck of Eniwetok, and this was initiated at 1155.

Lieutenant Colonel Mizony's command began its D-plus 3 daylight advance to the north shortly after 0800. Company L continued as the left flank unit, while Company K replaced Company I on the battalion right. Marine medium tanks continued to give close support, and engineers carrying pole charges, flame throwers and shaped charges materially assisted

in the reduction of enemy strong points. By nightfall the landing team was 1,000 yards from the northern tip of Eniwetok. The attack was resumed the next morning and continued in the usual manner. At 1430 on D-plus 4 (21 February) Mizony informed Ayers that the northern end of the island was secure. With Admiral Hill and General Watson on hand, the Stars and Stripes were raised on Eniwetok Island at 1721.

Altogether, it took three days to overrun Eniwetok, and the 3d Battalion, 22d Marines bore the brunt of the operation during a sustained 24-hour advance. Its area included the most heavily defended portion of the island. But it was clear that the commanding general was not pleased with the performance of the 106th RCT:

. . . In the assault against PRIVILEGE Island by the 106th Infantry . . . the assault troops did not move forward rapidly from the beaches (thereby causing a serious congestion), did not operate in close cooperation with tanks and failed to realize the capabilities of and to use to the fullest extent naval gunfire and close support aviation. [76]

---

[75] *Sperling.*

[76] *TG–1 Spt Rpt* 7; "It would be wrong and even un-

UNOPPOSED LANDINGS were made on a number of small islands in Eniwetok Atoll. Here a group of Marines goes ashore on one of them. (Navy photo.)

Although Eniwetok Island was secured, the battle for Eniwetok Atoll was not yet complete and movements were under way to bring this to an expeditious end.

SIDESHOW

While primary attention was focused on the assault of Eniwetok Island, other units were actively engaged in other portions of the atoll.

The chain of islands making up the eastern rim of Eniwetok Atoll had been assigned to Captain Jones' V Amphibious Corps Reconnaissance Company. On the morning of D-plus 2 this unit continued with its mission.

Operating from the APD *Kane*, the Marines secured ten islands and islets during the day without meeting any natives or enemy. At 1600 General Watson ordered the company to occupy Japtan (LADYSLIPPER) before dark, and two hours later the unit was ashore. A Japanese flag flying from a mast in the center of the island indicated the presence of the enemy, but it turned out that the invaders were the only human beings there.

Inasmuch as Japtan bounds Deep Entrance and lies immediately north of Parry, Watson selected it as a position for the 2d Separate Pack Howitzer Battalion to support the Parry operation.[77] The Reconnaissance Company selected landing beaches for the DUKW-borne artillery, and at 1000 the next day (20 February) guided the howitzer battalion ashore.

In the midst of these multiple activities, a survey of Jeroru Island (LILAC) was overlooked. This minute bit of coral lies just inside the lagoon between Japtan and Parry. On 21 February a reconnaissance patrol reported it unoccupied. The Corps Reconnaissance Company thereupon reembarked in *Kane*, awaiting the attack on Parry the following day.

The western chain of islands in the atoll was the responsibility of Company D (Scout), 4th Tank Battalion under Captain Edward L.

Katzenbach, Jr. As noted earlier, the northern portion of these small islands was secured by the evening of D-plus 1. The next morning the Marines began their landings on the southern group, starting with Rigili (POSY). Here enemy fire was received, and a brisk five-minute fire fight followed. When it was over nine Japanese lay dead. The remaining seven islands in the chain were secured during the day without meeting any natives or Nipponese. At the close of the day the scouts reembarked on *Schley* and stood by for the Parry attack.

Thus, when both Eniwetok Island and the islet of Jeroru were reported secured on the afternoon of 21 February (D-plus 4), there remained only one island to be taken in the entire atoll—Parry.

BREAKING HEARTSTRINGS

The first few hours on Eniwetok Island clearly indicated the original invasion schedule could not be maintained, but for a time General Watson still hoped that the island would be secured at the end of the day. By 2100, however, he was convinced that "the capture of PRIVILEGE Island would not be completed before the evening of 20 February at the earliest." Therefore, he decided to take the victors of Engebi (Colonel Walker's 22d Marines) off their island and turn the Parry (HEARTSTRINGS) mission over to them, with a target date of 21 February.[78] Walker was ordered to begin reembarkation immediately and arrive in the transport area by 1600 the following day.

At 0800 D-plus 3 (20 February) LT 1/22 was afloat in the transport area. Four hours later responsibility for Engebi was assumed by the 3d Army Defense Battalion, reinforced by Companies A and D, 111th Infantry Regiment.[79] And later that afternoon Landing

---

fair to ignore the brave and competent performance of many fine and highly trained individuals and small units who collectively made up the 106th Infantry . . . ." *Anderson II.*

[77] As has already been noted, the 104th Field Artillery Battalion would support the Parry assault from the island of Eniwetok.

[78] "When it became apparent that this operation [Eniwetok Island] would require two or three days, it became necessary to revise the entire operations for the assault on Parry Island . . . . The change in plans was effected very expeditiously and efficiently by Gen Watson and Col Walker, together with members of my staff." *Hill II.*

[79] These were forward elements of the 111th Infantry Regiment. That organization later relieved RCT 106 in its duties as garrison for Eniwetok Atoll.

PARRY ISLAND (looking south) under bombardment the day before the 22d Marines landed there. (Navy photo.)

Team 2, 22d Marines, arrived in the transport area.

Following a conference of unit commanders at 1400 on 20 February, General Watson issued Tactical Group-1 Operation Order 3–44. This postponed the attack on Parry until 0845 (later changed to 0900), 22 February. It also provided for the relief and reembarkation of the 3d Battalion, 22d Marines, and the 2d Separate Tank Company the morning of 21 February in order that these organizations might participate in the Parry assault. Further, additional forces were assigned the regimental combat team to bolster its striking power.

In the midst of this planning a shift was made in landing beach designations, which was to play an important part in the operation. As originally established, a small 20-yard-long pier on the northern lagoon shore of Parry separated Beach Green 2 and Beach Green 3, the latter being south of the marker. On Beach Green 3's southern flank was a larger 30-yard-long pier,

designated VALENTINE Pier. During the planning it was decided that too much territory was involved in this scheme, and the beach designations were shifted northward about 300 yards, Beach Green 3's southern flank then resting just south of the smaller of the two piers. "This information apparently was not known in time by all naval forces,"[80] and the effect of this will be subsequently seen. (See Map 14, Map Section.)

On 21 February Colonel Walker issued his Operation Order 10–44. The landings would be executed from the lagoon on the northern portion of Parry on Beach Green 2 (north) and Beach Green 3 (south). The northern one-third of the island constituted the first objective. Separating this area from the southern two-thirds was an 0–1 line running east-west. The attack south of the 0–1 line would be made on order by two battalions abreast, the battalion

[80] *Fromhold;* Historical Branch interview with Col Floyd R. Moore, 1Mar53, hereinafter cited as *Moore.*

boundary running north-south in the center of the island.

LT 1/22 would land on Beach Green 3 at Z-Hour, drive straight across the island and secure that area falling within its zone. It would then be prepared to attack south, being responsible for the eastern sector.

LT 2/22 would land on Beach Green 2 at Z-Hour, secure the portion of island in its zone, thoroughly mop up the northern one-third of Parry and then revert to regimental reserve.

LT 3/22 would land on Beach Green 3 on order and take over the western area in the drive to the south.

The 2d Separate Tank Company (medium) would land in the 4th wave, attack enemy defenses in the northern portion of Parry and prepare to support the attack to the south.

Major James L. Rogers' 708th Provisional Amphibian Tractor Battalion would once again take the troops ashore and support the landing in the same formation as was used at both Engebi and Eniwetok Islands.

Other organizations which would be prepared to land on order included Company C, 766th Light Tank Battalion (RCT 106), V Amphibious Corps Reconnaissance Company, Company D (Scout) of the 4th Tank Battalion, and a Provisional Landing Force consisting of five provisional companies organized within the 10th Defense Battalion (Marine).[81] Ticketed for Group reserve was BLT 106–3, which would be reembarked from Eniwetok the morning of 22 February.

One aspect of preparing for the Parry assault was the diligent search among the ships for hand grenades, demolition charges, and small arms.[82] These were now in short supply, as were artillery shells. Some grenades and demolitions were found, but it was necessary to fly in an additional 775 grenades and 1,500 demolition caps from Kwajalein. A number of BAR's and rifles were acquired from RCT 106 to make up deficiencies in RCT 22, and artillerymen were directed to reduce planned harassing fires.

At 2100 on D-plus 4 Colonel Walker reported to General Watson that his men were transferred to the LVT-bearing LST's and "all preparations for the attack on HEART-STRINGS Island on 22 February [are] complete."

While the Marines prepared for their landings on Parry, Warrant Officer Shionoya and his comrades on that island were impatiently awaiting the assault.[83] On the morning that the 22d Marines went into Engebi, the Japanese warrant officer wrote:

We thought they would land this morning, but there was only a continuation of their bombardment and no landing. As this was contrary to our expectations, we were rather disappointed.

The next morning preparations were underway for the landing on Eniwetok. To the defenders of Parry it seemed that they would be the target that day, and once more Shionoya recorded his reactions:

When I looked out to sea there were four transports and three destroyers lined up. That surely made me angry. At 0540 the enemy was in the midst of preparations for landing. Each unit got orders to prepare for battle and fell to its respective position. . . .[84]

On the basis of resistance encountered on Eniwetok Island, Admiral Hill decided to intensify the naval bombardment of Parry. On D-plus 3 (20 February), *Tennessee* and *Pennsylvania* lay a mere 850 yards off the island and "conducted a close, destructive enfilade bombardment."[85] The next day *Pennsylvania* delivered plunging main battery fire from 0740 to 1630, and both battleships repeated this from 1730 to 1900. That night the 2d Separate Pack Howitzer Battalion on Japtan Island and the 104th Field Artillery Battalion on Eniwetok

[81] 10th Defense Battalion (Marine) Operation Order 4-44, 21Feb44. This provisional group was not landed. The battalion operations officer later recalled, "enthusiasm ran high among the troops and there was much grumbling when, on the morning of the scheduled landing, the men were ordered to secure." Ltr Col Paul A. Fitzgerald to CMC, 12Mar53.

[82] "One of the basic reasons for shortage of grenades, equipment and workable weapons was because of the fact that casualties [on Engebi and Eniwetok] were not stripped of their equipment, weapons and ammunition prior to evacuation. A great proportion of this equipment, etc., was later found to be in the hands of ships' companies and was recovered. . . ." *Lanigan*.

[83] Whether Shionoya survived until the day Parry was assaulted is a moot question. The final entry in his diary is dated 19Feb44.

[84] *Shionoya.*

[85] *TU 51.17.2 AR*, 4.

placed harassing fire on Parry, as did four destroyers.

At 0600 on D-plus 5 (22 February) the two artillery battalions stepped up their harassing fire to preparatory strength, the Marine cannoneers augmenting their howitzer fire with bullets from sixteen .50 caliber machine guns.[86] At 0700 the Navy joined in with a full scale bombardment from *Tennessee, Pennsylvania, Louisville, Indianapolis,* and *Hailey.* At 0845 the first wave of Marines left the line of departure and headed for Beaches Green 2 and 3, accompanied by LVT(A)'s and preceded by LCI's. A string of buoys had been set up from the line of departure to within 500 yards of the beach to indicate the division between landing teams during the approach.[87] But the smoke and dust generated by the bombardment of Parry rolled out over the choppy water, curtailing vision and making the buoys little help. Moreover, as the LVT's butted their way toward shore, they were guided toward the original landing beaches rather than toward the ones newly established 300 yards northward.[88]

The LCI(G)'s supporting the right flank approached shore and began firing their 40mm batteries, when suddenly all three craft were struck by 5-inch fire from *Hailey,* apparently because they were further south than had been expected. The acting-gunboats lost 13 men killed and 46 wounded, as well as receiving extensive damage, but nevertheless they fired their rockets before retiring from the scene.[89]

On the 22d RCT's right flank, the first wave of LT 1/22 hit the beach at 0900 just south of VALENTINE Pier, some 300 yards south of its scheduled landing position; the second wave followed at 0908, landing 200 yards north of

the pier, and the third wave came in three minutes later, debarking in the gap between the first and second waves.[90] Units were intermingled on the beach, and as at Namur junior officers and noncommissioned officers used their initiative.

During hand-to-hand encounters in the shell holes which pockmarked the beach, officers and non-coms rose splendidly to the task of reorganizing confused men who were separated from their units and leaders.[91]

The Marines under Lieutenant Colonel Fromhold were meeting stiff resistance from intense Japanese machine-gun and mortar fire, and casualties on the beach were described as "fairly heavy."

It is well to note here that when landing on an enemy-held island, it is often difficult, if not virtually impossible, to determine whether the landing has been made on the correct beaches. Unless something is obviously wrong, it is generally assumed that the landing has been correctly performed. This was the case of both assault landing teams at Parry. Initially they were under the impression that they had landed some 300 yards north of where they actually were.[92]

In the combat teams' northern zone, Landing Team 2/22 hit the beach on schedule and in contact with the unit on its right. Thus, it too was some 300 yards south of its landing beach and accordingly had a greater area of responsibility than originally planned. Initially, resistance was light, but some men on the left flank were killed by an enemy mine field.[93] Lieutenant Colonel Hart's battalion began pushing across the island with Companies G, F, and E from left to right. The landing team moved roughly as a line, the left flank attempting to move along the northwestern and northern shore line, while the right flank remained in contact with Landing Team 1/22 to the south. As had been the case on Engebi, there was no organized Japanese resistance, only fanatical

---

[86] The artillerymen had 20 units of fire for these weapons. Ltr LtCol Alfred M. Mahoney to CMC, 25Mar53, hereinafter cited as *Mahoney.*

[87] Whether these buoys marked the old or new beach designations is not known.

[88] A possible factor in the confusion regarding the landing beaches was that the smaller, or northern pier, was destroyed by naval gunfire. Thus the only pier visible was VALENTINE Pier. *Martin.*

[89] At about the same time a spotter plane carrying the Marine artillery aerial observer flew too low and into the artillery barrage. It burst into flames and crashed.

[90] The components of each wave are unknown to the author. Inasmuch as the landing units were intermingled and based on available records, it is assumed for the purpose of this narrative that LT 1/22's line included Companies A, C, and B, from right to left.

[91] *Fromhold.*

[92] *Ibid.*

[93] *Reinhardt.*

defenders in isolated groups who had to be rooted from their spider traps and individual strong points.

The intensive fires placed on Landing Team 1/22 were not limited to the Marines ashore. Thirty minutes after the first wave of Marines touched the beach, Japanese mortar and machine gun fire grew so severe that both the *Pennsylvania* and the control vessel (*SC 1066*) had to shift position, the latter not regaining her original station until 1500.[94]

Meanwhile, assault elements of Companies B and C had knifed their way across to the ocean (eastern) beach of Parry within an hour after the landing,[95] but not in sufficient force adequately to clear the intervening ground. The bulk of Landing Team 1/22 was continuing to fight its way across, ably assisted by tanks of the 2d Separate Tank Company which had landed in the fourth wave. A short distance off the beach, three Japanese tanks had been emplaced to resist invasion, and these vehicles had remained in position until the Marine medium tanks came ashore. For reasons best known to the enemy, his light armor thereupon emerged from the emplacements and attempted to give battle to the Marine tanks, with disastrous results to the Japanese and no damage to the Marine armor.[96]

As enemy resistance increased, particularly from what were believed to be several 75mm guns on the right flank, Lieutenant Colonel Fromhold requested naval gunfire. As noted earlier, the landing team commander was under the impression he was considerably north of his actual position, and what occurred was subsequently recalled by him:

[Naval gunfire] was requested on the basis that troops had landed where planned, as the much bombarded pier and building foundations indicated. This request was denied by higher channels who, through air spot, had knowledge that the troops had been outside the planned area and would be endangered by this fire. However, a direct request from a naval liaison team spotter did get through. Five salvos were furnished as requested. . . . The Naval gunfire struck some

TANKS AND INFANTRY worked together to secure Parry in one day.

of our medium tanks . . . [and] also partially landed among our own troops. . . . Less than 10 of our troops were lost by this fire, whereas the Japs suffered heavily both in men and field pieces. . . .[97]

Captain Harry Calcutt, the tank commander, made his own caustic comments regarding the naval salvos:

Five-inch guns will penetrate the two-inch armor of medium tanks and generally raise hell with them. We would appreciate it if they would call their gunfire somewhere else, especially when we are forced to hold the tanks static in the gunfire in order to cover the infantry in the same area in an attempt to silence what we thought to be enemy opposition.[98]

The naval gunfire apparently broke the back of enemy resistance, for after it had ended the landing team, assisted by the tanks, moved forward with relative ease and rapidity. As the Marines reached the opposite shore shortly after 1100, between 150 and 200 heavily armed Japanese were seen moving along in column. Evidently they were caught by surprise and were able to put up only token resistance before being eliminated.

In the northern portion of Parry, Lieutenant Colonel Hart's Landing Team 2 had pushed to

[94] Transport Division 30, Action Report—Amphibious Phase of Eniwetok and Parry Islands, Eniwetok Atoll, 6Mar44, 5.

[95] Ltr LtCol Charles F. Widdecke to CMC, 10Mar53.

[96] *Scott.*

[97] *Fromhold.*

[98] 2d Separate Tank Company, Report on DOWNSIDE Operation, 26Feb44.

HEARTS CIRCLE, a cleared mound in the center of the unit's zone. Here Company H [99] placed all of its machine guns on line to provide overhead fire for the advancing troops. While this was in progress a hidden ammunition dump exploded under the machine gunners, wounding six men and eliminating a section of guns.[100] But this did not hamper the landing team's progress.

Landing Team 3/22, regimental reserve, was originally scheduled to land on Beach Green 3, but as it was dispatched from the line of departure at 0945, its destination was changed to Beach Green 2. Because Landing Team 2 had gone ashore south of its prescribed beach, the reserve battalion now landed north of all assault units at 1000, receiving "heavy machine-gun, rifle and mortar fire."[101] Moreover, a portion of the unit landed in a mine field and incurred several casualties.

Company I, reinforced by a platoon from Company K, neutralized the enemy positions on the beach, and Major Shisler directed his command south to ADONIS Road, where Company I relieved Company A at 1100. The latter unit thereupon reverted to reserve for Landing Team 1/22.

The 22d Marines' command post was estab-

[99] *Lanigan.*
[100] *Ibid.*
[101] *BLT 3/22 SAR,* 4.

lished just off Green Beach 2 at 1145, Colonel Walker having gone ashore an hour earlier. At noon General Watson ordered V Amphibious Corps Reconnaissance Company ashore to reinforce LT 2/22, and 45 minutes later directed Company D (Scout) to land and assist LT 1/22.

Landing Team 2/22 continued to press its attack northward and eastward, assisted by RCT 106's light tanks which had landed at 1100. Captain Jones' Reconnaissance Company was evenly divided between Companies E and F, providing about 55 additional men to each rifle company, and with this added strength the 2d Battalion pushed on across the island.[102] The northern portion of Parry was reported secure at 1400, but mopping up continued to engage the unit's attention until reembarkation.

Shortly after 1300, Landing Teams 1/22 and 3/22 were poised on the 0–1 line, ready to advance southward. This boundary was the line secured across the island by Lieutenant Colonel Fromhold's organization. Originally, of course, it had been drawn on the maps considerably north of its present position, but now it lay just south of VALENTINE Pier.

Landing Team 1 occupied the eastern half (left sector) of the jumpoff line, Companies B and C on the left and right, respectively. Both

[102] "We needed some extra zip to complete the job." *Lanigan.*

MARINES FOUGHT THEIR WAY through shattered coconut groves which the Japanese had filled with spider traps and log emplacements.

front-line units were reinforced by one platoon each from Company A, the remainder of that organization acting as battalion reserve. Responsibility for the western half (right sector) of the island lay with Landing Team 3/22, which would move forward in column of companies, Company I leading the attack, Company L mopping up, and Company K in reserve.[103]

Following a 15-minute artillery preparation, the two landing teams began their southward movement at 1330, the 2d Separate Tank Company moving in support shortly thereafter. It was the same story as before, the enemy putting up a static defense from spider traps and other subsurface positions. Landing Team 1/22 was reinforced by Company D (Scout) of the 4th Tank Battalion at 1422, the scouts joining with Company A (less two platoons) in the mission of mopping up and landing team reserve.

We were closely supported by medium tanks which, while moving very slowly, fired their machine guns at random and occasionally let go with their 75's. When the tanks had exhausted their ammunition the advance would halt, the tanks would leave to resupply, a 60mm mortar barrage would be brought down close to the front, a 75mm pack howitzer barrage would be laid down beyond the mortar barrage, half-tracks [104] and DUKW's would bring forward more supplies for the infantry.[105]

The advancing Marines had covered some 350 yards when Company I encountered an enemy strong point consisting of underground barracks and extensive tunnels.[106] All tanks in both landing team areas were quickly dispatched to Company I's assistance, and after a short, fierce fight the enemy positions were overrun.

Artillery was active all during the afternoon, combining with naval gunfire in shelling the southern portion of the island and softening

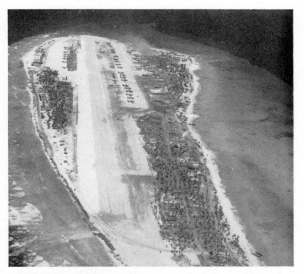

A 7,000-FOOT BOMBER STRIP was created on Eniwetok Island. (Air Force photo.)

the way for the advancing troops.[107] Additional support was provided by RCT 106's light tanks which moved southward after they were no longer needed by Landing Team 2 in the north.

After Company I's successful reduction of the Japanese strong point, the attack progressed with increasing velocity. Principal resistance came from Japanese in the heavy brush on Landing Team 1's left flank. By nightfall the two landing teams were some 450 yards from the southernmost tip of Parry (SLUMBER Point). Here the intervening ground narrowed to such an extent that there was danger of troops firing into each other if the advance were pushed, so the landing teams were directed to dig in for the night.

With a small area remaining to be covered, Colonel Walker considered Parry in his hands. Its possession meant the successful completion of the Eniwetok operation, and a general feeling of pleasure and satisfaction was reflected in the various radio messages that followed.

Colonel Walker started the ball rolling. He radioed General Watson: "I present you with Parry at 1930. Request this unit be relieved

[103] *Shisler.*

[104] "The battalion commanders' lack of mobile logistic support prompted them to use the attached half-track platoons to haul supplies and wounded. Also, as I recall, the tank company commander made repeated recommendations against the use of half-tracks in any zone which he was to work." Ltr LtCol Cecil D. Ferguson to CMC, 9Mar53.

[105] *Scott.*

[106] *Moore; McCabe.*

[107] ". . . [Army] artillery was firing directly at the troops who were advancing southward on Parry. This firing was handled most capably by a young Army captain who was liaison officer with the 22d Marines. . . ." Ltr BrigGen M. F. Schneider to CMC, 9Mar53.

ENGEBI'S AIRSTRIP was improved by the Seabees and taken over by the 4th Marine Air Wing.

for reembarkation in the morning." To which General Watson replied, "Well done, Johnny. My sincere congratulations to the 22d Marines and their supporting units. You have done a magnificent job."

The last congratulatory message of the night was sent to all units from General Watson at 2000: "With the capture of Parry at 1930 today, Eniwetok Atoll is now in our possession. My sincere congratulations to the officers and men of this group whose aggressive spirit and combat efficiency made the capture of this atoll possible. Well done."

CATCHPOLE CONCLUDED

The night of 22–23 February on Parry Island could hardly be described as "quiet" in the accepted sense of the word. Under the circumstances, however, it was a quiet night. There were no organized attacks against the Americans, but Japanese as individuals and in small groups emerged from camouflaged holes bypassed during the day and used rifles and grenades against the invaders. This was futile business at best. Naval vessels in the lagoon fired 5-inch star shells over the island all night, marking the first time in the Pacific that continuous illumination was provided.[108]

Enemy activity . . . during the night was light, and our casualties were few. The relatively peaceful night can be attributed to several things. Great care had been taken during the day to thoroughly mop up and remove ordnance and munitions from the areas covered by the assault units. Thus, any surviving enemy troops did not have loose weapons readily available to them. The star shells fired by the naval guns were invaluable. . . . The battalion night S. O. P. proved sound, and the troops followed it well—demonstrating the fact that they were seasoned troops.[109]

On the morning of D-plus 6 (23 February) elements of Landing Teams 1 and 3, Company D (Scout), and tanks of the 2d Separate Tank Company jumped off from the defense line of the night before. Enemy opposition was light between the jumpoff and SLUMBER Point, the Marines declaring the area secure shortly after 0900. But mopping-up operations continued.

---

[108] "Based on our experience at Tarawa and the known tactics of the Japs in regard to night infiltration and counterattack, we decided . . . that we would utilize 5-inch star shells from our Force to keep the island . . . under continuous illumination. . . . This was the first time that such a procedure had been developed, and as I watched the demand for them grow during succeeding operations . . . I always looked back on this with a great deal of satisfaction. . . ." *Hill II.*

[109] *BLT 1 Rpt.*

At 1045 the American flag was raised over Parry, indicating that the atoll, as well as the island, was in American hands.

The next few days were filled with the arrival, departure, and shifting of troops, debarkation and reembarkation, unloading and loading. The 10th Defense Battalion (Marine) had been released from its reserve status 22 February, and the next day began unloading at Eniwetok, assuming responsibility for that island on 25 February.

BLT 106–3, which had remained in floating reserve for Parry, was landed on the island 23 February and began policing and mopping up. Colonel Walker reembarked his Landing Team 2 and the 2d Separate Tank Company that day, followed by the remainder of the exhausted RCT 22 on 24 February. The next day the 22d Marines, reinforced, departed Eniwetok for Kwajalein, where it relieved the 25th Marines.[110] Various attached units were ordered to Hawaii at the same time. Of the assault force that had arrived at Eniwetok on 17 February, only RCT 106 (less BLT 106–2) remained. On 2 March it left the operational control of Tactical Group-1 and became a part of the Eniwetok Atoll garrison force.

General Watson departed Eniwetok by air on 3 March, arriving at Pearl Harbor the following day. And on 22 March Tactical Group-1 was disbanded.[111]

The combat elements assigned to Tactical Group-1 had been floating reserve for the Kwajalein operation, and on extremely short notice had gone in to take Eniwetok Atoll. They had entered Eniwetok's lagoon as men untried in combat,[112] but they performed like veterans in seizing their objectives. As added evidence for this view, the 22d Marines and virtually all the attached units were awarded the Navy Unit Commendation.

Marine and Army troops went into Eniwetok outnumbering the defenders roughly three-to-one. At the end of five days of intensive combat some 3,400 Japanese were buried and the Americans held the atoll. Statistically, the Marines lost 254 dead and 555 wounded. RCT 106 (less BLT 106–2) casualties numbered 94 dead and 311 wounded.[113] The figures by themselves are not representative. RCT 22 took both Engebi and Parry. RCT 106 (less BLT 106–2) assaulted only Eniwetok, and then it was reinforced by a tank company and a landing team from RCT 22. Thus, any comparison between Marine and Army casualty figures for the over-all operation must take into account the amount of combat experienced by the respective units as well as the number of troops involved.

After training in the Samoan area for some 18 months, the 22d Marines, reinforced, had at last experienced combat and was now a blooded regiment, as it capably demonstrated later at Guam and Okinawa.

In deciding to proceed ahead of schedule with the Eniwetok operation, Navy and Marine commanders had greatly advanced the war effort. Now the 2d Marine Division and the remainder of the 27th Infantry Division were free for other operations and would not be held down by the Marshalls. Eniwetok was secure in February instead of May. Admiral Nimitz was able to move up the target date for the Marianas by at least 20 weeks.[114] And Truk was revealed as being incapable of operations against U. S. forces.

---

[110] As noted in Chapter VII. Activities of RCT 22 after effecting this relief will be treated in Chapter IX.

[111] V Amphibious Corps General Order 51–44, 22Mar44.

[112] With the exception of the 708th Provisional Amphibian Tractor Company, VAC Reconnaissance Company, and Company D (Scout), 4th Tank Battalion.

[113] Marine casualty figures from Personnel Accounting Section, Records Branch, Personnel Department, HQMC, 1Aug52. RCT 106 casualty figures from *RCT 106 Rpt*, 15Apr44.

[114] *Isely and Crowl*, 303.

CHAPTER IX   Mopping Up the Marshalls[1]

FLINTLOCK, JR. BEGINS

The 22d Marines arrived at Kwajalein Atoll on 26 February 1944 and began the relief of Colonel Cumming's 25th Marines, that 4th Marine Division unit having remained as a temporary garrison force. By 5 March Colonel Walker's command was disposed as follows: 1st Battalion, Bigej Island; 2d Battalion, Roi-Namur; 3d Battalion on Edgigen, and the remainder of the regiment on Ennubirr and Obella Islands, with the regimental command post on Ennubirr. The 2d Separate Pack Howitzer Battalion relieved 1st Battalion, 14th Marines, on Edgigen,[2] but Company A, 10th Amphibian

---

[1] Unless otherwise indicated, this chapter is a synthesis of the following sources: 22d Marines Report of Operations into Lesser Marshalls, 6Apr44; Maj Paul H. Bird, "Atoll Hopping—The Lesser Marshalls," an undated report dealing with the 22d Marines in the Lesser Marshalls hereinafter cited as *Atoll Hopping;* Atoll Commander, Report of Occupation of Wotho, Ujae and Lae Atolls, 28Mar44; Atoll Commander, Report of Occupation of Ailinglapalap and Namu, 2Apr44; Atoll Commander, Report of Occupation of Ebon and Namorik Atolls and Kili Island, undated; Atoll Commander, Report of Occupation of Ailuk Atoll, Mejit Island, Jemo Island and Likiep Atoll, 12Apr44; Atoll Commander, Report of Occupation of Bikini, Ailinginae, Rongelap, Rongerik, Utirik, Bikar and Taka Atolls, 14Apr44; *Campaign; Sherrod.*

[2] "This consisted of a relief in place to continue the defense. . . . During this relief the pack howitzers of [1/14] were left in place and exchanged for those of

Tractor Battalion, was directed to remain at Kwajalein and work with the 22d Marines.

But if the tired victors of Eniwetok thought that they would merely occupy Kwajalein Atoll, this illusion was quickly dispelled. On 1 March Rear Admiral Alva D. Bernhard, Atoll Commander, received orders to neutralize and control the Lesser Marshalls, consisting of those atolls and islands thought to be undefended or lightly held. Specifically, the admiral was directed to:

1. Destroy Japanese installations or materials which might be of benefit to their submarines, aircraft or surface forces.
2. Make prisoner Japanese or suspicious natives.
3. Instruct the natives in the war situation and their changed sovereignty.
4. Assist them in any way practicable economically, and establish relations of friendliness and good will.

Admiral Bernhard and Colonel Walker set up a joint staff to direct the Lesser Marshalls campaign, which was dubbed FLINTLOCK, JR. Five areas of operations were established:

1. West Group (Wotho, Ujae, and Lae Atolls).
2. South Group (Namu, Ailinglapalap,

---

the 2d SepPkHowBn. Such procedure is often recommended but seldom accomplished." *Mahoney.*

Namorik, Ebon Atolls, and Kili Island.)
3. North Group (Bikini, Rongelap, Ailing-inae, and Rongerik Atolls).
4. Northeast Group (Bikar, Utirik, Taka, Ailuk, Likiep Atolls, Jemo and Mejit Islands).
5. Separate (Lib Island).

Each atoll and island was reconnoitered by low-level PBY flights prior to moving troops to the objective, and aerial photographs were delivered to the various naval and troop commanders. The naval force for each operation usually consisted of one LST transporting six to nine LVT's, two LCI's, one destroyer or destroyer escort, and one mine sweeper. Three

SBD's from VMSB–151 [3] were called on to furnish air support.

Inasmuch as native reaction was considered important in the scheduled operations, a flag-raising ceremony was evolved to be carried out whenever this formality took place. One civil affairs report best describes it:

After the proclamation explanation and posting formality, the American flag was raised . . . one platoon at present arms, staff officers at hand salute, natives in a group in the center. A Marine photographer made a picture record of each raising. The ceremony appealed to the natives, and was an aid in inculcating

[3] The squadron at this time was divided into two echelons, one based at Roi, the other at Engebi. The air support mentioned was to be provided from Roi.

THE AMERICAN FLAG was raised on a great many islands of the Lesser Marshalls in the six weeks following the Eniwetok operation.

the idea that they now were under American protection and no longer subject to Japanese rule.[4]

It was further planned that each force of Marines would be augmented by civil affairs officers, medical personnel to examine the natives, interpreters and native scouts from Kwajalein.

On 7 March the first reconnaissance group departed Kwajalein Atoll with the West Group as its objective. The Marines included two reinforced companies from 1st Battalion, under Major Crawford B. Lawton, battalion executive officer.[5] The next morning this force lay off Wotho Atoll where it was learned that the only Japanese at hand numbered 12, the stranded crew of a crashed bomber. On the morning of 9 March 180 Marines landed on Wotho Island without opposition. During the night the 12 Nipponese had fled to a nearby island where they committed suicide when later they were pursued by 1st Platoon, Company C. On Wotho the proclamations were read, the flag raised and the expeditionary group departed, but not before one Marine had been killed by the accidental explosion of a hand grenade.

At Ujae Atoll the following day, Major Lawton learned that only six Japanese were there, the crew of a weather station. Once again 180 Marines landed, and once again the enemy reacted by committing suicide—with one exception. One of the six, not so fervent as his comrades, made a halfhearted attempt at suicide and then permitted himself to be taken prisoner.

Lae Atoll was secured next. No Japanese were found, but the naval officer in charge of the task force noted that "the natives were not as friendly as at the other atolls." This unfriendly attitude was apparently due to an unfortunate event which occurred a few days prior to the Marines' arrival. A hand grenade box containing one grenade floated ashore. The bomb had exploded, killing a child. When the armed troops landed on Lae the natives connected them with the hand grenade and decided that the Marines were in some measure responsible for the child's death.[6] The reconnaissance force returned to Kwajalein, arriving there the evening of 14 March, mission successfully completed.

During the absence of the 1st Battalion group there had been a change in regimental command. On 10 March Colonel Walker was detached to V Amphibious Corps and was succeeded in command by Colonel Merlin F. Schneider, regimental executive officer.

One other reconnaissance took place during the 22d Marines' first two weeks at Kwajalein Atoll. On 11 March a reinforced platoon from the 1st Battalion landed on Lib Island, listed as a separate operation on the schedule. No trace of Japanese was found, natives were assembled and questioned, proclamations read, and at 1130 that day the American flag was raised. The platoon returned to its home base the same day.[7]

SECURE IN THE SOUTH

On 19 March, after a false start the preceding day,[8] two landing forces, each containing about 325 Marines, departed Kwajalein Atoll to clear the South Group. Both forces were taken from the 3d Battalion with Major Shisler and his executive officer, Major William E. Sperling III, the respective commanders. It was planned that the two forces would part company after securing Ailinglapalap Atoll, which objective was reached the morning of 20 March. Native scouts reported some 40 armed Japanese on Ailinglapalap Island, and that afternoon Major Sperling's force landed, followed the next morning by Major Shisler's group.

Company I, reinforced by both a heavy machine-gun platoon and an 81mm mortar platoon, made contact with the enemy the morning of 21 March. The Japanese defense line was entrenched across a narrow portion of the island, and the 81mm mortars began pounding it, the Marines overrunning it in the early afternoon.

[4] Report of Reconnaissance of Wotho, Ujae and Lae Atolls, Chief of Civil Affairs Section, 15Mar44, 1–2.

[5] Atoll Commander, Report of Occupation of Wotho, Ujae and Lae Atolls, 28Mar44.

[6] LtCol Crawford B. Lawton, comments on preliminary script.

[7] Report of Reconnaissance Unit, Landing on Lib Island, 11Mar44, 1–2.

[8] The force originally included an LCT loaded with medium tanks. Upon departing the lagoon on 18Mar44, however, the craft began shipping water and all vessels returned to the lagoon. There it was decided to dispense with the LCT and the tanks.

SEVENTH AIR FORCE B–24 banks toward Wotje during the bombing of the by-passed atolls. (Air Force photo.)

Two Marines were wounded and 39 Nipponese killed,[9] two surviving enemy escaping to other islands in the atoll where they were eventually picked up.

Having overcome this resistance, Major Shisler's force reembarked the afternoon of 21 March and steamed toward Ebon Atoll, the southernmost of the Marshalls. Major Sperling's unit remained to bury the enemy dead, scout the other islands in the atoll[10] and proceed with proclamations and flag-raising formalities.

Ailinglapalap Atoll is the residence of the clan which controls the Ralik (western) chain of islands in the Marshalls, and the civil affairs officers took pains to make clear the new order of things. Chief Jemata, the head of the clan, assured the Marines that his people would adhere to the proclamation notices, and that he looked upon all Americans as friends—as no doubt he had previously looked upon all Japanese.

Major Sperling's group next proceeded to Namu Atoll where native scouts were dispatched to reconnoiter the islands. The scouts duly reported that the Japanese on the atoll consisted of one policeman and one schoolteacher together with his wife and three children. The next day (24 March) the Marine commander sent a surrender note to the Nipponese who quickly gathered on the beach waving white flags. Major Sperling noted that the number of Japanese present was correct "with addition of one child." The seven interned civilians were taken on board ship, and the troops departed, arriving at Kwajalein the next afternoon.

Meanwhile, Major Shisler's command arrived at Ebon Atoll on the morning of 23 March. Native scouts landed, followed shortly by Marines. Only friendly natives were found during the day, but the next morning contact was made with the enemy on Ebon Island. A 20-minute fire fight ensued in which two Marines were killed and 17 armed Japanese wiped out.[11]

---

[9] Included in the enemy armament were several 1903 Springfield rifles, a Browning light machine gun, and two cases of United States hand grenades. *McCabe.*

[10] Seven Japanese civilians were found and taken back to Kwajalein.

[11] The Japanese force consisted of one woman, 11 male civilians, and five soldiers.

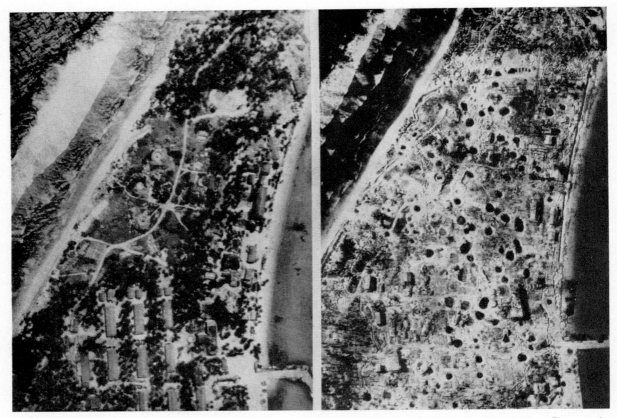

GRAPHIC EVIDENCE of the aerial pounding given the by-passed Japanese strongholds in the Marshalls. Six months intervened between these photographs of Emidj Island, Jaluit Atoll. (Air Force photo.)

Six civilians were picked up at Ebon for internment, and the troops thereupon proceeded to Namorik Atoll and Kili Island. No Japanese were found at either objective. Consequently, the usual formalities were expeditiously accomplished, and the Marines returned to Kwajalein Atoll, arriving there 28 March.

MEJIT, AILUK AND LIKIEP

Two days after Major Shisler's return to Kwajalein, a reinforced company from his 3d Battalion, under Major Earl J. Cook, moved toward the Northeast Group. The entire group was not assigned this force, however. Its objectives were Ailuk, Likiep and Taka Atolls, Jemo and Mejit Islands. Aerial reconnaissance indicated that Jemo and Taka were uninhabited, and inasmuch as native scouts confirmed this, it was decided to by-pass them.

Ailuk was reconnoitered by the Marines on 31 March and 1 April and the usual formalities followed. No Japanese were found, but an important question was settled as far as the natives were concerned.

> On Ailuk the question was raised [by Typhoon, the native chief] as to whether the people could now pray again, and considerable pleasure was expressed when they were assured that they could.[12]

The reconnaissance force stood off Mejit Island on the morning of 2 April, and six LVT's carried the troops ashore. Six Japanese assigned to a naval weather station there were killed resisting the landing.

During reembarkation, however, trouble developed. The LST ramp chains parted, leaving three LVT's still in the water with no way to be loaded on board. Rather than risk the vehicles falling into enemy hands, the naval commander ordered them stripped of equipment and then sunk by gunfire.

On Likiep Atoll, which was reconnoitered on 3 April, no Japanese were located, but the

---

[12] Reconnaissance of Ailuk and Likiep Atolls and Mejit Island, Report of Civil Affairs Section, 7Apr44.

Marines met a plantation owner, Carl F. Hahn, who said he had been an American citizen since 1900. Hahn, a native German, told the Marines he was shipwrecked in the Marshalls in 1891, had married a native woman and had lived there ever since.[13]

With its mission completed, Major Cook's reconnaissance force returned to Roi-Namur, arriving there at 0800 on 5 April.

FINALE IN THE NORTH

While elements of the 3d Battalion were reconnoitering to the south and north, a reinforced company of the 2d Battalion was equally active. On 27 March this unit, under Major Robert P. Felker, 2d Battalion executive officer, stood out to sea with the mission of raising the flag in the North Group and a portion of the Northeast Group. Aerial reconnaissance and native reports indicated that Ailinginae, Rongerik, and Bikar Atolls were uninhabited.

These were ignored, therefore, Major Felker concerning himself with only Bikini, Rongelap, and Utirik Atolls.[14]

From the morning of 28 March until the evening of 30 March the Marines scouted Bikini Atoll. Only five Japanese were found, but they committed suicide instead of resisting or surrendering. The proclamations were read, the flag was raised, and the miniature task force steamed toward Rongelap Atoll. Here the reconnaissance elements paused until 3 April, fruitlessly searching for a reported group of six Japanese soldiers.

Utirik Atoll was reached the morning of 5 April, but the naval commander decided the pass was dangerous and the lagoon "exceptionally full" of coral heads. He thereupon ruled that his vessels could not enter the lagoon. This made it necessary for the Marines to make a seven-mile run in amphibian tractors in order

---

[13] How Hahn could have established American citizenship in 1900 is not disclosed.

[14] Likiep Atoll was originally included in this list, but Adm Bernhard canceled it for Felker's group and turned it over to Maj Cook's force.

MARINE SBD'S such as this one over Majuro helped keep the Japanese "anchored aircraft carriers" ineffective until the war ended.

TWO COMMANDERS of the 4th Marine Air Wing during the tour of duty in the Marshalls were Generals Cushman (left) and Woods.

to land on Utirik Island. Fourteen armed Japanese resisted the invasion, but they were quickly overrun. A motor generator set was blown up, the flag raised, and the troops departed, reaching Kwajalein the next afternoon.

Major Felker's group arrived not a moment too soon, for the 22d Marines were loading transports. "The force [Felker's] . . . tied up alongside APA's and transferred troops just in time to sail with the regiment . . . to another staging area for preparations for further operations against the enemy." [15]

Between 7 March and 6 April 1944, elements of the 22d Marines, reinforced, had established American sovereignty over 12 atolls and three islands of the Lesser Marshalls, a water area of some 60,000 square miles. Thus the American forces fixed grip on what had been Japanese territory only three months earlier. And definitely on the profit side was the experience gained by junior officers in exercising command during actual landing operations.

As noted in Chapter VIII, Tactical Group-1 was disbanded on 22 March. On that same date the 1st Provisional Marine Brigade was organized and the 22d Marines assigned to it. A week later Colonel Schneider was alerted for a move to Guadalcanal, and on 6 April the 22d Marines, together with attached units,[16] departed for the new base.

LAST STAGE

During the month of April, Marine and Army forces reconnoitered three other atolls, the last to be secured in the Marshalls before the end of the war.

On 17 April a force of 199 Marines from the 1st Defense Battalion, VAC, embarked from Majuro on two LCI(L)'s with the mission of reconnoitering Erikub and Aur Atolls. Erikub lies a mere five miles from Wotje, and Aur only ten miles from Maloelap. Despite the proximity of the small atolls to the two formidable Japanese bases, no enemy was found on either. The Marines thereupon returned to Majuro only four days after departing it.[17]

The seizure of Ujelang Atoll, westernmost of the Marshalls, was virtually a repetition of the 22d Marines' landings in the smaller eastern atolls. A reinforced company from 3d Battalion, 111th Infantry, proceeded from Kwajalein 20 April and stood off the tiny atoll the next afternoon. For two days the infantrymen reconnoitered the various islands at Ujelang, killing 18 Japanese in the process. The American flag was raised and the soldiers reembarked, arriving at their home base on 24 April.[18]

---

[16] Included here is the amphibian tractor company. During the period just covered, the 10th Amphibian Tractor Battalion was at Maui and another LVT company there was designated Company A, 10th Amphibian Tractor Battalion. The LVT company then working with the 22d Marines was thereupon redesignated as a unit within the 11th Amphibian Tractor Battalion, then forming, and it sailed to Guadalcanal with the 22d Marines.

[17] War Diary for April 1944, 1st Defense Bn, VAC. Troops from this organization also conducted reconnaissance of Arno Atoll which had been reconnoitered shortly after the occupation of Majuro. No enemy was found on Arno.

[18] Company I, 111th Infantry, Report of Operations, Occupation of Ujelang Atoll, 27Apr44.

---

[15] *Atoll Hopping*, 10.

Remaining in enemy hands were Kusaie Island in the western Marshalls, and Wotje, Maloelap, Mille, and Jaluit Atolls in the east, and the Japanese garrisons of these were left to winter on the vine.[19] (See Map 15, Map Section.) To apply the heat necessary to keep them withered, the 4th Marine Base Defense Air Wing[20] (4th MBDAW) staged into the Marshalls. In mid-February 17 planes of MAG–31 arrived at Dyess Field[21] on Roi,

joining the ground echelon which had arrived a few days earlier. At the newly acquired fleet base of Majuro the Seabees completed an airstrip on 19 February, and the planes of MAG–13 flew in during the next seven days. Aviation elements also followed on the heels of Marine landing forces at Eniwetok Atoll. On 19 February a ground echelon of MAG–22 arrived at Engebi, planes setting down there 10 days later.

The 4th Marine Base Defense Air Wing's campaign against Mille, Maloelap, Jaluit, and Wotje, a campaign that was to continue until Japan's surrender, began on 4 March 1944 when VMSB–331 of MAG–13 conducted a bombing mission against Jaluit. Five days later Brigadier General Lewie G. Merritt, commander of

---

[19] The remainder of this narrative is taken principally from *Campaign; Sherrod.*

[20] The "Base Defense" portion of the Wing's designation was dropped 10Nov44.

[21] Named in honor of LtCol Aquilla J. Dyess, who was posthumously awarded the Medal of Honor for his actions on Namur, as previously noted in Chapter V.

JAPANESE SURRENDER OF MILLE ATOLL, 22 August 1945. Captain Masanori Shiga, IJN (left) and Captain H. B. Grow, USN (right). (Navy photo.)

the 4th MBDAW,[22] established his headquarters at Kwajalein.

Navy carrier planes had flown 1,671 sorties against Wotje, Jaluit, Mille, and Maloelap before the Marine pilots got in on the act. Since the preceding November, Navy and Army planes, principally the bombers of the Seventh Air Force, had struck at the four atolls. The Army planes continued attacking the by-passed targets until the Seventh Air Force moved to Saipan in June 1944, and Navy land-based planes struck at the atolls throughout the remainder of the year.

But the bulk of the dull job of pounding the enemy bases in the Marshalls until the end of the war fell to the Marine pilots.[23] For awhile the Japanese attempted to repair airstrips, just as they continued constructing realistic dummy gun positions. But a shortage of food and supplies, plus the progressive deterioration of morale, eventually put a stop to their efforts. As long as their antiaircraft guns were operational, the Nipponese continued to handle them against attacking planes, sometimes with telling effect.

But strength and time were on the side of the American forces. The Japanese on the by-passed atolls could only sit out the war, concentrating on a struggle for survival. Wotje, Maloelap, Mille, and Jaluit had been considered by the enemy as "unsinkable aircraft carriers," key links in the chain of defenses protecting Japan's eastern perimeter. Strong reinforcements had been rushed to them in order to contain or delay the inexorable American advance across the Pacific. But with war's end, the tattered, starving garrisons could only surrender.

---

[22] Succeeding commanders of the 4thMBDAW while in the Marshalls were BrigGen Thomas J. Cushman, MajGen Louis E. Woods, and BrigGen Lawson H. M. Sanderson.

[23] One pilot subsequently recalled that as he was returning from a mission he spotted two LCI(L)'s which had reconnoitered Aur Atoll and were on the way back to Majuro. Somehow the two vessels made an incorrect turn and were inadvertently heading for

---

Mille. The pilot flew low over the craft, sending them a message in Morse by means of a flashing light. He thus notified them of their error and in all probability saved the lives of the men on board. Capt Ernesto H. Giusti, comments on preliminary script.

APPENDIX I

Bibliography

This bibliography cites only those sources which were particularly important and helpful in compiling the monograph. Literally hundreds of records were consulted. Some duplicated others, and some merely confirmed information already available. Preliminary drafts of the monograph were sent to participants in the operations in order to solicit their comments, corrections, and elaborations. A great many individuals contributed invaluable material, which has been cited in the course of the narrative. Lack of space prevents a separate listing of them here. Letters and interviews are on file in the offices of Historical Branch, G–3 Division, Headquarters Marine Corps, and are available to bona fide students within the limitations of security and restrictions imposed by originators.

DOCUMENTS

CCS 239/1 "Operations in the Pacific and Far East in 1943–44," a JCS paper approved by CCS 21May43. Pertains to plans for operations in the Pacific and Far East during late 1943 and early 1944.

CinCPac–CinCPOA. Dispatch to CominCh, 1Jul43, serial 096. A tentative proposal for operations in the Marshalls, depending on the outcome of photocoverage.

CinCPac-CinCPOA. Operation Plan 16–43, 12Oct43. Serial 00218. Early FLINTLOCK Plan.

CinCPac–CinCPOA. Dispatch to CominCh, 25Oct43, serial 00247, revising Marshalls target date.

CinCPac–CinCPOA. Dispatch to CG, Army Forces, CenPac, 30Oct43, serial 022120. Directs that 106th RCT be made available for the Marshalls operations.

CinCPac–CinCPOA. CATCHPOLE Detail Plan, 29Nov 43. Early plan for seizure of Eniwetok. Serial 00272.

CinCPac–CinCPOA. Base Development Plan, Kwajalein Island, 29Nov43. Serial 001612.

CinCPac-CinCPOA. Dispatch to JCS, 13Dec43, serial 001685, regarding decision to drop Wotje-Maloelap and concentrate on Kwajalein.

CinCPac–CinCPOA. Memorandum Report of Conference held in the Office of CinCPOA, 18Dec43. Pertains to LVT and DUKW program. Discussion of LVT performance in the Tarawa operation and future possibilities.

CinCPac–CinCPOA. FLINTLOCK II, Joint Staff Study, 20Dec43. A staff study based on the assumption of seizing Kwajalein Atoll and neutralizing the more heavily defended atolls.

CinCPac–CinCPOA. FLINTLOCK II, Alternate Joint Staff Study, 23Dec43. A staff study based on the assumption of seizing Wotje and and Maloelap Atolls and neutralizing other atolls.

CinCPac–CinCPOA. Base Development Plan, Majuro Atoll, 2Jan44. Serial 000201.

CinCPac–CinCPOA. Operations in the Pacific Ocean Areas, December 1943. Serial 001035, 31Mar44. Naval operations in the Pacific during this period.

CinCPac–CinCPOA. Bulletin 126–44. A Guide to the Western Pacific. An island-by-island study of the Pacific.

JICPOA Bulletin 53–43, "Kwajalein," 1Dec43.

JICPOA Bulletin 3–44, 20Jan44. A study of Eniwetok Atoll.

JICPOA Bulletin 46–44, 15Apr44. An analysis of base installations found on Roi, Namur, and Ennubirr Islands. Accompanied by maps and photographs.

JICPOA Bulletin 48–44, Japanese Defenses, Kwajalein Atoll, 10Apr44.

JICPOA Bulletin 88–44, 1st Amphibious Brigade, Japanese Army. A study of the brigade from its organization through its defense of Eniwetok Atoll.

JICPOA Bulletin 89–44, 12Jun44. Information compiled from captured documents and prisoners-of-war interrogations pertaining to the Japanese defense plans for Eniwetok Atoll.

JICPOA Item 7005, Translation of Diary of Warrant Officer Shionoya, a member of the 3d Battalion, 1st Amphibious Brigade.

CenPacForce. Capture of the Marshalls, Outline Plan, 1Oct43, Serial 0053. Includes dispatch from CinCPac–CinCPOA to CominCh, 20Aug43, and from CinCPac–CinCPOA to ComCenPacForce, 22Sept43.

CenPacForce. Operation Plan Cen 1–44, 6Jan44. Adm Spruance's plan for seizure of Kwajalein and Majuro Atolls.

CenPacForce. War Diary, December 1943. Serial 0082, 27Feb44. A day-by-day account of activities of the Central Pacific Force during the period covered.

CenPacForce. War Diary, January 1944. Serial 0095, 1Mar44. A day-by-day account of activities of the Central Pacific Force during the period covered.

Task Force 51. Operation Plan A6–43, 17Jan44. Admiral Turner's operation plan for Kwajalein Atoll. Includes appropriate annexes.

Task Force 51. Operation Plan A9–44, 7Feb44. A detailed operation plan for the Eniwetok Expeditionary Group (Task Group 51.11) was signed by RAdm R. K. Turner.

Task Force 51. Report of Amphibious Operations for the capture of the Marshall Islands (FLINTLOCK and CATCHPOLE Operations), 25Feb44. A detailed report containing 11 enclosures, including a narrative of operations, intelligence, troop landings, beach and shore parties, naval and air bombardment, support aircraft, communications, LVT's and DUKW's, medical, ship loading and recommendations.

Task Force 52. Attack Order A1–44, 14Jan44. Contains appropriate annexes and maps for the attack on southern Kwajalein.

Task Force 53. Operation Order A157–44, 16Jan44. Includes Movement Order A156–44, 11Jan44, together with appropriate annexes, maps and charts for operations against northern Kwajalein.

Task Force 53. Report of Amphibious Operations for the capture of Roi and Namur Islands (FLINTLOCK), 23Feb44. Report of Commander, Group 3, Fifth Amphibious Force. Includes nine enclosures containing operations narrative, and comments on naval gunfire, air support, communications, intelligence, material, logistics, loading and unloading, casualties.

Task Group 50.15. Action Report, Marshall Islands Campaign, 15Feb44. Comments and summary of events for the period 29Jan–3Feb44.

Task Group 51.11. Report of Eniwetok Operation, 7Mar44. A comprehensive report of the Eniwetok Operation signed by RAdm Hill. It is divided into seven separate parts and deals with planning, conduct of the operation and unloading after combat was concluded.

Task Group 51.2. Majuro Action Report, 15Feb44. Detailed report of the Majuro operation. Includes composition of forces, narrative, training and rehearsal, air and fire support narratives.

Task Group 58.2. Action Report of Marshall Islands Operation, 25Feb44. Narrative and chronological account of the organization's participation in the Kwajalein operation. Includes three enclosures.

Task Unit 52.5.1. Operation Report, FLINTLOCK, undated. Transport Division 4's summary and comments pertaining to training for the Kwajalein operation and conduct of operations.

Task Unit 53.5.5. Action Report on the Attack, Capture and Occupation of Kwajalein Atoll, 9Feb44. Chronological account of the bombardment of the islands of northern Kwajalein, 30Jan–1Feb44.

Task Unit 58.2.2. Action Report of Bombardment of of Roi-Namur Islands, 3Feb44. Account of battleship and destroyer bombardment of Roi-Namur, 30Jan44.

Battleship Division Two. Action Report of Bombardment of Eniwetok Atoll, 28Feb44. A 19-page report containing a narrative of events, bombardment plan for Eniwetok, and two track charts of the flagship during the Eniwetok operation.

V Amphibious Corps. G–5 Estimate of the Situation, FLINTLOCK Operation, 21Oct43. Discussion of various proposed courses of action in the Marshalls.

V Amphibious Corps. G–2 Study of the Theater of Operations: Marshall Islands, 26Nov43. A detailed terrain study of Mille, Maloelap, Wotje, Jaluit, Kwajalein, and Majuro Atolls. Includes maps and annexes.

V Amphibious Corps. Memorandum to Chief of Staff, 29Dec43. Report of conference with Cdr Dodge, USS *Seal*. Attached is report by USS *Seal* of photographic reconnaissance of Kwajalein Atoll.

V Amphibious Corps. Estimate of Japanese Troops and Defense Organizations, CARILLON Atoll, 17Jan44. A study of enemy potentialities on the islands to be invaded in Kwajalein Atoll. Includes maps and overlays. Signed by LtCol St. Julien R. Marshall.

V Amphibious Corps. G–1 Journal. Résumé of messages received and sent during the period 17Jan–7Feb44.

V Amphibious Corps. G–2 Journal. Covers period 17Jan–7Feb44.

V Amphibious Corps. G–3 Journal. Résumé of dispatches and messages received and sent from 22Jan44 through 7Feb44.

V Amphibious Corps. Study of Japanese Defensive Works, Kwajalein Atoll, 15Feb44. A 61-page detailed report containing maps and photographs of Japanese defenses at Kwajalein. Signed by LtCol A. Vincent Wilson, CE, USA.

V Amphibious Corps. Operations Report of the FLINTLOCK Operation, 6Mar44. A comprehensive report of the Kwajalein operation. Contains narrative report of operations and nine annexes. These are: Corps Operation Plan 1–44; G–5 Report; G–3 Report; G–2 Report; G–1 Report; G–4 Report; Liaison Team Report; Special Staff Officers' Report; Reconnaissance Company Report.

V Amphibious Corps. Report of Logistical Aspects of FLINTLOCK Operation, 23Mar44. A 15-page report signed by MajGen H. M. Smith. It discusses all VAC logistical matters pertaining to the Kwajalein operation.

V Amphibious Corps. Special Action Report CATCHPOLE Operation, 1Apr44. Includes comments of MajGen H. M. Smith, Commanding General, VAC, pertaining to Tactical Group-1's Special Report; Naval Gunfire Report on CATCHPOLE; 70sth Amphibian Tank Bn, Special Action Report on Eniwetok Operation; Final Report of Civil Affairs, Eniwetok Atoll.

V Amphibious Corps. Miscellaneous Orders and Plans. Folder containing miscellaneous orders, plans, memoranda, maps, and charts. Majority of the material pertains to Eniwetok.

V Amphibious Corps. Units and Ships Upon Which Embarked, FLINTLOCK, undated. Breakdown of ships with units embarked including unit strength and preferred and alternate loading plans.

V Amphibious Corps. War Diary, Jan44, 4Feb44. Contains list of VAC components as well as all orders issued during the month. Narrative of VAC activities during the period covered is included.

V Amphibious Corps. War Diary, Feb44, 5Mar44. A narrative of VAC activities during February 1944. Includes a list of all VAC orders issued during the month. Signed by MajGen H. M. Smith.

V Amphibious Corps. War Diary, Mar44, 8Apr44. Contains list of VAC components as well as copies of all orders issued during the period. A narrative of events is included.

4th Marine Division. Operation Plan 3–43 (revised), 31Dec43. Sets forth the mission of the Northern Landing Force in the Kwajalein operation, and how it is to be effected. Contains appropriate annexes and maps.

4th Marine Division. Journal. Contains a résumé of all messages sent and received by the division from 31Jan44 through 2Feb44 and an operational narrative covering the period 13Jan44 through 2Feb44.

4th Marine Division. Final Report on FLINTLOCK Operation, 17Mar44. A comprehensive report of the division's participation in the Kwajalein operation. Includes division organization and training, preliminary planning and conduct of operations. Ten enclosures include narrative of operations; extracts from the division journal; Report of Commanding General, IVAN Landing Group; CT 23 Report; CT 24 Report; CT 25 Report; 14th Marines Report; 20th Marines Report; Medical report; comments.

4th Marine Division. Communications—Operations Report, 29Mar44. Enclosures include report of Landing Team 1, 24th CT; letter from Commanding Officer, CT 24; letter from Commanding Officer, CT 23; Reports of the 1st, 2d and 3d Bns, 25th Marines.

4th Marine Division. War Diary, Mar44–23Apr44. A day-by-day account of the division's activities during March. Contains a station list and combat readiness report.

4th Marine Division. Record of Events, 5May44. Day-by-day account of division activities from 13Jan44 through 8Feb44.

4th Marine Division. Intelligence Report on FLINTLOCK, undated. A collection of nine intelligence summaries, 31Jan–12Feb44, as well as POW interrogations, Japanese defense plan for Roi-Namur, and a D–2 analysis of the conduct of the Japanese defense.

20th Marines. Bomb Disposal Unit 1 Report of Activities in the FLINTLOCK Operation, 27Apr44. Report accompanied by 12 photographs.

23d Marines. Journal. Résumé of messages sent and received during the period 31Jan–4Feb44.

Landing Team 1, 23d Marines. Report on the FLINTLOCK Operation, 10Feb44. Bn commander's report of his organization's assault on Roi. Attached are reports by the Bn executive officer and each staff section.

2d Battalion, 23d Marines. Comments on Landing Operations on Roi-Namur, 14Feb44. Contains a narrative of operations, record of events, comments and recommendations. Attached are reports from the Bn commander and executive officer, each staff section, each company commander and each attached unit commander. Also sketches of Japanese defenses.

3d Battalion, 23d Marines. Record of Events, 12Feb44. Comments and recommendations of the Bn commander and executive officer and each staff section during the period 31Jan–5Feb44. Includes overlays and sketches.

1st Battalion, 24th Marines. Preliminary Report of Operations on Namur, 8Feb44.

2d Battalion, 24th Marines. Narrative, Battle of Roi-Namur, undated. Brief account of the Bn's participation in the assault on Namur.

2d Battalion, 24th Marines. Preliminary report of operations on Namur, 7Feb44.

3d Battalion, 24th Marines. Undated and incomplete report of operations on Namur.

Landing Team 1, 25th Marines. Report of Activities on D-Day and D-plus 1, 16Feb44. Narrative, followed by questions and answers pertaining to the Kwajalein operation.

Landing Team 2, 25th Marines. Report of Activities, 20Feb44. Chronological account of the Bn's activities on 31Jan–1Feb44.

Landing Team 3, 25th Marines. Report on D-Day and D-plus 1, 9Feb44. Brief account of the Bn's activities during the Kwajalein operation.

Landing Team 3, 25th Marines. History. A mimeographed paper, source not indicated, covering the period 11Jan–8Mar44.

4th Tank Battalion. Report of Activities in the FLINTLOCK Operation, 31Mar44. Contains summary of activities, comments and recommendations as well as combat reports by each platoon.

10th Amphibian Tractor Battalion. Report on Operations, FLINTLOCK Operation, 17Mar44. An analysis of the unit's activities during its organization, training and combat operations. Contains individual reports from each company, as well as an earlier Bn action report dated 17Feb44.

1st Joint Assault Signal Company. Report of Commanding Officer on the FLINTLOCK Operation, 6Mar44. Attached are individual reports from each liaison team. Carries endorsements by MajGen Schmidt and MajGen Smith.

7th Infantry Division. Report of Participation in the FLINTLOCK Operation, 8Feb44. Includes a narrative of operations, recommendations for future operations, proposed operating procedures for LVT's, and commendatory messages.

7th Infantry Division. Report on FLINTLOCK Operation, 6Mar44. A detailed list of questions and answers pertaining to the Kwajalein operation.

7th Infantry Division. Report of the Southern Force Artillery, FLINTLOCK Operation, 22Feb44. An account of planning and conduct of operations, followed by recommendations.

7th Infantry Division. G–3 Reports. G–3 daily reports of division's activities during the period 31Jan–5Feb44. Overlays.

7th Infantry Division. FLINTLOCK Report. Volumes III, IV, VII, IX, XI. The division's formal report of participation in the Kwajalein operation.

Tactical Group-1. Report of Attack on Eniwetok Atoll, 27Feb44. A 14-page narrative report concerning operations against Eniwetok Atoll. Carries endorsement of RAdm H. W. Hill.

Tactical Group-1. Special Report concerning FLINTLOCK and CATCHPOLE Operations, 1Mar44. A comprehensive report dealing with the attack on Eniwetok Atoll. Includes daily unit reports with overlays from 17Feb44 through 23Feb44; radio log for the operation; action report by Company D (Scout), 4th Tank Bn; action report, VAC Reconnaissance Co; Japanese map of Parry Island; Group Operation Order 2–44, DOWNSIDE, 10Feb44.

Tactical Group-1. Journal. Contains memoranda, dispatches, training orders, reports and maps. Covers period 7Dec43 through 22Mar44.

Tactical Group-1. War Diary, 5Nov43–29Feb44. A day-by-day account of TG–1 activities during the period covered.

Tactical Group-1. War Diary, March 1944. Signed by BrigGen T. E. Watson, with endorsement by BrigGen G. B. Erskine, CofS, VAC. Covers period 1Mar-22Mar44.

22d Marines, reinforced, Operation Orders. A folder containing combat instructions, field messages, regimental operations plans for FLINTLOCK, and regimental operations orders for CATCHPOLE. Inclusive dates are 26Sept43–21Feb44.

22d Marines. Record of Events. A folder containing various orders, reports, copies of war diaries, dispatches and records of events from 6Aug42 through 2Mar44.

22d Marines. Journal. A record of all messages sent and received by 22d Marines Headquarters, 17Feb–24Feb44. Included is a penciled report dated 15Mar44 dealing with activities of the Regimental Weapons Co during the Eniwetok operations.

22d Marines, reinforced. Report on DOWNSIDE Operation, 9Mar44. A detailed 25-page report dealing principally with an analysis of all aspects of the Eniwetok operation and containing pertinent recommendations for future activities.

22d Marines. Reports, undated. A folder containing reports relating to the Eniwetok operation from the following organizations: 2d Separate Transport Co; 2d Separate Pack Howitzer Bn; BLT 2; Service & Supply Plt, H&S Co.; 2d Separate Engineer Co; 2d Separate Tank Co; 2d Separate Medical Co; Regimental Weapons Co.

22d Marines. Action Reports on Lesser Marshalls. Detailed reports from each group participating in the occupation of the Lesser Marshalls. Also a regimental report covering the over-all Lesser Marshalls operations. Dates are 11Mar44 through 24Apr44. Each report carries the endorsement of the atoll commander and the Marine Administrative Command, VAC.

22d Marines, reinforced. War Diary, 3Mar44. Signed by Col. J. T. Walker, with endorsement by MajGen H. M. Smith, Commanding General, VAC. Covers period 1Jan44 through 29Feb44.

1st Battalion, 22d Marines. Report on FLINTLOCK II Operation, undated. A report on Landing Team 1's activities at Eniwetok Atoll and signed by W. H. Fromhold. Includes a history of operations, operation overlay, unit journal and message abstract and comments and recommendations.

2d Battalion, 22d Marines. Record of Events. A day-by-day report from 19Jul42 through 6Feb45.

106th Infantry Regiment. Unit Operation Report (DOWNSIDE), 15Apr44. A detailed report of the organization's participation in the Eniwetok operation. Includes operation plans and orders, maps, unit journal, casualty report and a report by BLT 106–3. Carries endorsements by VAC and the 27th Infantry Division.

1st Defense Battalion, VAC. War Diary for April 1944. A day-by-day account of activities during the month of April. Signed by LtCol J. H. Buckner, and carrying an endorsement from VAC.

708th Amphibian Tank Battalion. Report of 708th Provisional Amphibian Tractor Bn on FLINTLOCK Operation, 14Feb44. Includes a narrative of operations and recommendations for future operations. Signed by Maj J. L. Rogers.

708th Amphibian Tank Battalion. Special Action Report, Kwajalein operation, 12Mar44. A day-by-day account of the organization's participation in the FLINTLOCK Operation, 31Jan44–6Feb44.

708th Amphibian Tank Bn. Unit History, 22Jan45. A brief and generalized history of the organization covering its activation and participation in the Marshall Islands and Guam operations. Signed by K. C. Heise, Adjutant.

Company I, 111th Infantry. Report of Operations, Occupation of Ujelang Atoll, 27Apr44.

USS *Alabama*. Bombardment of Roi-Namur, 6Feb44. Report of bombardment on 30Jan44.

USS *New Orleans*. Report of Action, 8Feb44. Chronological account of activities during the bombardment of Roi, 30Jan44.

USS *Overton*. Action Report, 8Feb44. Chronological account of *Overton's* participation in the Kwajalein operation from 30Jan44 through 5Feb44.

USS *Arthur Middleton*. Report of Landing Phase of Operations at Eniwetok Atoll, 7Mar44. Contains narrative reports as well as operations plans and order for Eniwetok.

USS *Ashland*. Action Report, Eniwetok Atoll, 3May44. Chronological account and comments on the Eniwetok operation during the period 11–23Feb44.

Island Commander, Roi. Report of Action, 4Apr44. Chronological account of Japanese air attack on 12Feb44, with pertinent comments.

Fleet Orders. Folder containing orders issued by RAdm Alva D. Bernhard, Kwajalein Atoll Commander, pertaining to operations in the Lesser Marshalls. Orders issued between 27Feb44 and 24Mar44, inclusive.

Marine Corps Headquarters. Advanced Base Operations in Micronesia, 712. Approved by the Commandant on 23Jul21; this document was the plan for Marine participation in the event of war with Japan. It is a detailed estimate of the situation on each of the numerous possible targets in the Pacific.

Document submitted by Capt Buenos A. W. Young, dated 10Apr44 and believed to be the Action Report, 3d Bn, 22d Marines, on the Eniwetok Operation.

BOOKS, PAMPHLETS, PERIODICALS

Amphibious Operations in the Marshall Islands, January–February 1944. Issued by CominCh, United States Fleet, 20May44.

Bartley, Whitman S. *Iwo Jima: Amphibious Epic.* Washington: Government Printing Office, 1954.

Craven, W. F. and Cate, J. L. *The Army Air Forces in World War II*, Vol IV, *The Pacific—Guadalcanal to Saipan.* University of Chicago Press, 1950.

Crowl, Philip A., and Love, Edmund G. *United States Army in World War II, The Seizure of the Gilberts and Marshalls.* A forthcoming volume to be published by the Office of the Chief of Military History, Department of the Army.

Heinl, Robert D., Jr. *The Defense of Wake.* Washington: Government Printing Office, 1947.

Heinl, Robert D., Jr. *Marines at Midway.* Washington: Government Printing Office, 1948.

Hoffman, Carl W. *Saipan: The Beginning of the End.* Washington: Government Printing Office, 1950.

Hoffman, Carl W. *The Seizure of Tinian.* Washington: Government Printing Office, 1951.

Hough, Frank O. *The Island War.* New York: J. B. Lippincott Co., 1947.

Isely, Jeter A., and Crowl, Philip A. *The U. S. Marines and Amphibious War.* Princeton University Press, 1951.

Lodge, O. R. *The Recapture of Guam.* Washington: Government Printing Office, 1954.

Love, Edmund G. *The 27th Infantry Division in World War II.* Washington: Infantry Journal Press, 1949.

Marine Corps Gazette. "Personalities—Men Who Differed," by Maj Frank O. Hough, USMCR, November 1950.

Marshall, S. L. A. *Island Victory.* Infantry Journal Press, 1945.

Military Review. "The Marshall Islands Operation," by VAdm Harry W. Hill, USN.

Morison, Samuel E. *History of United States Naval Operations in World War II*, Vol VII, *Aleutians, Gilberts and Marshalls.* Little Brown and Co., 1951.

Proehl, Carl W. (ed) *The Fourth Marine Division in World War II.* Washington: Infantry Journal Press, 1946.

Rentz, John N. *Marines in the Central Solomons.* Washington: Government Printing Office, 1952.

Robson, R. M. *The Pacific Islands Handbook, 1944.* New York: The MacMillan Company, 1945.

Sailing Directions for the Pacific Islands. Washington: Hydrographic Office, U. S. Navy Department, 1938.

Saturday Evening Post. "The Marines' First Spy," by Maj John L. Zimmerman, USMCR, 23 November 1946.

Sherrod, Robert. *History of Marine Corps Aviation in World War II.* Washington: Combat Forces Press, 1952.

Smith, Holland M. *Coral and Brass.* New York: Charles Scribner's Sons, 1949.

Stockman, James R. *The Battle for Tarawa.* Washington: Government Printing Office, 1947.

The War Reports of General Marshall, General Arnold and Admiral King. New York: J. B. Lippincott, 1947.

United States Strategic Bombing Survey. *The American Campaign Against Wotje, Maloelap, Mille and Jaluit.* Washington: Government Printing Office, 1947.

United States Strategic Bombing Survey. *The Campaigns of the Pacific War.* Washington: Government Printing Office, 1946.

United States Strategic Bombing Survey. *The Reduction of Truk.* Washington: Government Printing Office, 1947.

Wendell, William G. *The Marshall Islands Operations.* Unpublished manuscript, 1945.

Zimmerman, John L. *The Guadalcanal Campaign.* Washington: Government Printing Office, 1949.

MISCELLANEOUS

Maj Paul H. Bird, "Atoll Hopping—The Lesser Marshalls," an undated report dealing with the 22d Marines in the Lesser Marshalls.

LtCol Austin R. Brunelli, Historical Tactical Study, The Capture of Namur Island, 1–2 February 1944, written for Amphibious Warfare School, Quantico, Senior Course 1946–1947.

Notes of LtCol W. F. Fromhold, undated. Prepared by Capt W. G. Wendell.

S. L. A. Marshall. Kwajalein Notes. Col Marshall was with the 7th Infantry Division during the Kwajalein operation and conducted a series of interviews with participants as soon as organized resistance ceased. Maps and sketches accompany his notes.

Ltr Col O. T. Pfeiffer to Col. G. B. Erskine, 23Oct43.

Memo BrigGen O. T. Pfeiffer to BrigGen G. C. Thomas, 23Feb44.

LtCol Richard Rothwell, A Study of An Amphibious Operation, The Battle of Namur, 31Jan44–2Feb44, written for Amphibious Warfare School, Quantico, Senior Course 1946–1947.

Maj William E. Sperling III, an undated paper titled "BLT 3/22 on Eniwetok Island," filed in Archives, HQMC.

Memo Adm H. R. Stark to SecNav, 12Nov40.

APPENDIX II

Chronology

1943

11 May	TRIDENT Conference in Washington; CCS decides to seize the Marshalls and to move against Japanese outer defenses.
Mid-June	JCS directs Adm Nimitz to submit plan for occupation of the Marshalls.
1 July	Adm Nimitz submits concept for operations.
20 July	JCS directs Adm Nimitz to organize and train forces for operations in the Marshalls on 1 January 1944.
15 August	4th Marine Division organized.
20 August	Adm Nimitz submits outline plan for occupation of Kwajalein, Wotje and Maloelap.
17–24 August	At the QUADRANT Conference at Quebec, routes of advance on Japan laid out and operations in the Marshalls agreed to.
24 August	Fifth Amph Force set up, RAdm Turner commanding.
1 September	JCS dispatches directive to Adm Nimitz, allocating troops and naval forces for the Marshalls.
16 September	7th Inf Div arrives at Oahu, T. H. to begin preparations for the Marshalls.
20 September	4th MarDiv assigned to VAC.
12 October	Adm Nimitz issues OP Plan 16–43, first formal operation plan for the Marshalls.
15 November	MajGen Smith issues OP Plan 2–43, first over-all troop directive for the Marshalls.
16 November	TG–1 organized under VAC GenOrd No. 55–43.
20 November	2d MarDiv assaults Tarawa.
4 December	First aerial photo coverage of Kwajalein Atoll effected.
5 December	VAdm Yamada assumes command of Japanese aviation in the Marshalls.
14 December	Adm Nimitz revises OP Plan 16–43; target date postponed.
20 December	Adm Nimitz issues final JCS Study, FLINTLOCK II in which all changes have been ratified.

1944

3 January	RAdm Turner issues OP Plan A6–43, listing components and setting forth mission of Joint Expeditionary Force.
4 January	1st Amphibious Brigade (Japanese) arrives at Eniwetok Atoll.
5 January	VAC OP Plan 1–44 released, superseding OP Plan 3–43.
13 January	Main body of TF 53 departs San Diego.
22 January	Joint Expeditionary Force sails from Hawaii.
31 January	D-Day in the Marshalls: Landings effected on small islands in both northern and southern Kwajalein Atoll. VAC Reconn Co lands on Majuro Atoll.
1 February	Combat Teams 23 and 24 land on Roi-Namur. RCT's 32 and 184 land on Kwajalein Island.
4 February	RAdm Harry W. Hill given command of Task Group 51.11, with the mission of seizing Eniwetok Atoll. Kwajalein Island overrun. 109th NavConsBn begins repair on Roi airfield.
7 February	Ground elements of 4th MBDAW arrive at Roi.
8 February	Kwajalein Atoll secured.
12 February	Japanese retaliate with air attack on Roi.
17 February	Landings effected on small islands of Eniwetok Atoll.
17–18 February	TF 58 attacks Truk.
18 February	22d Marines land on Engebi and secure it.

19 February	Landing by 106th RCT and 3d Bn, 22d Marines, on Eniwetok Island.
21 February	Eniwetok Island secured.
22 February	22d Marines land on Parry and secure it.
26 February	22d Marines relieve 25th Marines on Kwajalein.
1 March	RAdm Bernhard receives orders to neutralize and control the Lesser Marshalls.
4 March	4th MBDAW begins bombing campaign against Wotje, Jaluit, Mille and Maloelap.
10 March	Wotho Island taken.
11 March	Ujae Atoll occupied. American flag raised on Lib Island.
21 March	Ailinglapalap Atoll taken.
22 March	TG–1 disbanded; 1st Prov-MarBrig organized.
24 March	Ebon Atoll secured.
30 March	Flag raised on Bikini Atoll.
1 April	Ailuk Atoll taken.
2 April	Marines land on Mejit Island.
3 April	Likiep and Rongelap Atolls secured.
5 April	Utirik Atoll secured.
6 April	22d Marines depart for Guadalcanal.
17 April	Marines from 1st Defense Bn, VAC, land on Erikub and Aur Atolls.
22 April	Soldiers of 111th Inf raise flag on Ujelang Atoll.

1945

22 August	Mille Atoll surrendered to American naval forces; the first of the by-passed atolls to surrender.
2 September	Japan formally surrenders.

168

Casualties

APPENDIX III

MARINE ORGANIZATIONS [1]	Killed or Died of Wounds [2]		Wounded		Total	
	Officers	Enlisted	Officers	Enlisted	Officers	Enlisted
4th Marine Division:						
Hq Co, Hq Bn................			2	2	2	2
4th Sig Co....................				2		2
MP Co........................			1		1	
4th Spec Wpns Bn.............			1	8	1	8
4th Tank Bn..................	1	6	1	7	2	13
4th Serv Bn..................				2		2
4th MT Bn...................			2	2	2	2
4th Amph Trac Bn............				1		1
10th Amph Trac Bn..........		9		8		17
11th Amph Trac Bn..........		6				6
1st Armd Amph Bn...........		9		8		17
14th Marines:						
1st Bn.......................				2		2
2d Bn........................		1		6		7
3d Bn........................		5	1	2	1	7
20th Marines:						
H&S Co......................		7	3	17	3	24
1st Bn.......................	1	22	2	21	3	43
2d Bn........................	2	3	1	10	3	13
23d Marines:						
H&S and Wpns Cos..........			1	3	1	3
1st Bn.......................		2	2	13	2	15
2d Bn........................		13	1	36	1	49
3d Bn........................		3	2	10	2	13

[1] Marine casualty figures furnished by Personnel Accounting Section, Records Branch, Personnel Department, HQMC. These figures were certified and released on 26 August 1952, and includes those casualties incurred in the Marshalls within the period 31 January through 6 April 1944.

[2] Includes MIA and Missing, Presumed Dead figures.

MARINE ORGANIZATIONS	Killed or Died of Wounds		Wounded		Total	
	Officers	Enlisted	Officers	Enlisted	Officers	Enlisted
24th Marines:						
H&S and Wpns Cos..............	1	6	2	9	3	15
1st Bn.........................	3	44	3	64	6	108
2d Bn.........................	3	91	5	123	8	214
3d Bn.........................	6	72	5	94	11	166
25th Marines:						
H&S and Wpns Cos..............			1	3	1	3
1st Bn.........................		9	1	7	1	16
2d Bn.........................		13		8		21
3d Bn.........................		1		14		15
1st JASCO.....................	2	4		4	2	8
Reconn Co, VAC....................		7	1	11	1	18
10th Defense Bn.....................				1		1
15th Defense Bn.....................		5	1	39	1	44
22d Marines:						
H&S and Wpns Cos..............		8		19		27
1st Bn.........................	1	97	12	193	13	290
2d Bn.........................	1	60	1	128	2	188
3d Bn.........................	2	72	9	145	11	217
2d Sep Pk How Bn..............		2	2	8	2	10
2d Sep Tank Co.................		6	1	13	1	19
2d Sep Engr Co.................		5	1	23	1	28
4th Marine Base Defense Air Wing:						
MAG–13:						
VMSB–231.......................	1	2	1	1	2	3
VMSB–331.......................			2	2	2	2
MAG–22:						
Hq Sq–22.......................			1	2		3
AWS–1.........................			1	2		3
SMS–22.........................				4		4
VMF–113.........................				3		3
VMF–422.........................			1	4		5
MAG–31:						
Hq Sq–31.......................			9	16		25
SMS–31.........................			6	23		29
VMF–111.........................	1		4	9	5	9
VMF–224.........................		2	3	17	3	19
VMF–311.........................			2		2	
VMF–441.........................	1		4	2	5	2
Total [3].....................	26	610	81	1, 151	107	1, 761

[3] The following organizations suffered no casualties during the operation: 1st Defense Bn, 2d Sep Transport Co, 2d Sep Med Co and 3d Bn, 20th Marines.

NAVY MEDICAL [4]	Killed or Died of Wounds		Wounded		Total	
	Officers	Enlisted	Officers	Enlisted	Officers	Enlisted
4th Marine Division..................		1	2	15	2	16
22d Marines........................		6		13		19
MAG–31............................		2				2
Photo Sq No. 3.....................		1				1
Total........................		10	2	28	2	38

ARMY ORGANIZATIONS [5]

	Killed or Died of Wounds		Wounded		Total	
	Officers	Enlisted	Officers	Enlisted	Officers	Enlisted
7th Infantry Division:						
17th Inf...........................		16	2	77	2	93
32d Inf...........................	2	55	19	303	21	358
184th Inf..........................	1	64	17	252	18	316
13th Engr Bn......................		10		31		41
57th FA Bn........................		2	1	9	1	11
48th FA Bn........................	1				1	
49th FA Bn........................				5		5
145th FA Bn.......................		9		22		31
7th Div Arty......................	1				1	
7th Med Bn........................		1	1	1	1	2
7th Reconn Trp....................		2	2	18	2	20
7th Div Hqs.......................	1				1	
91st Chem Co......................		1		13		14
75th Sig Co........................				4		4
47th Engr Co......................		3		1		4
767th Tank Bn.....................		1	2	5	2	6
111th Inf..........................		2	1	5	1	7
867th AAA........................				1		1
4th Army Def Bn..................		1		1		2
Total........................	6	167	45	748	51	915
708th Amph Tank Bn [6].............		1	3	33	3	34

[4] Navy Hospital Corpsmen, Medical and Dental Officer casualty figures furnished by U. S. Navy Bureau of Medicine and Surgery, Statistics Division, World War II Casualties, 1Aug52.

[5] These figures taken from 7th Infantry Division FLINTLOCK Operation, ACofS, G–1 Report of Operation.

[6] This unit participated in both the Kwajalein and Eniwetok operations. Casualty figures are taken from the 708th Amph Tank Bn History, 27Oct43–31Dec44, which lumps together all casualty figures for the Marshalls.

ARMY ORGANIZATIONS [7]	Killed or Died of Wounds	Wounded	Total
RCT 106 (Reinf) (less BLT 106–2):			
106th Inf....................................	82	281	363
104th FA Bn.................................	2	8	10
104th Engr Bn...............................	6	10	16
Co B, 102d Engr Bn..........................	1	4	5
Co C, 102d Med Bn...........................	2		2
Det, 295th Sig Co...........................		1	1
Co C, 766th Tk Bn...........................	1	5	6
Det, 727th Ord Co...........................	1		1
Hq Btry, 27th Div Arty......................		1	1
Hq, 27th Inf Div............................		1	1
Yank Magazine...............................	1		1
Total..................................	96	311	407

[7] These figures taken from 106th RCT Operation Report, Eniwetok.   No breakdown into officers and enlisted was shown.

APPENDIX IV — Task Organization

NORTHERN LANDING FORCE—MajGen Harry
Schmidt

PHASE I

IVAN Landing Group—BrigGen James L. Underhill
Det Hq Co, Hq Bn, 4thMarDiv
Det Sig Co, Hq Bn, 4thMarDiv
25th Marines (plus Band Sec)
14th Marines
1st Composite Engr Bn (plus Cam Det, H&S Co, 20th
Mar)
Co A, 4th Tk Bn (less 1st Plat)
Btry B, 4th Spl Wpns Bn
10th Amph Trac Bn
1st Plat, Btry A, 4th Spl Wpns Bn
Co A, 11th Amph Trac Bn (plus Prov LVT(2) Plat,
1st Armd Amph Bn)
Cos B and D, 1st Armd Amph Bn
Co A, 4th Med Bn
Co A, 4th MT Bn
1st Plat, Ord Co, 4th Serv Bn
1st Plat, Serv & Sup Co, 4th Serv Bn
1st Plat, 4th MP Co
Det 1st JASCO
Co D, 4th Tk Bn (Scout)   (All less Rear Echelon)

PHASE II

Combat Team 23—Col Louis R Jones
23d Marines (plus Band Sec)
3d Composite Engr Bn (plus Cam Det, Com Plat,
H&S Co, 20th Mar)
Co C, 4th Tk Bn (Medium)
1st Plat, Co A, 4th Tk Bn
Btry C, 4th Spl Wpns Bn
3d Plat, Btry A, 4th Spl Wpns Bn
4th Amph Trac Bn
Cos A and C, 1st Armd Amph Bn

Co C, 4th Med Bn
Co C, 4th MT Bn
3d Plat, Ord Co, 4th Serv Bn
3d Plat, 4th MP Co
Dets 1st JASCO   (All less Rear Echelon)
Combat Team 24—Col Franklin A. Hart
24th Marines (plus Band Sec)
2d Composite Engr Bn (plus Cam Det, H&S Co, 20th
Mar)
Co B, 4th Tk Bn
Btry D, 4th Spl Wpns Bn
2d Plat, Btry A, 4th Spl Wpns Bn
10th Amph Trac Bn
Cos B and D, 1st Armd Amph Bn
Co B, 4th Med Bn
Co B, 4th MT Bn
2d Plat, 4th MP Co
Dets 1st JASCO   (All less Rear Echelon)
Division Reserve—Col Samuel C. Cumming
25th Marines (plus Band Sec)
1st Composite Engr Bn (plus Cam Det, H&S Co, 20th
Mar)
Co A, 4th Tk Bn (less 1st Plat)
Co D, 4th Tk Bn (Scout)
Btry B, 4th Spl Wpns Bn
1st Plat, Btry A, 4th Spl Wpns Bn
Co A, 11th Amph Trac Bn (plus Prov Plat, 1st Armd
Amph Bn)
Co A, 4th Med Bn
Co A, 4th MT Bn
1st Plat, Ord Co, 4th Serv Bn
1st Plat, Serv & Sup Co, 4th Serv Bn
1st Plat, 4th MP Co
Det 1st JASCO   (All less Rear Echelon)
14th Marines (less Rear Echelon)—Col Louis G.
DeHaven
Support Group—Col Emmett W. Skinner
Hq Bn 4th MarDiv (less dets)

20th Mar (less 1st, 2d and 3d Bns, and less Com
   Plat and Cam Sec, H&S Co, 20th Mar)
4th Tk Bn (less dets)
1st Armd Amph Bn (less dets)
4th Med Bn (less Cos A, B and C)
4th Serv Bn (less dets)
4th MT Bn (less dets)
1st JASCO (less dets)
4th Spl Wpns Bn (less dets)
15th Defense Bn (Marine)

SOUTHERN LANDING FORCE—MajGen Charles H.
   Corlett, USA

7th Infantry Division—MajGen Charles H. Corlett,
   USA
RCT's 17, 32 and 184
7th Reconnaissance Troop
13th Engr Bn
Co D, 34th Engr Bn
1st Bn, 47th Engr Bn
50th Engr Bn
7th Sig Co
75th Sig Co
GAU 7, 163d Sig Photo Co
767th Tk Bn
Det, 8th Chem Co
91st Chem Co
7th QM Co
MP Platoon
707th Ord Co
93d Bomb Disposal Squad
Cannon Co, 111th Inf
1st Bn, 111th Inf (less Co C)
708th Prov Amph Trac Bn
Co A, 708th Amph Tk Bn
7th Med Bn
31st Field Hospital
Btry A, 55th CA
Btrys E and F, 57th CA
Btrys A, B, C and D, 96th AAA Bn
Btrys A and C, 98th AAA Bn
Det, 296th AAA Bn
Co B, 376th Port Bn
Btrys A and B, 753d AAA Bn
Btrys A and D, 867th AAA Bn
Dets, 87th ASSRON

3d Army Defense Bn
4th Army Defense Bn

Division Artillery Group—BrigGen Archibald V.
   Arnold, USA

31st, 48th, 49th, 57th and 145th FA Bns

SUNDANCE LANDING FORCE—LtCol Frederick B.
   Sheldon, USA

2d Bn, 106th Inf (reinforced)
V Amphibious Corps Reconnaissance Co
1st Defense Bn (Marine)

RESERVE LANDING FORCE (Tactical Group-1)—
   BrigGen Thomas E. Watson

22d Marines (reinforced)
106th Inf (reinforced) (less 2d Bn reinforced)

ENIWETOK LANDING FORCES (Tactical Group-
   1)—BrigGen Thomas E. Watson

22d Marines
2d Sep Pack How Bn
2d Sep Engr Co
2d Sep Med Co
2d Sep Tank Co
2d Sep Transport Co
Co D (Scout), 4th Tank Bn
V Amphibious Corps Reconnaissance Co
10th Defense Bn (Marine)
Nav Const Co (Acorn 22)
106th Inf (less 2d Bn)
104th FA Bn
104th Engr Bn (less 1 Co)
Co B, 102d Engr Bn (less 1 Plat)
Cos C and D, 102d Med Bn (less 2 Plats)
Portable Surgical Hospital #1 (Prov)
Co C, 766 Tk Bn
Det, 727th Ord Co
Det, 97th Ord Co
Det, 295th Sig Co
Co A, 708th Amph Tk Bn
708th Prov Amph Trac Bn (less 1 LVT Grp)
Prov DUKW Btry
47th Engr Bn
3d Army Defense Bn

APPENDIX V

Command and Staff

KWAJALEIN ATOLL [1]

(31 January 1944–8 February 1944)

V Amphibious Corps [2]

Commanding General....	MajGen Holland M. Smith
Chief of Staff...........	BrigGen Graves B. Erskine
G–1....................	LtCol Albert F. Metze
G–2....................	LtCol St. Julien R. Marshall
G–3....................	Col John C. McQueen
G–4....................	Col Raymond E. Knapp
G–5....................	Col Joseph T. Smith

4th Marine Division

Commanding General.....	MajGen Harry Schmidt
Asst. Div. Commander....	BrigGen James L. Underhill
Chief of Staff...........	Col William W. Rogers
D–1....................	Col Merton J. Batchelder
D–2....................	Maj Gooderham L. McCormick
D–3....................	Col Walter W. Wensinger
D–4....................	Col William F. Brown

1st Armored Amphibian Battalion

Commander Officer.......	Maj Louis Metzger
Executive Officer........	Capt Richard G. Warga
Bn–3..................	1stLt Thomas M. Crosby

[1] Tactical Group-1 was in reserve for the FLINTLOCK Operation. Inasmuch as this unit participated in CATCHPOLE its command and staff organization is listed only under the latter operation.

[2] In the case of VAC staff, the officers shown herein occupied their respective billets during the important planning phase of FLINTLOCK, although not all of them accompanied MajGen Holland M. Smith on the *Rocky Mount* to Kwajalein.

4th Amphibian Tractor Battalion [3]

Commanding Officer.....	LtCol Clovis C. Coffman

10th Amphibian Tractor Battalion [4]

Commanding Officer.....	Maj Victor J. Croizat
Executive Officer........	Maj Warren H. Edwards

4th Tank Battalion

Commanding Officer.....	Maj Richard K. Schmidt
Executive Officer........	Capt Francis L. Orgain
Bn–3..................	Capt Leo B. Case

23d Marines

Commanding Officer......	Col Louis R. Jones
Executive Officer........	LtCol John R. Lanigan
R–1....................	Capt Frank E. Phillips, Jr.
R–2....................	Capt Richard W. Mirick
R–3....................	Maj Edward W. Wells
R–4....................	Capt Henry S. Campbell

Regimental Weapons Company

Commanding Officer......	Capt George W. E. Daughtry
Executive Officer........	Capt Raymond C. Kraus

1st Battalion, 23d Marines

Commanding Officer......	LtCol Hewin O. Hammond
Executive Officer........	Maj Hollis U. Mustain
Bn–3..................	Capt James R. Miller

[3] Executive Officer and Bn–3 not shown in available records.

[4] Bn–3 not shown in available records.

2d Battalion, 23d Marines

Commanding Officer......... LtCol Edward J. Dillon
Executive Officer............ Maj Lawrence V. Patterson
Bn-3........................ Capt James W. Sperry

3d Battalion, 23d Marines

Commanding Officer......... LtCol John J. Cosgrove, Jr.
Executive Officer............ LtCol Ralph Haas
Bn-3........................ Maj Robert J. J. Picardi

24th Marines

Commanding Officer......... Col Franklin A. Hart
Executive Officer............ LtCol Homer L. Litzenberg, Jr.
R-1......................... Capt Kenneth N. Hilton
R-2......................... Capt Arthur B. Hanson
R-3......................... LtCol Charles D. Roberts
R-4......................... Maj Clyde T. Smith

Regimental Weapons Company

Commanding Officer......... Maj Richard McCarthy, Jr.
Executive Officer............ Capt Edward J. Schofield

1st Battalion, 24th Marines

Commanding Officer......... LtCol Aquilla J. Dyess
    (KIA 2 February)
    Maj Maynard C. Schultz
Executive Officer............ Maj Maynard C. Schultz
    (to 2 February)
Bn-3........................ Capt Gene G. Mundy

2d Battalion, 24th Marines

Commanding Officer......... LtCol Francis H. Brink
Executive Officer............ LtCol Richard Rothwell
Bn-3........................ Maj Claude M. Cappelmann

3d Battalion, 24th Marines

Commanding Officer......... LtCol Austin R. Brunelli
Executive Officer............ Maj John V. V. Veeder
Bn-3........................ Capt Webb D. Sawyer

25th Marines

Commanding Officer......... Col Samuel C. Cumming
Executive Officer............ LtCol Walter I. Jordan
R-1......................... WO Daniel H. Nelson [5]
R-2......................... Capt Charles D. Gray
R-3......................... LtCol William F. Thyson, Jr.
R-4......................... Capt Edward Sherman

Regimental Weapons Company

Commanding Officer......... Capt James T. Kisgen
Executive Officer............ Capt Thomas H. Rogers
    Capt Delbert A. Graham
    (from 1 February)

---

[5] WO Nelson was actually assistant R-1 of the 25th Marines. He accompanied the regiment to Kwajalein, however, while Capt Francis A. Norton, R-1, remained with the rear echelon.

1st Battalion, 25th Marines

Commanding Officer......... LtCol Clarence J. O'Donnell
Executive Officer............ Maj Michael Davidowitch, Jr.
Bn-3........................ Capt Fenton J. Mee

2d Battalion, 25th Marines

Commanding Officer......... LtCol Lewis C. Hudson, Jr.
Executive Officer............ Maj William P. Kaempfer
Bn-3........................ Capt Victor J. Barringer

3d Battalion, 25th Marines

Commanding Officer......... LtCol Justice M. Chambers
Executive Officer............ Maj James Taul
Bn-3........................ Maj John H. Jones

14th Marines

Commanding Officer......... Col Louis G. DeHaven
Executive Officer............ LtCol Randall M. Victory
R-1......................... 1stLt Cecil D. Snyder
R-2......................... Capt Harrison L. Rogers
R-3......................... Maj Frederick J. Karch
R-4......................... Maj Richard J. Winsborough

1st Battalion, 14th Marines

Commanding Officer......... LtCol Harry J. Zimmer
Executive Officer............ Maj Clifford B. Drake
Bn-3........................ Maj Thomas M. Fry

2d Battalion, 14th Marines

Commanding Officer......... LtCol George B. Wilson, Jr.
Executive Officer............ Maj William McReynolds
Bn-3........................ Capt Ralph W. Boyer, Jr.

3d Battalion, 14th Marines

Commanding Officer......... LtCol Robert E. MacFarlane
Executive Officer............ Maj Harvey A. Feehan
Bn-3........................ Maj Donald M. Love, Jr.

4th Battalion, 14th Marines

Commanding Officer......... Maj Carl A. Youngdale
Executive Officer............ Maj John B. Edgar, Jr.
Bn-3........................ Maj Roland J. Spritzen

20th Marines

Commanding Officer......... Col Lucian W. Burnham
Executive Officer............ LtCol Nelson K. Brown
R-1......................... Capt Martin M. Calcaterra
R-2......................... Capt Carl A. Sachs
R-3......................... Maj. Melvin D. Henderson
R-4......................... Capt Samuel G. Thompson

1st Battalion, 20th Marines

Commanding Officer......... Maj Richard G. Ruby
Executive Officer............ Capt George F. Williamson
Bn-3........................ Capt Martin H. Glover

2d Battalion, 20th Marines

Commanding Officer...... LtCol Otto Lessing
Executive Officer........ Maj John H. Partridge
Bn–3.................. Capt George L. Smith

3d Battalion, 20th Marines [4]

Commanding Officer..... LtCdr William G. Byrne
Executive Officer........ LtCdr Thomas H. Flinn

15th Defense Battalion

Commanding Officer..... LtCol Francis B. Loomis, Jr.
Executive Officer........ LtCol Peter J. Negri
Bn–3.................. Capt Guy L. Wharton

7th Infantry Division

Commanding General..... MajGen Charles H. Corlett
Asst. Commanding General BrigGen Joseph L. Ready
Chief of Staff............ Col LeRoy J. Stewart
G–1................... LtCol Charles V. Wilson
G–2................... LtCol Robert G. Fergusson
G–3................... LtCol George B. Sloan
G–4................... LtCol David X. Angluin
Adjutant General........ LtCol Arthur J. Salisbury

7th Medical Battalion

Commanding Officer..... LtCol Robert J. Kamish
Executive Officer........ Maj Alan B. Eaker
S–3................... Capt Sidney Cohen

7th Reconnaissance Troop

Commanding Officer..... Capt Paul B. Gritta

13th Engineer Battalion

Commanding Officer..... LtCol Harold K. Howell
Executive Officer........ Capt George G. McCormick
S–3................... Capt Myrl A. Reaugh

17th Infantry Regiment

Commanding Officer..... Col Wayne C. Zimmerman
Executive Officer........ LtCol William B. Moore
S–1................... Capt Henry R. Sievers
S–2................... Maj Harry L. Beatty
S–3................... Capt James E. Simmons
S–4................... Capt Paul S. Foster, Jr.

1st Battalion, 17th Infantry

Commanding Officer..... LtCol Albert V. Hartl
Executive Officer........ Maj Maynard B. Weaver
S–3................... Capt Robert H. Johnson

2d Battalion, 17th Infantry

Commanding Officer..... LtCol Edward P. Smith
Executive Officer........ Maj Delbert L. Bjork
S–3................... Capt Robert J. Edwards

3d Battalion, 17th Infantry

Commanding Officer..... LtCol Lee Wallace
Executive Officer........ Maj Earl W. Nelson
S–3................... Capt Mervin A. Elliot

32d Infantry Regiment

Commanding Officer..... Col Marc J. Logie
Executive Officer........ LtCol John M. Finn
S–1................... Capt Jack L. Oliver
S–2................... Maj Charles F. Manov
S–3................... Maj Leigh H. Mathias
S–4................... 1stLt Wayne K. Yenni

1st Battalion, 32d Infantry

Commanding Officer..... LtCol Ernest H. Bearss
Executive Officer........ Maj Leonard E. Wellendorf
S–3................... Capt James R. Hurt

2d Battalion, 32d Infantry

Commanding Officer..... LtCol Glen A. Nelson
Executive Officer........ Maj Charles A. Whitcomb
S–3................... Capt Robert E. Goodfellow

3d Battalion, 32d Infantry

Commanding Officer..... LtCol Francis T. Pachler
Executive Officer........ Maj James H. Keller
S–3................... Capt John P. Connor

184th Infantry Regiment

Commanding Officer..... Col Curtis D. O'Sullivan
Executive Officer........ LtCol Merl W. Bremer
S–1................... Capt Charles J. Simon
S–2................... Maj Jackson C. Gillis
S–3................... Maj James K. Bullock
S–4................... Maj Otto G. Niemann

1st Battalion, 184th Infantry

Commanding Officer..... LtCol Roy A. Green
Executive Officer........ Maj Cortez A. Kitchen
S–3................... Capt Clark G. Campbell

2d Battalion, 148th Infantry

Commanding Officer..... LtCol Carl H. Aulick
Executive Officer........ Maj Richard W. Robison
S–3................... Capt John R. Palmer

3d Battalion, 184th Infantry

Commanding Officer..... LtCol William P. Walker
Executive Officer........ Maj Daniel C. Maybury
S–3................... Capt Paul L. Smith

Division Artillery Group

Commanding General.... BrigGen Archibald V. Arnold
Executive Officer........ Col William C. Lucas
S–1................... Maj Waldo W. Montgomery

S-2 . . . . Maj John W. Pritchard
S-3 . . . . Maj Ara G. Lindley
R-4 . . . . Maj Waldo W. Montgomery

31st Field Artillery Battalion

Commanding Officer . . . . . LtCol Stanley Sawicki
Executive Officer . . . . Maj Clement B. Harts
S-3 . . . . Capt Edward L. Smith

48th Field Artillery Battalion

Commanding Officer . . . . . Maj Harold S. Dillingham
Executive Officer . . . . Capt Stanley C. Anderson
S-3 . . . . Maj Ray D. Free

49th Field Artillery Battalion

Commanding Officer . . . . . LtCol Francis B. Harrison
Executive Officer . . . . Maj Jack D. Beck
S-3 . . . . Maj Carroll Mitchell

57th Field Artillery Battalion

Commanding Officer . . . . . LtCol Donald F. Slaughter
Executive Officer . . . . Maj Stuart M. George
S-3 . . . . Maj John F. Hanson, Jr.

145th Field Artillery Battalion

Commanding Officer . . . . . LtCol George D. Preston
Executive Officer . . . . Maj Ralph W. Morgan
S-3 . . . . Maj George F. Seacat

767th Tank Battalion

Commanding Officer . . . . . LtCol William G. Bray
Executive Officer . . . . Maj Walter S. Hahn
S-3 . . . . Capt Joseph L. Lohner

708th Provisional Amphibian Tractor Battalion

Commanding Officer . . . . . Maj James L. Rogers
Executive Officer . . . . Maj William Rossing
S-3 . . . . Capt John D. Kooken

50th Engineer Battalion

Commanding Officer . . . . . LtCol Leonard L. Kingsbury
Executive Officer . . . . Capt George S. Baumgart-
ner
S-3 . . . . Capt Charles J. Bainum

3d Army Defense Battalion [6]

Commanding Officer . . . . . LtCol Ralph W. Oakley

4th Army Defense Battalion [6]

Commanding Officer . . . . . Col Clifford R. Jones

---

[6] Executive Officer and S-3 not shown in available records.

MAJURO ATOLL
(31 January 1944–1 February 1944)

2d Battalion, 106th Infantry [7]

Commanding Officer . . . . . LtCol Frederick B. Sheldon
Executive Officer . . . . Maj Almerin C. O'Hara

1st Defense Battalion

Commanding Officer . . . . . LtCol Lewis A. Hohn
Executive Officer . . . . Maj Jean H. Buckner
Bn-3 . . . . Capt Charles S. Roberts

V Amphibious Corps Reconnaissance Company

Commanding Officer . . . . . Capt James L. Jones
Executive Officer . . . . 1stLt Merwin H. Silverthorn, Jr.

ENIWETOK ATOLL
(17 February 1944–24 February 1944)

Tactical Group-1

Commanding General . . . . BrigGen Thomas E. Watson
S-2 . . . . Maj Robert W. Shaw
S-3 . . . . LtCol Wallace M. Greene,
Jr.
S-4 . . . . Col Robert J. Straub
Artillery Officer . . . . Maj Joseph L. Stewart
Naval Gunfire Officer . . . . . Maj Ellsworth G. Van Or-
man

D Company (Scout), 4th Tank Battalion

Commanding Officer . . . . . . Capt Edward L. Katzenbach, Jr.
Executive Officer . . . . 1stLt James R. Barbour

V Amphibious Corps Reconnaissance Company [8]

22d Marines

Commanding Officer . . . . . Col John T. Walker
Executive Officer . . . . Col Merlin F. Schneider
R-1 . . . . Capt Curtis G. Callan
R-2 . . . . Maj Paul H. Bird
R-3 . . . . LtCol Floyd R. Moore
R-4 . . . . Capt Roland A. Wright

Regimental Weapons Company

Commanding Officer . . . . . Maj Theodore M. Sheffield
Executive Officer . . . . Maj Cecil D. Ferguson

1st Battalion, 22d Marines

Commanding Officer . . . . . LtCol Walfried H. From-
hold
Executive Officer . . . . Maj Crawford B. Lawton
Bn-3 . . . . Capt Peter R. Dyer

---

[7] S-3 not shown in available records.

[8] Command and staff for this unit shown under Majuro Operation.

2d Battalion, 22d Marines

Commanding Officer...... LtCol Donn C. Hart
Executive Officer......... Maj Robert P. Felker
Bn–3.................... Capt William B. Koren

3d Battalion, 22d Marines

Commanding Officer..... Maj Clair W. Shisler
Executive Officer......... Maj William E. Sperling,
III
Bn–3.................... Capt Leighton M. Clark,
(KIA 20 February)
Capt Harry D. Hedrick

2d Separate Pack Howitzer Battalion

Commanding Officer...... LtCol Edwin C. Ferguson
Maj Alfred M. Mahoney
(from 17 February)
Executive Officer......... Maj Alfred M. Mahoney
Maj Nathan C. Kingsbury
(from 17 February)
Bn–3.................... Maj Nathan C. Kingsbury
Capt Robert T. Gillespie
(from 17 February)

2d Separate Engineer Company

Commanding Officer...... Maj Paul F. Sackett
Executive Officer......... Capt Frederick G. Bloomfield

2d Separate Medical Company [9]

Commanding Officer...... Lt Llewellyn E. Wilson

2d Separate Tank Company

Commanding Officer...... Capt Harry Calcutt
Executive Officer......... 1stLt Robert Hall

2d Separate Transport Company [9]

Commanding Officer...... Maj Joseph A. Meyer

10th Defense Battalion

Commanding Officer...... LtCol Wallace O. Thompson
Executive Officer......... LtCol Robert E. Hommel
Bn–3.................... Maj Paul A. Fitzgerald

106th Infantry Regiment

Commanding Officer...... Col Russell G. Ayers
Executive Officer......... LtCol Joseph J. Farley
S–1..................... Capt George E. White
S–2..................... Capt William A. Foxen
S–3..................... Capt. George H. Temme, Jr.
S–4..................... Capt Jacob Ludwig

1st Battalion, 106th Infantry [7]

Commanding Officer...... LtCol Winslow Cornett
Executive Officer......... Maj John M. Nichols

3d Battalion, 106th Infantry [7]

Commanding Officer...... LtCol Harold J. Mizony
Executive Officer......... Maj Ernest C. Delear

104th Field Artillery Battalion [6]

Commanding Officer...... LtCol Van Nostrand

708th Provisional Amphibian Tractor Battalion [10]

3d Army Defense Battalion [10]

---

[9] Executive Officer not shown in available records.
[10] Command and staff for this unit shown under Kwajalein Operation.

Index

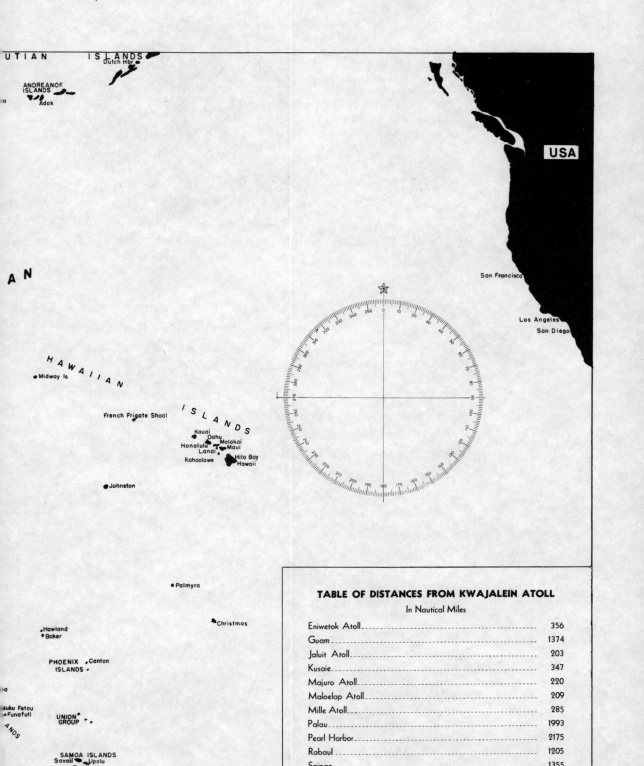

AUTIAN ISLANDS
Dutch Hbr

ANDREANOF
ISLANDS
Adak

USA

San Francisco

Los Angeles
San Diego

A N

H A W A I I A N
Midway Is

French Frigate Shoal   I S L A N D S

Kauai
Oahu   Molokai
Honolulu   Maui
Lanai
Kahoolawe   Hilo Bay
Hawaii

Johnston

Palmyra

Christmas

Howland
Baker

PHOENIX   Canton
ISLANDS

uku Fetau
Funafuti

UNION
GROUP

SAMOA ISLANDS
Savaii   Upolu
Tutuila

COOK ISLANDS

TONGA
ISLANDS
Tongatabu Gp

TABLE OF DISTANCES FROM KWAJALEIN ATOLL
In Nautical Miles

Eniwetok Atoll	356
Guam	1374
Jaluit Atoll	203
Kusaie	347
Majuro Atoll	220
Maloelap Atoll	209
Mille Atoll	285
Palau	1993
Pearl Harbor	2175
Rabaul	1205
Saipan	1355
San Diego	4368
Tarawa	540
Tokyo	2228
Truk	955
Wotje Atoll	156

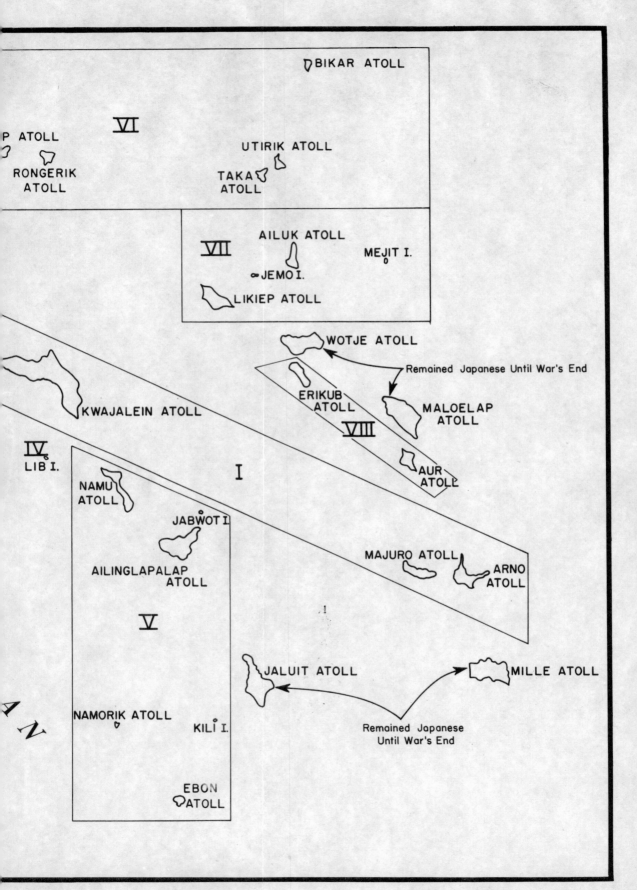

BIKAR ATOLL

VI

P ATOLL

RONGERIK
ATOLL

UTIRIK ATOLL

TAKA
ATOLL

AILUK ATOLL

VII

JEMO I.

MEJIT I.

LIKIEP ATOLL

WOTJE ATOLL

ERIKUB
ATOLL

Remained Japanese Until War's End

KWAJALEIN ATOLL

VIII

MALOELAP
ATOLL

IV
LIB I.

I

AUR
ATOLL

NAMU
ATOLL

JABWOT I.

MAJURO ATOLL

ARNO
ATOLL

AILINGLAPALAP
ATOLL

V

JALUIT ATOLL

MILLE ATOLL

NAMORIK ATOLL

KILI I.

Remained Japanese
Until War's End

EBON
ATOLL

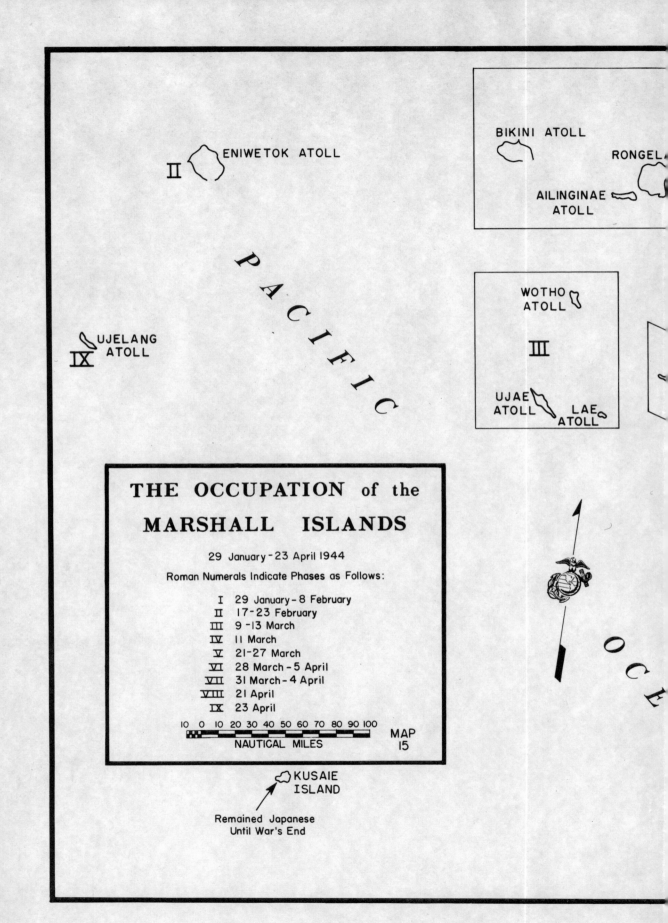

II ENIWETOK ATOLL

P A C I F I C

IX UJELANG ATOLL

BIKINI ATOLL

RONGELA

AILINGINAE ATOLL

WOTHO ATOLL

III

UJAE ATOLL   LAE ATOLL

THE OCCUPATION of the
MARSHALL ISLANDS

29 January - 23 April 1944

Roman Numerals Indicate Phases as Follows:

I	29 January - 8 February
II	17 - 23 February
III	9 - 13 March
IV	11 March
V	21 - 27 March
VI	28 March - 5 April
VII	31 March - 4 April
VIII	21 April
IX	23 April

10 0 10 20 30 40 50 60 70 80 90 100

NAUTICAL MILES

MAP 15

KUSAIE ISLAND

Remained Japanese
Until War's End

O C E

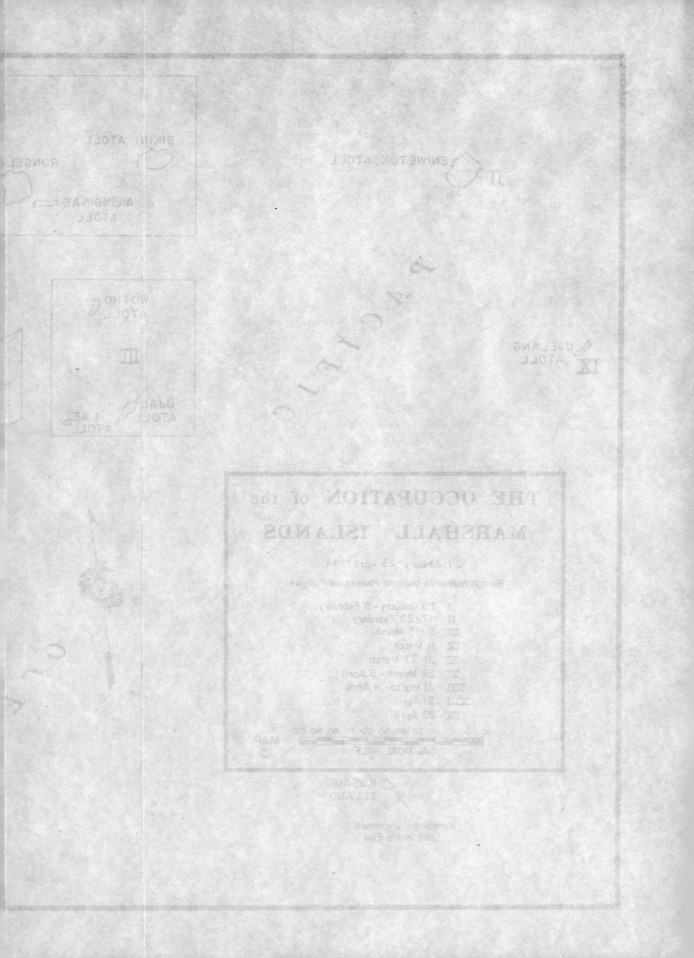